# TEMPTATION'S INFERNO

*Inferno Book 2*

### KAT MIZERA

Copyright @2017 by Kat Mizera, all rights reserved

All rights reserved. No part of this book may be used or reproduced in any manner whatsoever, including internet usage, without written permission from the author, except in the case of brief quotations embodied in critical articles and reviews.

These are works of fiction. Names, characters, places and incidents are either products of the author's imagination or are used fictitiously, and any resemblance to actual persons, living or dead, business establishments or locales is entirely coincidental.

Cover Design: Dar Albert, Wicked Smart Designs

Editing: Ashley Martin, Twin Tweaks Editing

Cover photographer: CJC Photography

Cover model: Joey Santa Lucia

❦ Created with Vellum

# ACKNOWLEDGMENTS

There are always so many people to thank, I'm afraid I'll forget some! However, this was a special book with a special theme and I'm so grateful to those who had my back the whole time I was writing it!

Special thanks to Jason Lavender for the sex Q&A—that's the most I've laughed in a long time! I'm not sure which one of us blushed the most...

There's no one as important on a daily basis as my writing and critique partner, Tiffani Lynn. You're always there when I need encouragement, a laugh or a swift kick in the ass—I'm so grateful that we're in this together!

Big thanks to all the bloggers and reviewers who help get the word out about these books—what you do is invaluable.

Thank you to my beta readers who jump in to help—sometimes a chapter at a time—whenever I need them. I couldn't get through the process without you.

As always, the biggest thanks go to Kevin, who does everything possible to support me in this endeavor...I can't imagine doing this without you. I love you.

# OTHER BOOKS BY KAT MIZERA

***Las Vegas Sidewinders:***
Dominic
Cody's Christmas Surprise
Drake
Karl
Anatoli
Zakk
Toli & Tessa
Brock
Vladimir
Royce
Nate
Sidewinders: Ever After
Jared
Dmitri's Christmas Angel
Ian

***Sidewinders: Generations:***
Zaan
Tore
Anton (2021)

***Alaska Blizzard:***
Defending Dani
Holding Hailey
Winning Whitney
Losing Laurel
Saving Sara
Chasing Charli
A Very Blizzard Christmas
Tending Tara (2021)

***The Royal Trilogy:***
Nowhere Left to Fall
Nowhere Left to Run

Nowhere Left to Hide

***Royal Protectors:***

Sandor

Cocky Protector (book 1.5, part of the Cocky Heroes Club series)

Xander

Axel

Dax *(A Royal Protectors/Sidewinders crossover novel)*

Gunnar *(short story, currently unavailable)*

***Inferno:***

Salvation's Inferno

Temptation's Inferno

Redemption's Inferno

Tropical Inferno (formerly "Tropical Ice")

***Romancing Europe:***

Adonis in Athens

Smitten in Santorini

Lucky in Lugano

***Other Books:***

Special Forces: Operation Alpha: Protecting Bobbi (Susan Stoker's Special Forces World)

Special Forces: Operation Alpha: Protecting Delilah (Susan Stoker's Special Forces World)

Brotherhood Protectors: Catching Lana (Elle James's Brotherhood Protectors World)

# AUTHOR'S NOTE

Dear Readers:

The Inferno series was born from two general ideas: the first was simply that Dante needed a book of his own and that led to the others. However, the second inspiration came from the simple need to promote acceptance. These books are fictional, and as authors we often push the envelope with things like insta-love, travel times, locale and more. We know they aren't always realistic but we hope that you enjoy them for what they are—escapism entertainment based on reality.

In the Inferno books, I deal with issues that are prevalent in today's society: Hate crime, the struggles within the LGBTQ community, divorce and blended families, and the many, many differences in how people from all walks of life live their lives. I don't promote nor condemn any of them, but I hope that you can discern the distinctions in these scenarios I've created. Not all of them are realistic and they truly aren't meant to be; these are fictional depictions of potentially real people and situations.

I don't in any way want anyone to assume that all BDSM clubs are like Club Inferno—because Club Inferno doesn't exist and is simply a place I created in my mind that these characters might enjoy. Not all bisexual people live like Jamie and Viggo. Not many divorced couples can have a relationship like Viggo and Emilie. The liberties I take with the BDSM lifestyle are not meant to portray it in any way other than the way that fit with this series—fun and sexy and occasionally over-the-top with both good and bad people involved in it, just as there are in real life. They are in no way meant to be realistic from the perspective of romantic fiction—just good fun, good sex and happily-ever-afters.

All the best,
Kat

*Please note: No characters were harmed in the creation of these books (except maybe the bad guys).*

# CHAPTER 1

He'd known it was coming, but hearing the actual words that made it official was a huge blow. Jamie Teller disconnected the call he'd just gotten from his agent and put the phone in his pocket. There'd been no rush, he'd told him just weeks ago, but it seemed that Ottawa had jumped at the chance to have him, and his current team had traded him away like yesterday's news.

*You asked for the trade*, he reminded himself with a grimace.

"Dumb-ass," he muttered, walking into the kitchen of his apartment and pulling a beer out of the fridge. He'd only gotten home to Las Vegas yesterday and it looked like he was going to have to get serious about packing. He'd agreed to the trade, but he really didn't want to leave. Now it was a done deal and he had no choice.

"You say something, mate?" His friend and roommate, Viggo Sjoberg, came padding into the room yawning.

"Nah, just telling myself how stupid I am." Jamie held up his beer. "I've been traded to Ottawa."

Viggo stared at him in surprise. "Really? That wasn't just gossip? You're moving?"

"Just got the call." Jamie leaned against the refrigerator and looked down.

"This is because—"

"Doesn't matter," Jamie interrupted him abruptly. "It's done and technically I asked for it."

"Then why don't you look happy?"

"Sometimes I guess you do what's right instead of what's easy. Or some bullshit like that."

Viggo frowned, staring at his lean, dark-haired friend and roommate. Viggo had come to Las Vegas last year on a tryout. There'd been almost no chance he would make the team, but somehow he'd impressed both the coaches and management and there'd been an introductory contract. Jamie's living situation had changed around the same time and he'd invited Viggo to move in. They got along well and had become close but he hadn't known what was going on when, just after winning the team's first championship back in June, Jamie left with no warning and went home to his native Ontario for the summer. There had been trouble, things Jamie hadn't talked about much, but Viggo knew most of it. What he didn't know was why Jamie was leaving. Viggo also knew Jamie loved it here and, despite some of his problems, loved this team.

"You need to talk?" he asked finally.

"There's nothing to say," Jamie grumbled. "I did this to myself."

"This is because of you and Becca?" Viggo asked, referring to a threesome Jamie had had with his friend Dante and his girlfriend that had been videotaped without their knowledge and released to the public. Becca worked for the Las Vegas Sidewinders, the team Jamie and Viggo played for, and there had been an unspoken expectation that one of them would leave to avoid any further scandal. Everyone assumed it would be Becca since she was now engaged to her wealthy baseball player boyfriend and would undoubtedly be starting a family soon. Instead, Jamie had asked for a trade but Viggo hadn't had the opportunity to talk to him about it.

"Yeah, kind of." Jamie ran a hand through his wavy hair, making it stick up for a moment before a long strand fell back onto his forehead, where it perpetually rested over his right eye. "Dante asked me to. He said she was humiliated and if she had to leave the team because of this she would never recover from it professionally. Even though she doesn't need to work anymore, since he's richer than God, he said it was eating her up inside and she didn't want her career to end this way."

"So you offered?" Viggo arched a brow doubtfully.

"He made me an offer I had a hard time refusing." Jamie met his friend's gaze. "He knows a lot of people and is involved in shit I don't understand, but he said he'd make sure the steroid use never got looked at again, that I wouldn't have to worry about the no-notice tests and that if anything ever happened financially, he'd take care of it."

"And the contract they offered was good?"

"Yeah." Jamie nodded miserably. "It's really good. More money than I've ever made."

"But you don't want to go."

"Fuck no." Jamie blew out a breath and downed the rest of his beer. He slammed it on the counter and stalked out of the room, heading to his bedroom.

Viggo followed, worried about his normally easygoing friend. "So you can't turn it down?" he asked.

"Too late, this is a done deal."

"You don't have to sign."

Jamie laughed even though it wasn't funny, throwing himself down on his bed and staring up at the ceiling. "One of us has to go, and remember, I asked to be traded. I'd look like a complete idiot. No, it's done and I have to get used to the idea."

"I'm sorry." Viggo sat on the edge of the bed and looked at him. "What can I do?"

"Nothing." Jamie paused, smiling at the much-bigger man he'd lived with for the last year. "You've got to go get your wife and kid, start a new chapter in your life too."

Viggo sighed. "Yeah. That."

Now Jamie frowned. "What's *that* supposed to mean? You don't sound like a newlywed."

"Nothing." Viggo felt a twinge of guilt. He had no right to talk about his troubled young wife and their even more troubling marriage.

"Nothing? Really?" Jamie sat up. "Did something happen?"

"No." Viggo shook his head. "It's just, you know, Emilie and I don't really know each other. We've known each other since we were teenagers, but we've never dated, never spent any real time together... Three months ago I didn't even know I had a kid. Now I'm a bisexual man married to a...very sexually liberal woman...and I'm moving both her and our baby to Las Vegas, where neither of us truly fit in."

"Why do you think you don't fit in?" Jamie asked, still frowning. "You fit in great with the team here."

"I speak English okay now—thanks to you—but I don't read or write very well and half the time I don't even get the jokes in the locker room. I know for a fact I'm the only openly bisexual man in the league and now I'm married to a woman. I don't give a shit what anyone says about me, but I don't want that for Emilie."

"Emilie's a big girl," Jamie said gently. "And she knew exactly what she was getting into. Karl's here—you know no one is going to say a word about either of you in front of him." Karl was Emilie's older brother and the starting goalie for the team.

"I can't count on Karl to protect her—or me," he groused. "I had a good season last year, but I'm worried about what kind of scrutiny she'll be under for being married to me."

"Are you worried about scrutiny or are you worried about being married to a woman I get the feeling you're not in love with?"

Viggo sighed. "I love her—I'm just not sure it's the forever kind of love. We care for each other and both of us feel that we need to try for Simone's sake, but it scares me. And now you..." He looked away, feeling somewhat foolish for letting Jamie see how unhappy he was that his closest friend in the U.S. was moving.

"On top of everything else I'm leaving," Jamie finished for him. "I'm sorry, man. I'm going to miss you too, but with Emilie and the baby coming, it wasn't going to be the same for us anyway."

"Ya, I know." Viggo met his gaze and gave him a lazy grin. "How the hell am I going to survive without Xbox tournaments at 3 a.m.?"

Jamie grimaced. "We can play online?"

"Three-hour time difference and travel schedules," Viggo grunted.

They locked eyes and Jamie slowly sat up. The room was suddenly charged with electricity and Jamie couldn't help but grin at the familiar excitement. "You wanna go?"

Viggo narrowed his eyes. "Now?!"

"When else? Tomorrow when you pick up your girls? This is it, man—we have less than 24 hours of bachelor-level Xbox." Jamie was already up and heading to the door, pausing to look back over his shoulder. "You comin'?"

Viggo laughed. "Hell yeah."

. . .

PACKING up her life and moving from New York to Las Vegas was stressful for Emilie, Viggo thought as she complained to him on the phone about all the items she had to take with her to the airport. She was a new mom and a new wife, and about to do it all with a new job in a brand-new city. If it hadn't been for the fact that they had a child together and he was partially responsible for the sex scandal she'd endured just over a year ago, he didn't know where they would be now. He didn't worry about things like that, though. From finding out she'd had his child without him even knowing she was pregnant to unexpectedly earning a spot on a professional hockey team to getting married with only a couple of weeks' notice, he'd been through a lot but wasn't nearly as stressed or out of sorts as she was. They had huge obstacles in front of them and they both knew it, but while she was nervous and edgy, he just wanted to take care of her and show her it was going to be okay. Even though they'd secretly had feelings for each other since they were teens, Viggo was openly bisexual and Emilie had so many demons when it came to sex, he was concerned that she might not be able to get beyond them.

For now, he was enjoying getting to know their daughter and bringing Emilie to Las Vegas where they would start their new life. She'd moved to New York to attend school to become a clothing designer, but that dream had faded when she realized her priority was her daughter and being wherever Viggo was so he could be a part of her life too. The opportunity to manage a new sex club owned by a friend of theirs was a way for her to have a bit of independence and something to do while he forwarded his career, but he wondered if there was more to it. Her sexual desires were far beyond anything he was familiar with or interested in, so maybe being at the club would feed some of her demons and she wouldn't have to act on them. Or maybe it would do something entirely different; maybe she would discover that a traditional marriage, especially to a bisexual man, wasn't for her. There was already evidence she was struggling with it and they'd only been married a short time.

"You sounded so serious just now." Viggo said, feeling a twinge of regret that he'd come home to Las Vegas instead of going to New York with her when they'd returned from Sweden. He'd had things to do to get the apartment ready, and they'd agreed it would be better for him to do that while she packed up her life in New York. "You all right?"

"I'm good," she said. "Just a little overwhelmed. New city, new apartment, new job—and still a new mum."

"You're a fantastic mum," he whispered.

"Most days I wake up and wonder what I'm doing."

"You're doing great and Las Vegas is going to be a wonderful new start for us."

"Viggo, what if it doesn't work out?"

"Stop saying that!" he cried. "Don't you trust me?"

"Not everything is about you," she spoke tenderly. "I'm totally fucked up and no more equipped to be in a monogamous relationship than a confused bisexual man who found out the girl he's always had a crush on had his kid."

Viggo scowled even though she couldn't see it. "I'm not that confused, so what are we talking about, Em?"

"You," she said softly. "You're such a kind, wonderful, sexy beast of a man—I've never truly even considered loving anyone else. But deep down I don't know if I'm capable of a normal, healthy relationship. My demons started long before Therese blackmailed me..." Her voice trailed off as she thought of her former best friend, who'd since betrayed and used her in ways she'd never thought possible. "She knew about them and used them against me."

"She also used me and that fool Otto." He and Otto had been friends before Otto tricked Viggo into a threesome with him and Emilie that Therese secretly recorded and used to blackmail her with.

"For sure, but after that video went viral and she killed those people...tried to kill my brother...I'm still struggling with it all. Humiliated in front of my family, traumatized knowing that both you and I were used by friends...and there's more, things I'm not ready to talk about even with you."

"You should see someone," he said after a thoughtful silence, a million things running through his mind as he listened to her sad voice. "A professional. Whatever it is, try to work through it."

"I'm going to."

"That's all any of us can do, Em." He kept his voice hopeful, but tiny pinpricks of doubt were beginning to creep in. Could they do this? Could he stay faithful to a woman who appeared to be an even bigger mess than he was? Would they be able to work through what felt like insurmountable issues? He wasn't sure, she appeared even less sure, and there wasn't a damn thing he could do about it.

## CHAPTER 2

Jamie stared at the packed boxes in his room with a sigh. He was Canadian, so technically he was going home but it sure didn't feel like it. Ottawa was only about two hours from his hometown of Kingston, Ontario, but the problem was that Las Vegas was home now. He didn't want to go back to Canada, and he didn't want to play in Ottawa. Sure, it was a great organization, and moving around was part of the job of a hockey player, but he wasn't ready to leave the Sidewinders. He loved playing here, loved his teammates and loved being part of a team that had won a championship last season.

He also had really good friends. His buddy Zakk had lived with him the first year they'd been on the team together and they'd been tight. When Jamie had gotten serious with his then girlfriend and thought he was going to propose, Zakk had moved in with another teammate, but then Jamie and Rachel had broken up. Jamie hadn't been sure whether he wanted another roommate or not, but one had fallen into his lap.

Viggo Sjoberg was a big, burly redheaded Swede who'd gotten invited to try out for the team because of his friendship with the Sidewinders' goalie, Karl Martensson. No one had been more shocked than Viggo when he'd been offered a position and Jamie had been quick to invite him to move in. It had been great, too. Even though Viggo was openly bisexual and had brought home men a few times, he was discreet, trustworthy and easygoing. He didn't hide his sexuality, but Jamie had never thought twice about it. They got along really well and it never occurred to him that Viggo might make sexual advances; it just didn't seem like a big deal and it turned out that Viggo was a really good guy.

It was convenient having someone to ride with to and from games, plus another single guy to go out with once in a while. With Zakk and probably more than half of the rest of the team involved in serious relationships now, Jamie had begun to feel like a third wheel. Viggo had been single until recently too and it hadn't taken them long to fall into a routine, working out together, working together and hanging out when they were off.

Though Viggo had struggled a little with English in the beginning, by spending time together he'd improved rapidly and one of the ways they'd practiced was by watching TV. They also played video games and listened to a lot of hard rock music on the radio. They were almost the same age and had a lot of the same interests, making their friendship a lot more solid than friendships with other roommates Jamie had had over the years. It had been a great season that ended with them winning the championship, and having to move across the country to start over was depressing as hell.

Trying to shake off his melancholy, he went into the bathroom and got into the shower. As the hot water sluiced over him, he breathed in steamy air that was so thick it looked like he was encased in a cloud. He closed his eyes and put his hands against the wall, letting his chin fall to his chest as he thought about the changes that were coming: a new city, new team, new place to live and no friends. Scowling at his self-deprecating thoughts, he forced himself to try to think about something else.

He wondered if there would be any interesting women in Ottawa and how he might meet them. After spending 18 months dating a movie star and having a handful of dates with Zakk's sister that hadn't gone anywhere, he was at a loss with women. Rachel Kennedy had been beautiful, rich, successful and surprisingly down-to-earth. They got along well and she'd been as into letting him spank her as he was into doing it, but his trouble with steroid use and the subsequent blackmail that arose had driven her away.

Zakk's sister, Danielle, was a fresh-faced 21-year-old hockey-playing college student, but he'd screwed that up too. When it became clear the blackmail situation wasn't going away, he'd gone home to Canada not long after they started dating. He'd taken a side trip to Manhattan and got caught coming out of a sex club with the Sidewinders' head of Media Relations, Becca Hernandez. He'd been involved in a threesome with Becca and her fiancé, baseball player Dante Lamonte, but since the pictures had circulated the internet, there was no way to deny he'd slept with someone else. He hadn't cheated on Danielle since they'd only gone out a couple of times, but his indiscretion made it clear that things between them weren't going anywhere.

Of course, it was those same pictures that had led Dante to make the deal with Jamie that he be the one to leave the Sidewinders. Either he or Becca had to go; it was too complicated for them to both work for the team after the scandal. If he asked for a trade, Becca could keep her job, and emotionally it had been important to Becca that she didn't sacrifice her professional reputation over illicit photographs that had been taken without permission.

When it was all said and done, Dante had sued the club owners and now owned the establishment where the pictures had been taken, but that hadn't helped Jamie. He was being shipped off to Ottawa and Becca was getting ready for another season. Yes, Dante had made it worth his while and had promised Jamie he would never have to worry about anything, but he was beginning to wonder if it was a worthwhile trade-off. He had no idea how Dante would keep any of the promises he'd made, but at this point it was moot.

Stepping out of the shower, he dried off and wrapped the towel around his waist. He brushed his teeth and dragged a comb through his hair as he stared in the mirror. He padded back into his bedroom and was about to dig out a pair of shorts when a shriek from the living room startled him. Viggo was supposed to be picking up his new wife and daughter at the airport and going to dinner at his brother-in-law's house, so who the hell was in the living room? Without a weapon of any kind, he wasn't sure what to do but he couldn't just sit here either. Had they come home unexpectedly? And who was yelling?

He grabbed his phone off the dresser and dialed 9-1-1, though he didn't press the send button, keeping it hidden in his hand as he slipped down the hall. Another yelp made him jump and then a woman's voice caused him to freeze in his tracks.

"Harder! Viggo, please!"

*Shit*. Emilie and Viggo were having sex and he was close to walking in on them. He was about to turn and go back to his room when he heard the sound of a hand slapping skin. Jesus, were they into spanking too? His cock twitched just thinking about it and he couldn't resist taking the last three steps to the end of the hall. He peeked around the corner feeling like a creep, but the moment he caught sight of them there was no way he was going anywhere.

Emilie was bent over the back of the couch, Viggo buried deep inside of her, one hand gripping her long blond hair, the other slapping her beautiful little ass. He watched in fascination as Viggo pounded into her, over and over, the muscles in his taut ass straining as he fucked her. She was panting, her long legs spread wide to give him deeper access, and Viggo's body was like that of a powerful animal as he took her. Jamie couldn't even blink as he watched. They were fucking *hot*, and he hadn't had sex in a couple of months, so he was already aroused.

"More!" she whimpered.

"Dammit, Em, I can't hit you any harder!" Viggo grunted.

"Please!" She whispered something in Swedish that made Viggo groan, but he stopped moving and let go of her hair.

"Em, I can't."

*I could*, Jamie thought, his hand unconsciously traveling to his erection.

"Viggo!" Emilie dropped her head, frustration practically oozing out of her.

"I'm sorry..." He seemed as unsatisfied as she was. "I just, it's not me. You know how I feel about this."

"But I like it!" she cried. "You're not hurting me!"

"I'm sorry..." His voice trailed off.

"I can hit her." Jamie wasn't even aware he'd spoken until Emilie and Viggo jumped in surprise, their heads whipping around to stare at him.

"Jamie!" Viggo's face flushed slightly. "Damn, I'm sorry, we thought—"

"I don't have to do anything else with her," Jamie continued slowly, walking towards them. "I can just spank her while you fuck her—nothing else. If it would help. You both seem irritated and...it's kind of my thing."

"Oh, Viggo, please!" Emilie reached back to clutch her husband's forearm.

Viggo hadn't moved, his cock still buried inside of her, and he met Jamie's gaze with interest. "You're sure? You don't mind?"

Jamie let his towel fall away, revealing his throbbing erection, his eyes meeting Viggo's. "Watching the two of you fuck is hot as hell—I've always enjoyed watching—and I don't mind jerking off when we're done."

The two men exchanged a look of mutual appreciation as Viggo slowly nodded. "Em, are you sure?"

"Oh, yes!" Her blue eyes were glittering with excitement.

"I'll be right back." Jamie turned and practically ran into his room, yanking open the closet door and grabbing the only belt he found. If she liked it rough, he'd give her rough; it was one of his favorite things when it came to sex.

Viggo's eyes widened when Jamie returned, and he glanced down at his wife. "Em?"

"Oh yes..." Her voice was a breathy whisper this time.

Jamie didn't hesitate, folding the belt into a manageable size and bringing it down on her left cheek, careful not to hit Viggo's crotch in the process. She yelped and he immediately did it again. This time she moaned, surging back to meet Viggo's hips.

"I hit, then you thrust," Jamie instructed Viggo, who nodded.

Jamie felt his cock getting stiffer and stiffer as he increased intensity and Emilie bucked like a wild woman, her chest rising and falling in an almost rhythmic pattern as she begged for more. She was whimpering, her skin getting redder and redder. He paused, running his hands over the inflamed area gently.

"Okay, baby, I'm going to hit you twice more," he said softly. "Once on each side, and then you're going to come. You can't take much more—you understand?"

"Wait..." she was breathing hard, her cheeks flushed, body covered in sweat. "We should come together...all of us...not fair...for you to just watch."

"I don't think—" Viggo began.

"It's okay—" Jamie said at the same time.

"But it's what I want," she whispered. "Both of you on your knees, one behind me, the other in front. We come together..."

"Yeah, all right." Viggo was battling the pure lust burning inside his gut with his need to protect his wife and their marriage. Feeling her squeezing him, her juices practically running down her legs each time Jamie hit her, was hot. Not to mention the sexy hunk of man whose cock was making his mouth water. Why had he never noticed Jamie like this before? They'd lived together for a year and it took a threesome with his wife to notice how sexy he was?

Emilie dropped to the ground on her hands and knees and Jamie knelt in front of her. Without hesitation, she took him into her mouth and he let out a long, low moan.

"I'm not going to last long," he muttered. "It's been a while."

"Em's on the verge too," Viggo murmured, positioning himself behind her and sliding in deep.

Jamie fisted Emilie's hair, using his hands to hold her head still as he pumped in and out of her mouth. "Can you deep throat me, Emilie?" he asked.

She nodded and he drove straight to the back of her throat, closing his eyes and enjoying the sensation of her warm lips and tongue enveloping him.

Viggo picked up the pace, holding her in place by the hips. He met Jamie's rhythm and they fucked her together, their bodies perfectly in sync, moving as though they'd done this a million times before. Viggo's big, muscular body was sheer perfection in Jamie's eyes; large, strong and pure masculinity. Emilie was the complete opposite, as feminine as any woman he'd ever seen with milky white skin, light blond hair, pale pink nipples and the softest skin he'd ever felt. Watching

Viggo fuck her had gotten him excited; having her suck him off at the same time was more than he could stand. Jamie lost control first, growling as he pushed his cock down her throat, shooting deep. Emilie never even blinked, swallowing without so much as a cough, continuing to suck until he nearly collapsed. Viggo yanked her against him, rocking back on his haunches without breaking contact and pulling her up so her back rested against his chest.

"Put your mouth on her," Viggo growled at Jamie.

Jamie didn't hesitate, crawling over to them and gliding his tongue right between her folds. She was completely bare and her clit puffed up between his lips. He bit down lightly, one hand sliding underneath to cup Viggo's balls. He had no idea what made him do that but the urge to touch his large, sexy friend was suddenly irresistible. Viggo's reaction was all he could've hoped for too, a moan escaping him as he briefly met Jamie's cautious gaze. Unable to resist, Jamie ran his tongue from her slit to the base of Viggo's shaft and wrapped his mouth as far around it as he could. Viggo shuddered against him and thrust up hard, both he and Emilie coming together.

Jamie lay back and collapsed, still breathing hard. Emilie crawled off of Viggo and lay on the floor on her stomach. Viggo didn't move, simply watching both of them with heavy-lidded eyes. The aftermath of what they'd just done was heavy in the air and Jamie sat up first.

"She'll need aftercare," was all he said as he started to get up.

"Yeah, and you'll be the one to give it to her," Viggo rumbled, reaching over to run a hand over Emilie's bright red ass.

"I thought—"

"You thought what? You'd come in here, have sex with us and walk away?"

"I figured that's what you'd want," he said quietly, crawling over to Emilie and gently running his hand down her back and onto her behind. "I didn't mean to interrupt but when I heard you say you couldn't hit her harder...it's my thing so I... I'm sorry. I didn't mean to overstep the boundaries of our friendship."

Viggo chuckled. "Did you hear her beg you for more? I can't give her what you just gave her."

Jamie hesitated. "I'm, uh, I'm not sure what to do now."

"Take care of her," Viggo murmured, getting to his feet. "I'll clean up a bit and be right back." He padded out of the room without a backwards glance and Jamie leaned over Emilie, moving her hair back so he could see one side of her face.

"How're you doing, hon?" he whispered softly, one hand trailing along her cheek. "I went at you pretty hard. You okay?"

"Oh yes." She smiled faintly. "It was lovely."

"I, uh, didn't know you liked this kind of thing."

"I didn't know you did." She opened one eye and grinned. "I loved having you both take me."

He smiled and used his hands to gently rub her bruised behind. "Honey, I think you'll need a cool cloth for this. You're awfully red."

"I'm fine," she murmured. "My skin's sensitive, but I'm not hurt. I promise."

"Still." He got to his feet and bent to lift her. "I'm going to put you in bed and get a towel—"

"I've got it." Viggo met Jamie's eyes and motioned with his head. "Go on, take her to the bedroom."

## CHAPTER 3

Jamie laid her on the bed and Viggo put the cool, wet towel over her throbbing cheeks. Jamie lay beside her, resting on one elbow while he used the other arm to gently massage her back. Viggo lay on her other side, his position almost a mirror image of Jamie's as he stroked Emilie's hair. Within minutes she was fast asleep, her deep breathing giving away just how much they'd worn her out.

They were quiet for a long time, both watching Emilie as she slept.

"I didn't know you were home." Jamie felt like he should explain. "I heard a noise and went to investigate."

"We came in and called out, but you didn't answer, so we thought we'd take advantage of some alone time because Kate has the baby."

"I was in the shower."

The two men looked at each other, Viggo's expression unreadable while Jamie fidgeted uneasily.

"Look, I hope we're okay," Jamie said at last.

"We're fine," Viggo nodded slowly, unsure how to best handle his friend's obvious discomfort. "I thought you'd had threesomes before?"

"I have, but never with a man I've lived with for almost a year, and his *wife*."

"I can't hit her like that," Viggo admitted abruptly. "My father beat my mother, and even though it's not the same thing, every time I do it I'm afraid I'm hurting her. I enjoy a little pain, but I can't do it to a woman, and Em really wants it."

"I'm glad I could, uh, you know, take care of that."

"We're good, okay?" Viggo met his gaze again. "I told you I was bisexual when I moved in, and you know I've brought men here but—"

"Yeah, I could hear you with them." Jamie looked down.

"Did it bother you?"

"No. It was kind of hot." He felt himself grow a little warm.

"So being together like this was okay?" Viggo yearned to touch him but didn't dare. "We're okay?"

"I'm not worried about you and me," Jamie interrupted brusquely. "I'm worried about you and *her*."

Viggo shook his head. "Em has needs I can't take care of, so it's okay."

"What about your needs?" Jamie wasn't sure why he put his hand on top of Viggo's, and the words came out of their own volition.

"Em and the baby come first," he responded gently. "Things like that aren't important."

"You mean your interest in men?"

Viggo managed a small shrug. "I don't think about it."

"You thought about it tonight." Jamie couldn't believe he was pressing the point, but couldn't seem to help himself.

"Hard to resist when it's so hot and sexy and right under my nose." Viggo wasn't sure what was going on with his straight friend, but it turned him on more than he wanted to admit. He was willing to bet his life Jamie had never had a one-on-one sexual encounter with a man before, but the interest he was showing now was hot enough to make Viggo think about things he'd never thought about before. Not with Jamie, anyway.

"Luckily, I'm leaving in three days, so this particular temptation will be gone." Jamie didn't understand what was happening between them but there was no denying something was there.

After a brief hesitation, Viggo looked up, keen interest in his blue eyes. "But think of all the fun we can have in three days."

JAMIE WOKE to the exquisite feeling of a warm and wet mouth sucking his cock. His eyes popped open and he gasped at the sight of Emilie bending over him as Viggo buried his face between her legs from behind. Jamie groaned when she sucked harder, his hips arching into her face.

"Holy shit," he groaned. "You two are gonna kill me!"

Emilie released his cock with a soft popping noise and slid down until one of his balls was nestled between her lips, working him into a frenzy. Jamie squeezed his eyes shut, trying to hold back, but the second she sucked him deep again he came so hard his hips shot up off the bed, ramming himself into her harder than he intended.

"We're going to have to work on your stamina," Viggo murmured, sitting up with a grin.

"Shit." Jamie shook his head. "Emilie's got my number with this."

She smiled, sliding up his body and stretching out on him. "Since you've gotten off, it's only fair you get us off now."

He raised his eyebrows, one hand gliding down the silky slope of her back. "What did you have in mind?"

She straddled him with a soft smile. "We have two days," she whispered. "How far are you willing to go, Jamie? Just the three of us. We can do anything and everything. I can take both of you, and I know Viggo can take the two of us. Can *you* take both of us?"

Jamie swallowed hard, looking into her sparkling blue eyes before cutting a nervous glance at Viggo. "I've never been with...a man—not like that."

Viggo moved beside him, one big hand digging into the shock of dark wavy hair that perpetually fell over his forehead. "Do you want to try? Em wants you, and I have to admit I'm not opposed to letting you top me."

A fluttering of excitement shot through Jamie at the thought of actually having sex with Viggo but it wasn't something he'd ever been tempted to try before. He'd never been with a man other than some secondary contact from both of them having sex with the same woman. He had to admit he'd always been vaguely curious, but now that he had the opportunity he wasn't sure what to do. He wanted to say yes and shove Emilie down on his still-erect cock while Viggo did whatever he wanted to him. Instead, he looked from one to the other hesitantly, torn between what his body wanted and what his brain told him was wrong.

"I'm willing to try," he whispered finally, the words sounding foreign on his tongue but escaping nonetheless.

"It won't feel much different with Emilie between us," Viggo whispered, spreading out beside him and putting a gentle hand on his arm. "We'll keep one-on-one contact minimal until you're comfortable."

"What if I can't do it?" Jamie looked down worriedly.

Viggo could see pure desire in Jamie's soft brown eyes, but there was also fear and insecurity. The only way to get past it would be to show him it was okay, so he leaned over and kissed him.

Jamie was startled when Viggo moved towards him but couldn't seem to turn away. Viggo's lips were soft yet his mouth was rough and demanding. He didn't hesitate to thrust his tongue against Jamie's, kissing him with vigor. Jamie was too shocked to respond at first, but his body knew what it wanted immediately and before he even realized what had happened he was kissing him back. Tongues swirled, lips locked and Viggo kissed him like no one had ever kissed him before. It wasn't until Jamie heard his own moan that he realized he'd wrapped one arm around Viggo's neck and was pulling him closer, so anxious for more he forgot all about the fact that Viggo was a guy. When their chests touched and they were skin-to-skin, Jamie was vaguely aware of Emilie taking him in her mouth again but he was far more interested in the kiss that was blowing his mind.

He wasn't sure what to concentrate on as Viggo held his mouth prisoner and used his larger body to keep him pinned in place. Jamie wouldn't have moved if his life depended on it, though, never having been overpowered like this before. It was hot, much hotter than when he was the one in control with a woman; he'd always imagined that being with a man would provide him with the roughness and intensity he enjoyed, but he'd never even considered trying it.

Now that it was happening his cock stiffened even more and his mouth was completely captivated by the burly hockey player who'd simply been a friend and teammate until just minutes ago. Viggo's lips were so spellbinding he was paralyzed with lust. It was unlike anything he'd ever experienced and instead of revulsion, he wanted more. The rough scrape of Viggo's beard, his firm grip, and his skill with his tongue left Jamie feeling scorched, raw, and aroused to the point it was painful.

He nearly cried out in frustration when Viggo pulled away, but Emilie's tongue drew his attention down to the pleasure flowing from his cock to his groin and back again. Viggo nudged Jamie until he was slightly propped up with a couple of pillows behind him. Emilie moved with them, her lips never leaving his penis as she sucked and licked him back into oblivion.

"Do you want to touch me?" Viggo asked quietly, lifting to his knees and straddling Jamie's chest as he wrapped a beefy hand around his own cock, careful to keep it a couple of inches from Jamie's mouth. There was no mistaking the anxiety in his friend's eyes and the last thing he wanted was to pressure him.

"I, uh..." Jamie's eyes rolled back in his head as Emilie relaxed her throat and let him slide down so far he had to gasp for air. "Jesus...*fuck!*"

Viggo waited patiently, lightly jacking his cock, until Jamie could focus again. "Do you want to try?" he asked, the look on his face so tender Jamie was willing to do almost anything he asked.

Instead, he closed his eyes, wondering how he would come back once he went down this road. The memory of Viggo's kiss, his strong body on his, made him helpless to do anything but lean forward and open his mouth. It felt wrong, completely foreign, but when Viggo put just the head against his lips, Jamie was strangely stimulated and surprised at the ease with which he took it.

"I, uh, I don't know how to do this," he admitted, turning his head.

"Just think about what *you* like," Viggo said quietly. "It's all good, however you want to do it."

"*Shit*." Jamie wrapped his hand around the other man's bulging cock and brought it halfway into his mouth this time. He closed his lips around it, exploring the head and cautiously running his tongue over the slit. His eyes flew open nervously at Viggo's sharp intake of breath, but his eyes were closed, mouth slightly open, the pleasure on his face obvious.

"He likes it hard," Emilie whispered. "Suck him deep, like I did to you."

Jamie did as she suggested, one hand around the base of Viggo's shaft, the other cupping his balls. He squeezed with enough pressure to make Viggo groan deep in his chest. It wasn't too bad, he thought, and there was no taste, unlike how there was with a woman. He tentatively sucked harder, drawing him in deeper, moving his hands to Viggo's hips. Viggo was perfectly still, allowing Jamie to set the pace and explore at his leisure. Emilie seemed to sense that she should pause and give Jamie time to get acclimated with something so new to him, so she rested her chin on his abdomen.

A plethora of emotions ran through Viggo. Jamie was sucking him like a pro, despite his nervousness, and the sensation of his wet tongue with his strong mouth created the holy grail of blow jobs for him. Every swipe of Jamie's tongue brought him closer to nirvana and he clenched his jaw tightly to keep from gripping Jamie's head and fucking his mouth for all he was worth.

"Enough." Emilie's gentle hands pried Viggo's cock from Jamie's mouth and both men groaned. "My turn," she said. She replaced Jamie's mouth with her own, swirling her tongue along the outside with sweeping motions that made both men groan all over again. Jamie slid further down between Viggo's legs and lifted his head to suck one of his balls into his mouth. He licked between them, moving forward as Emilie moved down. As their faces came together, he captured her mouth in a kiss that was brief but intense. They separated and this time Jamie took Viggo back between his lips, picking up where Emilie left off.

They moved back and forth, sucking, licking and kissing both Viggo and each other, until Viggo gripped each of them by the hair, tugging them up to their knees so that all three were pressed together. He kissed Emilie first, holding her firmly in place by the hair, before abruptly releasing her and turning to Jamie. This time Jamie was ready and his tongue snaked out to meet the bigger man's in a heated frenzy. They alternated kisses the same way they'd alternated blowing him, but it was Emilie who broke away, her rapid breathing belying her need for them.

"Both of you," she whispered. "I want the two of you at once..."

"She's not on the pill," Viggo said, giving Jamie an apologetic look. "We probably shouldn't take a chance..."

Jamie nodded with understanding. "Are you okay with anal?" he breathed against Emilie's ear, wrapping his arms around her waist.

"Yes." She leaned forward to reach into her nightstand and pulled out a bottle of lube, handing it to him as Viggo dug condoms out of his nightstand. Emilie sheathed them both while Jamie dripped a liberal amount of lube between her cheeks, easing one finger into her and pressing deep.

"So fucking smooth," he murmured, lining himself up behind her. She leaned forward, onto Viggo's strong torso as Jamie pushed past the resistance from the straining ring of muscles.

Emilie moaned when Jamie edged in, her body protesting the invasion. Jamie wasn't as thick as Viggo, but she and Viggo hadn't had anal sex in a long time, and it had been well over a year since she'd done it with anyone.

"Easy, baby, relax..." Jamie pulled back, giving her time to adjust before pressing forward again. He moved slowly, a fraction of an inch at a time, until finally he was completely immersed in her. His cock elongated and swelled as she tightened around him, her beautiful ass surging back to meet his thrusts.

"Fucking hot," Viggo growled, pulling them with him as he lay on his back. He tugged Emilie forward until her pussy was directly over his cock and slowly guided her down.

"Oh God, please, harder..." She was breathless, her fingers digging into Viggo's shoulders. "Both of you...harder!" Her head fell back, spreading her golden hair across Jamie's chest and he reached around front to cup her breasts with both hands. He watched as Viggo thrust up and into her, keeping his own cock buried in her ass without moving.

When he couldn't stand it anymore he began to glide in and out, thrusting as Viggo withdrew. Once again, they found a rhythm that was natural. Jamie rolled her nipples between his fingers, tightening until she cried out and then rubbing his thumbs across them to soothe the burn. He did it over and over, picking up speed with both his fingers and his cock. She was impaled on Viggo who was grinding into her, fingers digging into her hips as he took her.

Emilie couldn't move since she was held fast by both of them, and looking down at their entwined bodies, Jamie became aware of one sensation after another piling on top of each other until his breath left him in an explosive rush that made everything go black. The pleasure started at his feet and crept up his body like a heatwave. He felt Viggo pumping into Emilie as cries escaped them and Viggo thrust up a few more times before they all went completely still. No one moved, and Emilie slowly collapsed on Viggo's chest. Jamie rested partly on her back, partly off to the side. The only sound was of their breathing returning to normal and the thudding of their hearts.

Jamie finally moved away from her, careful not to pull out too fast. He rolled onto his side and off the edge of the bed, getting up and padding into the bathroom. He locked the door behind him and took a moment to clean up before resting his forehead against the bathroom door. What *the fuck* had just happened?

He'd had threesomes before but nothing like this, and...sucking another guy's dick had been as erotic as it had been humiliating. How the fuck was he ever going to look at Viggo again? He closed his eyes, willing himself to calm down. He would settle his mind, relax his body and go back out there coolly. He'd make an excuse and escape to his room where he could lick his wounds in private.

# CHAPTER 4

Lying together quietly, they were quiet and relaxed. Viggo's eyes eventually opened and he smiled at Emiie. "You all right?" he asked.

She smiled back. "I'm good. You?"

"Same." He wrapped his arms around her. "He's sexy as hell, yeah?"

"Oh yes." She glanced at the closed bathroom door. "But he's been in there a long time. Maybe he's not okay?"

Viggo frowned. They'd agreed to do this a little over an hour ago, as they'd watched Jamie sleep and conceded that they both wanted him. If it was just for these last couple of days, they were okay with that, but last night's sex had been as satisfying for them as any they'd ever had and they both wanted more. Personally, it had been a long time since a man had turned him on this much, and he didn't want to think about how much he'd enjoyed having the two of them take turns sucking his dick.

If he could wake up that way every single day, he would die a happy man. Emilie seemed equally content, and that made this so much better. But she was right: Jamie had been in the bathroom a long time and, as a man who'd struggled for years with being bisexual, it occurred to him Jamie might not be as accepting of that as Viggo had been. Especially since it had been his first time giving a man head.

With a regretful sigh, he pushed her to the side and sat up. "I should go," he said. "If it's because of me—because of what we did—I should talk to him."

She nodded. "Yes, of course." She leaned over and pressed her lips to his. "Don't let him regret this, darling..."

He met her gaze guiltily. "I'll do my best to sort it." He got up and walked to the bathroom, knocking on the door. "Jamie? You all right?"

"Yeah, just need a minute." Jamie's voice was strained and Viggo felt a twinge of guilt, remembering his own first sexual encounter with a man.

"Jamie, I know what's in your head. I've been there. I remember the first time I sucked a man's dick. Don't torture yourself. Talk to me."

There was a long silence but finally the door opened. Jamie stood there with a towel wrapped around his waist, looking completely bewildered.

"No, don't look like that." Viggo reached for him and tugged him forward, his arm around his neck. He led him to the bed and sat on the edge, patting the spot next to him. Emilie had disappeared, probably to one of the other bathrooms, and they sat in silence for a moment.

"No guilt, no regrets." Viggo didn't touch him, but made sure he was sitting close to him; he didn't want him to be uncomfortable but he also didn't want him to feel used or abandoned. "Have you ever thought that you were bi?"

Jamie shook his head. "No."

"If you weren't into it, we would have stopped."

Jamie snorted. "I practically swallowed your dick—there's no doubt I was into it!"

"But you're not now."

"Look, I have to finish packing and—" He started to get up but Viggo closed strong fingers around his forearm.

"I sucked my first cock at 17," he said quietly. "When I was done, he zipped up and laughed, asked me how it felt to be a faggot."

Jamie hissed under his breath and sank back down on the bed. "I'm sorry, man."

"I wasn't with another man for two years. Instead, I fucked any female with a pulse and made sure everyone knew it. Then I went to my first sex club, met a guy who knew instinctively that I was bi. He was older, a dom, and he showed me a whole new world. Made me understand that it was okay to like both—I didn't have to pick one sex or the other, I only had to pick people I liked and do things I enjoyed. I still struggled to figure out why I enjoyed both, why I needed both. I saw therapists, did a lot of soul searching..."

"And?" Jamie looked at him intently.

"There's nothing wrong with me. I like men. I like women. I love sex. I've never forced anyone, never been with a child, never touched someone who didn't want to be touched...please tell me I still haven't."

Jamie shook his head. "I definitely wanted to be touched. I, uh, well, you know. I never did *that* before, never thought I would enjoy it."

"Did you?" Viggo's voice was soft.

"Yeah." Jamie looked down. "It wasn't what I was expecting, to enjoy that with a guy... but I did and I'm already such a fucking mess—the timing could've been better for me to discover I'm bi."

"I'm always here," Viggo said. "You're only moving to Ottawa, not Australia. I'll see you next month, in fact. You'll be playing here at the end of October."

"Yeah." Jamie couldn't meet his eyes.

"Listen to me." Viggo gripped Jamie's chin and made him turn. "If you don't want to do this again, then don't. If we coerced, or—"

"No." Jamie's hand came up to squeeze Viggo's. "You didn't force me. You didn't trick me. You asked if I wanted to try and I did. I liked it. I'm not such a pussy that I'm going to pretend that this wasn't some of the most mind-blowing sex of my entire life. But I'm also not going to pretend I'm not confused as hell. I don't even know what it means to be bisexual—what am I supposed to *do*?"

"Nothing." Viggo ran a hand through Jamie's hair, something he was growing fond of doing. "Get ready for hockey season. Think about the move. Focus on your career. If you're up for it, tonight you might spank my wife again. If not, we'll leave you be and spend some time with the family. Either way, you're still you, Jamie. The steroids and the sex scandal are behind you—go to Ottawa with a clean slate and a bright future. One day someone is going to catch your eye and you're going to feel like having sex. When that happens, you'll know what you want and need."

"Guys." Emilie poked her head in. "I'm sorry to interrupt, but Kate is on her way up with the baby. You might want to get dressed."

"I'm going to take a shower," Jamie said hoarsely. He squeezed Viggo's hand once more and leaned over to brush his lips across Emilie's cheek as he passed her. Then he disappeared into his room and shut the door.

THAT NIGHT A GROUP of his teammates from the Sidewinders took Jamie out for a farewell dinner and drinks. Emilie had demurred, telling the men to have fun and that she and the baby would spend some time with Kate. Viggo and Jamie left together, driving in Viggo's truck to the restaurant where they were meeting everyone. The sound of the engine was the only noise for a while, leaving them with nothing to focus on but the vibrations.

"You're quiet," Viggo finally said, glancing at him. "You all right? I wasn't sure what to think when we didn't see you this afternoon."

"I needed a little time to myself," Jamie muttered, staring out the window. "I had to finish packing the non-essentials since the movers are coming tomorrow, and it gave me time to think."

"Anything you want to share?"

"You've probably thought about all the same things."

"Then you didn't find any answers."

"Nope."

Viggo nodded, knowing there was nothing else to say and it would probably help him relax if they found a more neutral subject. "You sure you want to leave most of the furniture and such?"

Jamie waved a dismissive hand. "Yeah, I'm going to be living with one of the rookies who's already there. He needs a roommate and they thought it would be a good match since they want someone older to look out for him. It's already furnished so it's perfect for the time being."

They were silent again until Viggo couldn't stand it anymore. "Are you pissed about last night or moving to Ottawa or something else?"

Jamie sighed. "All of the above."

"I'm sorry." Viggo pulled into the restaurant and parked, unsure what else to say. "You gonna be all right hanging out with the team?"

"These guys are a big part of the reason I don't want to leave—I'm just going to try to enjoy my last night with them." He got out of the truck and walked into the restaurant without waiting for Viggo. He was anxious to see everyone, have a drink and for a few hours forget all about this latest clusterfuck he'd gotten himself into.

Tonight, much later, he would think about the man who'd used nothing more than a kiss to turn his heart inside out.

"JAMIE!" With his friends calling to him, Jamie lost himself in the memories of the last two years. He'd been traded before, from Minnesota to Las Vegas, and he hadn't batted an eyelash. But this move, leaving this team, was turning out to be the hardest thing he'd ever done. Listening to their stories, as they drank and joked, he realized it was the closest he'd ever come to having friends that meant as much to him as family, and for the first time since it happened, he resented the hell out of Dante for getting him into this situation.

The party moved from the restaurant to a bar they often frequented and sometime after midnight he went outside to get some air, overwhelmed with emotion he didn't want his teammates to see. It was late and he'd had quite a bit to drink, the alcohol making him more melancholy than usual. The black sky seemed to match his mood; an endless, shapeless inkblot as far as the eye could see. There wasn't even the whisper of a breeze and he stared out at the bleak horizon without feeling the heat that, despite the lack of sun, seemed to be baking his skin.

Viggo had stopped drinking a couple of hours ago, offering to be their designated driver, so Jamie was glad he didn't have to think about that on top of everything else. He had enough on his mind.

"Hey." Zakk Cloutier came out and stood next to him. "You okay?"

"Why does everyone keep asking me that?" Jamie tried to smile but failed miserably and turned to stare back out at the dark sky.

"Because you don't look happy."

"Yeah, well, getting traded after winning a championship sucks."

"Talk to me, man." Zakk and Jamie were close after sharing an apartment and partying together for over a year. Zakk had a whole new life now that included a pregnant fiancée and her twin sons, but he would miss his kind, fun-loving friend. Jamie was not just leaving the team, he was leaving the country, and Zakk hated knowing that Jamie was going to miss so many of the important upcoming events in his life; his first child would be born in January and Jamie would be gone.

"I don't want to go," Jamie admitted. "I know it's part of the game, but I wasn't ready. It was me or Becca, and it had to be me because she was so humiliated, but that doesn't mean it doesn't suck."

"I know." Zakk clapped a hand on his shoulder.

Jamie momentarily froze, wondering how he would react to the touch of one of his best friends, but nothing happened. For a second he was confused, frowning slightly, and Zakk cocked his head. "You sure you're okay?"

"Yeah, sorry, just have a lot on my mind." He forced an easygoing smile. "You're not going to knock me silly when I come back next month, are you?"

Zakk smirked. "Maybe."

The two friends smiled at each other. "I'm going to miss you," said Jamie.

"Doesn't matter where you are," Zakk held out his hand, "we're bros. I'm always there if you need me."

"I know." Jamie shook his hand and flinched as Zakk drew him into a hug, clapping him on the back.

"Kick some ass in Ottawa, huh? Show 'em how we do it in Vegas."

Jamie nodded. "Thanks, Zakk."

"If I don't see you before you go, drop me a text, okay?" Zakk pulled out his keys. "I gotta get home. Tiff's been a little under the weather and I don't want to be out too late."

"Yeah, of course. Give her my love." Jamie watched him drive away and slowly said goodbye to the rest of his friends: Toli, Cody, Dom, Drake, Karl, Vlad and Brock. He was proud of himself for not showing them how hard this was for him, but by the time he and Viggo were walking out to his truck he was in a piss-poor mood again.

# CHAPTER 5

They drove home in silence, once again lost in their own thoughts, and took the elevator up to their apartment. Viggo unlocked the door and they stepped inside, careful to be quiet since Simone was undoubtedly asleep.

"I guess I'll see you in the morning," Jamie murmured, turning towards his room.

"Like hell." Viggo grabbed him, pinning him against the wall and finding his mouth with a swiftness that made Jamie's heart beat harder and his blood start the kind of simmer that would boil over sooner rather than later. Jamie growled deep in his throat, fighting the conflicting emotions that were battling with the alcohol in his system. He wanted this man like nobody's business but he'd spent all night trying to figure out why Viggo made him feel this way while he had absolutely zero interest in any of his other male friends.

He didn't have time to think because Viggo's body was pressed tightly against his and his mouth took ownership of Jamie's without mercy. His kisses were demanding, almost punishing, and he didn't relent until Jamie surrendered, letting Viggo take the reins.

Once his inner battle eased, the kiss changed, and Viggo's lips turned tender, almost loving. The intimacy nearly took Jamie's breath away and he slid his hands up under Viggo's shirt to caress his back, enjoying the feel of sinewy muscles underneath the skin and trying not to think about how much he liked it. Viggo released him abruptly, shaking his head.

"What the hell was that?" Jamie demanded in a frustrated whisper.

"You spent all night fighting this—us. I wasn't going to let you walk away because you're drunk and depressed about leaving. Now go into the bedroom and see if Em's awake. I'm getting a drink and I'll be right in."

Jamie hesitated and Viggo reached out to grip the erection bulging through his jeans. "Don't try to tell me you're not interested."

"Of course I'm interested." Jamie couldn't help but smile as he kicked off his Chucks and walked softly into the bedroom.

"I thought you two were going to start without me," Emilie whispered in the semidarkness. She was on the bed in something slinky and black, her hair piled on her head in a messy bun with long tendrils hanging in her face.

He reached for her, sliding across the bed and pulling her close. She nuzzled his neck, the smell of her fruity perfume wafting up and making him smile. "You smell good enough to eat."

"That's a good thing, because I was hoping you were hungry." She lifted her mouth to his and he kissed her. Tonight their kisses were unhurried, exploring, more patient than they'd been last night in their fury to be together. Her lips were sweet and pliable, exactly the opposite of Viggo's, and he was uncomfortably aware of how much he suddenly yearned for everything masculine about Viggo.

Realization dawned slowly: He was attracted to Emilie but wanted Viggo almost desperately. Deep down, that had been his worry, that he was developing feelings for the burly man who'd rocked his world the night before. He only had 36 more hours to enjoy a kind of pleasure he hadn't been aware he needed until Viggo had touched him. Then he would go to Ottawa and start a whole new life, trying to pretend this had never happened.

His lips caressed hers gently now, unhurried, his worries melting away as he allowed himself to enjoy this brief departure from reality. His unexpected need for Viggo didn't diminish the pleasure he got from touching her as well. When he felt Viggo behind him, his big hands moving over Jamie's back, he reached back with one hand and cupped the Swede's strong, tight ass. Even through the jeans he wore, Jamie could feel his solid, muscular cheeks and thighs. By the same token, Emilie was soft and sexy, her skin a silky contrast to Viggo's hairier limbs. He loved having them both, her mouth under his and Viggo's lips on his neck and ear.

Jamie gripped Emilie by the ass, lifting her against him, and paused when he felt her wince. He pulled back slightly, frowning. "Em? Are you still sore from last night?"

"A little." She shrugged. "It's okay."

"No." He gently put her down. "Turn over and let me look."

"Jamie, no, it's just—"

"It's not *just* anything. You know that in the BDSM world part of the gig means aftercare—not just five minutes after, but taking care of you for as long as we're together. Twenty-four hours after I gave you a pretty intense spanking, I need to see why you flinched or I won't be able to take care of you tonight."

She sighed, turning onto her stomach. Viggo reached for the small lamp by the bed and switched it on. Jamie let out a grunt of displeasure when he realized a deep purple bruise was forming on one cheek and a lighter bruise had begun on the other. He ran his hands over them softly, shaking his head.

"Honey, never ever let someone you don't know hit you like that. Promise me."

"But I like it," she said softly. "I enjoy the pain. You saw how much it aroused me."

"Yes, but I can cause pain that won't leave bruises like this. Your skin is very sensitive; it's not okay to leave marks. That's not how I do things."

"Em, he's right." Viggo ran his hands over her bruises, shaking his head. "This is why I can't do it. I don't know my strength, don't know how badly I could hurt you."

"I do know my strength and normally I can stop, but I've never had someone want to go so far the first time."

"I'll be careful," Emilie said. Her blue eyes were focused intently on his before she flipped over again.

"Okay, good." Jamie looked away suddenly, unsure what to do next.

"Jamie, I know you're out of your comfort zone," Viggo said quietly. "Tell us what you want to do."

"I don't know exactly," Jamie admitted. "But I couldn't walk away now if my life depended on it. I got into a threesome last night that picked up again this morning. I did things I've never done before, but after agonizing about it all day, I want to enjoy every minute of this until I have to go. I don't understand it, but since I'm leaving in two days, I guess I don't have to."

Viggo reached out and fingered the wavy locks that perpetually hung over Jamie's forehead. "I'm glad you feel that way."

JAMIE WOKE up first in the morning. Like yesterday, he was sprawled between Emilie and Viggo. Unlike yesterday, they were both fast asleep, with Emilie curled into Jamie's right side and Viggo on Jamie's left, with one arm draped across his torso. Last night had been amazing, but instead of confusion today, there was a tug of depression because he wasn't just leaving the team and city he loved, but also a man who'd become much more to him than a friend or roommate. He'd never been in a threesome where he was more attracted to the man than the woman, but that's what had happened. Viggo's touch brought him alive and he didn't know if it was the man, the sex or some combination of both.

His bladder was screaming for attention, so he slid out of bed as quietly as possible and used the bathroom. After washing his hands, he left Viggo and Emilie's room and went back to his. He had the master suite since Viggo had moved in later, and he wondered why the three of them had used Viggo's queen-size bed both nights instead of the king-sized one in his room. Maybe tonight. He grimaced, realizing he had every intention of spending his last 24 hours in Las Vegas in bed with a man. Later, when he was alone in Ottawa with nothing to do, he would figure out how he felt about all of this.

He was headed to the kitchen to make coffee when he heard Simone gurgling in the playpen she slept in. Since he was moving out soon, Viggo and Emilie were keeping her in a playpen in the living room at night. Once he was gone, they would move into the master suite and make a nursery for Simone in the room they were currently using.

"Good morning, little one," he smiled at the towheaded baby. She was sitting up, her bright blue eyes twinkling when she saw him. Glancing back to where Viggo and Emilie still slept, they had the monitor on and would wake if she started crying, so he picked her up. She was much lighter than he was expecting and he chuckled when she nestled her head in his shoulder. He didn't know a lot about babies; he was the oldest in his family and neither his brother nor his sister were married yet. His friends had kids, of course, but he didn't have much hands-on experience with them.

"I don't know what you eat in the morning," he said to her as he used his free hand to make coffee. "Probably no coffee, right?"

Simone blinked up at him, content to watch what he was doing, following his every move.

"You're a natural." Viggo's deep but soft voice made Jamie jump and he spun around with a grunt.

"Seriously? Dude, I could've dropped her!"

Viggo chuckled. "Sorry. Good morning." He leaned over to nuzzle his daughter's stomach, making her giggle.

"I was trying to let you two sleep."

"Bed is too small for two of us, much less three," he grunted. "Don't sleep worth a damn in it."

"Good thing I'm leaving you my king," Jamie said lightly.

"It's better with you in it." Viggo ran a hand along Jamie's bare back.

Jamie turned and their eyes met. A powerful surge of emotion he still didn't understand coursed through him and he turned away, reaching for a coffee mug and trying to concentrate on anything but the way it felt when Viggo looked at him. It was freaking him out that he was unexpectedly so attracted to him. He'd never thought of him like that in the year they'd lived together, but he suddenly couldn't think about anything else.

"Does being alone with me make you nervous now?" Viggo asked softly.

"No." Jamie shook his head, but wouldn't look at him.

"Then why can't you look at me?"

"Because when I look at you I want you to kiss me." Jamie nearly groaned when he realized he'd spoken aloud, but then Viggo was pulling Simone from his arms, tucking her under one of his, and using his free hand to cup Jamie's head. He brought his mouth towards him and hesitated when their lips were millimeters apart.

"Any time you want me to kiss you, just say so." He parted Jamie's lips and let his tongue snake in to curl with his. Reluctantly, he pulled away after just a few seconds, pausing to rub his nose against Jamie's. "Plenty of time for this later, yeah? I have to feed the baby and take a shower. I've got meetings today."

"Yeah, okay." Jamie nodded nervously and focused on his coffee mug. He didn't want to think about kissing Viggo, because it felt like that's all he'd been thinking about lately. What the hell was going on?

H*E WAS UP EARLY* the morning he was leaving for Ottawa, and slipped into the shower without waking them. Emilie had somehow convinced Kate to take Simone so they could spend their last 12 hours together uninterrupted, and Jamie definitely hadn't gotten enough sleep. He had to get going, but he didn't know what to say to either of them. Emilie, with her sweet, sensual body and desperate need for pain, had allowed him to thoroughly indulge in one of his kinks.

It would have been the best sex of his life if it hadn't been for his growing need for Viggo. Every fucking time Viggo touched him, his heart beat faster, his stomach flipped over and his dick got so hard it hurt. He didn't know what was happening between them, but he had to get away from it as quickly as possible. There was no universe in which he fell in love with a man. At least he hoped not, because this was beyond anything he was prepared to deal with. If only he could stop thinking about him and how intense his feelings had gotten in such a short time.

Viggo was in the kitchen having a cup of coffee when Jamie finished getting dressed. They looked at each other wordlessly until Jamie found himself walking over to him as if propelled by some erotic gravitational force. He leaned up and kissed him, a light, feathery mingling of tongues that didn't go any further but aroused them both anyway. They kept their mouths linked together for what felt like a long time, enjoying the closeness but managing to not let it intensify.

"I'm going to miss you," Viggo said, one hand on Jamie's cheek, wishing he was brave enough to ask him to stay. Staring at his long, lean form, he wondered why he'd never wanted him this much before. Jamie was just a couple of inches shorter than he was, but a lot slimmer. Though he wasn't huge or muscular, Jamie was hard and well-cut. His abs were so flat you could bounce a quarter off of them, and as a hockey player who'd been skating since he was practically a baby, his thighs were strong and well-shaped.

Viggo's eyes dropped down to the oblique muscles on either side of his torso, deep valleys that disappeared into his jeans and led to the most magnificent cock Viggo had ever had the pleasure of sucking. It wasn't the thickest, but it was long and perfectly formed, leaving him all but panting after it when they were in bed. He had to restrain himself from wrapping his hand around it now as they stood chest to chest.

Looking down into Jamie's long-lashed brown eyes, he couldn't resist kissing him just once more. He loved his mouth, the way he responded to him as if they'd always done this. Jamie neither wanted nor expected gentleness when they kissed, yet somehow it was always tender and loving, no matter how rough Viggo went at him. His lower lip was slightly bigger than the top one and Viggo nipped it between his own with a possessiveness there was no way to explain; the idea of someone else kissing this man made him want to claim him.

"So fucking good," Viggo murmured, unwilling to let go yet, hands and mouth exploring as if they hadn't touched every inch of each other in the last three days. He pictured his tight ass, long fingers and sexy smile even with his eyes closed. As he tried to focus on the gorgeous man in his arms, Jamie's change in body language told him he mentally coming out of their sexy interlude.

"I'm not good at goodbyes," was all Jamie said when he finally pulled away. "Tell Emilie I'm sorry, but I need to get going and I don't want to wake her. Maybe I'll see you guys when we're here at the end of October."

"Maybe?" Viggo frowned. "You won't be thinking of this?"

Jamie smiled, though he didn't look at him. "Yeah, I'll be thinking about it, but we said this was just three days of fun. Now it's done and I have to go."

"Without saying goodbye." Emilie stood in the doorway to the kitchen, looking sleepy but annoyed. "I'm beginning to think you like him better than me."

Jamie couldn't help but reach for her. "I have a tougher time saying goodbye to a woman."

"You want me to cry to prove I'm going to miss you?" Viggo asked with a twinkle in his eye.

"No." Jamie shook his head and reached out an arm to draw him into the embrace with Emilie. "I know you're going to miss me, and I'm going to miss you too. But I have a new life starting in Ottawa, and you guys are going to be busy with Simone, Club Inferno and all that. Let's chalk this up to a good time and move on. I think that's going to be best."

"You're probably right," Emilie said softly, resting her head on his shoulder. "Please keep in touch."

"I will." He kissed the top of her head.

"We'll see you in about six weeks, yeah?" Viggo ran his fingers through Jamie's hair, his heart deflating a little when he realized it might be the last time.

"Yeah." Jamie looked at them and nodded, trying to hide feelings he didn't understand and emotions that were beginning to frustrate him. He grabbed his keys and travel coffee mug, and walked out the door without looking back.

# CHAPTER 6

Emilie watched and swallowed the lump in her throat as she recognized the look in her husband's eyes. "Damn," she said after a moment. "You're going to miss him, aren't you?"

"Yeah." Viggo slid an arm around her shoulders. "But there's nothing we can do. His career is in Ottawa and our life is here."

Emilie chewed her lip as she thought of what to say next. Finally, in a half-whisper, she asked, "Viggo, have you ever been in love with a man?"

"What?" he asked, startled.

"You dated and slept with a lot of men—were you ever in love with any of them?"

"No." He reached out and grasped her chin, gently turning it so that she was looking at him. "You're the only person I've ever loved."

She nodded. "Yes, but we all fall in love—especially when we're teenagers. You never loved a man? A boy?"

"I didn't know I was bisexual until I was 17," he said. "And I was confused as hell, so I wasn't interested in that. I met you around that time as well, and there's never been anyone else in my heart."

"But that's just it—you were 17!" she protested. "How do you know this isn't just a sweet teenage fantasy?"

He let out a hiss of frustration. "Em, what's this about?"

"I need to know." She reached out to run loving fingers over his handsome face. "I've loved you since I was 15, but I've loved others too. Not in the same way, but I was in relationships, had feelings. Haven't you?"

"Not with a man." He shook his head as he pulled her close, wrapping his massive arms around her slight body. "It was always about sex, the power of being taken by a man. Never emotional. I took one look at you, more than 10 years ago, and that was it. Yeah, we were both young, but there's never been anyone else that was important. I thought my thing for men meant you would never want to be with me, but I was wrong, and look at us now."

"Viggo, I'm afraid we might have made a mistake."

"Because I'm bisexual and just enjoyed sex with a man?"

"Because you're bi and I'm...broken."

He looked into her eyes and saw love and fear and something he couldn't quite distinguish. Hesitation? Reluctance? "Why do you say that?"

"The things I've done..." She closed her eyes. "If I hadn't been pregnant, I don't know what would have happened to me. There's a darkness inside me that scares me—a fear that doesn't let up."

"Fear of what?"

"That I'll never be normal."

"I don't understand."

"I know." She blew out a breath.

"Em, if you don't love me—"

"It's so much more complicated than that." She shook her head. "I have... needs. Sexual proclivities that make me a bad candidate to be in a monogamous relationship."

"Such as?" He watched her intently.

"I like pain; severe, hardcore beatings. Whips and belts to the extreme."

He nodded. "Maybe I can figure out what you need in that department."

"But I'll never have a penis or gain 50 kilos of muscle."

"What?" He stared at her in confusion.

"You get off when you're taken by another man. How long before you miss the joy of getting off that way? I can't provide that, Viggo, and I would hate knowing something was missing in your life."

He grunted. "I have you, our daughter and a career I never dreamed of in the best hockey league in the world. There is *nothing* missing in my life."

She cocked her head. "It was very intense between you and Jamie—you can't deny it."

He swallowed, unwilling to admit she was right. "It was sex."

"Don't lie to yourself, Viggo."

He blew out a breath. "I never got the vibe he was attracted to men before, much less to me."

"Maybe you didn't notice."

"What does that mean?"

"The way he looked at you—it was different than how he looked at me."

"I don't understand." He did, but he didn't want to think about what it meant.

"He likes you."

He tried to shrug it off. "It was sex, Em. He's gone and we're moving on with our life. Don't make this into something it's not. Go get ready so we can get some things done today, okay?"

"All right." She didn't push it.

As she padded into the bathroom to shower, Viggo's mind wandered back to the last few days. How much of what happened had been simple sex, he wondered, and how much had been something else? Jamie had definitely gotten under his skin, but he would have to be careful not to let Emilie see it. He'd promised himself, and her, that he would be faithful and that he didn't need a man to keep him satisfied sexually.

Technically, that was still true, because although the three of them had done just about everything else, he and Jamie had kept their contact limited to oral sex. Somehow, they'd kept things from progressing beyond that point and he was relieved; he didn't know if he could stand letting a man like Jamie actually take him. That much intimacy would undoubtedly change things, and he wasn't sure why.

He'd had sex with dozens of men over the years, but Jamie Teller was different. Although he'd always found him somewhat attractive, Jamie wasn't his usual type. He picked the men he slept with based solely on looks and tended to prefer blonds. Except for a handful of dates over the years, there was usually nothing but sex involved, making it easy to recognize someone who wanted to get laid without any of the complicated emotions Viggo had never been willing to have with a man.

With Jamie, he'd been shocked to discover he was so attracted to him he wanted to actually spend quality time together. *Alone.* That had never happened before. Though he would never say it out loud, he was a little bit glad Jamie had moved to Ottawa because if he hadn't, he would have the ability to destroy the quiet, sensible life Viggo had always wanted.

---

Hockey season opened on a Wednesday but the Sidewinders weren't starting until the next day. Karl and Kate had invited several of the team members and their wives over for dinner and an evening of watching the league's other games on TV. Ottawa was playing New York, so they'd decided to cheer on their friend from afar. Viggo had only heard from Jamie twice: the day he'd arrived safely in Ottawa and the day after training camp started. Jamie had called the first time to tell him he was getting settled. The second time he'd merely sent a text saying camp had been good and he was looking forward to starting the season. There hadn't been anything else, so Viggo had texted him this morning to wish him luck on opening night. Jamie hadn't responded and Viggo didn't want to admit how much it hurt. Although he loved his wife, things had been different since the three of them had spent time together. It was as if she sensed his mind was on someone else but didn't care enough to ask about it.

Viggo tried to enjoy the company of his friends and teammates, but he'd started to feel a little depressed and couldn't put his finger on exactly why. Emilie seemed equally down, and he watched as she and Kate disappeared into the kitchen to start setting out the food for dinner.

"Hey, man." Karl took the chair next to Viggo's and gave his brother-in-law a look. "Everything okay?"

"Oh yeah." Viggo nodded. "Just a very different season this year with a wife and kid, you know?"

"Tell me about it!" Karl chuckled. "Kate came into my life a year and a half ago and there are days I don't know if I'm coming or going!"

"Is it worth it?" Viggo asked quietly. "I mean, changing everything about yourself for someone you love?"

"Well, yeah." Karl frowned slightly. "Is everything okay with you and Em?"

Viggo hesitated. "She's different. Quieter, more serious, less...something. I can't explain it. You know we're not the most conventional couple, yeah?"

Karl nodded. "I get that impression."

"She wants traditional on one hand and very nontraditional on another. It's a bit much to cope with sometimes."

"Don't you talk about it?"

"We do. We're close friends...but we're not like any other married couples I've spent time with, and I'm not sure why."

"Have you been faithful?" Karl asked, meeting his brother-in-law's gaze directly.

"Depends on your definition of faithful," he said after a moment. "If I've been unfaithful, she was there with me."

Karl sighed, understanding dawning. "So the two of you...share?"

"Threesomes." Viggo and Karl had been friends since they were young. They'd lived and played together for nearly four years before Karl had been drafted to the NHL, so they knew each other well. Though Viggo hadn't been aware of it, Karl had always known Viggo was bisexual, and it had never made a difference to him so he felt fairly comfortable talking about this to him. God knows, he didn't have anyone else to talk to now that Jamie was gone.

"If she's involved as well, and I know both of you well enough to know she's a willing participant, what's the problem?"

"She's pulling away from me, all but pushing me towards someone else. I don't understand it, but I feel like a spectator in my own marriage. I'm not sure what she wants, but when I ask her, she says all she needs is me."

Karl frowned. "Do you want me to talk to her?"

"I don't know. There's a lot going on inside her and she's holding on to me for some kind of strength she doesn't believe she has on her own. I think she needs help but she's not willing to get it—it doesn't seem as if she's ready."

"Are you going to leave?" Karl had noticed how withdrawn his sister was, but he'd assumed she was having an issue with Viggo's bisexuality. It never occurred to him she was the one pulling away.

"Not as long as she tells me she needs me to stay."

"But something is going on with you guys—something bad?"

"No." He shook his head. "Not bad...different. She's changed just in the couple of months we've been married and I don't know what I'm supposed to do. I don't think she's in love with me, Karl."

"Are you in love with her?"

Viggo sighed. "I thought I was."

"But?"

"I don't think I can be what she needs. Even in bed..." He froze. "Sorry, I won't go there."

Karl took a breath. "Yeah, we might want to leave that topic alone."

"Okay, I'm off to find another beer." Viggo started to get up.

"Hey." Karl touched his arm and Viggo paused, looking down at him. "If you need to talk, I'm here. We've been friends most of our lives—I know you don't have a lot of people you're close to, so we can talk about it if you need to."

Viggo grinned. "I'll keep that in mind, but I don't know if I can go there—even with you."

"I won't say I'm not relieved, but the offer stands." Karl met his friend's eyes.

"It'll be okay," Viggo said quietly. "But I appreciate the offer."

They moved to the dining room and soon everyone was eating and talking. When the game started, Viggo moved to Emilie's side and rested against her as he sought out Jamie on the screen.

"You've missed him," was all she said in a soft voice against his ear.

"Yes," he agreed mildly. "His easy laughter, the way he was always ready to go do something, playing Xbox on days off...we were inseparable for almost a year."

"Have you talked to him?"

"No." He shook his head.

"Hey, there's Jamie!" Kate called out. "He's number 24 now—same as you, Viggo! I guess there's already a 55 in Ottawa." Jamie had worn the number 55 in Las Vegas.

Viggo didn't say anything but Emilie saw the flush on his neck and put her hand on his shoulder.

"He looks good," Karl said, leaning back in his chair. "Fast."

"He looks great," Viggo agreed under his breath.

# CHAPTER 7

The ongoing construction and plans for opening Club Inferno on the night before Thanksgiving kept Emilie busy. With Viggo always doing something hockey-related, Emilie didn't have time to think about anything other than Simone and the club. The shipment from the building in New York was more than a week late and there was no way to continue getting the club ready until it got there so she sat on the phone with the shipping company for what seemed like hours.

"They're here!" She heard her new head of security, Darryl "Chains" Carruthers, shouting and wasn't sure what he was talking about. She moved the phone away from her ear and looked up as he came in.

"The shipment is here!" he grunted, sweat glistening on his bare chest as he lugged two big boxes and put them down.

She hung up the phone and hurried out to talk to the driver and sign for everything. "Dammit," she hissed as she followed him. "We don't have a crew here today to unload. This will take you and the driver days!"

Chains grunted. "Any chance your hockey-playing hubby and his friends could come give a hand?"

Emilie grimaced but realized how futile it would be for Chains and the driver to try to do this on their own. "I'll call Viggo, but they have a game tonight. Most of the guys are probably napping."

"Shit." Chains glanced over at the semi filled with furniture, decorations and supplies that included everything from reams of paper to blenders for the bar.

Emilie called Viggo but it went to voice mail which meant he was undoubtedly asleep. Most of the team napped in the afternoon before a game and she hated to bother him. "He's not picking up," she sighed. "I don't think we'll be able to reach anyone today. We'd better get—"

"Looks like it's a good thing I'm here." Jamie's voice made Emilie whirl around in surprise.

"Jamie!" Without thinking she ran and hugged him tightly. They kissed lightly before she stepped back to stare up into his face. "What are you doing here? I thought you were coming tomorrow."

"Told the team I had a few loose ends to tie up with my apartment and stuff, so I got permission to come in a day early."

"Hope you feel like working," Chains grunted in his clipped British accent, lifting another huge box off the truck. "The Sidewinders are incommunicado and this is a shit ton of work!"

Jamie looked at the load in the truck and at Emilie's somewhat stressed face and automatically nodded. "Of course." He pulled off his T-shirt and turned his baseball cap backwards.

"I'm going to change and put Simone in the shade over there," Emilie said. "Then I'll help too."

Two hours later they were all dripping with sweat and exhausted, but the truck was still only half empty. Emilie was taking a break to feed Simone while Chains, Jamie and the driver sucked down bottles of cold water. There were still several massive pieces of furniture to move and umpteen boxes; it was a daunting task and Emilie felt guilty because this wasn't Jamie's job and technically, it wasn't Chains' either. Her back was killing her and she hoped Simone would be able to nap in this heat, which the shaded overhang of the building was doing little to alleviate.

A familiar SUV pulled up and Dante got out with a grin. "Help has arrived!" he called out as three men they didn't know climbed out of his truck as well.

"Who are they?" Emilie asked, thankful she'd taken the time to tell Becca what was going on.

"Two are college interns for the Sidewinders in need of cash and the third is the roommate of one of the interns. We should be able to get this done quickly now." Despite being a multimillionaire and superstar baseball player, Dante pulled off his shirt and got to work with the rest of them.

As Dante had predicted, with the extra help, they were done in just over an hour and Emilie was glad she hadn't had to do anything more than direct them as they wound down. With a smile and a kiss to her cheek, Dante took the three young men home and told her he would pay them. The driver gave Emilie the last of his paperwork and got back on the road, leaving Chains, Emilie and Jamie staring at the mess inside the building.

"Tomorrow," Emilie said with a grimace. "I'm too tired and dirty to think about anything but a shower and food right now."

"I have to agree," Jamie said.

"See you in the morning then," Chains waved as he started to lock up.

"Thank you!" Emilie grinned over at Jamie. "Viggo's already gone to the arena. You coming back to our place?"

"I'm at the hotel where the team will be tomorrow," Jamie said quietly. "I don't think it's a good idea to—"

Emilie kissed him, pressing her lips to his and wrapping her arms around his neck. "You don't think it's a good idea to what?" she asked in a breathy whisper.

"Emilie, you and Viggo—"

She pulled out her phone and showed him a text she'd just gotten from Viggo: *Suck him off for me, yeah? Tell him he'll owe me when I get home tonight. Xoxo*

Jamie took a breath. "Damn, honey." He wanted to say no. He wanted to tell her how much he'd missed Viggo, how sleeping with the readily available women in

Ottawa held no interest for him and how he'd thought of nothing but her husband for weeks, no matter how hard he'd tried not to. But how could he tell her that? It was impossible, he realized. Instead, he followed her home to wait for the man he'd been aching for since he'd left Las Vegas. He was prepared for this to be the last time. It had to be, right?

JAMIE WOKE EARLY, despite how late they'd been up and how tired he was going to be tonight. The sun was peeking in through slits in the curtains and he needed to get going. His teammates would be arriving by noon and he had to meet them for lunch and a team meeting. Then he would take a much-needed nap before facing his friends on the ice. He hated having to play against the Sidewinders and he'd never felt that way before when it came to playing against friends and old teammates.

Zakk had texted him last night asking if he would have time for a drink after the game, and he'd heard from Cody and Brock as well, which only made it harder. Unsure whether he'd have time to see them after the game, he'd texted that he would let them know later. In the meantime, he had to get out of here. Last night had proven that he was absolutely in over his head with whatever this was between him and Viggo and he couldn't spend any time on a game day thinking about it.

He slipped out of the room and grabbed clothes out of his suitcase in the living room. He was digging around for socks when a voice startled him.

"You're the worst one-night stand ever," Viggo rumbled in his deep, slightly accented voice. "First, you're always trying to sneak out, and second, you keep coming back."

Jamie sighed. "Look, the sex is phenomenal, but the rest of it...I can't. I just can't, Viggo."

"You can't what?" Viggo folded his arms across his massive bare chest. "You're the one who said you can't look at me without wanting to kiss me, so don't pretend this isn't something you want."

Jamie shook his head. "Oh, no, I was 100% into it. That's why I have to go. That's why we can't do this again."

"I don't understand." Viggo squinted.

"You and Em, you're a couple," Jamie said quietly. "I'm nothing but a distraction for whatever you two are going through and, I'm sorry, but I can't be that. Not with you. I've done the threesome thing in the past, and the sex is un-fucking-believable, but this—well, I apologize for developing feelings over something that's just supposed to be physical, but I'm still human and—"

"Wait a second." Viggo held out a hand, shaking his head. "It's early and I've got a morning skate in a bit. What are you trying to say? Have you developed *feelings* for one of us?"

Jamie turned and stared at him. "Does it matter? You're married, I'm the outsider, and I'm not going to come between you. I have to get in the shower."

"Which one of us, Jamie?" Viggo moved closer.

"Come on, man, you already know the answer."

"Which. One." Viggo was staring at him intently, his blue eyes blazing.

"Why are you pushing this?" Jamie whispered, his voice dropping several octaves. "I don't want to get between you two but it's not fair that I get hurt either."

"Which one of us?" Viggo was up against him now, his hand in Jamie's hair as he practically growled the words.

"Who do you think?" Jamie closed his eyes as Viggo moved in for a kiss. "But I can't—" Viggo's hot mouth cut him off and he groaned as their lips came together. After only a few seconds of erotic bliss, he somehow found the strength to pull away. "Please. Don't."

"You're not some fuck toy," Viggo rasped. "We care about you—I fucking care about you."

"But we can't be together," Jamie whispered, frustrated his body was coming alive, aching with need. "Aside from mind-blowing sex, we can't be a *couple* with three of us in the picture. We can't be a family. I can't be Simone's father or stepfather or big brother. There's no future in this, and as kinky as I am in the bedroom, I'm still a regular guy. I want kids—*my own kids*. I want to share my life with someone. I need someone to love just me. This, what we're doing, is a disaster waiting to happen. Please, I have to go. *Please.*"

Viggo stepped back abruptly, nodding slightly. "I'm sorry, lover. We were selfish, Em and I. Never thought about that. But you're more to us than some sort of sexual diversion—know that we care about you too. Tell me you know that you mean something to us—especially to me?"

"I do know," he whispered. "That's what makes this so hard." He turned and disappeared into the bathroom.

WALKING through the tunnel towards the ice, Jamie wasn't sure if he was going to throw up or not. He'd never been nervous heading out for warm-ups, but tonight he was a little light-headed and queasy. The idea of seeing his friends and playing against them was a new experience. Yes, he'd played on another team before the Sidewinders, but it had been different. This sucked and he would have done anything to say he was sick, but that wouldn't fly after asking to come a day early. He had to get out there and do his job. They were paying him a lot of money, more than the Sidewinders had paid him actually, so he had to earn it.

"Hey, Jamie!" One of the arena ushers smiled and waved and Jamie nodded back as he skated onto the ice. He spotted Zakk and Dom skating nearby and he headed in their direction.

"Hey!" Zakk gave him a friendly grin as the three of them paused at center ice to chat.

"Good to see you," Jamie grinned back. "Remember, you promised not to hurt me tonight."

Zakk laughed. "Dammit, I forgot about that."

"I didn't promise anything," Dom joked.

They exchanged a few more pleasantries before skating off to warm up.

Jamie shot the puck in Ottawa's goalie's direction and was gratified to see it get past him. Maybe if he concentrated on the game he loved he wouldn't be so distracted by the redheaded Swede 50 feet away from him. Viggo had glanced in his direction and nodded, but kept his distance since Jamie had been talking with Zakk and Dom. Jamie figured it was best because he was still confused as hell about his feelings. One minute he wanted to run home to Ottawa, the next he would have done anything to bury himself inside Viggo. Maybe he needed a shrink or something because this level of attraction, where he hadn't been able to think about anything else, didn't make sense.

The start of the game was a good way to stop thinking about everything and Jamie couldn't believe he scored a goal less than two minutes in. It was his first time getting on the board for the new team and though he caught the look of annoyance from his ex-teammates, he also saw the quick wink Viggo sent him, which made his stomach lurch a little. He'd never been a big scorer, focusing more on setting up plays for the superstars, but occasionally the opportunity presented itself and he was glad it happened in front of his old team. Skating back to the bench, he'd just sat down when he heard Matt Forbes' voice carry over from the Sidewinders' bench:

"Thinks he's hot now that he's in Ottawa," he was laughing. "Couldn't score for shit as a Sidewinder!"

"Shut up, Matt!" Cody muttered.

"Sour grapes, eh?" One of Jamie's new teammates nudged him and he smiled, glad for the camaraderie but hating being on the other side. He'd been close to Matt for a while but after his break-up with Rachel, Matt had hinted incessantly about finding out if she would go out with him. Rachel was still Jamie's friend, though, and he had no desire to let one of his horny teammates go after her simply because she was a movie star. She deserved a nice guy who wanted to settle down with her, not a recently single jerk like Matt who notched conquests on his bedpost.

Jamie took his next shift feeling stronger. Scoring a goal had lifted his spirits but no matter how much he loved the Sidewinders, he loved hockey more. Skating after the puck, there was an opening and he shot it towards the winger closest to the goalie and moved back a few feet. The shot went wide and the Sidewinders took it back up to their end. Jamie followed the play, skating to the side when his defensemen took possession of the puck. One of them shot it in Jamie's direction and he wound up, hitting it hard and sending it down the ice towards where Karl was in net. It bounced from player to player and there was a momentary scuffle in front of the goal as different guys all went after the puck. Then it slid out from under them, right onto Jamie's stick. He pulled back and shot it into the net just before Matt Forbes slammed into him, catching him off guard. Jamie went down hard, the side of his head landing on the skate of someone who'd been involved in the melee seconds before.

# CHAPTER 8

The world stood still as Jamie lay on the ice. He was aware of the ref blowing the whistle and someone saying his name. He heard Zakk's growl, calling Matt a few choice words before kneeling beside Jamie and asking if he was okay. Jamie couldn't seem to answer, though, everything was a blurry cloud of haziness and the roaring in his ears was hard to explain.

"Jamie?" Viggo's voice cut through everyone else's and Jamie tried to look at him but couldn't focus. There was a sharp pain that had begun to shoot through the side of his head and he thought he moaned, but wasn't sure.

Then he heard Doc Levine's voice, soft and soothing. Jamie had always liked him, but it made him nervous that they'd called him out for someone on the opposing team. That meant he was hurt pretty bad. His limbs were paralyzed and panic began to set in.

"Jamie, I need you to lie still. You have quite a gash on your head from the blade of the skate. Let me put something on it, okay? Just relax, son, I've got this."

Jamie calmed a little, trying to nod but unable to. He closed his eyes, forcing himself to focus on slowing his breathing. It felt like someone was holding his head in a fishbowl and he wasn't sure what to do, so he just lay there.

"We need a stretcher," Doc Levine was saying. "He's out of it. Let's get him to a hospital."

Jamie's eyes flew open and he wanted to protest but his mouth was frozen.

"Easy, man," Viggo's voice was deep but soft, his hand heavy on Jamie's shoulder. "We'll see you later at the hospital."

Jamie closed his eyes, calmer after hearing that Viggo would be there.

THE NEXT TIME Jamie opened his eyes he was in a hospital; he figured it out from the beeping machines and hushed voices around him. He tried to focus on the figure standing next to him, but everything was blurry again. He blinked a few times and felt a cool hand on his arm.

"Mr. Teller? I'm Sarina, your nurse. You had quite a hit to the head and the doctor said your vision might be blurry for a few days. How are you feeling?"

"Weird," Jamie croaked out. "Can't see."

"Is it blurry or no vision at all?"

"Blurry."

"Just relax. It's perfectly normal after a concussion and should clear up in a few days."

"What time is it?"

"About midnight. You have a lot of people out there worried about you. I don't think your friend Viggo will leave without seeing you. He's been pacing the halls for a long time. Is he someone you want to see?"

Jamie couldn't help but smile. "Yeah, my old roommate."

"All right." Sarina bustled out and a moment later Jamie heard footsteps just before Viggo's deep voice filled the room.

Rough fingers briefly skimmed his cheek. "How are you?"

"Been better," he admitted, his voice still hoarse.

"Do you need some water?"

"Yeah, thanks." He parted his lips as Viggo put the straw between them. "I can't see very well."

"You hit your head hard."

Jamie ran his hand along the side of his face and realized it was bandaged. "I haven't seen the doctor yet, so I don't know what happened."

"Forbes took you down after you shot the puck."

"No surprise."

"Words were exchanged after the game."

"Between who?"

He grinned. "Me. Zakk. Matt."

"You and Zakk went after Matt?"

"Maybe." He chuckled. "We let him know what we thought of what he did. He might have a bruise on his back tomorrow. He might have hit the boards. Or the corner of the lockers. Not sure."

Jamie smiled. "Thank Zakk for me."

"Emilie wanted to come but she's home taking care of Simone so I can stay with you."

"You don't have to stay," he whispered. "I'll be okay."

"Shut up." He pulled a chair up next to the bed and gripped one of Jamie's hands between both of his. "I'm not leaving you alone."

"It's going to look weird!"

"I'm your friend."

"You're holding my hand."

"You can't see and you have a bad gash to the head—no one will think anything other than I'm comforting someone who's been seriously hurt."

"If it's serious, they'll call my mother." His head was starting to pound and he felt himself getting sleepy.

"And when she gets here, I'll go. Until then, shut up."

39

Jamie closed his eyes, too exhausted to think, but oddly comforted by his friend's strength and perseverance. "Thank you," he murmured as he drifted off.

JAMIE'S DAY started early with the doctor arriving just after 6:00 a.m. and telling him that he had a concussion and a deep gash on the side of his head that had required more than 20 stitches. A neurologist would also be coming soon to talk to him a little more about the head injury. Jamie was just grateful he could see again, though he had the headache of a lifetime and it didn't help that he was exhausted. They'd woken him every hour all night and now he yearned to sleep even though there was going to be a parade of doctors and tests going on for a while.

"Good morning!" Viggo, Zakk and Cody came in together. Viggo had stayed most of the night with him before going home at dawn to shower and get ready for the day.

"Morning." Jamie yawned and sat up.

"How's it going, man?" Zakk shook his head. "Damn, I was ready to throttle Forbes last night."

"It's all good. He didn't know I was gonna fall on a skate." Jamie tried to shrug it off.

"He hit you after the play," Viggo grunted.

"Did Coach Barnett say anything to him?"

"Not in front of us," Zakk said. "But I'm pretty sure he did in private. Especially after a few of us took him to task in the dressing room."

"Dude, I feel like we should apologize," Cody said after a moment. "I can't believe he did that."

"Part of the game," Jamie said lightly. "I'm fine."

"You're not fine!" Cody grunted. "You have a grade 2 concussion and stitches in your head. It was bullshit!"

"Did he get called?" Jamie asked. "I don't remember."

"Do you remember scoring?"

"Scoring?" Jamie frowned.

"The puck went in, my man," Viggo grinned. "You had two goals last night."

"Figures." Jamie rolled his eyes. "I had a great night and can't remember!"

"Your boys were pretty protective," Viggo said. "They went after Dom and Drake a few times after that—nice they had your back."

"They're good guys," Jamie said absently. "I need to call my roommate but I can't remember what room he's in at the hotel." He looked up helplessly. "Can one of you try to find out?"

"Haven't any of them been here?" Cody asked.

Jamie shook his head. "I don't know."

"Hang tight, buddy, we'll figure it out." Cody got out his phone and stepped into the hall.

"Hey, can you give us a minute?" Zakk asked Viggo.

"Yeah, of course." Viggo nodded at Jamie and followed Cody into the hall.

Jamie looked up at Zakk curiously. "I'm okay," he said.

"You didn't want to leave and now this happens on your first game back. I'm really pissed off at Dante right now."

"Not his fault." Jamie looked away. "This is about my size, being smaller than—"

"It's not about your size!" Zakk growled. "It's about one guy being a dick and not having guys like me looking out for you. I promise, Matt Forbes isn't long on this team, 'cause no one wants to play with someone who plays dirty, especially with a friend."

"Don't make this about me," Jamie said. "Go back and tell everyone I'm okay and that I'm not mad at Matt. Tell Matt he and I are good."

"What?! No!"

"Zakk, can you do this for me, please?" His dark eyes met Zakk's bright green ones. "I'm asking you to diffuse this situation. You were my closest friend here in Vegas—do this for me."

Zakk scowled. "I'll do anything you need, but are you sure that's what you want? He trash-talked you the whole game."

"I know. I heard him. Just do it my way, okay? Two wrongs don't make a right."

"You really want to take the high road like this?"

"Yeah."

"Hey, I just talked to your roommate," Cody stuck his head in the room. "He said he'll meet Emilie in the lobby in 10 minutes. Viggo's calling her now. He's going to give her your stuff 'cause the doctor said you can't get on a plane for a few days."

"Okay, thanks." Jamie nodded, fighting off a wave of dizziness.

"We're going to let you rest," Zakk said quietly. "Call if you need anything, okay? Anything at all."

"I'm fine, man. I appreciate you coming by."

THE NEXT FEW days were filled with tests and diagnoses. Luckily, Jamie's vision was returning quickly and his headache started to fade but the neurologist wanted to watch him and didn't want him traveling yet. He was finally released and went to stay with Zakk and Tiff since they had a guest room for him. Not to mention, he didn't want to be with Viggo and Emilie in this condition. He still got dizzy spells a few times a day and the thought of dealing with his feelings for Viggo while living under the same roof wasn't even an option. As much as he hadn't wanted to leave Vegas, now that he'd made the break he just wanted to get back to Ottawa.

Jamie was quiet at dinner that night but the twins kept up a steady stream of chatter about their day, their toys and anything else they could think of. Tiff fed them and made a point of ushering them upstairs to bathe them while Jamie and Zakk cleaned up the kitchen. He sensed Jamie had something on his mind and decided to bring it up.

"What's up with you tonight?" Zakk asked, closing the dishwasher and drying his hands.

"Are people talking about me?"

"Like whom?"

"The team? Matt? Anyone?"

"No, why?" Zakk met his gaze in confusion.

"I've had a lot of crap go on and I don't need people talking shit about me across the league. I'm trying to start fresh in Ottawa, away from the sex scandals and steroids and all of that. I can't have anyone stirring shit up. I don't have..." He sighed, frustrated. "I don't have a lot of friends, Zakk, and I don't have *any* in Ottawa."

"Your teammates were pretty fired up when you got hit the other night," he said slowly. "Seemed to me they had your back."

"They had my back as a teammate who'd just scored two goals. I've just met most of them—they don't know me and if there was another scandal, this soon..."

"Jamie, what aren't you telling me?" Zakk asked quietly. "You keep saying I'm one of your closest friends but you don't want to trust me with whatever it is that's going on with you. It's been going on for a while, so just spit it out."

"I can't." Jamie took a breath. "I haven't even... I can't even admit it to myself, much less to anyone else."

"You're gay." Zakk's voice was soft and calm.

Jamie groaned as he shook his head. "No." His voice dropped so low he wasn't sure if Zakk could hear him. "But I think I'm bi."

Zakk cocked his head. "So?"

"I figured it out because I'm falling in love with a *man*."

"Okay."

"Another hockey player."

"And? Is he interested too?"

"Dammit, don't act like this isn't a big deal!" His head snapped up, eyes blazing. "You know *no one* in the league is out! They talk about being accepting, providing a friendly environment and all that bullshit, but at the end of the day? *No one* is out! The first thing people focused on when they saw the video of me, Becca and Dante was about how much I appeared to be enjoying going down on Dante! Not the part where I was fucking another guy's girlfriend, but the part about me and him! I could lose everything if this got out!" He slammed his hand down on the counter and then swayed as a wave of dizziness washed over him.

"Hey!" Zakk grabbed him before his knees gave out. "All right, come on." He helped him to the family room, making him sit back on the couch. "You okay? Should I call the doctor?"

"No." Jamie took a slow, deep breath. "It'll pass. I've been getting these dizzy spells... Doc said it's normal. Should go away in a few weeks."

"Okay, just relax. Don't think about anything else right now."

"I'm fine. I just, I need to nip any rumors in the bud, Zakk."

"So you're just going to go directly into the closet? Why? Viggo's bi and everyone knows it. I don't think—" He paused. "Holy shit, is this about you and Viggo?"

"Not like you think!" Jamie said, sitting up abruptly and wincing as pain shot through his head. "It's been the three of us—with Emilie."

"All right, we need to table this discussion." Zakk put a hand on his shoulder. "I don't give a fuck what you do in the bedroom, okay? Are you listening? Look at me, Jamie."

Jamie took a breath and opened his eyes, the pain easing a little.

"You're my friend. I don't care if you're homosexual, bisexual, or asexual. Makes no difference to me—I have no issue with what you do in your personal life. But it's obvious this is stressing you out, so you really, really need to put this on the back burner until your head is better."

"I don't know how much longer I'll be in Vegas," said Jamie. "I have to make sure no one is talking shit about me."

"Jamie, let it go, man." Zakk frowned. "You have a concussion—what good is worrying about this going to do? You know people can be assholes, but trust me and the guys to handle it if anything comes up. Really. That's what friends are for, right? Wouldn't you do the same for me?"

Jamie met his friend's eyes and slowly nodded. "Okay, yeah. Thank you."

# CHAPTER 9

Jamie heard his phone buzz and rolled over lazily. It was early the following morning and he reached over to grab it off the nightstand.
*I need to see you. Can we meet after practice? Leaving on a road trip tomorrow, so you'll probably be gone when I get back. Just need a few minutes.*

Viggo. Jamie sighed. There was no way in hell he would say no and he began typing the response even before he'd thought it through.

*Sure. When?*
*Pick you up about noon?*
*I'll be ready.*

Jamie lay back with his hands behind his head. Seeing Viggo was going to be a mistake, but he was damned if he could stop himself from saying yes. It was like the guy had crawled under his skin and attached himself to Jamie's insides. No matter how hard he tried, he thought about him, wanted him, all the time. He didn't understand it; he was confused because he wasn't gay. He'd never been attracted to a man before, and he'd had plenty of opportunities. *I can't do this*, he thought to himself. He would talk to him, though, try to make him understand that their attraction didn't mean anything; it was just good sex and solid friendship making them think it was something else. Once he convinced Viggo of that, he would work on convincing himself.

VIGGO WAS RIGHT ON TIME, honking the horn, and Jamie slipped out without talking to Zakk or Tiff, who were both lying down. He got into Viggo's truck and looked at him warily.

"Hi."
"Hi."

Neither of them spoke as Viggo pulled down the street, his eyes focused straight ahead. He slowed to a stop in a nearly empty parking lot and finally looked at Jamie. "I understand what you're going through," he said. "I've fought who I am all of my adult life. It's been years of therapy and terrible relationships and hiding my sexuality, so if there's anyone you can talk to, it's me."

"It's not that cut and dried," Jamie said, staring out the window. "How did you know you were bisexual? Because I don't even know what that's supposed to feel like. I mean, thinking a guy is attractive but not doing anything about it doesn't make you bisexual, does it? And what's this thing with us? It's just sex, right?"

Viggo didn't say anything, staring straight ahead again, his jaw working as he struggled to string together a set of words that might possibly make sense. "I realized I was as attracted to guys as I was to girls when I was about 16 or 17. I figured out that made me bisexual when I was 17, but I've never had a relationship with a man. Plenty of sex, but nothing emotional. Half the time not even friendship. So I'm confused too. Even after all these years. Whatever this is, it's not like my other relationships with men."

"This isn't a relationship!" Jamie ground out.

"Of course it's a relationship!" Viggo laughed bitterly. "You're my friend. You were my teammate and my roommate for a year—so there's a relationship there by default. Adding the sexual part to it is what's different."

"I had a threesome with Dante too," Jamie responded. "And I'm most definitely not in a relationship with him."

"Did you kiss him like your soul was on fire?" Viggo whispered. "Did you wrap your arms around him and beg him not to stop?"

"No." Jamie swallowed hard. "No, that was definitely new."

"Jamie, I swore to my wife, my family—everyone—that I loved her and would be faithful to her. I had every intention of doing that. I love Emilie—since the first time I laid eyes on her." He paused and found Jamie's big brown eyes focused on his. "But then I met you."

"Dude..." Jamie closed his eyes.

"I know you're having a hard time with the attraction between us, but I need you to know."

"Know what?" Jamie's voice came out in a small whisper.

"That I feel what you feel and I know why you're running away."

"I don't even fucking know what I feel!" Jamie cried in frustration.

Viggo leaned over and found his mouth, sucking on his tongue until Jamie moaned and dug his fingers into Viggo's hair. Their breathing grew labored as they kissed and caressed with gentle hands, exploring each other's mouths without resistance. "That's what we feel," Viggo whispered when he pulled away. "And we both know it. You can walk away from it, Jamie, but don't deny it."

"If I was still living here we could try to figure this out..." His voice trailed off. "But we can't, so there's no point in having this conversation."

"So you're just going to walk away? Without even giving us a chance?"

"What chance?" Jamie asked, his eyes darkening. "You're married, with a kid! Where do I fit in? I can't be the third wheel. The only thing that's going to happen here is that I fall in love with you and get my guts ripped out. So no thanks, that doesn't sound like fun."

"I don't know how to let you go," Viggo admitted. "I love my wife, but I've never felt...like this. I don't know what to do either—but I can't stay away from you."

"We don't even understand what we're feeling and we're going to break up your marriage, hurt other people, and completely fuck up both our lives? Come on, man. We lived together for a year without a second glance—what changed? 'Cause I never looked at you like anything but a friend. It never even crossed my mind."

"Neither did I. Until you let me kiss you." He looked down. "It wasn't planned—you were only supposed to take care of Emilie. But the minute you touched me, separate from her, something changed."

"Then we need to change it back, because I can't do this. I can't fall in love with a man." The words came out in a rush and he turned away.

"Is that how you see me? Just some man?"

Jamie let out a long, slow breath. "It doesn't matter how I see you—it's how the world sees *us*. You're a man. I'm a man. Us being together isn't...acceptable."

"To whom?"

"Does it matter?!" Jamie cried out in frustration. "You're fucking married! I'm going back to Ottawa! What is there for us?!"

Viggo gripped the back of Jamie's neck and pulled him forward so that their faces were millimeters apart. "I'm going to show you. Come home with me."

"But Emilie..."

"Emilie's at the club all day."

"That would be cheating."

"You should know me better than that. It was her idea. She told me to come see you, told me we needed to do this, alone, to either get it out of our systems or explore what it is. She knows I asked you to meet, knows we're going to do this."

"I don't understand," Jamie said, confusion lurking just beneath the surface of his handsome face.

"She knows me, understands me, and saw the attraction between us. Emilie isn't like other women. She has all kinds of demons, things she hasn't dealt with. Our relationship is based on friendship, trust and acceptance—I told her I needed you, needed to figure this out, and she gave her blessing."

"Now I'm even *more* confused."

"Come home with me," Viggo whispered. "And I'll try to help you understand."

"Okay." Jamie wasn't sure what else to say.

Walking into the apartment he'd lived in for two years felt like home, despite not living there anymore. Jamie kicked off his sneakers and ran a hand through his hair, unsure what he was doing here. This was so damn wrong, but saying no apparently wasn't an option.

"You want a drink?" Viggo called from the kitchen.

"No." Jamie sank onto the couch, leaning back against the cushions and closing his eyes. "I just want you." He spoke the last part in a whisper but Viggo heard him and closed the distance between them more quickly than he intended.

"Part of me wants to apologize," Viggo admitted, sinking down next to him.

"For what?" Jamie glanced at him in surprise.

"For introducing you to this, showing you something you didn't know you wanted."

"Yeah, I *am* kinda pissed about that." Jamie grinned over at him before sobering. "Dammit, Viggo, I don't know how to do this. What do we do?"

"Whatever we want." He leaned over and found Jamie's lips, forcing himself to take it slow. He had him for the rest of the day, just the two of them, and he wasn't going to rush anything. He sensed Jamie wasn't ready to explore the things Viggo wanted to share with him, but he was going to make him want to.

"Kiss me back, lover," he said softly, pulling back a little so Jamie could take the lead. "The other night you fucking devoured me when I kissed you—do it again. Forget about the outside world. It's just you and me now. This is how you figure it out, how you decide what you need."

"I need you," Jamie growled, grabbing Viggo's head and pulling it back to his. This time when their mouths came together it was erotic and raw. Jamie had never kissed anyone like this, unable to open his mouth wide enough or get his tongue any deeper. Viggo pulled him astride him and Jamie could feel his erection rubbing against Viggo's, right through their clothes.

"Take your damn clothes off and get on the bed," Viggo growled, yanking his shirt over his head as he stood up and moved towards the bedroom.

"Fuck." Jamie followed, pulling off his shirt, unable to believe how hard he already was. He got on the bed and Viggo crawled on top of him.

"Tell me what you want," he said. "How you want it."

"I don't know. You have to show me...how this works." If Jamie's heart slammed any harder, he would've been afraid he was having a heart attack. "Tops, bottoms—do we pick?"

"We can do anything we want—and no, we don't have to pick. We'll go slow until you're comfortable with what you want to do."

"I don't know!" Jamie whispered.

"I've got you." Viggo ran his hands down Jamie's flat, rippled stomach and bent his head to kiss him again. He'd never met a man he wanted to kiss like this, without abandon, all the fucking time. Running his tongue along the seam of his lips, he felt Jamie shudder, his tongue seeking Viggo's almost urgently. The moment they touched, the fire that always burned when they were together started like the flame of a candle and quickly became a fiery inferno.

Swirling, curling, dueling with the desire to take control, Jamie forgot all about his inhibitions and uncertainty. All he knew right at this moment was he needed this man to keep touching him, to fulfill every fantasy he'd never been able to articulate. His love of rough sex had always been tempered by the need to be cautious so he wouldn't hurt a smaller, physically weaker woman. With Viggo, that wouldn't be an issue and this was blissfully sexy.

"I like it rough," he ground out, his fingers closing around Viggo's throbbing cock. "I like to be in charge but I can't right now because I don't know how."

"You can be rough," Viggo gave him a slow, sexy smile. "I can't wait to let you top me."

"Except I still don't know how," Jamie chuckled helplessly.

"Tell me what you want." Viggo tossed a handful of condoms on the bed next to them and met Jamie's smoldering gaze. "You want to take me? What do *you* want, Jamie?"

"Is it the same as with a woman?" Jamie asked, clearing his throat as his face burned with embarrassment.

"Angle is a bit different, depending on the position, but yeah. And you can be as rough as you want—that's hot as fuck."

Jamie slid the condom down his aching shaft and stared at Viggo as if he'd never seen him before. They'd been naked together hundreds of times between living together, being in showers and locker rooms together, and of course their recent sexual activities, but he'd never looked at him like he was now.

He was a big guy: close to six feet four inches and probably over 250 pounds. He had red hair that had gotten bleached to a reddish-gold over the summer and hung just a little too long over his ears in what Jamie thought was a sexy mess. His blue eyes were deep-set and wide, with a firm, square jaw and a nose that probably had been nice and straight before it had been broken a few times. He wasn't cut and ripped like a lot of athletes either; he was thick, made of solid muscle. His shoulders were huge and wide, topping muscular arms and a massive chest, which provided a lot of the power that made him so strong. His stomach was flat and hard, his abdominal muscles hidden by sheer bulk. His hips were lean, almost small sitting atop thighs that were bigger than some women's entire torsos.

The overall package was absolutely breathtaking to Jamie, and whatever else was going on with them, the physical attraction was new. He'd never noticed any of this stuff before and now it was almost more than he could stand. He'd had no idea how much he liked a really big guy. He bent his head and closed his lips around Viggo's thick erection, sucking until his cheeks hollowed out.

He was comfortable doing this now and teased him for a while, sliding his tongue down his shaft and kissing the sensitive spot at the bottom that met the soft, heavy sacs. With gentle brushes of his lips and swipes of his tongue he continued until he heard Viggo moan deep in his throat. Jamie replaced his mouth with his hand and moved it between Viggo's legs, running it across his groin and over his pelvis. Viggo handed him a bottle of lube, but didn't say anything, merely watching with hooded eyes that were glittering with anticipation.

"I know how rough you like it, so use plenty," was all he said.

Jamie poured a liberal amount on his hand and tentatively reached between Viggo's cheeks. God, he felt like a dork, completely unsure of himself and desperately hoping he didn't do something wrong, even though he'd done this with women.

"Use your fingers, lover," Viggo said in a throaty whisper. "Rub it in and have at it. You're not going to hurt me."

Jamie's hand trembled a little as he rubbed the lube into the tight hole, closing his eyes as he slid a finger inside of him. It was odd, but when Viggo pushed himself closer he was able to follow his lead, stroking him until he was comfortable with the motion.

"You familiar with the prostate?" Viggo asked gently, startling him.

Jamie shook his head. "Not outside of a medical exam."

Viggo grinned. "Next time I'll show you where yours is...right now your goal is to find mine."

"How?"

"Finger me, move around. You'll know when you find it. Trust me."

Jamie curved his finger up inside of him, slowly turning his hand and watching Viggo's face. Instinctively he added another finger and pressed deeper. A groan escaped Viggo and his hips shot up off the bed, his ass surging against Jamie's fingers. "I guess I found it," Jamie murmured, massaging that spot until Viggo was clutching at the sheets and breathing hard.

"Stop teasing," he growled. "Give it to me, Jamie."

Jamie pulled out his fingers and positioned himself between the bigger man's legs. He'd thought sex with a man would be weird, something out of a bad porn flick, but he'd never been more wrong. He was about to make love to this man as if it was the most natural thing in the world. Adding a little more lube, he pressed the head of his cock into the small, constricted entrance, closing his eyes against the incredible tightness that gripped him as it started to give.

He slid in slowly but effortlessly, and when he opened his eyes he was balls deep in the most beautiful human being he'd ever seen. Viggo's eyelids were at half mast, staring at him with so much intensity Jamie couldn't resist leaning down to capture his mouth in a kiss that sizzled like a drop of water on sunburned skin.

"Okay?" Viggo asked, reaching up to run his fingers through the untamed lock of hair he loved so much.

"Yeah." Jamie was breathing hard. "Fuck yeah." He started to move, gliding in and out as he struggled to find a rhythm in this ridiculously erotic yet unfamiliar position.

"Stop babying me," Viggo growled. "Do it like you want to—fuck me, Jamie."

Jamie rose to his knees, pushed back Viggo's legs far enough to lift his hips, and found an angle that allowed for maximum penetration. He snapped his hips forward and had to take a deep breath as waves of pleasure washed over him. This was better than anything he'd ever experienced and it was all because of the Swedish god beneath him. He had to stop deluding himself now that he was about as intimate as he'd ever been with anyone.

He wanted this man so bad it hurt and as his heart nearly exploded in his chest, he started to fuck him. He thrust hard and deep, grinding against his pelvis until pleasure and pain all but morphed into the same feeling. Pulling back slightly, he increased speed, jackhammering against him, and drawing a grunt from Viggo each time he bottomed out. With every thrust he felt Viggo clench around him and Jamie knew neither of them would hold out much longer.

Viggo reached for his own cock and started to stroke it in time to Jamie's thrusts.

"I need to feel you when I come," Jamie whispered. He lowered his body to cover Viggo's, digging his cock in so deep Viggo groaned. Whether it was pain or pleasure Jamie didn't know, but he was too far gone to stop. His balls had drawn up tight and when Viggo clamped down around him, he lost control, stabbing his cock into him again and again, shooting off with so much force he was afraid the condom would break. Viggo wound his arms around his back and gripped him tightly, his lips pressed against Jamie's shoulder as he shuddered through the aftershocks.

"*Fuck.*" Jamie collapsed against him, his body covered in sweat, heart still beating wildly.

"How was your first time?" Viggo asked with a soft chuckle, hands running down his back in a gentle caress that was completely at odds with their intense coupling.

"There are no words," Jamie huffed, his breath still coming in gasps. "I'm gonna need to do that again."

Viggo nodded. "Yeah, but first you're gonna need to suck me off before I explode."

"I'll do anything you want," Jamie muttered, licking a trail down his body with his tongue. Taking him into his mouth was truly second nature now; he loved the way Viggo's body reacted whenever he did it. Viggo trembled with need and desire, arching up and fucking his mouth the way Jamie had just fucked his ass. He would never get enough of how this made him feel, and he focused on the sexy man in his mouth instead of thinking about how he was going to leave him.

Viggo came with a roar, shooting so much come into Jamie's mouth he had to swallow twice. Slowly he released him, resting his head on Viggo's hip and letting the sweet aftermath wash over him. Tomorrow, he would regret this, but right now he didn't give a damn. It had been almost surreal, not just sex with a man, but going harder at him than he'd ever gone at anyone and watching him enjoy it.

"Hey." Viggo's fingers were digging into Jamie's hair, pulling him up towards his face.

"Hey." Jamie hesitated, unsure if he was capable of cuddling with a guy, but the sexy bastard gave him a smile that made his heart skip a beat and he gave in. He crawled up and rested his head on Viggo's shoulder, loving his strength and size. It was the craziest thing he'd ever experienced, but this was the most relaxed he'd been in a very long time. Lying there together felt more right than it had with anyone Jamie had been with before. One of Viggo's big hands was casually caressing his hip and the curve of his ass. The sheer tenderness of his touch made the gooseflesh raise on his skin and he nestled deeper, unable to look at the man making him feel this way.

"Are you freaked out?" Viggo asked softly, moving his hand up to Jamie's face and gripping his chin. "Look at me."

"I'm good," Jamie responded, turning slightly to press his lips against the underside of Viggo's jaw.

"You're full of shit and trying to distract me," Viggo rumbled, chuckling. "Remember, I was you before you were you."

Jamie chuckled too. "You were me? Really? Which one of us scored those two goals the other night?"

"That was all you, lover."

# CHAPTER 10

On the fourth day of Viggo's five-day trip, Jamie still hadn't gotten clearance to fly. Bouts of dizziness still came on unexpectedly and yesterday he'd had a headache so bad the doctor had to call in a prescription for the pain. Though everyone assured him he would be fine, in the back of his mind he worried his career was over. Although all athletes lived with the fact one injury could potentially end any career, he'd never given it much thought. Today it was the only thing on his mind.

There was nothing for him outside of hockey, and for the first time he realized how lonely he was. He had no one to share anything with—good or bad—and now that he'd developed all these irrational feelings for Viggo, he missed him like crazy.

That night, he broke down and texted him. Not talking to him was ripping him apart, and after yesterday's scare with the headache, he desperately needed something positive in his life.

*Ready to come home?*
*You waiting for me?*
*Much as I hate to admit it...yeah.*

The phone rang and Jamie couldn't hide his smile when he picked it up. "You know I'm not going to say sappy shit on the phone."

"I know," Viggo chuckled, his deep voice rumbling over Jamie like a medicinal salve that made everything hurt less.

"Nice win tonight."

"No thanks to me."

"You've been off your game this week."

"Been thinking of home."

"Miss your daughter?"

"Definitely, but she's not the only one."

"I miss you too," Jamie admitted grudgingly.

"Why do you say it like that?"

"Don't mind me, it's been a shitty couple of days."

"Why?"

Jamie told him about the headache and dizzy spells. "They seem to be getting more frequent instead of less. That's why the doctor won't let me fly."

"Maybe you should see a specialist, Jamie. Don't dick around with this, you know? You know how serious a concussion can be."

"Believe me, I know. My whole life could be over."

"Your life isn't over," Viggo said gently. "Even if you can't play hockey—"

"I'm 27 years old!" Jamie hissed. "What the fuck am I going to do if I can't play anymore? I barely finished high school! You think I'm the kind of guy who can sit in an office all day?"

"You could coach, scout, work in the back office..."

"Yeah, that's a great alternative to being a fucking hockey player!"

Viggo sat quietly, waiting for Jamie to finish venting. There was nothing anyone could say to make him feel better; he understood exactly what he was feeling because he worried about injuries too. The only difference was that Jamie was now living that nightmare and Viggo only worried about the possibility.

"Sorry I snapped at you," Jamie said after a moment, sighing heavily. "It's just...it's really fucking hard. Everyone asks me how I'm feeling every single day and every day I tell them I feel the same! I don't know what to do! The doctors don't have any answers. My parents want me to come home. I haven't heard from anyone in Ottawa—they just talk to my doctors. I have like two sets of clothes and don't know if I should buy more or what!"

"Hey, it's going to be okay." Viggo spoke softly, feeling his friend's pain and wishing there was something he could say or do to help. "I'll be home tomorrow night and I think we're off the next day. After I work out, we can hang out. Emilie can take Simone with her to the club and we can go do something...isn't the World Series going on in L.A.? I bet we know someone that could get us tickets."

Jamie paused. "You hate baseball."

"But you love it and I...want to do something you enjoy doing."

"You'd go to a baseball game with me?"

Viggo smiled even though Jamie couldn't see it. "Hell yeah."

"I'll call Dante and see if he can get us tickets."

"I'll call you tomorrow, see how your head is, okay?"

"Okay."

"Good night, Jamie."

"Good night."

JAMIE WAS in a better mood the next day, knowing he would be spending time with Viggo tomorrow, but he was bored. His friends on the team were out of town and even Becca had gone on this trip, so he borrowed Tiff's car and drove to Club Inferno to see how preparations were going for the grand opening. It was only two weeks away now and Emilie was working long hours every day overseeing everything. He had nothing else to do and honestly, despite their complicated relationship, he liked Emilie and wanted to make sure she was okay on her own like this, working crazy hours and taking care of Simone by herself.

The doors were open, indicating workers were there and he heard the sound of construction as he walked through the now painted and decorated main rooms. The big room on the ground floor would be similar to any regular nightclub, with a huge bar along one mirrored wall, a fantastic dance floor and lots of chairs and high-top bar tables with stools.

The difference would be the random restraints and chains hanging from the ceiling in a variety of places, along with nooks and crannies specially designed for couples who wanted to indulge in a sex act without the full audience of a scening room or the expense of a private one.

Looking at the changes since the last time he'd been here, he was impressed. It was going to be a high-class, private club that catered to the elite of the BDSM world. Though there would undoubtedly be a good number of members who were into voyeurism or the intense arousal offered by simply being in a sex club, there would also be the most hardcore and kinky members of the community. Hopefully, Chains and the security team would keep tight reins on membership approval so no one nefarious managed to sneak in.

He caught sight of Emilie arguing with a construction worker and he ambled over curiously. "Hey, Em."

"Jamie! Hi!" She smiled at him before turning back to the worker. "You have until six today. If it's not done, we'll be hiring someone else and the cost will come off of your contract. If you couldn't afford extra people, you shouldn't have underbid." She turned on her heel and snagged Jamie's hand, tugging him along with her as she trudged back to her new office.

"Oh, wow, this is great!" Jamie's eyes widened in surprise. While the rest of the club was still in various stages of construction and design, her office was finished. Painted in a warm, soft yellow color with light brown carpeting, black furniture and a striking red leather couch. He sank into the chair across from her desk and raised his eyebrows as she immediately began typing something on her computer.

"You want coffee? That's all I have right now," she murmured, typing away.

"Nah, I'm good. Just wanted to see if there was anything I could do to help. I'm kinda bored and sitting around wondering if my head is going to get better is making me a little nuts."

She glanced up. "Still getting the dizzy spells?"

He nodded. "Some."

"Well, if it would distract you from worrying, I could use someone to count bottles of liquor. I know it's mindless, tedious work but we're working on the liquor license and everything has to be accurate and accounted for."

"I can count bottles," he grinned. "I may not have a college degree, but addition and subtraction are no problem."

"Really?" Her eyes lit up. "You truly don't mind?"

"No." He shook his head. "Tell me what to do."

She handed him a clipboard with sheets containing lists. "The storeroom is over here..." She got up with a massive key ring and led him down the hall and around the back. "You have to open the boxes and make sure what's inside matches what's on these invoices. We've only gotten the one shipment, so it's everything that's in here. Will you be okay moving boxes around?"

He nodded. "If I feel a dizzy spell coming on, I'll stop. Promise."

"Oh, you're a lifesaver!" She blew him a kiss and was gone.

Jamie looked down at the sheets in his hand and almost laughed. He'd never had a job that didn't involve hockey. He hadn't gone to college or learned anything about any career other than being an athlete. He knew how to balance a checkbook, use basic word processing, email and internet programs on a computer, and he knew a little about cars because his father was a mechanic. Other than that, this was the first time in his life he actually had a job to do. Chuckling to himself, he held out the invoices and took a selfie pointing to the boxes of liquor. Then he texted it to Viggo without any explanation; the response made him laugh.

*??????*

*Your wife has put me to work—counting liquor bottles. I've never had a job before!*

*Fucking pansy! Do some work and stop slacking off by taking selfies!*

Being called a pansy by Viggo made him laugh, but it occurred to him if anyone found out about them they would call him much worse than that and for a moment he was so focused on that, he only realized he hadn't responded because another text came in.

*Be careful, though, yeah? With you getting dizzy, don't lift anything too heavy.*

*I've already been lectured, Dad. Thank you.*

*Don't want you to make it worse.*

*I know. I'm kidding. Dante got us kick-ass seats for tomorrow, by the way.*

*Right on! Looking forward to it!*

*What time will you be home tonight?*

*Probably late, but I'll come straight to the club if you're still there. Try to get Em to hire a sitter for the evening, will you? It's too much, working 16-hour days and taking care of Simone.*

*I'll do my best.*

*Talk tonight.*

*Later.*

Jamie stuck his phone in his pocket and got to work.

# CHAPTER 11

Two hours later he was tired but feeling extremely accomplished. He'd accounted for every bottle of alcohol they'd been invoiced for and he'd separated the boxes by type: tequila, vodka and rum. Picking up his clipboard, he headed back to Emilie's office and found her rocking Simone, who was whimpering.

"Hey," she smiled faintly. "I don't know what's wrong with her but she's been like this for 30 minutes."

"She probably wants to leave," he said gently. "She'd be happier at home with a sitter. Why don't you call someone?"

"I tried. Everyone is busy and Kate had her the last two nights."

"Emilie!" Chains' voice reverberated through the room, making them all jump.

"In here!" she called back.

"They just delivered the chandeliers," he said, coming into the room and nodding at Jamie. "The *wrong* bloody chandeliers."

"Again?!" she cried, staring at him. "Are you kidding? We went over the order in detail when the last ones were wrong! Shit! The electrician is coming tomorrow! If we don't have the light fixtures they may not get back before the opening! Shit! Shit! Shit!"

"Hey, now, little ears shouldn't hear bad words like that!" Jamie said with a grin, reaching for Simone. "Go deal with the chandeliers. I'll take care of her."

"Jamie, she's really cranky and—"

"Would you go already? We get along just fine, don't we, sweetheart?"

Simone took one look at him and burst into tears.

"Jamie..." Emilie hesitated.

He held up a hand. "Really? She's six months old. I can handle this."

"O-kay." Emilie followed Chains back into the club and Jamie rocked back in Emilie's big leather chair.

"Okay, darlin', what are we going to do now? If you want to cry, you might bring

55

on one of my headaches and then what will we do? Hey, let's call Daddy." He dug out his phone and dialed Viggo's number as Simone continued to whimper.

"Hey, there." Viggo answered on the first ring.

"Houston, we have a problem."

"Jamie? Who is Houston?" Viggo was confused.

Jamie paused. He sometimes forgot Viggo hadn't grown up in North America and even though his English was good, he often missed nuances of slang or references to pop culture. "Sorry, it's an American thing—never mind. Anyway, Emilie has an emergency at the club and I thought maybe if you had a minute we could FaceTime and cheer up Simone."

"We're at the airport," Viggo grunted. "Flight's delayed, so yeah, I'll ring back." He disconnected and a moment later the FaceTime app flashed. Jamie answered and held the phone up in front of Simone.

"Look who's there, sweetie. It's Daddy. Do you see Daddy?"

"Da-da-da!" Simone chirped and Jamie froze.

"Dude, has she said Da-da before?"

"N-no." Viggo's eyes were huge. "Em is going to be pissed—she hasn't said Mama yet!"

"Ma-ma-ma!" Simone bobbed her head.

"Holy crap," Jamie breathed. "Look at that!"

"Aren't you the smart girl," Viggo cooed into the phone. "But you said Da-da first, didn't you?" He said something in Swedish Jamie didn't understand, but Simone was gurgling happily now, as if seeing her father solved all her problems.

Viggo spoke to Simone in soft, soothing tones, both in English and Swedish, and within 10 minutes she'd curled into Jamie's shoulder, her eyelids drooping.

"Flight is about to board," Viggo murmured softly. "I'll see you in a few hours—wait up for me?"

Jamie swallowed. "Sure."

"Be a good girl, Simone. Daddy loves you." Viggo disconnected and Jamie stared at the dark screen for a long time.

*Wait up for me? Sure.*

The words echoed in his head over and over as he rocked Simone. What the hell was this?

*Wait up for me? Sure.*

Sex was one thing, but having a video chat while babysitting for his daughter was...what was it, Jamie wondered. It wasn't something he could put his finger on. There wasn't anything emasculating about it—most of his friends had kids these days and calling home before bedtime was something many of them did. He and Viggo certainly hadn't been flirting or doing anything that someone watching would consider inappropriate, but it felt ridiculously intimate. In some ways, even more intimate than when they were in bed together. It felt real, like two people who could count on each other to know what their family needed. *Family.* Fuck, he wasn't part of their family.

Staring down at Simone, with her rosy cheeks, pink lips and pure white hair, she was like a little doll. He could only imagine what his own child would look like, and that was the type of problem that lurked in the back of his mind more than almost anything else. Someday he wanted kids, his own kids, and that would never happen if he...settled down with a man. Yes, they could hire a surrogate or adopt, but that's not what he wanted. He wanted a child whose mother meant something to him. Didn't he?

*What the fuck was he thinking?!* He wasn't going to be in a serious relationship with a guy. Not even with a guy he was falling in love with. Not even with Viggo. They didn't live in a world that readily accepted same-sex couples and he wasn't the kind of man who could live in hiding. No, he had to stop thinking about that kind of thing and focus on getting better in order to get back to Ottawa and his career.

He leaned back in the chair and continued to rock Simone. A few minutes later Emilie peeked her head in and smiled.

"You got her to sleep!" she whispered happily. "Oh, you're a lifesaver, Jamie! That's twice today. I owe you!"

He shrugged. "Nah, it was fun. Got me out of the house and I really wasn't responsible for her settling down. We got Viggo on video chat and she calmed down the minute she saw him."

Emilie rolled her eyes. "Of course she did. Mommy spends hours every day catering to her every whim but one phone call from Daddy and all is right in her world!"

He chuckled. "I'm pretty sure that's how it works."

"Why don't you put her in the playpen?" she suggested. "You want dinner? I'm going to order food. Franny's coming in and we've got a long night ahead of setting up the furniture in the dungeon."

"Who's Franny?"

"She's an experienced Domme who's been working at sex clubs to support her two kids since her husband was killed in Iraq. She and Chains know each other from somewhere—I don't remember—but he sings her praises and she's really excited to work with us."

He raised his eyebrows. "And you guys are putting that stuff together yourselves?"

"Chains and Franny want to personally oversee the installation of all the equipment in the dungeon for safety reasons. I've got a dozen boxes of toys that arrived that also have to be counted, checked in and stored until we've got the scening rooms finished, so that's what I'll be working on."

"Don't you have people to do this stuff?" he asked, laying Simone down in the playpen.

Emilie got out her keys and locked the door behind her after checking her phone to make sure she was getting the live video feed from the security cameras their security expert, Joe Westfield, and his crew had installed. The system allowed her to watch Simone in her office from anywhere, right on her phone, so she didn't mind leaving her while she napped.

"We currently only have four people on the payroll: Joe is the security consultant we hired. He owns a big firm in New York and, I don't know if you remember this, but he was involved with Dante's friend Trey before he was killed. Other than me, Chains and Franny are the only other full-time employees. We've hired a general contractor to do the actual renovations and next week the interior designer will be here redecorating. We have more than a dozen applications from people but we don't want to hire anyone until we can give them a start date and I'm not sure we'll make our goal of having the grand opening the night before

Thanksgiving." She headed into the main room where Chains and Franny were laughing at something, and they looked up with friendly smiles.

"Hey, Jamie!" Chains grinned. "How's the head?"

"Haven't had a headache or dizzy spell since the night before last," he said. "I'm keeping my fingers crossed."

Franny held up crossed fingers on each hand. "Me too! I'm Franny, by the way!"

"Hi, Franny!" Jamie grinned at the bubbly redhead with massive breasts and the brightest smile he'd ever seen.

"What shall we order for dinner?" Emilie asked. "Pizza?"

Franny wrinkled her nose. "We had pizza the last two times we worked late. How about Italian? I could sink my teeth into some garlic rolls and a big plate of carbonara..." The look on her face was pure rapture as she closed her eyes and licked her lips.

"Damn, baby doll," Chains snickered. "If you're that hungry, I have something you can chew on." He playfully reached for his belt buckle and Franny slapped his hand.

"Pervert! Ruining a perfectly good food-gasm!" She rolled her eyes and got to her feet as Chains laughed.

"I think there's a menu from that Italian place a few blocks from here," Chains said good-naturedly.

"I could do pasta," Jamie nodded.

"All right, just get me a Caesar salad," Emilie said absently, glancing down at her phone. "You've got the corporate card number, yes?"

"Got it!" Chains patted the wallet in his shorts.

"Salad?" Franny made a face at her. "Damn, girl, is it because you're Swedish or just too young to know life is too short to eat salad all the time?"

Emilie frowned. "I modeled for so long, I guess it's habit now. Plus, after having a baby, I wanted to lose the weight quickly and—"

"The weight's gone," Jamie interjected mildly. "Eat something, will you?"

She smiled. "All right. Get me an order of chicken parmesan. Viggo can eat what's left."

After the order was placed they headed down to the dungeon and got to work. The construction crew was still there, installing sawhorses and a St. Andrew's cross. Jamie watched in fascination as everything was bolted down and Chains and Franny both tried out every piece personally, making sure even Chains' massive body couldn't budge them or topple them over. At one point, all four of them climbed onto the St. Andrew's cross, testing to ensure it would hold anyone's weight as well as the force involved when subjects moved.

"Not nearly as erotic while it's under construction, eh?" Emilie chuckled as she climbed down.

"Not even a little bit," Jamie agreed.

"Damn, it's been an age since I've been on a St. Andrew's..." she murmured, half to herself.

He cocked his head. "Need a spanking, little girl?"

She chuckled. "More than you know."

# CHAPTER 12

Viggo was exhausted after playing three games in four days and then waiting an extra two hours for the delayed flight, so he nearly groaned when Emilie texted him to say they were still at the club. This would be short-term, because they had a tight deadline to get everything ready for the grand opening, but he found it hard to concentrate on hockey with her constantly on the go with the baby in tow. However, when she mentioned Jamie was still there his heart leapt a little and, instead of going home, he headed in that direction. He grabbed his bag from the back, which contained a change of clothes, since he was positive there would be work to do, no matter how late it was.

After he changed he headed down to the dungeon and found Chains, Jamie and Franny stretched out on the floor, while Emilie sat in the only chair in the room, holding Simone, who did not appear to be anywhere near ready for sleep. Glancing at his watch, Viggo frowned, noting it was almost 11:00. He didn't have strong opinions about what time Simone went to bed and got up; she was six months old and healthy as could be. Emilie took good care of her; she was always clean and smiling, with good reports at each check-up. But they could afford to get babysitters for nights like this, when Emilie was working against a deadline. There was no reason for her to have Simone with her as they got closer to the opening.

"How are my two favorite girls?" he asked, bending to lightly kiss Emilie and scoop Simone from her arms.

"Da-da-da!" Simone giggled as Viggo blew a raspberry on her belly.

"Long week for you, eh?" Emilie met Viggo's eyes.

"Looks like a longer one for you," he said pointedly.

"I've had help."

"She killed us," Jamie called out, still on the floor. "I'm in shape—I'm a freakin' professional hockey player—and she kicked my ass. I'm cooked. I'm going to sleep right here 'cause I can't get up."

"He's fallen and he can't get it up," Franny snickered, starting to giggle.

"Nobody said anything about getting *it* up," Jamie shot back with a grin. "I said I can't get my body up. My dick is fine."

"Put your money where your mouth is," Franny playfully kicked out with her leg, catching him in the thigh.

"Bloody hell, I've been offering you my services all week and you've blown me right off, but this wanker shows up—Mr. Big Shot Professional Hockey Player—and you're goin' on about his dick?!" Chains demanded in faux indignation. "Bloody insulting, this is!"

"You're all gonna have to wait unless you want to take me right here." Jamie pretended to sigh heavily. "Mistress Emilie kicked my ass and unless I can lie right here, I don't think anybody's gettin' anything tonight."

Viggo felt a twinge of jealousy at the camaraderie between them; Emilie seemed more at ease here with Chains, Franny and Jamie than she did at home sometimes. And after just a few days, Jamie had fallen in with them as well. Where the hell did that leave him?

"It's late, Em," he said curtly. "Simone should've been in bed hours ago."

Emilie raised her eyebrows, glancing at him in surprise. "I couldn't find a sitter and the construction crew was here until after nine. We—"

"It's after 11:00 now and she's tired!" Viggo eyed his wife defiantly. "I'm going to take her home."

"Would you excuse us for a minute, please?" Emilie tugged her husband's arm and pulled him out of the room. "What the hell was that about?" she demanded in Swedish, assuring that no one would understand them. "The sitter is coming tomorrow morning at 9:00 and will be with her all day! Things got a little out of control today and it's not like you were here to help! I'm a single mum during hockey season for the most part, so I don't think it's fair for you to come in here acting like I've done something wrong by keeping her with me while I work—she's been perfectly well-cared-for!"

He sighed, meeting her gaze guiltily. "You're right. I'm sorry. But there's no reason you can't hire more help—Becca and Dante have a substantial budget. You, Chains and Franny are killing yourselves, and that's not what she pays you for! She pays you to manage—not do all the work."

Emilie dropped her gaze, absently playing with one of Simone's tiny feet. "It keeps me busy, keeps the bad thoughts and bad...tendencies...at bay."

"Have you called to find a therapist?"

"Not yet." She shook her head. "It's been crazy."

"Em, I have fantastic insurance with the team—go see someone."

"I don't really want to talk about it," she admitted.

"So instead you're going to let it eat away at you? How is that good for anyone, least of all Simone?" He met her eyes.

"Hey, I should probably take off," Jamie peeked around the corner. "It's late and although I was kidding before, I really am tired."

"Jamie, stay a bit." Emilie glanced from him to Viggo and back again. "Please?" She looked at Jamie meaningfully and he hesitated.

"Em..." Viggo blew out a breath.

"Tomorrow the two of you will go off to L.A. overnight and leave me here to deal with everything. There's only one thing that brings me any relief right now..." She bit her lip. "And Jamie's the only one who can do it."

"We don't have to go tomorrow!" Jamie said quickly. "We can hang out here, it's fine. I don't—"

"No, I want you to go," she interrupted. "I do. I'm not jealous or angry—truly I'm not. I just need...release. I promise, as soon as the club opens I'll look for a therapist! But I don't have a lot of options until then! Please, Viggo?"

He ran tender fingers over her cheek. "If Jamie's okay with it, you know I don't mind. In fact, you two can start without me while I try to get Simone settled in your office."

"We're taking off," Chains and Franny came out, ready to leave.

"I'll be back in the morning," Chains said with a wave.

"Me too," Franny nodded, hiding a yawn.

"Good night—thanks for your help!" Emilie waved back.

"I'll put Simone down," Emile said, gently prying her from her father. "I see the look on Jamie's face so I'll let you two discuss tonight's activities." She winked at Jamie and followed in the direction Franny went.

Instead of talking, Viggo took two long steps in Jamie's direction and covered his mouth with his own.

"You're a manipulative bastard," Jamie chuckled, grabbing the back of his head. "You know the minute you kiss me I'll do any goddamn thing you want!"

"Actually, the thought of you fucking anyone but me kind of pisses me off," Viggo ground out, gripping him by his T-shirt.

"She doesn't want me to fuck her—she just needs some pain and a good orgasm."

"But someone has to fuck her for that orgasm."

"That would be you," Jamie whispered, finding his lips again. "And while you're doing that, I'm going to fuck *you*."

Viggo's dick instantly came to life and he managed to nod between kisses. "Yeah. Yeah, you are."

THEY LEFT for Los Angeles after Jamie made a quick stop at the mall to buy some new clothes. He'd been alternating between shorts and a pair of sweats for a week and he was sick of it. The only other thing he'd brought on this trip was his suit, but he had no need for that now. He bought another pair of shorts, a pair of jeans, two more T-shirts, and a few pairs of socks. Now it felt like he wouldn't have to throw in a load of laundry every single day.

"You ready for some baseball?" Jamie grinned as they got on the freeway heading south.

"I'll be ready by the time we get there," Viggo chuckled.

"You're really just doing this for me, aren't you?" Jamie eyed him.

"I love sports," Viggo shrugged. "But we don't have baseball in Europe. I follow hockey, rugby, soccer...like that. Baseball still makes me scratch my head. It moves a bit slow for me, I'm used to sports with more action, but if it's something you enjoy, I'll learn more about the game."

"That's nice." Jamie reached out and tentatively wrapped his hand around Viggo's. He'd never held a man's hand before and it was definitely strange, but as Viggo's big fingers laced with his, all he saw was the man he was starting to have really intense feelings for.

"Seems like a small thing for someone you care about," he answered, staring out at the highway.

"You think Emilie's okay with us being gone overnight?" Jamie changed the subject, trying to focus on one thing at a time. Holding hands for the first time felt like they'd just gotten engaged or something, so it was easier to bring up Emilie. "I feel kind of guilty...like we're cheating."

"Em is struggling with something that has nothing to do with us," Viggo said after a moment. "After what happened with her friend Therese—the way she used and manipulated her—she hasn't been the same. She forced her to have sex with random men, on camera, by threatening to send both her parents and mine the video of the threesome she and I had. I think there's more to what happened, but she doesn't talk about it. I believe it was a lot like being raped. It wasn't violent—she had a choice—but it was still against her will. I guess she thought us getting married would somehow make the pain of what she had to do go away, and it hasn't. I'm worried about her, but not because of you and me. She knows there's something between us and, believe it or not, she's encouraging it."

"It almost sounds like she has PTSD," Jamie said thoughtfully.

He nodded. "She promised she would get some help once the club opens and she's not working 18-hour days."

"Are you even in love with her, Viggo?"

"I honestly don't know anymore," he admitted. "I'd always loved her from far away. Then she showed up at this club two years ago, and I was with this guy I used to hook up with—my buddy Otto. We all got wasted and next thing I knew we were back at Otto's place. I had no idea this woman we knew—Therese—had paid him off and was there secretly taping everything. The three of us got down and dirty that night, you know? Then all that other stuff happened, with Em's brother and Therese, and she came to me, told me I owed her one night...she wanted to make love with me just one time, so we could officially say goodbye."

"Did she get pregnant on purpose?" Jamie asked curiously.

Viggo frowned. "That was my first thought when I found out, that she'd done it as a way of hanging on to me because she'd admitted that she'd always loved me, but now I don't think so. She would have told me as soon as she found out she was pregnant if that had been the case. By the time she finally got up the nerve to tell me what she'd done, I didn't know what else to do, so we got married..." He sighed. "But now I don't think either of us is in love. We have a history—our shared experiences with Therese and the baby and such—and we wanted to try. It didn't take long for us to figure out we weren't going to live happily ever after, but she needs someone to look out for her. Her need for pain has escalated; she didn't used to enjoy anything that intense and I'm worried."

"She *is* pretty intense," Jamie admitted.

"In spite of everything, I'm a traditional guy. I want a family. I don't want to sleep around; I want to go to bed and wake up with the same person every day."

"Me, too," Jamie murmured, looking down. "But I never considered doing that with a man."

"Nor did I. I got married and planned to be faithful to her, Jamie. I didn't plan this."

"When did it change? We lived together for a year. I never looked at a man, not like that. I've seen you naked a hundred times and never even blinked. When did we figure out we were attracted to each other?"

"I don't know. I always thought you had a nice ass," he admitted. "But not in a perverted way—just a generic, he-or-she-is-hot way, like when you pass someone on the street. Of course, we get on great, since we first met. Good friends, good roommates, good teammates, and apparently, a physical attraction too. I don't know when it became something more."

"When you kissed me," Jamie said thoughtfully. "It changed when you kissed me."

"I've been told I'm a pretty good kisser," Viggo answered with a shy smile, "but to make a straight guy go gay? I should bottle that shit."

Jamie burst out laughing. "We could probably retire."

"Ah, I don't know that my magical kiss would work on anyone but you. I think you just happen to like the way I kiss."

"Yeah, I can't deny it—I really like the way you kiss."

"I plan to spend most of tonight doing just that."

"I hate not being able to touch you in public."

"I hate it too, but I don't think the world is evolved enough for guys like us to be open about being lovers. It's even hard with your friends and family."

"I can't imagine telling my parents. I don't think they're ready for me to tell them I have a male lover."

"They're never going to be ready," Viggo said after a moment. "In a way, I'm almost glad my parents found out the way they did."

"Are your parents still married? I thought your dad left?"

"The man I call my dad is not my biological father—that rotten bastard died in a bar fight about two years after he left. Good riddance. My stepfather is the man I consider my father. He married my mum about a year after my dad left. He and Mum worked together at the factory and as soon as she was free, he moved in. I have a half-brother too."

"You've never mentioned him."

"Mattias hasn't spoken to me since he found out I'm bisexual." He glanced over at Jamie. "Luckily, my parents handled it better than he did."

"I don't know what my parents will think," Jamie admitted. "My sister, Maddie, will be fine. She's only 11 months younger than me and we're close."

"You have a brother too, yeah?"

"Dwight is 24, two years younger than Maddie. He played hockey for the University of Michigan but he blew out his knee sophomore year."

Viggo winced. "How'd that go?"

"He was bummed for a while but he graduated—they honored the scholarship—and I paid for him to get his master's degree. He got an MBA last spring and now he works for some big technology company in Toronto. He's doing well."

"And you're close to your parents?"

"Yeah." Jamie nodded. "When the sex tape got out of me and Rachel, my mom was a little embarrassed but my dad and brother, behind her back, were like, 'Yeah! You're our hero!'" They both chuckled. "Then with the steroid situation, they weren't mad but they were worried, you know, about my health and stuff."

"Of course."

"When the video of me, Becca and Dante got out my dad was pissed. He didn't say much about the content, but he had some choice words about me needing to grow up, be responsible, and how I needed to start thinking about my career instead of my dick. He never said a word about the fact there was a man involved. I don't know if it was because he was embarrassed or because he was so pissed I got caught again."

"I think my dad knew I was bi," Viggo said after a moment. "There were a couple of times I was with guys—you know, that I met playing hockey—and I would catch him watching us, like he knew something. But I had girlfriends too, so I think he figured it out. My mother was more hurt that I hadn't confided in her, that she had to find out online."

"That's good, that your parents are okay with it." Jamie was thoughtful. "I think my parents will still love me, you know, the way parents say they'll love you no matter what? But I think they'll be disappointed. I don't know that they'll understand that two men can truly be in love. To be honest, I don't know that two men can either."

"You and me both," Viggo murmured. "This is new territory for me too."

"I'm sorry I've been so...wishy-washy."

"Wishy...?" Viggo frowned.

"You know, unsure of everything to do with us, sending you mixed signals."

"Believe me, I understand better than anyone. At least we got to get away today, where no one knows us."

"I'm really excited that we're going, especially since I didn't think you'd ever want to go to a baseball game with me."

"It's the World Series!" Viggo laughed. "Aside from the fact that I want to spend time with you, no one I know has ever been to a World Series game, so this is one of those things you get to brag about."

Jamie chuckled. "Please tell me you're an L.A. fan."

Viggo frowned. "Is that mandatory?"

"Well..."

"I'm a bit of a Bandits fan."

"Because of Dante?" Jamie snorted. "Kiss up!"

"What's that?!" Viggo looked bewildered.

Jamie laughed and explained what it meant.

## CHAPTER 13

They got to the game and found their seats. They were incredible, so close to the field they could practically touch it, and not far from the dugout. Seats like these probably couldn't even be bought and Jamie knew they only had them because of Dante. This was by far the most exciting sporting event of his life, with the exception of his own participation in the hockey championships earlier this year. This was different, though. These were the kinds of seats celebrities and big shots sat in and he wondered if Viggo realized how cool this was.

"This is fucking amazing," Viggo muttered, practically reading Jamie's mind as he looked around.

"Dante seriously hooked us up," Jamie agreed. "I fucking love live baseball."

"I can tell." Viggo met his gaze and there was no mistaking the ever-present spark between them.

Jamie just smiled and turned back to the field, suppressing the urge to lean over and kiss him. It was okay, though; they had all night for that.

"Jamie!" A voice called his name and Jamie turned, surprised to see Dante approaching.

"Hey! Thanks for the tickets, man! These seats are amazing!"

"Yes, thank you!" Viggo nodded, shaking Dante's hand. "I'm off to get us some beers. You want one, Dante?"

"No, I'm good, thank you." Dante nodded, watching as Viggo moved to the bar. "You look like you're having fun. I could see you from up in the box."

"Yeah, it's a great game," Jamie grinned. "I love baseball. Trying to teach Viggo a little; they don't have baseball in Sweden."

"No, not a very European sport," Dante agreed.

"Not at all."

"Jamie, what's happening with your concussion? When do you see the doctor again?"

"Next Friday."

65

"I don't want you to worry," he said quietly.

"What do you mean?"

"If something happens—if you can't play—don't worry about the future."

Jamie frowned. "Do you know something I don't?"

"I know you've been injured and it's somewhat serious. You must be worried about your ability to earn an income should you be unable to play. But you don't need to—I told you when I asked you to get traded that I would always take care of you, that I would owe you."

"I'm going to be fine," Jamie said firmly. "Lots of guys get concussions. But I appreciate it."

"Take your time getting better and let your body heal." Dante looked at him intently. "I'm serious. Don't ruin your life so you can get back a few weeks earlier."

"I won't. Besides, it gives me a little more time in Vegas." He glanced in the direction Viggo had gone.

"And with Viggo."

Jamie snapped his head back. "Is it that obvious?"

"Don't worry, my friend. It's not a judgment. I see the way he looks at you—and the way you look at him. It's good, isn't it?"

Jamie looked down. "I don't know what it is."

Dante laughed. "Do you think I don't know who you are, Jamie? Come, give me a little credit. My fiancée says I have super powers, that I'm able to bend people to my will, but you know the truth, don't you?"

"I'm afraid to ask," Jamie muttered.

"I read people," he said. "And I learn about them. Usually it's by watching and listening. Sometimes it's instinct. Once in a while I hire people to do a background check."

Jamie chuckled. "Now that I believe."

"But seriously—do you think you were a random choice for our threesome?"

"What?" Jamie blinked.

"I chose you for a variety of reasons. First and foremost was safety and health. I wasn't going to take a chance that someone with a disease would get near either of us. Condoms break, so that wasn't a chance I was willing to take, especially not with the woman I love. As a professional athlete and a friend, I was as sure as I could be that you were clean."

Jamie nodded with understanding. "And the other reasons?"

"I knew you were experienced in both being dominant with a woman and in threesomes with other men." His eyes bore into Jamie's. "But the main reason was that I knew you weren't going to fall in love with her."

"How could you possibly know that?!" Jamie demanded. "She's smart and beautiful and sexy—except for being terrified you would kill me, there was nothing stopping me from falling for her!"

Dante smiled as Viggo approached, taking in the bigger man's presence. "Yet there obviously was." He touched Jamie's shoulder, nodded at Viggo and headed back in the direction from which he came.

"Thanks." Jamie accepted the beer and took a long pull.

"What did Dante have to say?"

"That we look happy."

"Aren't we?" Viggo seemed confused.

Jamie couldn't help but smile. "Yeah, I guess we are."

IT WAS LATE when they got back to the hotel. The game went into extra innings and then they'd gone out drinking with Dante and a group of his friends. Jamie couldn't drink much because of the concussion but he had one more beer and Viggo had a decent buzz going. They'd been careful not to show any affection or touch each other throughout the evening so now they were aching with desire. They'd barely walked in the door before they were shedding their clothes and falling onto the bed together. Viggo grabbed a handful of condoms and a bottle of lube, keeping the items on the bed next to them as they kissed.

Their bodies pressed together tightly, cocks rubbing together, mouths practically fused into one. Jamie refused to let his mind wander and focused solely on enjoying this moment. Every time he thought he was satisfied, Viggo made him want more. Instinctively, he sensed it was just as much emotional as it was physical, but his raging hard-on didn't allow him to think about anything but the strong, sexy body all over him.

"Are you ready to try something new?" Viggo murmured, running his hand over Jamie's taut ass and slowly fingering his crease. Jamie stiffened, so Viggo merely continued to tease without going any further, running his finger along the crack.

"I don't know…" Jamie whispered, his eyes meeting Viggo's anxiously.

"Trust me," Viggo nibbled Jamie's bottom lip. "Relax. It's just a finger, yeah? I know you're not ready for the rest."

Jamie nodded, closing his eyes against this new form of exhilarating torture. All the things he'd thought were hard limits suddenly became fair game. It was going to be hell walking away from this—whatever this was—because Viggo made him feel like a new man. He didn't understand it, but he wanted it. Just looking at Viggo's firm, strong body and the lips that gave him so much pleasure, there was no chance he'd move away. He didn't want to think about what all of this meant, but he was aware his feelings were now just as entangled as his body.

VIGGO KNEW BETTER than to go too far. Jamie was struggling with the emotional part of this and too much ass play would definitely send him running for cover. There was nothing stopping him from teasing him, though, bringing him right to the brink of ecstasy. Then he would back off and see what signals Jamie sent. Jamie's cock was already starting to stiffen against his leg and Viggo felt a pang of desire so strong it would have brought him to his knees had he been standing.

Instead, he grabbed the bottle of lube and drizzled it into Jamie's crack, rubbing it in before pressing his finger into muscles so tight he couldn't imagine fitting his cock in there. Jamie was an anal virgin—on the receiving end anyway—and the thought made Viggo's stomach clench a little. Being the first—the only—man to ever have sex with Jamie this way was heady. He'd never imagined finding a virgin at this age, and he was falling hard.

"So tense…" he whispered against Jamie's ear. "Relax and let me make you feel good."

"Viggo, this might be too much…"

"Shh." Viggo sought his lips, the one thing Jamie couldn't resist and always surrendered to. The moment their mouths came together Jamie gave him all he had. It was spectacular, the way it felt when they kissed, and this was no exception. Jamie didn't struggle, his lips pressing against Viggo's with no urgency, just pure and simple desire. Viggo used the opportunity to press his finger inside of him again, slowly, letting him adjust to the intrusion.

"I don't know if I like this…" he murmured.

"You will. Trust me." Viggo pushed deeper, exploring him with gentle strokes.

Jamie's eyes fluttered closed as he tried to breathe through the new sensations. It didn't hurt, but he didn't find it particularly pleasant either. When Viggo added a second finger, the slight burn made him wince and Viggo intensified their kiss, successfully distracting him as their tongues tangled and danced. God, he loved kissing him. It was different than with anyone else; with Viggo, it was an out-of-body experience, transcending sex and time and emotions. This kind of kissing was ethereal, perfection in its truest form. Jamie couldn't recall a kiss that had ever made him fall in love, but that's what had been happening.

Just when he thought nothing could bring him out of the kiss-induced coma Viggo had led him into, pleasure shot through his groin, so intense he almost vaulted off the bed.

"What in holy hell…" his voice faded as Viggo rubbed some magical spot in his ass over and over, leaving him incapable of thought, much less speech.

Pushing him onto his side, Viggo added a third finger and kept the pressure just right so Jamie was practically howling with need. He rubbed against the spot, working his fingers in and out until Jamie cried out.

"Oh fuck, god damn, what are you…shit!" Viggo bent over, sucked him deep in his mouth and Jamie came with no warning, thrusting his hips forward and his cock down Viggo's throat. Everything exploded around him with such force the room started to spin, lights shooting across his field of vision. Heat seared his skin and his cock jerked over and over, his body acting of its own volition.

It seemed like a long time before Jamie could think again. He was wrapped tightly in Viggo's arms, lips pressed against his chest, as he came down from a high he'd never felt before. He finally stirred, bringing his hand up to find Viggo's face and bring it closer to his.

"Told you to trust me," Viggo smiled down at him, but his eyes were tender and unsure, the unspoken question about whether or not Jamie was okay as plain as day.

Jamie nuzzled his face into the hollow of Viggo's shoulder, nestling into him and soaking in his warmth, understanding he was worried about him and loving him for it.

Viggo ran his fingers through Jamie's hair, and Jamie almost shivered with pleasure. It was such a simple gesture but it left him craving more. The emotions rocked him like a jetty in a stormy sea, yet instead of wanting to get away, he wished it would never end. They couldn't have this forever, but they could have it for a while. Everything about it was foreign, but he didn't have it in him to break away. Eventually he'd go back to Ottawa and leave this behind, but there was no chance he was going anywhere yet. Right now, he was all in, whether he wanted to be or not.

# CHAPTER 14

When he woke in the morning, Jamie was still tangled up in Viggo, arms and legs entwined. He managed to pull free to go use the bathroom and brush his teeth. He slid back into bed and wrapped his arms around Viggo from behind, moving into the spooning position as if they'd been sleeping together for much longer than a few weeks.

"Is brushing my teeth mandatory before touching you in the morning?" Viggo rumbled, moving against him.

"No, but I was up, so I figured I might as well."

"Fine." Viggo reluctantly pulled free but turned to eye him. "I'll do it this time because it's our first time waking up like this, but I'm not going to get up and brush every day before I can kiss you good morning!"

Jamie chuckled but his stomach dropped a little. Every day? They weren't going to be together much longer, much less every day, so that wouldn't be an issue, but the idea of not waking up with him ever again was gut-wrenching. It occurred to him Viggo probably had no idea he was planning to put some distance between them and he needed to address that.

The problem was that not only did he not want to talk about it, he also didn't want to do it. Normally he had no trouble cutting someone he was dating loose, but Viggo wasn't just someone he was casually dating; he was falling for him and Jamie believed it was mutual.

Viggo came back to bed and this time he was behind Jamie, pulling him close against his chest. He pressed light kisses on his shoulder before resting his head there.

"What time do we have to get back?" he asked.

"Up to you. You're the one with responsibilities—I'm completely free."

"I'd like to spend some time with Simone," he admitted. "Sometimes I feel like I don't see her enough."

"She's still little," Jamie reminded him. "She'll need you more when she starts communicating and developing her personality."

"I can't wait," he admitted. "She's this little part of me—it's amazing. I never thought I'd want to be a dad, but now that I am..."

"I've always wanted to be one," Jamie said. "I mean, not immediately, and I obviously wanted to wait for the right person, but it's always been in the back of my mind."

"You'll be a great dad. I see you with Simone—you're a natural."

Jamie didn't say anything, wondering how that would happen if he didn't marry a woman. If he allowed himself to fall in love with Viggo, he would never have a family, and he didn't think that was something he was willing to sacrifice. Not even for someone who made him happier than he'd ever been.

"What are you thinking?" Viggo murmured, running a hand along Jamie's hip.

"That I love being here with you and that when we're together everything is great, but the outside world comes crashing in the minute we step outside. And I hate it."

"I'm sorry."

"Not your fault."

"If I had my way, I would stand in the middle of a room full of everyone we know and kiss you like I do when we're in bed."

Jamie smiled. "That would go over like a ton of bricks."

"But it's my fantasy." He grinned. "Well, one of them."

"This is *my* fantasy," Jamie whispered, leaning back against him.

"This?"

"You and me...just the two of us. When we're like this, it feels real."

"It *is* real." Viggo leaned over to kiss him and, as always, the moment they touched thoughts of anything else were far, far away.

JAMIE DIDN'T SEE Viggo for the next few days. Viggo was spending time with Simone and kept busy with team practices, working out and the two home games that week. They had dinner one night with Emilie, followed by another threesome that left Jamie feeling oddly out of sorts. He'd actually felt a pang of jealousy watching Viggo fuck Emilie, and he didn't like it at all.

It was irrational since Jamie wasn't ready to let Viggo top him, but watching them together had set his teeth on edge. They didn't have any more time alone together either, and by the time Jamie saw his doctor on Friday, he was in a piss-poor mood, horny as hell and frustrated that though they were in the same city, Viggo was too busy to spend time together. Once he went back to Canada it would be over, so he resented all the commitments that kept them apart.

"How have you been, Jamie?" The doctor's question snapped him out of his gloomy reverie.

"I was having a good week until yesterday."

"What happened yesterday?"

"I got really dizzy after I went for a run, and then I got another one of those headaches that was so bad I had to take a pain pill."

The doctor nodded. "But you went almost a week without any headaches at all?"

"Yeah."

"That's good. You're not having them every day anymore, and that's important. I think you'll be able to fly home soon. Go ahead and make your plans. Avoid strenuous activity, and if you go the weekend without a headache, I'll make the call to your team doctor in Ottawa. If you get one before Monday, though, call my cell phone." He handed him a business card with a handwritten number on the back. "It's very important, Jamie. I don't want you on a plane at 30,000 feet getting one of these spells."

"I'll be careful. Thanks." Jamie walked downstairs and got in Tiff's Mercedes, which he'd borrowed for the appointment. He took a deep breath, pulled out his phone and sent Viggo a text.

*Looks like I'll be going home next week.*
*Shit. Let's get together tonight. I'll get a sitter for Simone and we can do something.*
*I'd rather stay in.*
*I'll see if Kate will take her.*
*I have a couple things to do today. Text me before you come get me.*
*About 5?*
*See you then.*

JAMIE WAS a nervous wreck when Viggo picked him up. He didn't know what he was going to say, but he had to find a way to explain they couldn't continue their relationship long distance. He'd done everything possible to keep himself from developing feelings for him, but it was too late. He was prepared for the broken heart that was in his future, but actually saying the words—telling Viggo he didn't want to see or talk to him once he went back to Ottawa—was going to suck. Part of him wanted to just leave and simply stop returning calls and texts, but that would be a dick move and Viggo didn't deserve that.

"You want to get some wings and have a few beers?" Viggo asked him as he pulled onto the street.

"I'm not real hungry, but sure." Jamie nodded. Maybe doing it in a public place would be easier? Probably not.

Viggo glanced at him with a frown, but decided not to say anything. Jamie ran hot and cold, and though it was getting a little tiresome, he figured he'd had more than a decade to come to terms with being bisexual; Jamie had only had a short time. It hurt a little, but he vividly remembered the pain and confusion at his own revelation, so he was determined to be patient.

They got to the bar and ordered wings and a couple of beers. There was a hockey game on, Chicago against Nashville, so they kept conversation to a minimum as they watched. Jamie only picked at his food, though, the first twinge of pain behind his eyes indicating a headache was coming on. He hoped he was wrong, but by the end of the second period, the dull thud had become a distinct ache and he pinched the spot between his eyebrows.

"You all right?" Viggo was watching him with concern.

"Headache," Jamie murmured. "I'd better get home."

"You know how many times I've heard that excuse?" Viggo tried for levity and earned a small smile.

"Definitely a first for me," he responded, rubbing his temples.

"Come on, let's get out of here." Viggo had just taken a step when Jamie's knees buckled. He managed to catch him around the waist before he fell, and eased him back onto the bar stool.

"Damn." Jamie hung his head. "Dizzy spell. I need to sit for a second."

"Sure." Viggo yearned to reach out and push his unruly hair out of his eyes, but this was a big Sidewinders hangout and they were easily recognized. He hated not being able to comfort him, but there was no help for it.

"Let's go," Jamie whispered, managing to get to his feet. Viggo kept an eye on him as they walked to the truck and helped him inside.

He put the truck in drive and turned towards Zakk's house.

"No," Jamie whispered. "They'll make a fuss. Can we go to your place?"

"Sure." Viggo made a U-turn and headed home, wondering if he needed to call Jamie's doctor.

They were almost home when Jamie grasped his arm. "Stop!" he hissed. "Pull over, dammit!"

Viggo eased onto the shoulder and slowed to a stop just as Jamie threw open the door and heaved onto the pavement.

"Shit." Viggo reached into the back and grabbed a towel out of his bag, handing it to him.

Jamie felt another wave of nausea and leaned over the side again, emptying his stomach. Viggo gently rubbed his back and Jamie was grateful for the support. When his stomach seemed to have settled, he sat back in the seat and closed his eyes. "I should be able to make it home."

"You sure?"

"Yeah."

"All right." Viggo eased back into traffic and was gratified they didn't hit any lights the rest of the way. He pulled into his parking spot and jumped out, hurrying to the other side to help Jamie. His skin felt a little clammy and he was extremely pale. Viggo had been an EMT before he'd known he would be able to make a living playing hockey, and his training kicked in automatically. He felt Jamie's forehead; there was no fever, but his skin was damp as hell.

He slid an arm around his waist as they made their way to the elevator. Once the doors closed behind them Jamie practically fell against him, his head landing on Viggo's chest.

"I'm gonna need a bathroom quick," he murmured.

"I've got you." Viggo half-carried, half-dragged him to the apartment, unlocking it with one hand and just making it to the guest bathroom as Jamie lost it once again. Digging in the closet, he found a washcloth and got it wet. As Jamie sank to his knees over the toilet, Viggo pressed it against the back of his neck.

"You don't have to stay," Jamie rasped. "I'll be okay."

Viggo rolled his eyes. "Shut up, will you?"

Jamie couldn't help but smile. "Thanks."

## CHAPTER 15

Viggo watched Jamie vomit over and over for the next 30 minutes. He'd suggested going to the emergency room twice, but Jamie was violently opposed. Finally, Viggo slipped out of the room and called Zakk.

"Hey, man." Zakk sounded half-asleep.

"I have a problem," Viggo spoke quietly, so Jamie wouldn't hear.

"What's up?"

"Jamie's sick and won't let me take him to the hospital."

"What happened?!"

"We went for something to eat and he started complaining he had a headache. On the way home I had to pull over for him to throw up. He's been puking on and off for an hour and I'm afraid he's going to get dehydrated. He's clammy and his pulse is a little fast."

"I'll be there in 15 minutes," Zakk said after a moment. "If it gets worse call Doc Levine."

He disconnected and Viggo went to sit with Jamie again. He'd never had to take care of someone who was sick, outside of the year he'd spent as a paramedic. Those people had all been strangers, though, and Jamie wasn't just a friend, he was his lover and the man he now realized he was in love with. Watching him suffer like this made his gut clench with worry, but he was more concerned that if he forced him to go to the hospital Jamie would never forgive him.

He understood the need for privacy, especially now that the hockey world would be watching him carefully for signs he wouldn't be returning to the game. Two weeks after the injury, it wasn't normal to start vomiting like this. Though nausea and vomiting were common after concussions, it usually happened sooner; this much of a delay bothered him. Jamie had had headaches and some dizziness, but nothing like this and it didn't make sense that it would get so much worse after two weeks.

He heard the buzzer and went to let Zakk up. Opening the door, he watched him come down the hall.

"What were you two doing?" Zakk grunted as he came in, giving Viggo a dirty look.

"We were at a bar, watching a game and having wings!" Viggo shot back. "Do you think I'd let him do something stupid?"

"I don't know. Would you?"

The two men glared at each other until Jamie's voice reached them. "Stop it. This isn't Viggo's fault. Someone come help me up."

Viggo eyed Zakk warily but went into the bathroom and held out a hand to help Jamie to his feet. Jamie stumbled twice on the way to the couch, but managed to make it and lie down.

"How long have you been puking?" Zakk asked, squatting next to him.

"I don't know...about 45 minutes?"

"You're fucking white as a sheet and really clammy," Zakk said, touching his arm. "We need to call the doctor."

"No!" Jamie scowled. "I'll be okay. It's normal."

"It's not normal—this is pretty severe for so long after the fact."

"Jamie." Viggo's deep voice always demanded attention and both Zakk and Jamie looked in his direction. "We're not going to let you hurt yourself because you're stubborn. Either we call the doctor or we're taking you to the E.R."

Jamie sighed. "What about Doc Levine? Can we call him first? If he says I need to go, I'll go."

"Fine." Zakk pulled out his phone and called the Sidewinders' team doctor. Though he didn't usually make house calls, Zakk knew he would make an exception for this.

They didn't talk while they waited for Doc, and Jamie had to be helped back to the bathroom once more. He was on the couch when the doctor arrived and Viggo let him in gratefully.

"What's happening, Jamie?" Doc asked, kneeling beside the couch.

"Not sure." Jamie's voice had gotten raspy from vomiting so much. "Was headache free for almost a week and tonight I felt one coming on. Then I started puking. Been going on for over an hour."

Doc asked him a few more questions, frowning as he listened. "What else have you been up to, Jamie? Working out? Drinking? Partying?"

"I ran a mile twice this week," Jamie replied, holding his stomach. "Had a couple of beers last weekend, and didn't even finish one tonight. No drugs. No steroids. No partying." His eyes closed.

"Rest a bit," the doctor told him. "Let's see how your stomach does while I'm here." He motioned with his head to Zakk and Viggo, who followed him into the kitchen.

"I don't know if it's anything serious," Doc said, "but I'd be happier if we took him in."

"What do you think is going on?" Zakk asked.

"I really don't know," Doc sighed. "What else has he been doing? Has he been on the ice?"

"No!" Viggo said firmly.

"Has he been having a lot of sex?" Zakk asked, fixing Viggo with a pointed look.

Viggo coughed. "I'm pretty sure he's been seeing someone."

"Could this have happened from having sex?!" Zakk demanded of the doctor.

Doc Levine shook his head. "In and of itself? No. But if it was overly strenuous, maybe. Any exertion can be dangerous right now. That's why he shouldn't be working out, skating, or doing anything physical. Completely sedate for a while."

"Viggo!" Jamie's voice wasn't loud but there was no mistaking his panic.

Viggo rushed into the room just as Jamie heaved all over the coffee table. "Sorry," he groaned. "I tried to get up..."

"All right." Doc Levine shook his head. "You need to go, Jamie. You can't keep this up. I'll call ahead to have you admitted under a different name. No one will know you're there and we'll make sure it's kept quiet."

"All right." Jamie was on his knees, leaning over the coffee table.

"Let me get you a clean shirt," Viggo said quietly.

"I'll clean up the table," Zakk turned to find paper towels.

"It's going to be all right, son," Doc Levine said quietly. "Let's get you something to settle your stomach and we'll figure it out."

After taking Jamie to the hospital and getting him checked in, Viggo and Zakk sat in the waiting room. They didn't speak for long minutes and Viggo had a feeling Zakk knew exactly whom Jamie had been seeing. Part of him was mortified, but another part of him wanted to stand up and tell Zakk to go fuck himself. He loved Jamie, and even though it was complicated and would be a nightmare if people found out, he refused to be ashamed of how he felt. He'd worked too hard to come to terms with his sexuality and Jamie meant a lot to him.

"What the hell were you thinking?" Zakk finally growled, his voice low but distinctly irritated.

"Oh, it's my fault?" Viggo demanded. "I kept him from having more than one beer. He didn't do any working out while I was around—he waited until we were on the road because he knew I'd have stopped him."

"How about the sex? Really?! After a concussion like that?"

"Not like I could stop him!"

"Don't." Zakk held up a finger. "*I know*. Aside from the fact that he's one of my closest friends and I noticed something has been different lately, I see the way he looks at you, the way his voice changes when he talks about you."

Viggo looked away.

"Don't fucking pretend you're not involved with him."

"I'm sorry."

"For what? Getting caught? Cheating on your wife? Dragging Jamie into whatever life you had before you moved here?"

Viggo's eyes narrowed as his head snapped back. "If you think I'm going to apologize for the way I feel about him, you're dead wrong. And I'll be damned if I apologize for being bisexual. But I am sorry this is happening *now*, at a vulnerable time in his life."

"Did it ever occur to you this might be happening *because* he's at a vulnerable period in his life?"

Viggo clenched his jaw. "I know that. I've tried to stay away. We both have, but..." He sighed.

"But what? Does Emilie know?"

"Of course she knows!" He scowled at him. "You might hate me for being bi, but do you think that little of me? That I'm carrying on with someone else behind her back, right under her nose?"

"I don't know!" Zakk admitted in frustration.

"I would never go behind her back! We had a threesome...several of them. And something changed with Jamie and me—even Emilie saw it. I've never lied to her and I've had her blessing to explore this thing we have. Whatever you may think of my unconventional lifestyle, I'm not an asshole."

"I don't know you that well," Zakk shrugged. "But I know Jamie and he's... dammit, he's not like you and me! He's gentle on the inside—don't you see that? He's a sensitive soul, the kind of guy who needs someone to take care of him. He's always getting into trouble because he's too trusting, too easy to manipulate. The steroids started because the guys he played with in junior hockey teased him about being too scrawny. The threesomes started because being with two girls made other guys think he was more of a man. He's always getting into things because he doesn't feel like enough of a man. And now he's involved with one. Something that's ultimately going to destroy him."

"He's going back to Ottawa," Viggo ground out. "I'm letting him go, so he'll forget about me."

Zakk grunted. "You don't know him very well, do you?"

"Well enough to know he's never going to come to terms with having feelings for a man and I'm going to be the one who gets hurt."

Zakk had the grace to look embarrassed because he also wondered if Jamie would ever be okay with being bisexual. "Just for the record," he said after a moment, "I don't hate you. Not for being bi or anything else. I wouldn't be a fan of you cheating on your wife, but if she's okay with this, it's none of my business."

"Emilie's emotional scars from what happened with Therese have her torn up inside," Viggo said quietly. "She's struggling so I can't abandon her, but she knows I have feelings for Jamie and he understands she needs me right now. It's complicated and I wish it wasn't like this—but it is."

"When it's all said and done, where does it leave Jamie?"

"If I had my way, he would be with me," Viggo admitted quietly, looking down. "But like you said, Jamie isn't like us. He doesn't have our 'fuck-you' attitude. I don't care what people think of me being bi. Sure, I wish it was more acceptable and that I didn't have to be careful who I'm open with so I don't embarrass people like my parents, but in general, I'm good with who I am. Jamie...well, we both know he won't stand up to that kind of scrutiny. I should have stayed away from him, but I couldn't help falling for him. I tried."

"Does he feel the same?" Zakk couldn't believe he was having this conversation with a guy about another guy, but Jamie needed someone to look out for him and apparently Zakk was going to have to be the one to do it because he hadn't confided in anyone else.

"I don't know." Viggo could only hope.

# CHAPTER 16

Jamie was released the next day. After a multitude of tests and all kinds of blood work, the doctors concluded it was merely a case of food poisoning, probably from leftovers Jamie had eaten the day before. After giving him something to settle his stomach and help with the nausea, he fell asleep.

Viggo went home but was back in time to pick him up after practice in the morning. Though Jamie knew it irritated Viggo, he went back to Zakk and Tiff's, determined to put a little distance between them. If they continued down the road they were on, Jamie wasn't sure what would happen. One way or another, he was going back to Ottawa and Viggo was staying here, which was only going to be a disaster.

He'd hoped staying with Zakk and Tiff would dull his need for the big Swede, but the longer he kept his distance, the more he realized how deep his feelings went. After eight days of no physical contact and strained telephone conversations, he'd tortured himself enough; he was going to give in to the emotions that were tearing him up inside. He was in love with a man and didn't know how to deal with it, so he'd tried to shut him out. Keeping him in the friend zone had been hard, but he hadn't known what else to do.

Continuing to see each other, touch each other, and share those blisteringly hot kisses would only delay the inevitable. He'd never imagined being in a relationship with a man long-term, and that was what it really boiled down to. Except he'd never loved anyone like this before. Never needed someone so much. Never hurt so much from being apart. It was the kind of love that burned hot on the outside, but somehow even hotter on the inside. Viggo didn't just make him happy, he made him whole. He filled every single need Jamie had—emotional, physical, intellectual and even professional. How the hell was he supposed to walk away from something that bordered on perfection?

When Emilie had announced they were doing a dry run for the grand opening of Club Inferno two nights before the real event, Jamie figured that would be his opportunity to talk to Viggo. He still didn't know what he was going to say, but being apart this past week had nearly destroyed him. Even though he wasn't supposed to do anything strenuous, he desperately needed to touch the man who'd taken his soul apart piece by piece and then handed it back to him put together better than it had been originally. Because that's what had happened.

Viggo had taken the confused, insecure man Jamie had been and loved him so much, and so well, Jamie now knew the reason he'd been the way he was before was because he hadn't realized a piece of him was missing. Being with Viggo had shown him what it was like to be complete—and even though he wasn't sure about settling down with a man, he'd learned so many things about himself. Those revelations made him stronger, and whether or not he embraced his bisexuality, he would be forever grateful Viggo had shown him a part of himself he'd been mostly unaware of.

In retrospect, he'd had inklings. There had been times he'd been with a woman and another man in a threesome and had felt stirrings of arousal for the man, but who wouldn't? People of both genders were sexy—he'd heard many a woman say another woman was beautiful. Guys didn't admit things like that out loud—it wasn't masculine—but that didn't mean they didn't think it. Jamie had assumed all guys occasionally found another man attractive.

He'd never even thought about asking a man out or kissing him, much less having sex with him. It had all been surface-level attraction, and he hadn't considered words like *bisexual*. Then suddenly being bisexual had bowled him over and he wasn't just thinking it; he was living it. Except he wouldn't be for much longer. Being bi meant liking people of both sexes, which meant he still liked women, and was just waiting to find the right one to settle down with.

Shaking his head, he shaved and dressed in the new clothes he'd had to buy since he had nothing to wear for a nice evening out that didn't require a suit. Black jeans, a black button-down shirt and a pair of boots made him feel at least a little dressed up. He was going to see a lot of people tonight, and although it was a private gathering to make sure the club was ready to open, he had a feeling it was going to get wild. The entire Sidewinders organization had been invited and almost everyone was going, even those that were married, had a pregnant spouse or weren't interested in sex clubs in general. It seemed as though everyone wanted to support the club and he was glad to have had even a small part in that.

Jamie got to the club with Zakk and Tiff, who made their way to the bar while Jamie detoured for Emilie's office. The door was open and he heard her on the phone, confirming a reservation for the grand opening. She smiled when he came in, and got up to hug him as soon as she hung up.

"So good to see you!" she whispered, holding him tightly. "I'm glad you came."

"Did you think I'd miss it?"

"Viggo said you've been distant. I didn't know if it was because of me."

"No." He touched her cheek. "It's my own demons, you know? It's not easy to deal with something life-changing on top of a concussion, getting moved to a new team and a new city…it's been kinda hard and I've been taking it out on him."

"Jamie, I know it's strange, but I truly want what's best, for you and for him." She stared up at him earnestly. "I love Viggo, but now that we're married I realize it's not what we thought it was. Something inside me is very, very dark and the only time I see light is with Simone. That's not fair to Viggo and I care for him enough to let him find the love he needs."

"But you'll get better," Jamie said gently, his hands at her waist. "You're going to—"

"Yes, but he loves *you*." She smiled. "I see the way he looks at you, the way he looks when he talks about you...and that's okay. As long as he doesn't abandon Simone, I want him to be happy. I need time to work on me, and honestly, it's a bit of a relief not to have to worry about whether or not I'm going to break his heart."

"Are you sure?"

"Yes. Now go find him and make up—he's been miserable watching you struggle with your feelings."

"I'll be around in case you need anything tonight," he said after a moment, trying to digest what she'd said. "Just let me know."

"Thank you." She kissed his cheek and went back to her desk, immediately picking up the phone.

Dismissed, he wandered back out to the club. Not a lot of people had arrived yet, but Becca was sitting at the bar with Dante and some friends. Chains was behind the bar mixing drinks and Franny sat at a table, flirting with a couple of young guys from the Sidewinders that Jamie knew by face only. Finally, Viggo came around the corner and their eyes locked. Jamie walked towards him purposefully, his eyes never leaving the other man's face.

"Hi." Viggo stuck his hands in his pockets. "How are you?"

"Good. You?"

"Pretty good."

"Can we talk?"

"Isn't that what we're doing?"

"Alone?"

"Is there something you need to say that we need privacy for?" Viggo was annoyed that Jamie had been avoiding him.

"I'll kiss you right here and give those two rookies a heart attack," Jamie said, eyes blazing with intensity.

"So it's not talking you have in mind." Viggo couldn't help a small smile.

"No, I do have talking in mind. *After* I kiss you. For about an hour."

Viggo chuckled. "Come on." He led him down a hall to the VIP elevators. The private rooms wouldn't be open tonight, but he had a set of keys so he unlocked the elevator and they stepped inside. Jamie turned and pushed him against the wall, finding his mouth and grinding against him roughly.

"Damn if you don't change your mind every five minutes," Viggo muttered, grabbing the back of Jamie's head and thrusting his tongue into his mouth. They swirled together, vying for dominance, yet still as tender as they were passionate.

"I'm sorry," Jamie panted against him. "I know I've been an ass, but it's my own shit, has nothing to do with how I feel about you or how much I want you."

"I know." Viggo pulled away as the elevator doors opened. Grabbing Jamie's hand, he led him to one of the rooms at the end of the hall. He unlocked it and they went inside. It was one of the nicer rooms, with a large bed, two chairs, a table, an armoire filled with every possible amenity and a private bathroom with a shower.

"Forgive me for being a dick?" Jamie whispered as he pushed Viggo onto the bed.

"Always," Viggo sighed, letting Jamie straddle him as they both pulled off their shirts. Bigger and stronger, Viggo lifted his torso to capture Jamie's mouth with his and press their chests together. Jamie's arms slid around his neck and as their tongues mated it was like coming home. Touching each other was more natural than almost anything, even if everything else about their relationship was strange and complicated.

Jamie grunted when Viggo flipped him onto his back and covered him with his larger body. They were a tangle of lips and limbs, groping and touching as though they'd been starved without each other.

"Did the doctor say this was okay?" Viggo was breathing heavily.

"Yeah. Saw him today. Just nothing too rough."

"Lie back, handsome—I'll take care of everything." Viggo kissed him again, yanking off his slacks and boxers with one sweep of his hands.

When they were both naked, Viggo slid down his body until he reached his cock. There was already pre-come leaking out and he licked it as one big hand closed around the base and the other groped beside him for the lube he'd grabbed as they'd approached the bed. Pouring a liberal amount on his fingers he slid one into Jamie, knowing exactly where he needed to go to make him howl.

"Fuck, I really do have to work on my stamina," Jamie grumbled, knowing he wouldn't be able to hold out.

"You've been without," Viggo soothed, not letting up and closing his mouth around him as Jamie shot off, grinding against his face.

"Sorry," Jamie sighed after a few minutes. "It seems like I have zero control when it comes to you. I swear, it's never been like this before!"

Viggo laughed. "I would hope not!" He moved up and kissed him, letting his mouth linger on Jamie's lips, tasting them, memorizing how they felt when Jamie gave them to him. He was in love with this man, but he wasn't blind; Jamie was closer to walking away than giving them a chance.

"Roll over, big guy," Jamie said, pushing gently on his chest. "Let me take care of you."

Viggo rolled onto his back and closed his eyes. Would this be the last time? Just thinking about it made him sick, so he didn't, focusing instead on how incredible it felt when Jamie wrapped his lips around him and sucked him deep. For a guy who'd never done this until two months ago, he knew exactly how to fulfill him. Viggo had always prided himself on his own stamina, and though he lasted longer than Jamie had, there was no doubt he lost control much quicker than usual when they were together. Something happened when they touched that made everything—even prolonging their pleasure—impossible to control.

When they were finally lying close together, Jamie's head resting on his chest, Viggo dug his fingers into the long locks that hung over his eye and tugged.

"Hmm?" Jamie murmured, half-asleep.

"I thought we were going to talk."

"Maybe." Jamie didn't want to pop this bubble of contentment, but Viggo had begun to ease away from him. "Don't go," he whispered.

"You can't be touching me," Viggo whispered back. "If you do, I won't be able to think straight."

"Fine." Jamie sat up and looked over at him sadly. "Doctor's letting me go home on Monday, assuming there are no more vomiting or headache episodes between now and then."

"And?"

"I don't know what to do."

"About?" Viggo's blue eyes darkened as he scowled.

"Come on, don't do that." Jamie rested his arms on his knees. "You know how I feel about you."

"Then why are you fighting it? Why is it hard to be with me? I know it's a little complicated, but damn, it's so good when we're together."

"I know, but..."

"But what?"

"I don't picture myself with a man—I picture myself settling down with a woman."

"Then why *the fuck* are you involved with me?" Viggo set his jaw angrily.

"I'm involved with you because—" He froze, unwilling to admit how he felt.

"Because why?" Viggo asked in a stony voice. "Why are you involved with me, Jamie?"

"Because you're you," Jamie fumbled, unsure how to articulate his feelings without using the "L" word. "I'm not with you because you're a man—I'm with you because there's never been anyone, of any sex, who's made me feel like you do. I'm just not sure what that means or how I feel about it, so you're going to have to give me time to sort it out. You've had years to deal with being bi—I found out a few weeks ago! I can't even begin to wrap my head around having these kinds of feelings for a guy. In addition to having a concussion. And going to a new team. And moving across the continent! Do you have any idea how hard this is?"

Viggo didn't say anything for a long time, trying to decide how best to explain how he felt. "At some point, you're going to have to come to terms with your feelings," he said at last. "You have to decide what's important overall and where I fit into your life. You don't have to answer now," he continued slowly, "but you're going to have to figure out if you think you can ever love me. Only you can decide if the obstacles involved in being with a guy are worth the rewards of being together. I struggled for years, but I know who I am. I've only ever been in love with one person before—and it wasn't until you that I realized what I feel for her isn't true love. I *thought* what I felt for her was the real thing, but now that I've found you, I see it wasn't."

Jamie swallowed hard, unable to look at him for fear he would say something he shouldn't.

"Em needs me right now." Viggo continued when he realized Jamie wasn't ready to reply. "I can't leave her until she's gotten a grip on her demons and she'll always be in my life because of Simone. I don't know if you can handle that."

"I don't know either," Jamie admitted finally. "Is what we feel strong enough for you to wait a little while? You'll be in Ottawa in January, right? Can we take some time apart, after I leave next week, to figure out if I can do this? You'll be able to help Emilie and hopefully I'll get back to hockey so I can think about something other than whether or not I'm going to be okay."

"Six weeks," Viggo said slowly. "We play there in early January. When we see each other we can reassess our feelings and what we want to do."

"We have four more days to be together," Jamie leaned closer to him. "And then we can talk on FaceTime and text. It'll be hard, but we can make it six weeks, right? No commitments, no demands, just letting it go at its own pace while we sort out how we feel."

"Are you going to date other people?" Viggo hated himself for even asking, but he had to know. He already knew how he felt about him, but Jamie wasn't ready to hear that yet.

Jamie met his gaze. "I don't know for sure, but I need to be willing to test the waters. That's how I know when it's serious—when the desire to be with anyone else goes away. Please say you understand. I need some distance so I can make sense of this."

"Of course I understand." Viggo put his hands on either side of Jamie's face. "You know I'd wait a lot longer than six weeks for you, don't you?"

Jamie looked into his eyes and the emotion reflected there nearly undid him. How had he gotten lucky enough to find someone who looked at him with so much selfless longing? And was he really in love with this incredible man? He turned away, blinking rapidly to control his emotions. "I know, big guy. I know."

## CHAPTER 17

Jamie went back to Ottawa the first week of December and was cleared to start working out again the following week. He got up early and ran every day, even though he wasn't used to the cold anymore and couldn't believe how quickly he'd become accustomed to the much warmer weather in Las Vegas. He'd spent his first week back seeing doctors and getting into something of a routine again.

This week he was running and lifting light weights. If he continued to remain headache-free, he would intensify his workouts next week and be back on the ice by Christmas, even if he wasn't cleared for contact. All of his tests had come back clean so the doctors were gradually getting him back in the game. The stomach bug was long gone and he'd been feeling good. Well, he felt good physically. Emotionally, he was a mess.

Leaving Las Vegas again had been even harder than the first time. He and Viggo had gotten closer than ever those last few days together. There was something about him that went beyond the physical attraction and the friendship. Of course, they had a lot in common, both being hockey players and enjoying so many of the same things. It was more than that, though. Everything was relaxed when he was with Viggo.

In his head, being physical with a man was awkward, but in reality, when they were together it was perfectly natural. He didn't think twice about putting his head in Viggo's lap when they watched TV or grabbing his ass if they were both standing at the refrigerator. When Viggo grabbed him by the back of the head and pulled him close for a kiss, he didn't even hesitate.

His only hesitation had been with anal sex. He hadn't been able to allow Viggo to take him that way. He'd topped Viggo countless times since they'd begun sleeping together, but when it came time to reciprocate he just hadn't been able to get himself to a place where he was willing to try. Viggo had been understanding, and hadn't pushed it, but Jamie sensed he was hurt. It wasn't the sex itself—they could spend all night sucking each other off because it was that good when they used their mouths and hands—but it was a glaring example of his unwillingness to commit emotionally. That was the final physical barrier, and by saying he wasn't ready, it was obvious he was holding back a huge part of himself.

"Hey, man!" A blond guy about his age fell into step beside him as he ran. He lived down the hall and they waved or said hello whenever they passed each other.

"Hey!" Jamie gave him a friendly smile.

"When do you get back on the ice?" the guy asked, keeping pace with him.

"Not sure," Jamie shrugged. "Waiting for the okay from the doctors. They're really careful with concussions." Jamie hadn't known for sure whether or not people in the building knew what he did for a living, but this was Canada, after all, and Canadians loved hockey.

"That was a dick move, when that Forbes idiot hit you in Vegas," the other man continued. "Your boys shoulda knocked him out!"

Jamie shrugged again. "The team had my back, but it's part of the game. It's all good."

They turned the corner that led back to the building and slowed down. "Hey, I'm Collin, by the way."

"Jamie." Jamie shook his hand.

"Listen, a group of us are having some friends over tonight. Nothing big, just some beer, gonna watch some movies, order pizza, hang out. Some real fine girls are gonna stop by."

"I, uh..." Jamie faltered. Why shouldn't he go? It might be good to get out of the apartment, make some new friends, and stop thinking about Viggo. Like *that* was going to happen. But it might be a distraction for a few hours.

"I think you'll like Misty," Collin teased, his blue eyes gleaming. "She strips and she's smokin'."

"How come you're not hittin' it?" Jamie raised his eyebrows.

"I got a girl," he chuckled. "Misty is my girlfriend Jill's friend, so probably not okay with her! Anyway, come on by around eight. We'll be chillin', nothin' fancy."

"Yeah, all right. I'll bring some beer."

"Right on, man! See you later!" he fist-bumped him after telling him the apartment number, and jogged off in the other direction.

JAMIE KNOCKED on the door a little after 8:00 and could hear laughter and music inside. Collin opened the door with a grin.

"Hey, it's Jamie Teller! Come on in!" He moved aside and Jamie followed him in. "That's my friend Ron, his brother Lance, and my buddy Felix. That's Jill, my girlfriend, her friend Misty, and our neighbor Valerie, who lives on the first floor."

They exchanged greetings and Jamie opened a beer after putting two six-packs in the fridge. He joined them in the living room, getting in on the tail end of a conversation about James Bond movies. It was easy to chime in since he was a big fan and soon they were immersed in *Octopussy*.

"So, are you single, Jamie?" Misty sank down on the floor next to him when the movie was over and blinked up at him with big blue eyes. She was petite, but had a pretty face and perfectly round breasts that were most likely fake.

Jamie smiled, unsure whether to take her up on what she was obviously offering. "Kind of," he said vaguely. "There's someone back in Vegas but we're keepin' it casual until we figure out if I'm going to play again this year."

"If you can't play, will you go back?"

"Don't know yet. Still getting settled, you know?"

"Do you like living in Canada?"

"I'm Canadian," Jamie grinned. "From Kingston, so this is home, and a lot closer to my family."

"But you're not happy to be back?"

"I haven't lived here in nine years," he said with a shrug. "I don't have any friends here and with this concussion, everything has been harder than it was supposed to be."

"Well now you have a friend!" she smiled.

"I can use them!" he smiled back.

They drank beer and watched another movie, laughing about random topics and generally having a good time. Jamie liked the somewhat forward brunette but there was something almost desperate about her, and he wasn't sure why.

She was beautiful and seemed able to carry on a conversation about multiple topics. There was a guarded look in her eyes, though, and he noted how she stayed close to him, almost as if she was afraid of the others. Although he was having fun, there was a strange dynamic in the room and a unexpected sixth sense left him inexplicably on guard.

"When do you find out when you can start playing again?" Misty was asking him as *Goldfinger* came to an end.

"There's no date," he said. "The team doctors watch my progress and decide when I'm allowed to play."

"That means you'll be in Ottawa for a while?"

"Most likely." He glanced at her curiously.

"And you could fool around without cheating, right?" She ran a hand up his chest and Jamie gently gripped her fingers.

"I could, but I'm not looking to rush into anything."

She laughed. "A big, strong hockey player like you probably has a girl in every town."

"Maybe every other town," he teased, trying to relax and remember what it was like to be single and hook up with a beautiful woman.

"Then you should have one here." Her eyes twinkled.

He dipped his head to brush his lips across hers. It had been a while since he'd slept with a stranger, and part of him wondered if he could even get it up for anyone with the way his feelings were all tangled up in Viggo. Misty lifted to her knees and slid one leg over to straddle him, her full breasts almost eye level. He felt his cock stir and blinked in surprise.

Jamie heard a moan on the other side of the room and glanced over to see Jill in Collin's lap, her skirt hiked up around her hips as she rode him. His jeans were down around his ankles and he was leaning back on the couch, letting her do all the work. Ron and Lance had Valerie on the floor, one kissing her, the other pulling off her jeans. Felix was on the recliner, his cock in his hand, watching the festivities as he jerked himself off.

"Come on," Misty whispered. "Let's join the fun. I'll have to sleep with Felix if you don't want me—and you're way hotter than him."

Jamie hesitated. He hadn't been expecting this, but he'd promised himself he would be open to dating between now and when he and Viggo saw each other again. Viggo was undoubtedly having sex with Emilie, after all, so it was only fair Jamie got to test the waters too. He would have a much better idea of his feelings for the Swedish hunk that made his heart beat faster after he'd been with a woman other than Emilie again.

"You takin' her, Jamie?" Felix called out. "'Cause I will if you don't."

"I don't have a condom," Jamie said, one hand closing around her ass possessively; he felt a little protective knowing she didn't want to sleep with Felix even though he really didn't have it in him to romance anyone right now. He glanced at her warily. "This is only sex," he said quietly. "You know I have someone back home I'm still involved with?"

"Sex is all I want," she whispered with a wink.

He wasn't sure where it came from, but a foil wrapper landed next to him 10 seconds later and he grabbed it. "Nothing like being prepared. Anybody got lube?" Since she'd told her he wasn't interested in a relationship, his only interest was to fuck her and get the hell out, plain and simple.

"Got some of that, too." Felix got up, disappeared down the hall and came back with a bottle he tossed to Jamie.

"Flip over, honey," Jamie said. "You good with me going in the back door?"

Misty's eyes widened slightly but she nodded. "Whatever you want, handsome."

He unbuttoned his jeans and let them slide down but didn't take them off. He wasn't going to get comfortable—this had obviously been planned ahead of time so he would take what she was giving and then go home. He rolled the condom down his already throbbing shaft and lifted to his knees.

Misty had shed her clothes and was poised over the couch, her firm round ass ripe for the taking. He squirted a liberal amount of lube between her cheeks and rubbed it in. He leaned over and kissed her, their lips locking tentatively at first. As he warmed to her slender body and sweet, soft lips, he gripped her hair and let her kiss him. Damn, it was nothing like Viggo's kiss and he had to force himself not to think about him.

He let one hand drift around to cup one of her soft, round breasts, tweaking her nipple as she arched against his hand. A few months ago he would have been all over her, fucking her in every room of the apartment, in every position imaginable. Tonight, he just wanted to find relief from the ache of wanting someone else.

She moaned with unmistakable desire and he closed his eyes. Then he positioned his cock right at her tight little hole, eased the head in cautiously and waited for her to adjust. As she relaxed, he thrust in a bit harder than he intended, pausing when she whimpered. He reached over to smooth his hands across her shoulders and down her arms in a comforting motion.

"You okay?" he asked gently. He didn't want to date her, but he didn't want to hurt her either.

"Just wasn't expecting that much at once," she panted, "but I'm fine."

He closed his eyes again and gripped her hips, thrusting in and out with practiced strokes.

"Damn, that's hot," Felix was standing over them watching, eyes gleaming. "You like it in the ass, Misty? How come you never let me do that?"

"'Cause you're not as hot as he is," she muttered.

"Oh yeah?" He laughed and climbed onto the couch in front of her, straddling her face. Grabbing a fistful of her hair, he lifted her head and stuffed his cock in her mouth.

"Hey, what's the deal?" Jamie paused again, waffling between getting himself off and making sure they weren't making her do something she didn't want to do.

"She's fine!" Felix grunted.

"I want to hear *her* say it," Jamie said, drawing back and meeting the other man's gaze. He lifted her by the shoulders, pulling her up against him. "Misty, you good? No one said anything about both of us doing you."

"I'm okay," she said quickly. "We do this all the time." She leaned forward and opened her mouth, allowing Felix to start pumping in and out again.

Jamie followed his lead and thrust back in between her cheeks, wondering why they needed another guy to join their sex club. Apparently, this wasn't a first for any of them and they'd simply added him to the fold without any explanation. He'd think about that later, though. Right now he was going to fuck her tight little ass until she came as hard as he did.

Felix only lasted about two minutes before he jerked in Misty's mouth and leaned back with a satisfied growl. Misty moaned as Jamie jackhammered into her, her lithe body straining back against his.

"Damn, that's good," she whispered, burying her face in the cushions of the couch.

"You wanna come, honey?" Jamie was ready to go, but he was damned if he was going to be a selfish bastard like the rest of them. Collin had groaned like a lame bear when he got off but Jill had merely sat back and pushed down her skirt, a look of disappointment on her face. Lance and Ron were pounding into Valerie, one from behind and the other in her mouth, but she hadn't made a sound, so he assumed she wasn't any happier than Jill.

"Oh, yes, please..." Misty breathed.

He reached around front and slid his finger between her legs, content to find her dripping against his hand. Her clit hardened under his finger and he rubbed it absently, his mind drifting to Viggo, missing his larger body and unrivaled strength. There was something primal about fucking Viggo that was missing now; though he was going at her pretty hard, he was still holding back. With Viggo, he hadn't had to; Viggo wanted everything he dished out and more.

"Oh, shit, Jamie, yes!" She bucked against him, her cries drowning out both the others in the room and the TV as Jamie slammed home one last time. He made sure she'd stopped shuddering before slowly pulling out and sitting back. Damn, it had been good as far as sex went, but all he felt in the aftermath was let down and lonely. The last thing he wanted to do was cuddle; luckily, she seemed content to pick up her clothes and pad into the bathroom.

Jamie pulled up his jeans and made his way into the master bedroom, where there was another bathroom. He cleaned up quickly and was just about to come out when Misty slipped inside. She put her finger to her lips and pressed herself up against him. Instead of trying to kiss him, however, she moved her mouth to his ear and whispered so softly he almost didn't hear, "Don't leave me here with them—I'll leave, I promise, just say you're taking me home with you. Please, Jamie."

He nodded, frowning slightly as he took in how she nervously clung to his neck. "All right, doll, come on home with me and we'll go another round." He spoke loudly as he wrapped his fingers around hers and they stepped back into the hallway together.

"Where you goin'?" Collin asked, standing up. "I figured you'd want a go at Val next."

Jamie had to force himself to smile at Collin, whose bare chest revealed a huge swastika tattoo right in the middle. Though his heart started to pound, he managed to reply, "Misty and I have plans for another go at my place. Maybe next time." He waved before tugging Misty into the hall as they headed to Jamie's apartment. He unlocked the door and let her walk in ahead of him.

"I'll go in just a few minutes," she said softly. "I just, ugh...they're such Neanderthals."

"Misty, what the hell is going on?" Jamie asked, tossing his keys on the counter and kicking off his shoes. "If you don't want to sleep with those guys, why do you?"

She frowned and ignored the question. "You seem like a nice guy—why are you hanging out with them?"

"I was jogging and ran into Collin this morning. He said he was having some people over, but I didn't know it was going to be like this—he didn't say anything about a fucking orgy." Jamie sank down on the couch. "Look, I'm really sorry if you wound up doing something you didn't want to do."

"It's not your fault I had to suck off Felix," she murmured. "But I definitely wanted to do you." She paused, cocking her head. "You're not really single, are you? You fucked me like a man thinking about something, or someone, else."

Jamie flushed. "No, I'm single—at least from the perspective of having sex with you. Just left something complicated behind and we haven't decided what we're going to do. I'm not the kind of guy who cheats."

"I, uh, I feel like I should thank you," she chuckled. "It's been a long time since I've had an orgasm brought on by anyone other than myself."

Jamie raised his eyebrows. "Sorry about that, doll, but if that's the case, it seems to me you should be having sex with different people."

"Yeah, well, sometimes you fall in with bad people and can't get out." She got to her feet and smiled wanly. "Be careful around Collin, okay?"

"Something you're not telling me?"

"Just that he and his boys aren't the best people—I put up with them because I have to. I'm saving money, though, and the minute I have enough I'm gone. As soon as I can make a new start in Vancouver, I'm out of here."

"You going to be okay until then?" he asked.

"I'll be better if I can have you get me off once in a while instead of those dickless wonders."

He chuckled. "I can probably help out for a bit. Things might change with my situation in Vegas, and then I can't make any promises."

"Hopefully, I'll be on my way to Vancouver by then!" She blew him a kiss. "If you're ever bored, come find me. I work Wednesday through Sunday nights, eight p.m. to four a.m." She gave him the business card of the club where she stripped.

"Drive safe," he said, watching her leave. He lay back on the couch and put his hands behind his head. Maybe he'd misjudged her. She seemed like a nice enough girl but she definitely wasn't telling him everything. Something was going on with those guys to make her have sex with them and then want to screw a stranger instead of one of them the first chance she got. What the fuck had he gotten himself into? He was going to take her subtle advice and stay away from Collin and his friends.

# CHAPTER 18

Jamie kept to himself for a few days, keeping an eye out for when Collin ran so he went out at a different time. The festivities from the other night had left a weird taste in his mouth and although he wouldn't mind having sex with Misty again, he didn't want to use her either. She seemed on board for casual sex, but he would wait for her signal instead of an invitation from Collin. He'd asked his roommate about them, but he'd shrugged and said he wasn't home enough to know them more than to wave. That left Jamie spending what felt like night after night hibernating in his apartment, missing Viggo, missing hockey and wondering what was going to happen with his career. He hadn't had any headaches, at least, so the doctor said he might be cleared to play by Christmas, which was only two weeks away. Then, if he continued to heal, he would be back to full-contact by New Year's. It seemed like a really long time, though.

He picked up his phone and smiled to find a text from Viggo.

*34 more days...*

He answered immediately.

*Until?*

*I kiss those sexy lips of yours and make you come in my mouth.*

Jamie groaned, the phone shaking slightly in his hand as he tried to think of how to respond to that. He wanted those things too, dammit. He just didn't know how to share this kind of intimacy with a man; it felt foreign and a little uncomfortable, despite how much he missed him. Spontaneously, he picked up the phone and dialed.

"Hey." Viggo's voice was subdued, which meant he wasn't alone.

"What are you doing?"

"At the airport, getting ready to fly home."

"Okay, you don't have to talk, just listen."

"Sure."

"I'm struggling. I don't know how to flirt with you, I don't know how to talk dirty to you...I don't know how this works. You have to help me because I'm lost, big guy."

"Your timing kind of sucks," Viggo chuckled, glancing around at all his teammates. "But why is it different? Do what you would do with anyone else."

"It feels weird...you know? Do I call you baby? Sweetheart? Do I talk about how hard I get thinking about you? Is it the same as it is with a woman?"

"If that's what makes you happy, then yes."

"Does it make *you* happy? Hearing me say those kinds of things?"

"More than you know."

"So...uh, I'm really looking forward to bending you over my couch and fucking you into the middle of next week."

Viggo laughed. "I'll text you my reply when we hang up."

Jamie laughed too. "I was just practicing because I know you're at a disadvantage since you're with the team right now."

"Yeah, and I might make you pay for that."

"Fuck yeah."

"Gotta go, we're boarding."

"See you soon." Jamie disconnected and put the phone down, a smile on his face. A moment later it buzzed with Viggo's text:

*When you're done with me I'm going to suck your dick so hard you're going to think I swallowed it. Then I'm going to put my fingers against that spot that makes you shiver...right before I fill you with my cock.*

Jamie closed his eyes and moaned, lost in the fantasy. He needed to see Misty sooner rather than later.

SHOWING up at the club where she worked, he got a table in the back and sat, watching a scrawny brunette on stage stagger around like she was drunk. He scowled, suddenly wondering why he was here. He wanted to see Misty, who was head and shoulders sexier than the women he'd seen so far. He wondered why a knockout like her was working at a low-class place like this, but he figured everyone was entitled to their secrets. He had a big one of his own, after all.

A waitress came by and he ordered a drink, asking if she knew where Misty was.

"I'll send her out, sugar," the woman said, winking.

Jamie was surprised to see Misty come out a minute later in a skimpy robe and high heels, her hair still in curlers. She sank into the seat next to him with a smile.

"Hey!"

"Hey." He looked her up and down. "You're a beautiful woman, but I have to say this isn't how I was expecting to find you here at the club."

She laughed. "You think I wake up beautiful? My hair sticks up and I definitely need makeup before anyone finds me presentable."

"I bet you look great when you wake up," he said softly.

She looked into his eyes and cocked her head. "You okay? You look sad."

He rubbed a hand across his forehead and massaged his temples. "Living in a new city and not playing hockey is hard. I'm bored. I'm lonely. I miss—" he cut off abruptly.

"You miss your girl back home."

"Yeah." *Well, I miss my man back home*, he thought to himself.

"She won't come?"

"She has a really good job," he hedged. "She can't right now."

"But you guys knew there was always a chance you'd get traded, right?"

"We didn't get together until right after I found out I was leaving," he admitted. "We were friends and then shit happened and we tried to stay apart, but we couldn't. It sucks."

"Can't you go back to Vegas while you're not playing?"

"It's complicated. The team wants me here so they can monitor my progress and as soon as I'm ready I'll get back on the ice."

She nodded and they were quiet.

"It's dead tonight," she said after a moment. "Want to go out? I go to this great little drag club—it's a hoot. The show is good, most of the audience is gay so they won't bother us, and they know me so I rarely pay for drinks."

He hesitated. A bar with a mostly gay clientele. That sounded like a great idea. Not. He made a face. "I don't know, maybe it's not a good idea."

"Come on, we'll have a few laughs and it'll get you out of your funk."

"You can just leave work?"

She motioned with her hand. "You see much of anything going on?"

He chuckled. "I guess not."

"Give me 10 minutes to fix my hair and get dressed and we'll go." She kissed his cheek and hurried into the back. He glanced down at his phone and opened up the pictures. The first one was of Simone, a big toothless grin on her face. Viggo's big hands were around her middle, holding her up, and although you couldn't see anything else of his, Jamie liked looking at the hands that were so brawny but could be so tender.

With a grunt, he shoved his phone back in his pocket and left money on the table. He was going to figure this out one way or another, and stop obsessing like a lovesick moron. His feelings for Viggo were one thing, but he needed to know if he was gay or bisexual or what, because going over it in his head was beginning to make him crazy. He wasn't sure what he needed to do to get the answers he sought, but maybe a drag club would offer some kind of opportunity.

THE CLUB WAS JUST what he expected, filled with drag queens of all kinds, straight couples, gay couples and everything in between. Jamie and Misty moved among the throngs of people drinking, dancing and talking. It was busy, filled to the brim with people having a good time, and for the first time in a long time, Jamie was in the mood to have fun.

He'd spent so long focusing on hockey—then Rachel, the plethora of scandals, and now his injury and the situation with Viggo—it had been a long time since he'd gone out just to enjoy himself. Maybe tonight, instead of finding a gay guy who might turn him on, he would just dance with the pretty woman beside him, have a few drinks and forget about everything for a few hours.

They ordered drinks and Misty dragged him onto the dance floor. Jamie had always loved to dance, and most of his girlfriends over the years had appreciated it. He had a feeling it wouldn't be a big deal to Viggo, and he nearly groaned out loud when he realized he was thinking about him. *Again*. What's wrong with me, he wondered. Part of him wanted to fly back to Vegas and beat the shit out of Matt Forbes. If he hadn't hit him, he wouldn't have this concussion, wouldn't have had to spend all that extra time in Vegas, and would be focusing on hockey now instead of a man.

"You seem tense." Misty swayed her hips, putting her arms around his neck. "Do you want to leave?"

"No." Jamie shook his head. "I'm fine."

Misty twirled around him, her long hair flowing behind her and a smile on her face. She seemed more relaxed too, laughing easily and completely uninterested in anything sexual. He had to wonder, seeing her behaving so differently tonight, what Collin and his friends held over her head to make her attend their little fuck fests. Eventually he'd ask her, but not tonight.

"Misty!" A petite redhead with big green eyes threw her arms around Misty and they hugged tightly.

"Jamie, this is my friend, Robin. Robin, this is the guy I was telling you about."

"Nice to meet you." Robin nodded. "Thanks for getting her out of there the other night."

Jamie nodded. "No problem."

"You guys want to go to a party?" Robin asked, grinning.

"Yes!" Misty nodded.

"I don't need to get into another situation like the other night." Jamie glanced at Misty meaningfully. "I'm new here—I don't know a lot of people and it's probably better if I don't take any chances...drugs, underage girls, that kind of thing could be a world of trouble for me."

Misty hesitated. "Oh, then maybe..."

"No, go on," Jamie said. "I'll be fine. I'll have a beer, maybe find someone to dance with and then head home. Go have fun."

"Are you sure?" Misty frowned.

"Positive." He hugged her. "We'll hang out on another night off."

"Hey, listen..." She looked undecided.

"What's up?"

"Look, they're blackmailing me," Misty said against his ear since it was too loud to talk in a regular voice with the music blasting. "I can't explain it now, but I will. Just promise me you won't say anything about...this. Collin and those guys would lose their minds if they thought I came to places like this—they already think I'm a lesbian because I moved in with Robin when I left my ex."

"Not a word." Jamie held up his hands. "I don't plan to hang out with them again, so don't worry. Go have fun with your friend—I'm going to have one more and call it a night."

"Thanks, Jamie!" Misty gave him a hug and disappeared through the crowd with Robin.

Shaking his head, Jamie moved to the bar and found a seat. How the hell did he get into these situations? He didn't even know what had just happened, but he'd begun to get used to the craziness that had taken over his life. It seemed like nothing was going right lately.

"Did your date just abandon you?" a deep voice beside him asked.

Jamie turned to stare into a face with a pair of hazel eyes, long lashes and a great smile. "Yeah, I guess she did," Jamie managed to respond.

"I'm Josh," the man said, holding out his hand.

"Jamie." Jamie shook his hand.

"Can I buy you a drink?"

Jamie opened his mouth to say no but then realized this guy was probably hitting on him. *How else are you going to figure out if you're into it, dumb-ass?* he thought to himself. He took a breath. "Uh, sure, thanks. Scotch, neat."

The man ordered two and they sat without talking for a few minutes, while Jamie stared into his drink and Josh watched him.

"I'm going to go out on a limb and guess you're not gay," Josh said after a moment.

Jamie started to shake his head but then chuckled. "I have no idea."

Josh raised his eyebrows. "At your age, my friend, either you are or you're not."

"Trust me when I tell you it's not that simple."

"I'm happy to listen," he said with a friendly smile. "I've known I was gay since I was young, probably 10 or 11. Well, I knew I was different at that age, but I didn't know what it meant until I was 13 or 14."

"And you were okay with it at such a young age?" Jamie met his eyes.

"I'm not sure how to answer that," he admitted. "Was I scared and confused? Sure. But I was lucky. I told my parents when I was 15 and they were great about it. I had love and support, so I was able to take my time, learn the difference between men who were gay, men who were experimenting and men who made a practice out of finding lonely little fags they could pretend to be interested in just long enough to humiliate them. I was too savvy for that, and managed to avoid it, but I've seen it happen to a lot of my friends."

"That's terrible," Jamie frowned. "I've never thought about men like that—and certainly never to humiliate them!"

"I don't get it either." He paused. "So, why are you confused?"

"I have feelings for a man but I've never been interested before, never even thought about it."

"Are you sure?"

"Three months ago I would've been positive, but now..."

"Now?" Josh watched his face.

Jamie chuckled. "I've always thought a handful of specific men were attractive, but I never thought about them in a romantic context until about three months ago. I was in a threesome that took a turn I wasn't expecting."

"And you liked it."

"I like *him*," Jamie said. "I'd never done anything like that before and because we were already friends, it was easy to turn it into something more, but..."

"Now you're confused because you can't figure out why you were never attracted to any other men."

"Exactly."

"Would you like to go out on a date with me, Jamie?"

Jamie's mouth fell open. "What?"

Josh laughed. "Look, I'm 37, single and a pretty nice guy. I have a good job, lots of straight friends and, I'll be honest, I'm a big hockey fan so I know who you are."

Jamie grimaced. "I don't know if that's a good thing."

"Hey, I'm not the press. I'm just a regular guy who sees how confused you are and can give you the opportunity to explore your sexuality in a stress-free environment. You don't know me, but I give you my word I'm not interested in publicity or anything that would embarrass either of us."

"You really want to go out with me?"

"Why not? You're a nice-looking guy and we seem to be getting along. What else is there?"

Jamie chuckled as he looked him up and down. He was tall, a couple inches taller than Jamie, with sexy eyes, high cheekbones and a straight nose. He had a beautiful mouth with lips that were made for kissing and a great smile. His dark hair was cut short and he seemed fit, with a flat stomach and a trace of muscles showing through his long-sleeved shirt.

"You're right," he said after a moment. "You're a good-looking guy and I started telling you things I've never told anyone."

"Sometimes there's more to it than looks, eh?"

Jamie nodded. "Oh yeah."

"Come on, relax, have a drink, let's shoot the shit. If you have a good time, I'll take you to dinner next week and you can see how you feel. Contrary to popular belief, homosexuals do not possess magical powers that turn straight men gay."

Jamie laughed. "Well, you know, one kind of did, but that might just be me..."

They talked and drank for a while and Jamie found himself enjoying the older man's company. He was a big hockey fan and it was fun to talk to someone who knew nuances of the game but didn't actually play. He'd been a fan of Jamie's in Las Vegas, saying he appreciated his ability to set up plays for the bigger, faster players. It was rare that Jamie met someone who didn't work in the hockey profession yet was cognizant of what most coaches considered Jamie's greatest skill on the ice, so the conversation was both laid-back and gratifying.

"I have to work in the morning," Josh said just after midnight. "I need to get some rest. Would you like to go to dinner next week?"

"I'd like that," Jamie nodded.

They walked out to the parking lot and exchanged numbers.

"Look, don't think so much," Josh said, sticking his hands in his pockets and looking at Jamie intently. "Life's short, my friend. I'll call you in a couple days and we'll set something up." He leaned over, brushed his lips across Jamie's and then got in his car and drove off.

Jamie ran a finger over his lips as he glanced down. Nothing. Not a tingle, twinge or tremor from his cock or anything else. The kiss had been a spectacular fail from the perspective of arousal. With a grimace, he got in his truck and headed home.

## CHAPTER 19

Getting cleared to skate with the team ahead of schedule put Jamie in a much better mood. Though he still wore the no-contact jersey, it felt good to be out on the ice and working hard again. He was so busy nearly a week had passed before he realized Josh had never called, but that night he got a text from him.

*Sorry, had a bad week. One of my patients committed suicide. If you're up for something casual, maybe we could hit a sports bar and watch a game? Not sure if I'll be very good company but I need to get out of the house.*

Jamie remembered he'd told him he was a psychologist, but he'd never imagined he had patients that were disturbed enough to kill themselves. There was an air of sadness in his text that made Jamie feel bad, so he texted back with a time and place.

They went out a few times that week and Jamie was relieved Josh didn't try to kiss him again. He liked him, but he had no desire to get involved with him and he was hoping Josh sensed that. They had a lot in common, though, and Josh had gotten out of a five-year relationship only a few months before, so they were both lonely and somewhat new to Ottawa. Josh had decided to leave his hometown of Winnipeg and take a job in Ottawa as a way of making a clean break after his boyfriend had broken things off.

"It looks like I'll be in the lineup on the 27th," Jamie told him a couple of days before Christmas as they sat in a sports bar eating burgers. "You want to come to the game?"

"I'd like that," Josh nodded, grinning.

"I'm going home to Kingston for the holidays," he said. "Make sure you text me the night before the game so I don't forget."

"Will do."

They sat in companionable silence, watching the Sidewinders' game on TV. Jamie tried not to watch number 24 skate across the ice, but couldn't tear his eyes away. *I missed him*, he thought. Regular, casual sex with a beautiful stripper and evenings with a handsome, intelligent gay man hadn't helped at all. In fact, it only made him miss Viggo that much more. He was counting the days until the Sidewinders came to Ottawa and he fell asleep every night envisioning Viggo's strong body around his.

"You haven't brought it up, but I don't think you're gay, Jamie." Josh's eyes were warm and filled with concern.

"I don't know what I am."

"I'd venture to say you're bisexual."

"Just because I haven't fallen into bed with you doesn't mean—"

"No," Josh laughed, "it doesn't. But I've taken you to all my favorite places—bars and restaurants with patrons that don't look askance at a gay couple holding hands or kissing—filled with guys checking you out. You've been oblivious. However, I've seen you take a second look at specific women more than once. You definitely have a thing for brunettes with big boobs."

Jamie looked down. "I guess."

"You know, it's possible to be in love with a man without labeling yourself anything but in love."

"What do you mean?"

"Why does your love for this man mean you have to be gay or bi or anything else? Can't you just be Jamie, who happened to fall in love with whatever-his-name is?"

"Viggo," Jamie whispered. "His name is Viggo."

"Ahhh...a red-haired man in Vegas with a very distinct name." He squinted up at the TV. "Number 24, I presume."

Jamie flushed. "Yeah."

"Do you have a picture of the two of you together?"

"Why?"

"It will tell me everything I need to know."

"It's not just the two of us, but this was taken at my going away party back in September." He pulled up a picture of himself, Viggo and Zakk, holding up beers, arms around each other's shoulders.

"Ah." Josh nodded. "Body language shows me you're not just sexually attracted to him, you also genuinely like him. The smile on his face reaches his eyes, which tells me he likes seeing you happy. Your big blond friend is also pleased to see you happy—does he know about the two of you?"

"He didn't then, but he does now."

"He already suspected."

Jamie shook his head. "I didn't think shrinks were supposed to be psychic."

"I make a living reading people."

"What about this one?" Jamie asked curiously, pulling up a picture of Viggo and Emilie, taken on the night of the grand opening.

Josh frowned. "That's Viggo and a woman—his girlfriend?"

"Wife."

"Her eyes are sad but not broken-hearted. She cares for him deeply and is emotionally dependent on him, but not in love with him. Did something happen to her?"

"I think so." Jamie nodded, watching as Josh continued to study the picture.

"She hurts. There's a desperation I can't quite figure out, but it's written all over her."

"She begs me to hit her—you know, in a sexual context—but it scares me. I know how to make sure she doesn't go too far, but I'm afraid she'll find someone else to do it that won't stop, because she never uses a safe word. Ever."

Josh frowned. "She's done something she's deeply ashamed of and believes she should be punished. I'm assuming she already had a proclivity towards this behavior before, so now it's self-inflicted punishment. And whatever it is, since she never says it's enough, she doesn't believe she'll ever make amends for it."

"Right again," Jamie nodded. "But neither Viggo nor I know what it is. That's part of the reason he won't leave her. He's afraid of what she might do—or let someone do to her."

"But you spank her."

"I know her limits; I've dabbled in some BDSM."

Josh grimaced. "Not my thing, I'm afraid."

"Too bad. Club Inferno in Vegas is a great place. You could meet someone interesting."

Josh smiled. "Maybe someday we can go there together—and I can meet your friends."

"Joe, the security consultant for the club, is gay and also not interested in the lifestyle. His boyfriend, Trey, was killed about 18 months ago...hang on." He scrolled through the pictures and found one of Joe, Becca, Dante, Chains and Franny, posing just before the club opened. "Joe's the silver-haired fox in the back."

Josh smiled, inclining his head. "I'd be lying if I said he wasn't my type."

"If *he's* your type then why the hell did you hit on me?!" Jamie laughed. "I'm half his age, with dark hair and not at all a tough guy!"

"I recognized you," Josh chuckled. "And who doesn't want to sleep with a hot hockey player?"

Jamie rolled his eyes but couldn't help laughing. "Really?!"

Josh was laughing too. "You knew I was attracted to you because I asked you out—is wanting to sleep with you a surprise?"

"No, but now you know I'm not interested that way..."

Josh shrugged. "I assumed we'd become friends and would remain so."

"We will if you're okay with it... I didn't want to lead you on."

"We're good, Jamie. I knew from the beginning you weren't truly interested in dating me."

"I'm glad," Jamie sighed in relief. "I don't have a lot of friends and I really enjoy your company."

"The feeling is mutual."

"Go!" Jamie grunted under his breath, his eyes cutting to the TV and watching Viggo move the puck up the ice towards the goal. He shot it past the other team's goalie and Zakk and Brock skated up to throw their arms around him. "Yes!" Jamie grinned as he met Josh's eyes. "Sorry."

"You don't have to apologize. That was a beautiful goal."

"I miss playing with them," Jamie admitted.

"When do you see Viggo again?"

"They come to town the second week of January."

"And what will you do?"

Jamie frowned. "What do you mean?"

"What have you decided? Are you okay with being in love with a man?"

"I never said I was in love with him."

Josh burst out laughing. "You don't have to admit it to me, but I sure hope you've admitted it to yourself, because you're so crazy in love with that man it's practically tattooed on your forehead!"

Jamie groaned. "Fuck. That's not funny."

"Jamie, you know how you didn't want to lead me on?"

Jamie frowned. "Yeah?"

"It's not fair for you to lead *him* on either. If he shares your feelings, he's expecting this to be a meaningful reunion. If you're not ready to make that commitment—in whatever context works for the two of you—you need to tell him sooner rather than later. You can't let him think there's hope if you're not comfortable with the relationship."

"I don't know how I feel about the relationship," Jamie admitted. "I only know how I feel about him."

"Unfortunately, those are the same thing, so you're going to need to figure it out before you see him again."

"Fuck." Jamie motioned for another drink.

THE FOLLOWING WEEKS FLEW BY, between Christmas, getting back to playing hockey, a New Year's Eve party with Misty that was epic, and a road trip at the beginning of January that took him away for 10 days. It irked him he'd been unable to get to Las Vegas for Dante and Becca's New Year's Eve wedding and missed the birth of Zakk's daughter a week later—a little girl named Savannah—but that was part of the life of a professional athlete. He'd spoken to them on the phone and sent gifts, but it wasn't the same. He was tired and missed Viggo, his friends and his old life. It was weighing heavily on him when he got back to Ottawa late on a Sunday night and he was looking forward to sleeping for 10 or 12 hours. His roommate was going straight to his girlfriend's house so Jamie let himself into the apartment and was in the bathroom brushing his teeth when someone banged on the front door. Padding out to the door in nothing but a pair of sweats, he peered through the peephole and was surprised to see Misty standing there crying. He opened the door with a frown.

"Hey, what's going on?"

She brushed past him and pushed the door shut behind her, leaning against it and closing her eyes.

"I'm sorry," she whispered. "I just don't know what to do!"

Now that she was inside there was no mistaking the bruise on her cheek and he reached out to gently run his thumb over it. "What happened?"

"Collin and his jerky friends!"

"Misty, what can they possibly have on you to make you put up with this?" Jamie demanded in frustration.

"My little boy," she said, tears spilling down her cheeks. "I'm in a custody battle with my ex and Jill's dad is the judge. One word from them and I'll lose him! That's why I let them do whatever they want with me! I have a little money, but I spend most of it on lawyers. My ex got custody because I'm a stripper and the judge hates strippers."

"Why didn't you tell me?!"

"They threatened to hurt you if I told you the truth."

"They threatened to hurt *me*?" he grunted. "Fuck them. Why don't you just talk to your lawyer and stay away from them?"

"Every time I have sex with one of them, I get to spend an hour with my son."

"That's practically rape, Misty!" He shook his head in frustration.

"They've never gotten violent before. It was always just sex and I don't care about sex—you're the only guy who's made me come in ages and those guys can barely get it up half the time. I would do anything to see my baby and I've been biding my time until the trial. It's only a few weeks away."

"Fuck." Jamie ran his hand through his hair. "All right, you should sleep here tonight. My roommate's out and I'll make sure they don't bother you."

"Thank you," she whispered. "I don't know what I would have done if I hadn't met you."

"I need to be careful, Misty." He looked at her intently. "You know about the sex scandals and past steroid use...if I get into trouble again, Ottawa can cut me loose. I can't do anything to jeopardize my job."

"You won't!" she promised. "I'll make sure they don't bother you. Don't worry!"

He rolled his eyes. "Now you don't want me to worry?"

She sighed. "I'm really sorry, Jamie. I didn't know where else to go."

"It's all right." He reached out to drape an arm around her shoulders as they sank onto the couch. She nestled against his chest and they were quiet for a while.

"Thanks for being my friend," she whispered. "I don't have many either."

"What about Robin?"

"I don't see her much. My ex thinks we're lesbians and threatened to kill her, so I keep my distance. I haven't seen her since that night at the drag club."

"I'm sorry," he said softly. "But don't worry—I'll help you figure this out."

"Thank you." She closed her eyes.

# CHAPTER 20

After getting some of Misty's things from her apartment and paying for her to stay at a hotel for a week, Jamie forced himself to think of nothing but hockey. He was careful not to come and go from his apartment alone, trying to match his schedule to his roommate's without being obvious, and making sure he wasn't home very often on his days off.

He was already searching for a new place in a building with tighter security, and his roommate seemed amenable to moving after Jamie had told him about the crazy neighbors that blackmailed young mothers. His plan would be to try to make a move during the All-Star break at the end of January, but it wasn't that far away so he was scrambling to find a place that his roommate liked, as well as a moving company that could do it while he and his roommate were away for a few days so they didn't have to deal with Collin.

On the bright side, Viggo and the Sidewinders had arrived a few hours ago and they'd been texting all afternoon. He felt like a kid again with butterflies in his stomach as he stepped onto the ice for the warm-up. Seeing Viggo already out there made his heart beat a little faster and he missed the net twice when he shot the puck. Making sure he focused, he tried to ignore the presence of the big man 50 feet away from him, but it was hard. Any time Viggo was in the general vicinity, Jamie felt different.

It was difficult to explain because he'd never felt that way about anyone else he'd been in love with. Sure, there was always an element of excitement in any new relationship, especially one where they were forced to be apart, but whatever this was with Viggo was all-encompassing. His throat felt tight, his stomach lurched and it seemed relief would only come from being in his arms.

Jamie's ears burned at the thought and he wondered, after all this time and confusion, if he would ever be comfortable with this new development in his life. How had he gone more than 27 years without ever being attracted to a man and then fell in love with one as if it happened every day? No matter how much he tried to come to terms with this, he always went back to the idea that there was no way for him to have a *relationship* with a man.

He'd hoped that would change once they were apart, but although he yearned for Viggo, he still couldn't fathom them living together, or having a family. Lots of gay men did it, but for him, it felt so far from the norm it wasn't going to be something easy to live with. Which meant ending things. They were already emotionally invested, but it had only been a few months. If he waited any longer, the pain and heartbreak would be much worse, so it was only fair to end things now... If only the thought of never seeing him again didn't make him feel like someone was peeling away his skin, one layer at a time.

Skating to center ice, he came face-to-face with the handsome Swede and the minute their eyes locked Jamie knew he was in trouble.

"Hey." Viggo spoke under his breath.

Jamie couldn't stop the curve of his lips at the sound of Viggo's voice. "Hey."

"Am I going to have to protect you from Forbes tonight?" Viggo's eyes twinkled.

"You're going to have to protect him from *me*," Jamie chuckled. "I owe him."

"Are you two plotting Matt's demise?" Zakk inquired, smiling as he joined them.

"Just me," Jamie laughed, bumping gloves with Zakk.

"I'll text you when I get back to the hotel," Viggo murmured as he and Zakk skated away.

Jamie nodded and turned his attention back to the upcoming game.

JAMIE LINGERED at the arena longer than usual, taking his time showering and getting dressed, talking with his teammates and the press, and finally heading out to his truck. Since the Sidewinders had lost—and he'd scored another goal against them—they hadn't hung around long and had left for the hotel nearly 30 minutes ago. Hopefully, Viggo would be texting him soon.

His phone rang just as he turned onto the street where the hotel was and he grabbed it, putting it to his ear.

"I'm ready." Viggo's voice was deep and resonating, causing the nervousness to morph into excitement.

"I'm at the corner," Jamie said.

"I'm walking out of the hotel."

"I'll circle the block and pick you up on the west side of the street." Jamie disconnected.

When he spotted Viggo standing there, his large form even more imposing in a long black overcoat, Jamie couldn't stop his heart from beating a little faster. He slowed to a stop and rolled down the passenger side window.

"Hey, mister—you need a ride?"

Viggo's eyes met his with a look so intent Jamie nearly got a boner right there. "Looking for the ride of my life, baby."

"Get in the truck, you goofball!" Jamie laughed, trying to use levity to temper their obvious desire.

They pulled down the street and Jamie turned towards home.

"How are you, handsome?" Viggo reached over and took his hand.

Jamie curled his fingers into Viggo's and let out a sigh of contentment. "Better now that you're here."

"Been watching you play—you look good."

"Been working my ass off," he admitted. "With me not juicing anymore, I'm going to look like a scrawny 12-year-old boy if I don't work it every damn day."

"You don't look like a 12-year-old anything," Viggo said gently. "You look like the man I'm going to get off a few dozen times tonight."

"A few dozen?" Jamie cut his eyes to him in amusement. "I'm good, but I don't think I can manage that many..."

"That's because you haven't been with me enough," Viggo chortled.

"Okay, no offense, but I was screwing Rachel Kennedy for almost two years—and I didn't manage that. And, no offense, but she's fucking gorgeous."

"And famous," Viggo agreed. "But she isn't me, and you two didn't have what you and I have."

"What do we have?" Jamie asked softly, not daring to look at him.

"Magic."

"My dick just got hard," Jamie moaned.

Viggo grinned. "First of, say, 10 times tonight."

Jamie sighed. "You're going to kill me, you know that?"

"You'll die with a smile on your face."

They talked about the game the rest of the way home and while they walked to the elevator, but the moment the doors closed behind them, Viggo grabbed him. His lips caressed Jamie's with feathery light strokes, completely at odds with the rough way he'd grasped him.

"Did you miss me?" he murmured, continuing his assault on their senses with teasing flicks of his tongue and the gentle flutter of his fingers on the back of Jamie's neck.

"Hell yeah." Jamie opened his mouth and let himself be consumed.

As the doors opened, they pulled apart abruptly and Jamie dug his keys out of his pocket. With Viggo behind him, his erection pressed discreetly into Jamie's lower back, he struggled to get the key in the lock.

"Something distracting you, lover?" Viggo teased.

"Yes, you big jerk!" Jamie was laughing, managing to get the door open, all thoughts of breaking up becoming the furthest thing from his mind.

They stumbled inside and Jamie had barely locked the door behind them before Viggo yanked him up against him.

"The first time is going to be quick," he grunted. "Then I'm going to take my time and make you beg."

"Maybe I'll be the one making you beg," Jamie muttered, his head thrown back in sheer ecstasy as Viggo's teeth scraped along his Adam's apple.

"I'm really looking forward to that." He pulled his shirt over his head and watched as Jamie's eyes darkened with appreciation. "Let's go to bed, yeah?"

"Yeah." Jamie tugged him towards his bedroom, holding on to his hand tightly. He kicked the door shut with his foot and turned to find Viggo right up against him. "You really like overpowering me, don't you?"

"Don't *you*?" Viggo countered, his hand moving to Jamie's waistband and unbuttoning his slacks.

"I do...I guess I'm just used to being in control."

"You can be in control." Viggo slid his lips up Jamie's throat, his tongue licking a trail from his chin to the sensitive spot just below his ear. He nibbled gently, keeping Jamie's hands pinned on either side of his head against the door.

"I don't feel very in control," Jamie breathed, his breath choppy as he yearned for Viggo to kiss him.

"Not yet," Viggo murmured, his lips continuing to tease and caress his ear, jaw and throat.

"I thought the first time was going to be quick?" Jamie taunted, his head lolling to the side as gooseflesh broke out on his skin.

"Patience, handsome..." Viggo found his lips with deliberate precision that bordered on torture. He nipped Jamie's lower lip, tugging it with his teeth before running his tongue over it. He did it over and over, carefully evading Jamie's attempts to kiss him until Jamie growled deep in his chest.

"Viggo..."

Viggo released Jamie's hands and slid his own down Jamie's back to cup his ass cheeks. Their mouths finally locked together in a kiss that went from gentle and teasing to spicy hot in seconds, their bodies grinding together. Viggo slipped one hand between them, wrapping it around both of their aching cocks. He jacked them hard, never breaking their kiss, and slowly slid down to his knees. Jamie's head fell back against the door, planting his feet as Viggo sucked him halfway down his throat in one fluid motion.

"Holy fuck!" Jamie couldn't breathe as Viggo licked and sucked, his tongue making him wet and slippery and deliciously hard. His head bobbed up and down, keeping him buried until Jamie started to pant. "Oh fuck, god damn! Jesus, Viggo, I'm gonna come!" He shot off into his throat, fingers digging into his hair as each spasm shook his body.

"Quick enough, yeah?" Viggo grinned, standing up and finding his mouth again.

Jamie shuddered slightly as Viggo drew him into his arms, kissing him with the combination of emotional tenderness and physical roughness Jamie had come to crave. No one else had ever affected him this way; while his mind battled conflicting messages, his body and heart were completely immersed in everything Viggo gave him.

"I need you," Viggo whispered, fingers exploring Jamie's crease.

They somehow made it to the bed, falling together, groping and touching with an urgency that hadn't lessened while they'd been apart.

Jamie's hand closed around Viggo's throbbing cock and he slid down to take it in his mouth. Viggo sucked in his breath, hips pumping in time to Jamie's movements. "Jamie...lover...I don't want to come in your mouth."

Jamie raised his head, his eyes meeting Viggo's in confusion. "No?"

"I want to be inside you," Viggo whispered, pulling him close. "It's time."

"I..." Jamie's mind went blank, trying to breathe through the uncertainty and fear. "I don't...I don't think I can."

"Don't you trust me?" Viggo's breath was warm on Jamie's neck.

"I do, but..."

"Are you afraid?"

"Kinda. Not exactly." He sighed, the moment lost as he rolled to the side, and covered his eyes with his arm.

"You're still not ready, are you?" Viggo muttered. "All these months, and you're still not invested."

"Of course I'm invested!" Jamie moved his arm and scowled at him. "You think this is easy? You think wanting you so much it hurts makes it any easier to deal with?!"

"Then why did we get together tonight? The sex can't be that good. In fact, we're not even having sex—you can get a blow job anywhere."

Jamie gave him a dirty look. "Really? You're going to throw it in my face that I'm not ready to let you top me?"

"How the fuck do you think it makes *me* feel?" Viggo snarled, getting off the bed and grabbing his boxers. "You come at me like you can't wait to be together, but the minute it gets serious you're ready to run."

"This is why I can't do it," Jamie protested. "I don't want to lead you on or hurt you! I care about you, but you have Emilie and Simone and the Sidewinders! I've got to deal with my career and a life on the other side of the continent! I keep walking away because I don't know if I can do this!"

"Really?" Viggo was buttoning his shirt but paused to look at him. "Because I think you've *been* doing it—not five minutes ago, a man was sucking your dick! Does that not count as *doing this*?"

"That's not fair!" Jamie snapped, reaching for a pair of sweats.

"And what you're doing is fair?"

"You're okay with who you are," Jamie whispered, walking up to him and looking into his eyes. "I don't even know who I am anymore. I was a straight guy who occasionally liked to get a little kinky. Then you kissed me and something inside me broke...in a good way. Every bad thing in my world melted away with that kiss and I fell in love with you. But this—" He waved his hand in the air. "*What is this?* How does a straight guy fall in love with another guy? How do I tell the world I'm straight but I'm with a man?!"

"Why do you have to tell the world anything?" Viggo asked gruffly, recognizing the indecision in the other man's eyes; he'd had that same look for many years before he'd come to terms with being bisexual. "Why can't you just love me?"

"Because that's not how it works!" Jamie sighed, suddenly defeated, sadness washing over him like a tidal wave of heartache. "The world will have distinctly ugly thoughts about us sleeping together, being together, loving each other..."

"I don't know what you think this is," Viggo said quietly, his fingers trailing a path along Jamie's jaw as the other man's tear-filled eyes broke his heart. "But this isn't about being bisexual or homosexual—this is about you being part of me. I don't see you as a man or a woman—I only see the person who makes me feel whole. There's never been anyone, of any sex, that makes me feel like you do— when I touch you I don't feel different anymore. I don't feel *bisexual*—I just feel like a man in love. You've given me the ability to be the man I've always wanted to be. Making love to you would be the physical display of the way my heart beats for you. If you still have to think about it, you don't love me enough."

Jamie couldn't stand the anguish on Viggo's face or the lump in his own throat as he wrapped his arms around him. "I love you enough," he rasped. "More than enough. You don't understand...there's no hesitation, no doubt—and physically I want you as much as I've ever wanted anyone—but our love can't be a dirty little secret. And as long as the world looks at gay men like it does...I can't take this step, because once I give that to you, I will never be able to be with anyone else ever again. Don't you understand?"

"All this time I've been falling in love with you and you've known you wouldn't give yourself to me?" Viggo looked crushed, despite his attempts not to let it show.

"All this time I've been trying to find a way for us to be a couple, but it's not going to happen. We're going to be two guys that don't fit in anywhere—not in sports, not in society, not anywhere except behind closed doors. Don't you see how degrading that would be?"

"All I see is you walking away from me."

"Do you see my heart breaking?"

"I do." Viggo rested his head on Jamie's. "I don't want to let you go, lover. I don't think I'll survive without you."

"You have to," Jamie whispered. "Emilie and Simone need you. Please don't let me be the reason you can't make your marriage work. I love you enough to want you to have the forever you and I can't have. Please."

Viggo found his mouth with a sweep of his head that left them both breathless. Their intimacy was tangible, the way their lips and bodies moved together with no hesitation. Tongues twirling, bodies so close they were almost one. Despite being unwilling to take the final step in their sexual relationship, Jamie was no longer reluctant to admit his feelings for this incredible man who made his life so much better every day he was in it.

He loved Viggo with everything he had, but the inability to be in an open relationship made it impossible for them to move forward. His heart was already shredded and if he gave up this last part of himself—the last scrap of who he'd been before he fell in love with Viggo—he might never recover. As much as he loved him, he had to love himself just a tiny bit more because he had no choice but to move on. Alone. When he walked away this time, all he would have was what was left of the old Jamie, something he had to keep intact.

JAMIE PULLED AWAY SLOWLY, gripping the sides of Viggo's face with his hands. "Emilie needs someone to take care of her, so it's going to be up to you to make sure she doesn't get too crazy with the pain stuff. Can you do that, babe? So I don't have to worry about you two?"

*Babe.* He'd never used a term of endearment with him before. It made Viggo's eyes feel scratchy and his throat got tight, but he nodded. "You know I'll take care of her."

"Chains can spank her on occasion," Jamie said after a moment. "He can take care of it when she gets a little too wound up."

"Jamie..."

"This is for the best." He met Viggo's gaze with a look Viggo had never seen before. "I love you. I swear on everything I believe in I have never loved anyone the way I love you. Being without you will be a slow, torturous death for me, but we have to be strong. If we got together like this, it would just re-open the wounds. You have Emilie to get you through it, but I'll be by myself, so I need you to be the stronger one and keep your distance because it's better for *me*. I have to try to get over you."

Viggo groaned deep in his chest. "I'll never get over you."

"I know, babe. Believe me, I know." Jamie pressed his forehead to Viggo's and they didn't move, eyes locked and bodies pressed close together.

"I can't bring myself to say goodbye."

"Then don't—just tell me what we had was real."

Viggo swallowed. "I shouldn't have to tell you."

# CHAPTER 21

It had taken every ounce of the control Viggo possessed to keep his heart from shattering into a million pieces in front of his teammates, but as soon as he saw Emilie he started to break down. It had been three days since he'd walked out of Jamie's apartment and his life, and he couldn't hold in his emotions another second.

"Viggo?" Her eyes filled with concern as soon as she looked into his eyes. "Sweetheart, what is it? What's happened?"

"I can't...shit, I'm sorry." He sank down on the couch and covered his face with his hands. He'd never had a broken heart before, not like this, and tears squeezed out of his eyes even though it was humiliating to cry in front of her.

"Viggo, what is it?" Emilie dropped to her knees in front of him, wrapping her arms around him as best she could.

"Jamie...he, he said he couldn't..." He took a deep, shuddery breath, unable to continue.

"Oh, no!" She hugged him tightly, wishing there was a way to somehow take this pain from him and wondering why Jamie was fighting something that was obviously so right. "Oh, darling, I'm here...I'm so sorry." She held him as tears slipped from his eyes. He didn't make a sound, internalizing the despair she practically felt seeping out of him.

"Do you feel better when someone hurts you?" he asked, raising red-rimmed eyes. "I mean, the spanking and whipping?"

"The physical pain releases the internal. For me, the temporary distraction from the internal pain is such a relief it gets me off. Why? Do you think you need that?"

"My soul is as black as the devil himself right now," he whispered. "I want to hurt on the outside before what I feel on the inside destroys me."

"Are you sure?" she whispered, pressing her forehead to his, stroking his hair.

"I've done everything you've ever asked of me," he said in a ragged breath. "This is the only thing I'll ever ask of you."

"Oh, darling, you don't have to explain—I'll always be here for you." She rose and held out her hands. "The club is closed tonight, so it's the perfect time. I prefer we didn't engage in this sort of behavior with Simone in the house. Even though she's asleep, you'll undoubtedly scream before it's over—and I don't want to chance her hearing it."

"No, of course not." He took her hands and got to his feet.

"I'll call a sitter. Go change into something comfortable." She leaned up on her toes and gently kissed his lips. "The relief is temporary," she said softly. "You know that, yes?"

"I'll take anything."

EMILIE SAT on the couch with Kate, staring moodily into the fireplace. Kate was trying to have a conversation but she was thinking about everything that had happened in the last few months. It had been just under two weeks since Viggo's break-up with Jamie and he wasn't the same. Her gentle giant of a husband was curt and short-tempered, snapping at her and getting into fights on the ice. He'd been at the club every single day he had off, allowing both her and Franny to hit him with a variety of toys until his ass, thighs and back flamed red.

Even when Emilie drew the line, refusing to go any longer or harder, he craved the pain. But Viggo never got off, never even got an erection; he merely stood there, usually on a St. Andrew's cross, his face a complete mask, as stoic as she'd ever seen anyone.

"Earth to Emilie!" Kate laughed. "What's going on with you? You're a million miles away."

Emilie smiled at her pretty sister-in-law, grateful for their close relationship. "Can you keep a secret, Kate?"

"Of course."

"You've heard the rumors about Jamie and Viggo?"

"Yes."

"Viggo is in love with him."

"What?!"

Emilie looked away. "I'm so confused because I love him—but I'm not jealous. What does that mean? I want them to be happy, I want them to be together, but I also want to keep him with me because I don't want my daughter to lose her father."

"Everything else aside," Kate said slowly, "why would Simone lose her father? Because you divorced? You wouldn't take her back to Sweden, would you?"

"Oh, no. I have a job here, and I wouldn't do that to either of them. I just...I guess I can't imagine my child growing up without having her parents together."

"Don't you love him, Emilie? Because I can tell you right now, this isn't a conversation I could ever have about Karl. I couldn't breathe when we broke up— it was like a piece of me was missing. Not just figuratively, but literally. When we were apart, my soul broke. I know that sounds stupidly romantic, but it's true. The thought of Karl with someone else—not even sexually, but the thought that he *loved* someone else—would destroy me."

"That's just it," Emilie whispered. "I don't feel that way. My own happiness isn't defined by his loving me and I'm actually *happier* thinking that he might have the kind of love I'm not capable of. What does that mean?"

"What it means," Kate said softly, "is that you're not in love with him. You care for him and you're possibly the best of friends—but he's not the man for you. I promise you, Em—whether it's a man or a woman—when you find the relationship that makes your heart whole, you'll know. What you have with Viggo can't possibly be true love if you're happy that he's in love with someone else, but that means you're free to find that person."

Emilie's eyes misted slightly. "If only it was that simple," she whispered. "Jamie ended it right before Viggo left Ottawa."

"Oh hell."

"He's shattered, Kate." She met her eyes sadly. "I've known him since I was 15 and I've never seen him like this. The light has literally gone out in his eyes. He's been...going to the club, letting me and Franny...whip him. He says the physical pain makes the emotional pain subside temporarily, and I understand because it works for me too. But I'm worried about him. He's not like me—he needs love, not pain."

"Should I have Karl talk to him?"

"I don't know."

"What can I do?"

"I don't know that either." Emilie pulled her knees up to her chest. "Since that whole thing happened with Therese, he's looked out for me. Even when we were apart and I was secretly pregnant, he checked in to make sure I was okay. Then he married me and has watched me fall apart, but he's never wavered. He's always there—my big strong, reliable husband—even while falling in love with someone else. Yet now? I barely know him. He's raw, hurting, angry and broken...just like me. And I don't want him to be like me—I don't want anyone to be like me! I need to help him, Kate, or I don't know if I can survive. Without him holding me up, I don't know how I'll go on."

"You have to," Kate said gently. "Simone needs you. She needs both of you. You have to power through, Emilie. Aren't you seeing a therapist now?"

"Not yet," she swallowed. "I have an appointment next week, but..."

"No buts! I swear to God, if you don't go, I'll smack you around myself!"

Emilie smiled. "That, I'd like to see." Kate was six months pregnant with twins.

"I won't be pregnant forever!" Kate reminded her.

"I know." Emilie dipped her head. "Thanks for listening."

"I want to do more than listen!"

"There's nothing we can do. I've no idea how to heal a broken heart, and Jamie didn't just break it, he pulverized it."

JOSH'S monthly poker game was usually a good time with an eclectic group of friends. He'd never invited Jamie before because he was a bit of a celebrity and Josh knew his friends would be over the moon that a local hockey star joined them. Jamie was a mess, though, and Josh hadn't been able to break through his misery with anything else he'd tried, so he extended the invitation and hoped he would show up. He hated seeing him suffer and Jamie had resisted every attempt to help him come to terms with his bisexuality, so Josh was trying another tactic. Maybe introducing him to new—and somewhat unconventional—friends would be more cathartic than trying to talk to him.

Jamie arrived a little late, just as they were about to start the first hand, and Josh got up to get him a drink and introduce him to everyone. It was a small group tonight, a few of his closest friends, and he hoped they would offer Jamie some sort of distraction from the gloom he'd been feeling since breaking things off with Viggo.

Josh had to swallow a laugh as he watched his friends slowly recognize Jamie and gradually become more and more star-struck. His buddy Keith seemed to lose his ability to speak and simply sat gaping at the younger man, his eyes wide and confused. He turned from Josh to Jamie and then back again, almost sputtering as he said, "For real?! You're friends with Jamie Teller and you never told us? Wait— are you guys *dating*?!"

Josh cringed, ready to shut his friend up, but Jamie just chuckled.

"Nah," he said, winking at Josh. "He's too old for me."

The men stared for a moment before realizing he was joking. Everyone laughed and the ice was broken, allowing Jamie to settle in without any more fanfare, although the guys didn't hesitate to ask him about playing for a new team and his move to Ottawa.

"How's it going since the concussion?" Tom asked, his blue eyes trained on him with genuine concern. "I played when I was a teenager and got two of them—that was the end of that."

Jamie nodded. "It's scary, but you learn to move past the fear that something bad is going to happen. It's like car accidents, you know? They happen—every single day—but you still get in your car and go to work, go on vacation, whatever. You can't think about what might happen or it would paralyze you."

"Are you happy to be home?" Keith asked.

Jamie frowned. "Honestly, I haven't lived in Canada since I was 18. I got drafted and sent to the AHL in Iowa. I got called up to Minnesota and then traded to Vegas. I've never lived in Canada as an adult—so it's kind of weird."

"Didn't you miss it?"

Jamie shook his head. "I missed my family, but like I said, I left when I was 18 so coming back doesn't feel like home because I never lived here on my own."

"Are you going to stay?"

Jamie chuckled. "As long as the team wants me, yeah. This is what I do, although I don't want to get traded again any time soon."

"Are you single?" Scott asked, cocking his head.

Jamie swallowed, unsure what to say but Josh was quick to jump in. "Are we gonna fawn over the hot, rich hockey player all night or are we gonna play cards?"

They started the game and Jamie was grateful for the distraction. It had been just under two weeks since the break-up with Viggo and he was drowning in a cocktail of despair: a full shot of desolation with a splash of loneliness and a dash of frustration. He'd had his heart broken before, but never anything like this.

He had to force himself to eat, push himself to work out, and most nights he stared at the ceiling for hours, unable to sleep. It was brutal and he wondered if Viggo was equally miserable. Based on his performance on the ice, he was. He'd been in fights and hadn't managed so much as a shot on goal in nearly two weeks; Coach Barnett was probably riding his ass.

Jamie was the opposite. The only time he felt any relief was when he was playing; he'd scored a goal every single game since they'd broken up. His coach and teammates were ecstatic and Jamie was optimistic about his future in hockey, if nothing else.

"How'd you and Josh meet?" Scott asked, bringing Jamie back to the present.

"At Lula's," Josh grinned. "He got dumped by his date and I bought him a drink."

"Are you gay?" Keith asked, no censure in his voice.

Jamie hesitated.

"Hey, we're all cool here," Scott said quietly. "What's said here stays here."

"Absolutely," Ralph nodded.

"It's okay if you don't want to talk about it," Keith said. "I guess no one is out in the NHL so you don't have to—"

"I'm bi," Jamie spoke quietly, lifting his chin slightly. "I, uh, I never knew until a few months ago. I went to Lula's that night to dance and Josh bought me a drink. We got to be friends."

"He's definitely not gay," Josh said, rolling his eyes in an attempt to lighten Jamie's obviously heavy mood. "All he could do was stare at chicks with big tits."

"Boobs are my thing," Jamie spoke with more conviction than he felt.

"Boobs are good," Keith grinned.

"Dicks are good too," Scott wiggled his eyebrows. "I'm bisexual too, Jamie."

Jamie glanced at his wedding ring. "Are you married to a man or a woman?"

Scott coughed and glanced at Josh, who nodded. "Both. I'm legally married to a woman but we have a third, a partner. A man. Craig. He and I dated before I met Samantha, my wife. She always said she was happy to indulge in threesomes with other men, but while the kids were young and stuff, it just didn't seem right. Plus, who has time? Wait till you have kids! Anyway, now that the youngest has gone off to university, we decided to explore some things outside the norm. We ran into Craig at a concert and the next thing you know, he was in our bed three, four times a week. Eventually Sam got emotionally invested in him too, so he moved in. The kids know we're all involved and he's just part of the family."

No one said anything for a few seconds until Jamie frowned. "So, he doesn't play poker?"

Josh snorted and Ralph laughed loudly.

"He does," Scott chuckled. "But one night a month he and Sam do date night. I come to poker night and they go out like a regular couple. It's their time to bond, have their own intimacy—and I'm not talking about sex."

Jamie cocked his head. "You're not jealous?"

Scott smiled. "No. She has girls' night out once or twice a month, and then he and I have our time together, although we're more likely to sit on the couch and watch a hockey game. She makes him dress up and take her to five-star restaurants or the opera, shit like that."

"So, nothing you need to hide here, my friend," Josh smiled at Jamie. "You can talk about Viggo or not."

Jamie sighed.

"Who's Viggo?" Tom asked.

"I thought we were playing cards?" Ralph grunted.

"Jamie recently went through a break-up," Josh said quietly. "I didn't invite him here to talk about it—I only wanted to distract him—but he can if he wants to. You guys are my closest friends and this is a judgement-free zone. Ralph, Tom and Keith are straight, Scott is bi, and our buddy Nate, who's away at a hockey tournament with his son this weekend, is gay. He and his husband have been married about 10 years, but together more than 20, and they adopted two boys about 11 years ago."

"They're openly gay?" Jamie asked after a moment.

"Yup. Chad, his husband, is a fundraising wizard and gets all kinds of donations for the kids' school. He's very involved and everyone loves him."

"What does he do for a living?"

"Journalist," Josh said. "And Nate is a psychiatrist."

"And they're not...outcasts? In the community? At their kids' events? It's just status quo?"

"There's an asshole now and again," Josh said. "But it's no different than an interracial marriage or something. Most of the time it's fine. Once in a while someone says something stupid, but they love each other. One idiot doesn't destroy that kind of relationship. What if your wife of many years gained weight after having a baby? Would you stop loving her because one of your friends called her fat? Or would you tell him to fuck off and say that she's still the most beautiful woman in the world in your eyes?"

Jamie lowered his eyes, suddenly feeling like an idiot. "I'd definitely tell him to fuck off."

"You and Viggo will have issues—without a doubt. But if you love each other, and I'm pretty sure you do, you'll get through it. We're still a long way from general acceptance of that kind of thing, but it boils down to one thing: *love*. It's not gay love or bisexual love—it's just love. How much do you love him?"

Everyone else in the room was busily inspecting their cards or cell phones, but Josh's eyes were intently fixed on Jamie's.

"Well?" he pressed.

"A lot." Jamie's voice was barely a whisper.

"Do you miss him?"

"You know I do."

"Is your life better without him in it?"

"Not even a little."

"Then stop being a pussy!" Josh folded his cards and laid them down. "Seriously, call him and apologize. Tell him how much you love him, that you want to see him."

"Wait...Viggo? Sjoberg?" Keith asked, his eyes glued to his phone. "Holy shit, he's hot!"

Jamie's brows knitted together. "I thought you were straight?"

Keith burst out laughing. "Yeah, but two of my best friends are gay, and another is bisexual. I've learned it's okay to think guys are hot—I just don't want to sleep with them."

"He *is* hot," Scott said, also looking at his phone. "Damn, he put up some good numbers this season too—except for the last two weeks. What'd you do to him?!"

Jamie flushed. "I guess I broke his heart."

"Douche nozzle." Ralph shook his head. "That's fucked up, man."

"Call him," Keith said.

"Listen to us," Josh nodded.

"Totally." Scott grinned. "Now, can we please put away our vaginas and play some poker?!"

"Are you gonna call him?" Ralph asked, his eyes twinkling.

Jamie took a deep breath. "Tomorrow. Yes."

"Now be prepared to lose money," Josh grinned. "We're hard core around here."

Jamie made a face at him. "Bring it." He put a handful of chips in the middle of the table with a thump, feeling better than he had since Viggo had left his apartment. He still had to think about a few things but hearing these men talking about their gay friends was enlightening. Maybe it wasn't so bad. Maybe he wasn't as much of a freak as he'd been afraid he was. Maybe Viggo would forgive him for fucking up the best thing either of them had ever had. Unfortunately, that was the biggest maybe of all.

# CHAPTER 22

Viggo had just gotten to the arena for a game when his phone buzzed. Thinking it was Emilie, he opened the text program and froze. His heart thundered when he read Jamie's name, and a faint crease formed between his brows as he read the message:

*I know I said you should stay away but we need to talk. I'm lost, babe. Can we talk? After your game? Please give me a chance to explain. J.*

Viggo stared at the phone for long minutes. What the hell should he say? Had Jamie finally realized he'd been an idiot? Or was he just lonely and horny, looking for temporary relief from the pain of his broken heart? He had to find out, because his own heartache wasn't getting any better and he was having a hard time explaining the marks on his back from the whip to his teammates. He had to be cautious, though, so he kept that in mind as he typed out a reply:

*If you're not ready to commit, be with me, then no, we can't talk. I don't have it in me to lose you again. But if you're ready to make it work, I'm here day or night. Always, V.*

He put the phone in his bag and took a breath. There was hope. There had to be. Jamie wouldn't have contacted him if he wasn't thinking about him. He'd seen the pain in his eyes when he'd told him they couldn't be together. He understood his fear of being ostracized, that society would never truly embrace them as a couple, because he'd also grappled with that issue for years. That was why he'd never allowed himself to become emotionally involved with a man.

Although there were plenty of publicly gay couples, it was usually celebrities or the ultra-rich who got away with that kind of thing. He and Jamie were just a couple of middle-of-the-road athletes whose careers and million-dollar contracts could end at any time. He knew what Jamie was afraid of, but he didn't understand how he'd been able to just walk away from what they had. Being apart had shredded him into ugly, seemingly irreparable pieces; Jamie had to be suffering at least half that much, didn't he?

He wouldn't look at his phone until after the game. That was the only way for him to focus. Otherwise, he'd be a mess all over again and he was just starting to get his groove back on the ice.

JAMIE DIDN'T KNOW what he was going to say when he talked to Viggo, but going through the last two weeks without him had been the worst of his life. He'd been an absolute mess and if it hadn't been for Misty and Josh, he didn't know if he would have gotten through it. Last night's poker game had been cathartic, talking to regular guys who didn't think anything was wrong with two men being in love.

He had to talk to Viggo and be more forthcoming than he'd been before; he had to talk about the specific things that made a future together seem impossible. They had to discuss the difficulties of fathering a biological child, not being able to be affectionate in public, and most of all, not being able to have what he considered a traditional family.

The one thing he'd neglected to consider when he'd made the decision to end things was that his life would never be the same after giving up the kind of love he'd found with Viggo. Loving Viggo had changed him—and everything he'd ever thought he knew about love. He wasn't sure why, but without him he wasn't just heartbroken; he was empty. It felt like every ounce of pleasure in his life had been sucked away and all that was left was the tattered shell of his soul. It was an ache he'd never experienced before, and one that left him inconsolable. He went through the motions each day but felt absolutely nothing. No joy, no pain, no excitement; he was 100% empty.

Thank God for Josh, he'd thought, as he'd typed his text to Viggo. He'd made him see that being in a relationship with a man didn't change who either of them were. He was still Jamie Teller, heartthrob hockey player who loved brunettes with big tits. Even now, though he had no interest in dating anyone, he couldn't tear his eyes away from a fabulous pair of breasts. He had no desire to go out with anyone else, though, no matter how attractive or interesting they were.

He'd met quite a few nice guys through Josh, and as he'd sat in a room full of educated, interesting and handsome men last week, he'd realized not one of them did anything for him. He might be bisexual, but as he'd watched some of them laughing, flirting and hooking up, he'd known there would never be anyone for him but Viggo. There would never be anyone else, man or woman, Viggo owned him.

Though the issues they faced seemed insurmountable, he had a feeling that would all change once he allowed Viggo to become a permanent part of his life. He had to make things right sooner rather than later, and he sighed with relief when he read Viggo's reply. He was about to text him back when another text, this one from Misty, came in and distracted him.

*They're going to hurt me! You have to help me! Please come upstairs—Collin is really drunk and he hit Jill so hard she's out cold. I'm sorry, I was supposed to see my boy but he's not here and they won't let me leave... I'm scared, Jamie. Please!!!*

*Now what?* he thought with irritation. Grabbing his keys, he slipped his phone into his pocket and headed down the hall. As soon as he was done getting Misty, he'd send Viggo a nice text that would be waiting for him after the game. This situation with Collin and his friends had gotten old, and he needed to get her away from them once and for all, or he'd never be able to concentrate on fixing things with Viggo.

"Well, well, look who it is," Collin said as he opened the door, his eyes bloodshot and red. "Our hero hockey stud. You gonna save poor Misty?"

Jamie arched his brows. "What's going on, man? Why don't you leave her alone? I'm not sure what you get out of pushing her around."

"I get the satisfaction of knowing that she'll do what I say, when I say it." He moved aside so Jamie could enter the apartment. "Kind of like you and your big, redheaded studmuffin."

Jamie got a bad feeling in his gut, but managed to keep his face neutral. "What are you talking about?"

Collin laughed. "You think we don't know what you are, homo? We saw you groping each other like disgusting pigs in the elevator... You had me fooled, faggot."

Jamie scowled. "Look, you must've smoked too much weed, 'cause I don't know what you're talking about."

"You don't?" He glanced over at Lance. "Bring her out."

Lance got up and a minute later dragged Misty out of the bedroom by her hair. There was a big purple bruise over one of her eyes and blood dripped from her lips. She was crying, but didn't make a sound as Lance deposited her at Collin's feet.

"Misty here left her husband for a woman—did you know that?"

Jamie shrugged. "So? She still lets *me* fuck her. That's all I care about."

"I think that's a cover for all your secret activities with men like that red-haired fairy. He stick his dick in your ass?" Collin advanced on him menacingly. "What's the matter, faggot? You ain't too shy to do it but you're too shy to talk about it?"

"I'm not shy about anything," Jamie ground out. "What do you want to know?"

"I want you to admit it—admit you're a homo."

"I'm not."

"Get my knife, Felix," Collin called out.

Jamie took a deep breath and squeezed his keys in his hand. He didn't know what he was going to do, but he was outnumbered four to one. Misty would help, but she was tiny and already beaten down. He'd been in more than a few fights in his time, but he didn't know if he could take all four of these guys.

The look Misty gave him told him she was thinking the same thing and he mentally calculated how far it was to the door. He might make it out, but chances weren't good she would be able to get away too, and he refused to just leave her behind.

"I think an *L*, right in the middle of her cheek, would look good," Collin said, looking at Jamie pointedly, the blade of the knife gleaming in his hand.

"An *L*?" Jamie frowned.

"Lesbo," Felix chuckled.

"Come on, man, what do you get out of this?" Jamie demanded. "Who cares who she fucks? She's a dumb stripper—what difference does it make?"

"It's because of people like her—and you—that the world is the way it is. The human race needs to be cleansed of the filth—the blacks, the gays, the unholy. Once that's done, our race will be pure again, and the Aryan brotherhood will rise again."

Jamie blinked, trying not to show his disgust.

"So, tell me, Jamie—what's your boyfriend's name?"

"I don't have a boyfriend," Jamie growled.

Collin dug the tip of the knife into Misty's cheek and she screamed. Jamie swung his fist, keys between his fingers, into Felix's face as he brought up his foot and caught Collin in the jaw. Misty scrambled to her feet and Jamie grabbed her hand. They were almost to the door when Lance grabbed Jamie by the back of his shirt. He swung around with his fist poised, yelling over his shoulder.

"Run, Misty!"

She yanked open the door, but Ron grabbed her around the waist, hauling her back inside.

"Dammit!" Jamie jerked free of Lance but froze as Ron held the knife to Misty's throat.

"Now you're gonna pay, you little queer," Collin hissed, standing up and holding his face.

Jamie was ready to fight but he didn't expect the blow to the back of the head that dropped him to his knees. He didn't have time to duck before something hard smashed into his skull again. The last thing he heard was Misty screaming his name.

## CHAPTER 23

It had been a great game and Viggo had both a goal and an assist. It was the first time since he'd left Jamie that he felt good, if not a little deflated he had no one special to share it with. Not yet anyway, but hopefully that would change once he talked to Jamie.

He was looking forward to having a day off tomorrow and spending some time talking to Emilie about what she wanted to do. She'd told him repeatedly she only wanted him to be happy and as long as he was around to help with Simone, she would do whatever he wanted. First, he had to figure out what Jamie wanted, but he had a feeling these two weeks of separation had made him realize what he'd walked away from. He hoped so anyway.

"You were hot tonight," Karl was saying to him. "Whatever it is that lit a fire under your ass, keep doing it!"

Viggo laughed but turned away, fishing in his bag for his phone. It seemed like a very long time ago Emilie had asked him if he'd ever loved a man, and he was still surprised it had happened. Loving a man, this man anyway, was the hardest thing he'd ever done, but being without him hurt more and more every day.

If it hadn't been for hockey and Simone, he wasn't sure how he would have gotten through this. He'd never had a lot of time or interest in exploring feelings. With the exception of Emilie, Jamie was the only non-family member he'd ever loved. Ironically, he had no problem with it; loving Jamie was as easy as waking up every morning. It simply happened, without any effort, which was why he didn't understand how Jamie had just given up.

He glanced up when Coach Barnett walked into the dressing room. They'd already had their post-game briefing, so he wasn't really paying attention until Cody let out a sharp whistle, alerting them Coach wanted their attention.

"Boys, I hate to come back in here with bad news, but I guess I should give it to you straight from the league, instead of you hearing it on the news." He took a deep breath. "There was an incident in Ottawa tonight."

Viggo's heart started to pound the moment he heard the word *Ottawa*. He instinctively sensed something had happened to Jamie and he gripped the side of the bench he was sitting on so hard he thought he might split the wood.

"Coach?" Cody was looking at him with concern.

"Jamie Teller was attacked in his apartment building tonight. The police haven't released the details, but it's been deemed a hate crime."

"Sonofabitch." There was no mistaking the anger in Zakk's voice.

"Is he dead?" Viggo's voice was a whisper.

"Coach?" Zakk's voice got louder when it became clear Viggo couldn't bring himself to repeat the question. "Is he okay?"

"They don't know if he's going to make it. He was beaten and left for dead. Right now, all they'll tell us is the assailants hit him repeatedly with a baseball bat, smashed his wrist with a sledgehammer, broke four ribs, shaved his head and... branded him."

"Branded him?!" Viggo shot up so fast his bag and its contents tumbled to the floor. His fists were clenched at his sides and he didn't even realize he'd begun breathing hard. It felt like fire was running through his veins and the heat was collecting between his ears. He barely kept control of the roaring in his brain as he yanked off his jersey and stared at Coach Barnett.

"This is *hate crime* because Jamie is gay?" Vladimir Kolnikov spoke in heavily accented English as he stood up and looked at the coach as well. He was dating Jamie's ex-girlfriend, Rachel, and she maintained Jamie was a good guy. Vladimir thought so too; he'd been a stellar teammate and a lot of fun off the ice as well. He couldn't imagine Jamie doing anything to invoke such a violent attack because he was generally a soft-spoken, easygoing guy.

"What happened, Coach?" Cody looked a little pale as he asked.

Coach Barnett cleared his throat. "What the coach in Ottawa told me was that they carved the word *faggot* into his back."

A hushed silence fell over the room as everyone tried to digest what he'd just said.

"When you say 'carved', do you mean with a knife, cutting into his skin?" Zakk could barely choke out the words and Coach Barnett managed to nod.

"No!" Viggo let out a roar of pure fury and pounded the side of his fist into the locker at his side, the metal unforgiving and causing a bone in his hand to snap, though he was too furious to notice.

"Viggo." Zakk stood and gripped the big man's arm, holding him back.

"My fault," Viggo growled in Swedish.

Karl quickly moved to his other side, responding in kind, "It was not. You're not responsible for what those assholes did!"

"He's in love with a man because of me!"

"He's in love with a man who loves him!" Karl shot back. His sister had told him everything and he felt for both of them, especially now.

"What can we do, Coach?" Cody was asking as Karl and Zakk huddled over Viggo.

"They don't know if he'll last the night," Coach responded sadly. "If you're the praying kind, you might want to do a little of that."

"Coach..." Viggo's voice was scratchy as he held back tears he didn't dare shed in front of his teammates. "I have to go...this is my fault...I have to be with him...*fuck*." He sank onto the bench and broke down, despite his best efforts not to.

His teammates were staring in confusion, looks of disbelief, embarrassment and compassion drifting across their faces.

"Come on." Zakk practically had to lift the big man off the bench as Karl slid an arm around his waist.

"Let's give them some privacy," Cody said quietly. "We should get going."

"What else can we do?" Vlad asked suddenly.

"I'm flying to Ottawa as soon as we can schedule a charter," Coach said. "Whether he makes it or not, I want to show his family that Jamie is still one of us and we don't give a rat's ass about his sexuality."

"Jamie isn't gay," Viggo said, stopping in the doorway and turning to them, his eyes gleaming with intensity. "Don't mistake his love for me with him hiding something. Jamie wasn't a closet homosexual, or a closet anything. Maybe by definition you would call him bisexual, but I'm telling you that until we got together, he was a guy like any of you, who unexpectedly met his soulmate—it just turned out his soulmate was a man. He broke things off because neither of us was prepared to deal with what that meant. And I let him go because I thought it would be better for him, *safer* in the long run. I should have been there to have his back, to protect him from hateful people..." His voice broke and Karl gently tugged him towards the showers again.

"I don't care who he sleeps with," Cody said quietly. "I only care about the kind of friend and teammate he was—and he was an exceptional one of both those things."

"I am not going to All-Star game," Vlad said. "I will go to Ottawa."

"Me too," Brock got to his feet.

"Count me in," Zakk spoke quickly.

"Me too." Toli stood up.

"You don't have to..." Viggo's voice broke as more voices echoed that they would go too. "I'm grateful to have friends like you. Jamie would be...happy to see that you care."

VIGGO'S HAND had swollen to double its size by the time they got to Ottawa in the early morning, but he wasn't even cognizant of the pain. Though they'd gotten a flight attendant to bring him ice during the flight, Viggo hadn't said a word, merely staring off into the distance at nothing.

The owner of the Sidewinders had chartered a plane, and according to the hospital, Jamie had still been alive when they'd left just after one a.m. There were 15 people on board, including Dante and Becca, Coach Barnett, Viggo, Karl, Zakk, Cody, Vladimir and several other players. Just before they'd taken off, Chains had appeared, sneaking into a seat next to Dante and Becca. Though his face was calm, there was an intensity in his eyes no one had ever seen before and everyone chose to give him space.

"Do the police know who did this?" Brock asked the question that had been on many of their minds.

"No one's been arrested," Coach Barnett said. "They found a woman in his apartment, also badly beaten, but have no idea who she is. His roommate was the one who found them and he thinks it was residents in his building, a group of guys Jamie used to hang out with until he found out they were skinheads and tried to stay away. The police haven't been able to find them."

"They will," Chains grunted, not looking up from the newspaper in his lap. "Or I will."

By the time they got to the hospital in a rented limousine, Viggo could barely contain himself and took the stairs up to the top floor where Jamie was in a special wing of Intensive Care with round-the-clock protection. Viggo's name had been added to the list of people allowed to visit and he froze outside the door to his room.

"You must be Viggo," a nurse said, coming up behind him and startling him. "He's been calling for you."

"He has?" Viggo turned in surprise.

She smiled. "When he came out of surgery he kept asking for you, but his injuries are so severe the doctor wanted him sedated. The only way I could get him to calm down when he woke up was by telling him you were coming."

Viggo felt tears prick his eyelids and managed to nod. "Can I see him?"

"He's sleeping but you can sit with him." She paused. "Are you aware of his injuries?"

"I, I don't know all of them...the wrist and some ribs?"

"Bruised kidney, dislocated shoulder, broken collarbone, trauma to the brain... they're not sure if there will be any permanent damage."

Viggo closed his eyes as she listed so many injuries he didn't know how Jamie would survive. So much pain. Just the thought of kind, gentle Jamie being attacked by those men, alone and overpowered, made him want to vomit.

"I'm sorry—are you okay?" She noticed his hand for the first time. "That doesn't look good. May I check it?"

"It's probably broken," he said absently. "It hurts like hell, but I really need to see him before I can think about it."

"Go on in. I'll send someone to look at your hand in a few minutes."

"I don't need—"

"Go on." She was soft and gentle, but her tone brooked no argument and Viggo didn't have it in him to argue with anyone.

# CHAPTER 24

He walked into Jamie's room and everything in his field of vision started to swim. Bandages covered most of his body and his handsome face had morphed into a plethora of overlapping, ugly purple bruises. He had scrapes and dried blood where the animals who'd attacked him had roughly shaved his head. It was so horrible Viggo had to take slow, steady breaths.

Staring at the prone figure on the bed made his soul hurt; if it hadn't been for the monitor reflecting a strong, steady heartbeat, he could have been dead. *Dead.* Even thinking that word tore through him and he had to lower himself into a chair just to catch his breath.

"I'm here, Jamie." He scooted his chair close to the side of the bed, and rested his forearms on his thighs. Underneath the bruises, Jamie was so pale and still. Reaching out, he found one of his hands and slowly closed his own around it, gratified to feel the warmth that signified he was still alive. The other hand was in a cast that went from his fingers to his elbow and then rested in a sling against his chest.

"I need you to wake up, yeah? I need you, period. We're meant to be together. If you need to stay in Ottawa, I'll find a way to get traded or find another job. Em and I will work out a custody agreement, but I'm not leaving you alone. Whatever we have to deal with, you won't be alone. I'll always have your back. I'm sorry, handsome. Forgive me for leaving you to face whatever this was alone. I'll never forgive myself. I love you, Jamie. Please don't leave me." His shoulders shook as he broke down, resting his head on Jamie's thigh.

"It's okay, he knows you love him." A soft voice spoke behind him and Viggo lifted his head as a hand squeezed his shoulder. The face looked familiar and he realized it was Jamie's sister, Maddie.

"You're Maddie," he whispered.

She nodded, tears sliding down her cheeks as she held out her arms. Viggo got to his feet and wrapped her in a huge hug.

"I'm sorry I let this happen," he whispered. "I shouldn't have left him...I thought he'd be better off if we weren't together."

"He loves you so much," she whispered back. "He told me everything the night before it happened. He was going to fly to Vegas during the All-Star break to find out if you still loved him."

"God, yes."

"So you're the man that made my Jamie so happy," a woman's voice startled them both.

"Mom! This is Viggo." Maddie turned, her fingers linked with his.

"Hello, Viggo. I'm Evelyn." She looked a lot like her son with big brown eyes, curly dark hair that bounced around her shoulders, and a slender frame.

"Mrs. Teller." His voice broke again and she shook her head.

"Just call me Evelyn. Or Mom."

"Your hand!" Maddie cried, suddenly noticing the way he cradled it at his side. "What happened? Did someone hurt you too?!"

"No." Viggo cleared his throat. "I, uh, I lost control when they told me what happened. I hit something." He looked down at his hand as if seeing it for the first time.

"Viggo Sjoberg?" A tall man with cropped salt-and-pepper hair and sharp blue eyes stepped into the room. "I'm Dr. Franklin. I was told you injured your hand?"

Viggo swallowed. "Yes, I, uh..." He simply held it out.

The doctor did a cursory examination and shook his head. "You're going to need an X-ray."

"I don't want to leave him." He glanced back at the bed.

"It'll take five minutes and you'll just be downstairs. Come." He gently took Viggo by the elbow. "You know, I think I saw you play at the World Championships in 2010 in Finland. Didn't you score..." Their voices faded as the doctor led him away and Maddie sank into the chair he'd vacated.

"He's quite handsome," Evelyn said after a moment.

"He's quite large," Maddie smiled. "Jamie said he was really big and gruff on the outside, but very sweet and tender on the inside."

"Just what Jamie needs," Evelyn said softly, staring at her son sadly.

"Excuse me, Mrs. Teller?" Zakk knocked on the door and stuck his head in. He'd met Jamie's parents during the playoffs last season and she immediately jumped up to hug him.

"Zakk! So good to see you!"

"I wish it was under better circumstances." Zakk had to breathe slowly as he looked at his friend's battered body.

"Would you sit with Maddie while I go make a phone call?" Evelyn asked.

"Of course." Zakk nodded. He glanced at Maddie. "Where's Viggo?"

"Doctor dragged him out to look at his hand," she answered.

Jamie moaned and they both hurried to his side.

"I'm right here, Jamie. It's Maddie." She took his hand and held it against her cheek. "Jamie, Viggo is here. Did you hear me? Viggo is here."

Jamie whispered something they couldn't understand and then he was asleep again.

. . .

CHAINS DIDN'T GO to the hospital with the others. Instead, he rented a car, bought a burner phone and made a few phone calls. By the time he'd finished, he knew what he needed to do and where he needed to go. He stopped by a hardware store and then drove to Jamie's apartment building. He sat in the car and watched for a while, getting the lay of the land and figuring out exactly how this was going to go down. He'd been a pilot for the Royal Air Force and then an agent for MI6 for nearly a decade. Although he'd retired from that life, he still knew what to do to get information he needed.

He smiled, drumming his fingers on the steering wheel. Those dumb, bigoted little fucks had no idea who they were up against, or what he was capable of doing to them. He snapped a few pictures with his phone and put another address into the GPS. He had one more errand before going back to the hospital. He'd take care of the skinheads who'd beaten Jamie later tonight. The rest of the time, he'd hang out at the hospital in case anyone needed anything.

VIGGO WATCHED Jamie sleep for the rest of the day and all night. He never closed his eyes, merely watching the man he loved fight for his life. Doctors and nurses came in and out regularly. Sometime after midnight Maddie fell asleep in the chair on the other side of the room and Evelyn went to lie down in the lounge. Dante and Zakk came in to check on Viggo at regular intervals and just before dawn Chains slipped into the room.

"Hey, mate." Chains squatted down beside him. "How're ya hangin' in?"

"Numb."

"Maybe this will cheer you up." Chains brought out his phone and pulled up some pictures.

"I don't understand." Viggo frowned. "Who are these people?"

Chains flipped through a couple until he got to the video he'd taken. A young man was on his back, completely naked, tied spread-eagle to the bed with a ball gag in his mouth. There was a huge tattoo of a black swastika on his chest and Viggo frowned as the scene unfolded. A woman in nothing but a mask, a black corset and fishnet stockings appeared with a whip. He watched in a kind of morbid fascination as she slashed the whip across the man's chest with expert precision. Each slice of the whip cut the skin where the swastika was inked until his chest was a mass of ugly gashes with blood running off his body and onto the bed.

"Bring in the next one!" the woman called out.

A massive black man brought in another young man, also naked and gagged, with his hands tied behind his back. The black man, whose face was never seen, bent him over the side of the bed and shoved his cock into the man's ass. The young man screamed through his gag, but the bigger man pushed his face down into the mattress and continued to pound into him until he appeared to pass out. Viggo watched in fascinated horror when the third man was brought in. He was the biggest of the three, and it appeared he'd put up a fight because his face was bloody and his knuckles bruised.

"Is this..." He pushed the video away from him slightly, shaking his head, and met Chains' gaze. "Are you sure these are the guys?"

Chains gave a barely perceptible smile. "I was a spy for almost a decade, mate. I know how to get people to talk—believe me, they're the ones that did this to Jamie."

"And you..."

"Made sure they understood that what they did would not just be punished by law, but was something they had to pay for in blood as well. No one died. No one has injuries they can't recover from. The punk with the swastika will have some scars, but so will Jamie, and our boy still might not make it." He glanced over to the bed. "He doesn't have to know about this—the only people who know are you, me, Dante and the friends who helped out." He paused. "The police should be on their way there now."

"Vigilante justice," Viggo said after a moment. "Not my thing, but I don't feel an ounce of pity."

"Nor should you." Chains rose to his feet. "Let me know if you need anything. I don't want to leave Emilie alone at the club too long, so I may leave later today."

"Thank you." Viggo nodded at him.

# CHAPTER 25

The hours passed with no progress. Jamie would occasionally cry out in his sleep, but the medication kept him from waking up and the doctors assured everyone this was giving his body time to heal. Either Viggo, Evelyn or Maddie was always at his side and friends and teammates would come in one at a time to sit with whomever was with him at the time.

On the third day after the attack, the doctor cut back the medication and they waited for a change. Evelyn left to go take a shower and Maddie went with Zakk, Dante and Becca to eat something other than hospital food. It was just after noon and Viggo was dozing in the chair when Jamie moaned. He instantly got to his feet, leaning over the bed and brushing a hand over Jamie's cheek.

"I'm here, Jamie. Can you open your eyes, lover?"

Jamie shifted his legs and twisted his torso slightly. Something must have been painful because he moaned again and slowly blinked.

"Good morning, handsome. Do you know who I am?"

Jamie's eyes narrowed slightly as they drifted shut again, but he nodded. "Duh." His voice was hoarse and barely a whisper.

"Just making sure."

"Is he awake?" A nurse came in, quickly and efficiently moving around Viggo to check the monitors.

"He opened his eyes and nodded at me."

"Not. Asleep." Jamie managed to say the two words.

"Jamie, can you try to open your eyes again? You've been asleep three days and we'd really like to see you awake for a little while."

Jamie's eyes fluttered and he blinked. "Hurts."

"What hurts?" she asked softly.

"Breathe."

"You have four broken ribs," she said. "Don't try to take deep breaths. Shallow and slow."

"Back. Burns."

"You have some lacerations on your back," she said. "We'll check those in just a bit, but we haven't wanted to move you because of your ribs."

"Mm." Jamie was struggling to stay focused.

"Is there any internal pain? Kidneys? Stomach? Anything like that?"

"No." Jamie's eyes were closing again.

"A little longer, Jamie." She moved the sheet back and ran her hands down his bandaged torso. "What about your head? Headache? Any nausea?"

"No." Jamie sighed. "Viggo."

"Right here."

His voice was soft. "...shouldn't be here."

Viggo felt a twinge of hurt but reminded himself Jamie had been through a terrible ordeal. "We're all here, Jamie. The Sidewinders came as soon as we heard what happened."

Jamie's eyes opened in confusion. "Sidewinders? Here?"

"Cody, Zakk, Coach Barnett...you have a lot of people that want to see you."

"My mom?"

"Your mom and sister are here too. They've gone to clean up."

"Jamie, I'm going to call Dr. Levesque. Try to stay awake for me, okay?" The nurse was heading for the hallway.

Jamie managed to nod even as his eyes started to close. "Heard you," he whispered when the nurse was gone.

"What did you hear?"

"Heard you...tell me...things."

"You heard me tell you I love you?" Viggo leaned down and pressed his lips to Jamie's forehead. "Heard me say I'm not letting you go? That I'm going to take care of you?"

Jamie nodded.

"You don't get to push me away anymore, Jamie. I love you and I know you love me. We're not going to continue this bullshit, trying to be apart—we're going to make this work."

"So much hate for guys like us." He sighed sleepily. "What did they do to me, Viggo?"

"They beat you," he said gently, "but you're going to be okay."

"My wrist." He closed his eyes. "How bad?"

"I don't know." That, at least, was honest. He didn't know what he was going to say if Jamie asked about the marks on his back.

"Sledgehammer. Said a fag like me...wasn't...man enough...to play hockey."

Viggo felt burning behind his eyelids but shook his head. "Doesn't matter what they said—you *do* play hockey. Doesn't matter that they tried to hurt you. It doesn't take away from the fact you're one of the one percent. Less than one percent of all hockey players get to this level—and you did. They may have tried to take it away from you, but you've played hundreds of games, thousands of hours on the ice. You *are* a professional hockey player. Getting hurt doesn't change what you've accomplished."

"How did you know to come?" Jamie asked after a moment, his sleepy eyes meeting Viggo's.

"It's, uh...a big deal. All over the news. Hate crime and all that."

Jamie didn't react at first, simply trying to understand. "How do they know it was a hate crime? No one heard the things they said to me."

Viggo swallowed.

"Viggo?"

"We should wait until you talk to the police, so they—"

"Stop." Jamie closed his eyes and breathed as deeply as he dared. "Tell me the truth." He was still trying to pull out of the haze created by the drugs in his system. "If you love me, treat me like your partner, not a kid."

Viggo grit his teeth. "They used a knife to carve the word *faggot* into your back." Viggo hadn't known what he expected Jamie to do, but he wasn't prepared for tears. Jamie didn't move or say a word, but as he lay there, tears leaked out and ran down his face. He was completely silent, but the pain on his face brought Viggo to his knees next to the bed. He put his head against Jamie's side and rested his hand on his chest. "I'm sorry. This is my fault. I should never have pursued you —forgive me."

"No." Jamie's good hand moved to Viggo's hair and he stroked it gently. "Not your fault. I have regrets, but loving you isn't one of them."

"You didn't even know you were bi—I showed you what that was. If I hadn't pursued the sex, this wouldn't have happened."

"Stop." Jamie paused to swipe at his eyes, forcing them open despite overwhelming fatigue. "Babe. Stop."

Viggo raised his head, his own tears still wet on his cheeks.

"Aw, Viggo, don't." Jamie tried to wipe them away, though he wasn't quite coordinated enough to manage.

Viggo shook his head. "This is on me—I brought this on you."

"No." Jamie brought his fingers to Viggo's cheek. "I'm bisexual. Deep down I suspected, but didn't want to face it. When we got together, I had no choice."

"If I hadn't shown you what that—"

"I knew. I refused to acknowledge it, but I knew. The thing is, it doesn't matter anymore. Don't you see? I'm not in love with a man. I'm in love with *you*. Until you, I didn't know it was even possible to be loved the way you love me. I wouldn't trade it for *anything*."

"They tried to kill you..." Viggo couldn't stop the tears and he swiped at them angrily. "And I wasn't there! They hurt you and I couldn't stop them."

"And if you'd been there, they might have hurt you too," Jamie rasped, trying to focus, stay awake and breathe through the pain in his ribs. "I'm glad it was just me."

"No!" Though his voice was barely a whisper, it was filled with agony and guilt. He hung his head and broke down, wishing he could change something that would have kept Jamie from getting hurt.

"Please don't do this," Jamie finally whispered, gripping his hand firmly. "I need you to be strong for both of us right now."

"Always." Viggo rubbed his hands down his face, trying to get himself together.

"Are you two done crying?" Maddie stage-whispered. "I'm sorry, but Mom is coming down the hall and she's going to freak if she sees you guys like this!"

"Maddie." Jamie would have been embarrassed had it been anyone else, but he loved and trusted his sister implicitly.

"I'm so happy to hear your voice!" Maddie threw herself across him, though she didn't put any weight on his torso.

"I'm here, kid." He stroked her hair, surprised when she started to cry. "You just yelled at *us* for crying," he whispered, teasing her.

"You almost died!" she cried. "I was so scared! I'm allowed to cry."

"I'm sorry, sis." He hugged her with one arm.

"Jamie!" His mother's cry was so loud it made all three of them jump, but Jamie looked up with a tired smile.

"Hi, Mom."

"You're awake! You're okay!" She leaned down and kissed his forehead and cheeks. "We've been so worried!"

"I'm sorry."

"I'm going to go tell the boys the news," Viggo said quietly, straightening up. He figured Evelyn would want some time with her son and he needed a few minutes to compose himself anyway.

"You're coming back, right?" Jamie met his eyes worriedly.

Viggo smiled. "Always."

"Don't be long." Jamie watched him go.

"He's a wonderful young man," Evelyn said softly, taking Jamie's hand in hers. "He seems to love you very much."

Jamie looked at her for a moment. "Did he tell you...?"

"About the two of you? No. Maddie did, after we got the call from the team."

He nodded. "I'm sorry."

"Sorry? For what? Falling in love with a handsome, kind and loving man? Isn't that what we imagine for our children? Do you think I'd prefer you to fall for some gold-digging bimbo just because she's a woman?"

"I don't know," he admitted. "I don't know how you feel about this kind of thing."

"It's not what we're used to, that's true, but you're my son. I don't care what you do in private as long as you're not hurting anyone and no one is hurting you."

"I'm not going to be able to give you grandchildren."

She raised her eyebrows. "Why not? Is something wrong with your sperm?"

He blinked. "Uh, well, I don't know anything about my sperm since I've never gotten anyone pregnant, but I assume it's healthy."

"Then there's no reason you can't have children—adoption and surrogates are just the beginning. And my understanding is that Viggo already has a child. She would be my granddaughter too, wouldn't she?"

Jamie met his mother's eyes and felt tears pooling in his again. He'd never imagined this level of support from his parents. He frowned suddenly. "Where's Dad?"

"He's not here," she said softly. "I just sent him a message that you'd woken up and he's coming. He's been a bit uncomfortable with the press camped out here."

"The press is camped out here?"

"It was a hate crime, Jamie. That's big news. We don't get a lot of this kind of thing, and you're a professional athlete. It's been on sports networks all over the world."

"All over the world?" Jamie sighed. "So the whole world knows I'm gay."

"No." Maddie spoke for the first time. "The whole world knows you're *bi*. And the entire sports community has your back. Not just Ottawa and Las Vegas, but the entire league. Most of the other sports' leagues have issued statements condemning hate crimes. You probably have 25 job offers to be an announcer for pretty much any sport you want!"

He sighed. "I guess that means my wrist is toast."

"It doesn't mean anything except that people are supporting you."

"I'm really tired," he said after a moment.

"Close your eyes. We'll be right here."

## CHAPTER 26

"Jamie, I'm afraid I have both good news and bad news," Dr. Levesque said in his quiet, efficient voice.

"What's the bad news?" Jamie glanced at Viggo, who reached over to take his hand.

He'd been awake for two days now and was slowly feeling better, but his injuries were so extensive it was hard to keep up with how much treatment he needed. Luckily, Viggo and his mother had been by his side helping him work through each new development. Today it was just Viggo; his mother had gone home to Kingston to deal with a few things and would be back the following day.

"Your kidneys have shut down as a result of the trauma to your body. You have less than 10% function on the right side, and only about 15% on the left."

"What does that mean?" Jamie asked, his mouth going dry.

"It means we need to do dialysis. I believe that after a couple of treatments, your kidneys will have enough rest to heal and work on their own, but there's no way to know until we try."

"What happens if they don't?"

"You'll need dialysis the rest of your life."

"Dialysis." Jamie felt sick to his stomach and closed his eyes.

"Let's not get ahead of ourselves," the doctor said gently. "You're young and in extremely good shape. I believe this is a minor setback, your body's way of rebelling against all the trauma. Trust me to do what I do. I think you're going to be fine. I want you to sign off on the dialysis. We'll do it this afternoon and again the day after tomorrow. Then we'll give it a couple of days and run the numbers again."

"Okay." Jamie could only nod numbly.

"You said there was good news." Viggo finally found his voice.

"The scans all came back clear—no brain damage and just a minor concussion. By sleeping those first few days you gave everything a chance to heal."

"Except my kidneys," Jamie murmured.

"That's great news," Viggo said, giving Jamie a look.

"Jamie, try not to stress about the kidneys," Dr. Levesque said, putting a hand on his shoulder. "You're healing amazingly well. Forty-eight hours ago we weren't sure you were going to make it. Today you ate solid food. One day at a time."

"I know."

"There will be papers for you to sign for the dialysis and I'll see you tomorrow."

"Thank you."

"It's going to be okay," Viggo said once they were alone.

"Dialysis?" Jamie squeezed his eyes shut. "It's a fucking nightmare. I'll never play hockey again. I'm going to need a job, and the only thing I know is hockey. How the fuck can I even be a coach or a scout if I have to have dialysis two or three times a week?"

"You're getting ahead of yourself." Viggo stood and leaned over him, putting a hand on his face. "It's going to be okay. I make plenty of money for—"

"Seriously, don't!" Jamie's face tightened. "I love you, okay? So don't take this the wrong way—but I'm still a man. I'm not the *woman* in our relationship. I'm not going to be the stay-at-home mom taking care of the kids and the house while you go be a hockey player."

Viggo nodded. "I don't expect you to be a woman—of any kind. But if I was the one that was hurt, would you not want to take care of me?"

Jamie took a breath. "Yes, of course, but I would expect you to *want* to do something once you were better, not sit home all day. It's not even about money; it's about being a contributing partner."

"So, before the job at the club came up, Emilie was going to stay home and take care of Simone and our home so I could play hockey. Was something wrong with Emilie? Was something wrong with me for wanting to provide for my family? I'm a little confused. What part of this is emasculating for you?"

Jamie looked down. "I don't know. I don't think less of Emilie for staying home but...it's not me. I can't, Viggo. What if you were a woman? Would it feel right for your man to stay home while you worked?"

"If my man was almost beaten to death and needed time to get back on his feet, yes, it absolutely would." Viggo shook his head. "You've come so far, but you've still got these perceptions of what a man is. A man shouldn't be a stay-at-home dad. A man shouldn't have sex with another man. A man shouldn't be in a relationship with a man...babe, don't you love me?"

Now Jamie was annoyed. "Of course I fucking love you! What kind of question is that?"

"The kind of question someone asks the person they want to spend the rest of their life with when that person is being a dipshit."

They glared at each other until Jamie finally chuckled. "Fine. Yes, I love you. Yes, if roles were reversed I would take care of you. And yes, I'll take time to heal before I freak out. Happy?"

"Only if you mean it and you're not going to silently agonize while pretending everything is fine."

"My wrist was smashed into eight pieces," he said softly. "I don't know if I'll ever be able to hold a hockey stick again. I just found out my kidneys have shut down. I had an ugly word literally carved into my skin. So, yeah, I'll be agonizing over everything. But not whether or not you'll take care of me—I already know that."

Viggo leaned over and kissed him, letting his lips linger on Jamie's for the first time in weeks. It felt so good to touch him he let out an involuntary moan of pleasure.

"Miss me, big guy?" Jamie whispered, looking up at him, his dark eyes gleaming.

"You have no idea." Viggo ran his hand over Jamie's bald head, gently fingering the scabs and bruises.

"Viggo?" The vulnerability in Jamie's eyes tugged at Viggo's heart.

"Yeah?"

"How bad is it?"

"What?"

"My head."

He shrugged. "You look like a guy who shaved his head—but you weren't very good with the razor."

Jamie looked down. "You can't possibly be attracted to me right now."

Viggo burst out laughing. "Jamie, I would be attracted to you covered in dog shit. You were violently attacked...you think I don't see past the bruises and the cast and all that? In a few months, you'll be healthy, your hair will grow back and we're going to move on, together."

"We have to talk about that."

Viggo groaned. "Now what?"

"I don't know what's going to happen, but I'm still part of the team here in Ottawa. This is also closer to where my parents are. My mom is probably going to have to take care of me for a while—don't look at me like that! This would be the same even if you were a woman with a job that required travel. I'm going to need full-time care for at least a month or two and you can't do it. I'll either be here or in Kingston and you have to go back to Vegas."

"It's short-term," Viggo said grudgingly.

"Most likely we're going to be apart until hockey season is over," he said gently.

"No." Viggo shook his head. "Not happening. As soon as you get permission to travel and are feeling a little better, in four or five weeks, you'll come to Vegas. And if you have to go back and forth, then so will I."

"You have to focus on hockey," Jamie reminded him. "One of us has to work."

"You're still getting paid."

"I know, but I'm trying to be practical. You can't give up your career because I might need long-term care."

"Jamie." Viggo put his hands on his hips. "Would you listen to yourself? I keep repeating myself, but let's do this one more time... If you were a woman, and you'd been hurt like this, or you had cancer or some other awful thing that required a lot of care, what do you think would happen?"

"My mother would help because you'd *still* have to work!"

"Yes, but it's my responsibility to take care of you. Just as it's your responsibility to take care of me if I need it. Don't you get that yet?!" With a grunt, he turned towards the door. "I need to get some air, all right? I'll be back."

"Viggo..."

"I'm not mad," Viggo said over his shoulder. "I just need to clear my head."

"Shit." Jamie rested back against the pillows with a grunt. He was already going stir-crazy but he wasn't even strong enough to take a piss on his own yet. His ribs hurt like a bitch and the slightest movement made his wrist throb. He essentially ached all over and though he'd insisted on cutting back on the pain medicine, he still needed it at night in order to sleep.

Viggo had been by his side nonstop and he felt guilty for arguing with him. It wasn't Viggo's fault this had happened but Jamie didn't know how to behave with him sometimes. He wasn't attracted to any other men, but he was in love with and about to explore a serious, permanent relationship with one.

That meant he was gay, didn't it? Or bisexual? It was so damn complicated. He now recognized he'd been attracted to Dante the night they'd had their threesome with Becca, but he hadn't acted on it because he'd known Dante most likely wouldn't have been interested. So did that mean he *was* attracted to other men? And what did that mean going forward?

It was confusing and every time he tried to work through it he felt the same twinges of fear. He had to stop getting irritated with Viggo whenever he said something alluding to their future together because he'd already tried breaking things off and knew that was a futile endeavor. He loved the big lug, and somehow, he had to make peace with it. It was just so hard with everything going on, and they absolutely had to talk about money and finances; that wasn't something Jamie would bend on.

"Son?"

His father's voice startled him and Jamie turned his head in surprise. He hadn't seen him since before the attack and having him standing a few feet away now was something of a shock. He'd been going over in his head what he would say to his father and hadn't yet come up with an explanation for what had happened, so now he just stared at him.

"Uh, hey, Dad."

"Damn, son." His father looked sad and Jamie self-consciously reached up to run his hand over his bald head.

"I'm a pretty ugly bald guy, huh?"

"No." His father shook his head. "You're a pretty beat-up bald guy."

"That too."

"I, uh, sorry I didn't come before now. I wasn't sure how to handle the press and everything. It's been a circus and I didn't want to say the wrong thing."

"About what?" Jamie frowned. "I was almost beaten to death—what is there to say about that?"

"Just the other questions, you know, about..."

"About me being gay?" Jamie met his father's eyes. "Dad, I'm bisexual but I didn't realize it until this happened..."

"You didn't?" James Teller looked confused.

"I'm sorry if this is a disappointment to you and—"

"Wait, no." He held up a hand and then rubbed it down his face. "I knew you would think that—that I'm ashamed or disappointed. I'm not. I don't give a shit about that kind of thing. You should know me better than that. I'm just *confused*. You're 27 and not that long ago you were engaged to this gorgeous female movie star...before her there were quite a few great gals. We've been out together and I've seen you chase skirts, both literally and figuratively. As your father, I feel a little betrayed, like you were purposely duping me, and that's what I couldn't handle. Not your ultimate choice."

"I didn't," Jamie whispered. "I swear to you, I didn't. I still love women—I just fell *in love* with this particular guy. I didn't even realize it. I've been in some threesomes and that's how it started, with him and his wife—"

"He's married?!" Now James looked annoyed and Jamie quickly shook his head.

"Yeah, but it's not what you think. It's complicated. I'll tell you everything, I promise, but he's going to be back any minute and I need you to give him a chance. Please, Dad? He's an amazing guy."

"Is he cheating on his wife?"

"No. She knows about us and is encouraging our relationship. They have a kid together, and that makes it complicated, but she's great. In fact, she called me this morning, to check on me. He's here with her blessing."

James slowly nodded. "Your mother and sister really like him."

"What about Dwight? He hasn't come either."

"He wouldn't come until...he's been bombarded at work with the press trying to get a statement so he's hiding out at home."

"I'm sorry this has affected everyone...we're going to try to keep things private going forward but—"

"No." James looked at him firmly. "How would you have felt if Rachel decided to make you her "secret" so the press wouldn't hound you guys? Wouldn't you have felt cheap, used? If you love this man enough to be talking about a relationship, don't do that to him or to yourself. If you love him, show it. Be proud of who you are and what you have with him. True love means something."

"I know. I just... Fuck, Dad, look at what they did to me! For no reason, other than the fact that I fell in love with a guy!"

"I know. The world, unfortunately, will always have people like that. Hitler created his own brand of hate in the 40s and we still see it now—especially in the LGBTQ community... The only way to fight it is to stand up proud and let the world know you're not doing anything wrong."

Jamie stared at his father in awe and disbelief; he'd had no idea his father was this enlightened and he was damn proud to be his son.

# CHAPTER 27

After so many days of not leaving Jamie's side, Viggo hadn't been aware of what a media circus the lobby of the hospital had become. Though the others on the team had told him what was going on, he hadn't realized how bad it was. So when he stepped out of the elevators on his way outside to take a walk and was immediately mobbed by cameras and reporters, he blinked in surprise. Momentarily caught off guard, he was surrounded before he knew it, microphones and cameras in his face. It took him a few seconds to get acclimated and finally his attitude kicked in and he scowled.

"Excuse me!" It always sounded like a roar when he used his deepest voice and the crowd seemed to grow quieter. "If you want any type of statement, you need to behave like civilized human beings and take a few steps back. I'll talk to you, but not if you're going to cage me in like an animal."

At first no one moved and the questions continued, but as Viggo planted his feet and folded his arms across his massive chest, a scowl of disapproval on his face, they slowly began to settle down. The two men with the biggest cameras took several steps back and eventually everyone grew quiet.

"Will you answer some questions, Viggo?" a tall man with glasses asked.

"I'll answer anything you want as long as you remain respectful and talk one at a time. This is my life, not a circus, and to be fair, English is my second language so it's difficult for me to concentrate when you all speak at once."

Someone nodded. "Viggo, are you and Jamie Teller lovers?"

He sighed. Not because he didn't want to answer, but because he didn't want to expose Jamie to anymore hurt. The alternative, however, was to lie and if they were going to be together—and he was going to do everything in his power to make that happen—they would undoubtedly get caught in that kind of lie.

"I love him," he said finally. "And he loves me."

The questions began in earnest again and he simply stared, refusing to speak until they stopped. He spotted Zakk out of the corner of his eye, moving towards the crowd briskly, and he smiled to himself; they would definitely get out of the way for Zakk.

"Does your wife know?" someone called out.

"Okay, let's set a few ground rules," he said. "My wife is off-limits in this conversation. She's aware of my relationship with Jamie and we're all close friends. Since she isn't here, I don't feel right answering questions for her."

"How long has your relationship with Jamie been going on?"

"We've been friends for a while, but we didn't develop feelings for each other until recently." He glanced at Zakk gratefully as he stepped up behind him.

"Is it true an ugly word was carved into his back?"

Viggo's lips tightened and he took a steadying breath. "Yes, and I'm going to say something about this: I've always been bisexual. I'm not ashamed of it, I'm not hiding it, and I'm not going to lie about it. I've had both men and women as lovers all of my adult life. Jamie, on the other hand, has not."

"What about that video of him and Dante Lamonte?!"

With his hand tightly wrapped around Becca's, Dante appeared as if by magic and walked right through the middle of the crowd, holding up a hand as the press went nuts again. Questions started coming one after the other and flashbulbs practically blinded them. Becca was pressed close to Dante's side but she held her head high as she looked out at the sea of reporters.

"The same rules apply to me if you want a statement," he said. Once again, it took a little while, but the crowd eventually grew quiet. In the meantime, Cody, Coach Barnett and Toli had all pushed in behind Viggo in a show of support.

"As you know," Dante said once it was quiet, "I've sown plenty of oats in my day. I'm not bragging or complaining; it's a fact and I'm not particularly concerned with who knows. When Becca and I started dating, we wanted to explore different sexual adventures before we got serious. We ran into Jamie at that club in New York and spent an evening together. Jamie and I were not *together*, in the sense that everyone seems to think. We were both with Becca—the video was edited to make it look like something it wasn't. That being said, I'm not particularly interested in your interpretations or judgements. We were three consenting adults who had sex and were recorded doing so without our permission. As a result of that, we sued the owners and Becca now owns Club Inferno. It has never been our intention to broadcast what goes on behind closed doors—we're married and planning to start a family—but what happened to Jamie last week was something else entirely.

"That wasn't just a crime, but something that should never happen to *anyone*. Our sexual encounter was one night of fun, nothing more. If you choose to turn it into something ugly, it would be both untrue and unethical, but I have no control over your choices. I only control what I do, and I choose to live without judgement, without shame, and most of all, without hate. What Becca, Jamie and I did didn't hurt anyone. The relationship that Viggo and Jamie have doesn't hurt anyone either. At some point, we have to let go of what we consider right and wrong in the world of love. So what if two men love each other? Or two women? Or a man and a woman? As long as everyone is old enough and healthy enough to give consent, what harm is there in people loving each other and wanting to be together?

"What those men did to Jamie was far more disgusting than anything two people in love do. Those are the men you should be hounding and asking difficult questions of. Those are the men who should be ashamed, not me, not my wife, and certainly not Jamie. He was a *victim*. If any of you here print something distasteful about him or his relationship with Viggo or me, I promise you that it will be my mission to make sure no professional sports team in North America has anything to do with you or the paper you represent."

"Is that a threat, Dante?"

Dante chuckled. "No, my friend. I just told you—it's a promise."

"Viggo, can you update us on Jamie's condition?"

Viggo glanced at Dante gratefully and stepped forward. "He's healing, but there were some unexpected internal injuries we're dealing with now."

"What about the branding on his back? What's he going to do about that?"

"You'll have to ask him," Viggo said. "Personally, I would have 'Fuck you, skinheads' tattooed on top of it, but Jamie isn't that kind of man. He's much more forgiving than I would be. One of many reasons I love him."

More questions came and Viggo answered them as best he could. It was exhausting, but he refused to back down or feel ashamed.

"Look," he said after he'd been answering questions for nearly 20 minutes. "This is what I'm going to end with: You can't help who you fall in love with. I know Jamie didn't want to fall in love with me. I was in a difficult situation with my marriage, but I wasn't looking either; it just happened. As a professional athlete, being in a relationship with someone of the same sex is an uphill battle. It's not fair, but it's reality, so those of us that have lived it do the best we can. Jamie didn't live it. Jamie wasn't, and still isn't, some closet homosexual. He's a man who wound up falling in love with another man—the only man he's ever been involved with. Not everything needs a label. The only label it should have is *love*. I love him and he loves me. That's it. Those men not only tried to take his life, their goal was to also take away his greatest love—hockey. They smashed his wrist with a sledgehammer, while telling him he's not man enough to play a sport like hockey. Well, I have news for you—he *is* man enough because he has and he does. He currently has a five-year contract that proves it. Even if he can't ever play another day, this is his ninth season as a professional hockey player—his record speaks for itself.

"As for this other stuff..." He frowned. "He almost *died*. I've been at his side for four days and he's still not out of the woods. They hurt him physically, emotionally and, most likely, professionally. His wrist was broken into *eight pieces*. That's going to leave an emotional scar just as disturbing as that ugly word on his back. I implore everyone who sees this—please stop the hate. If you have a moral issue with same-sex relationships, it's your prerogative not to have one, but that doesn't mean you have to hate people who do. Open your hearts and let go of hate—it would go a long way towards making the world a better place. Thank you."

He stepped back and felt Zakk's hand on his shoulder. "Let's go back inside," Zakk whispered.

Viggo nodded. "Yeah." He followed his friends inside, where security kept out the press. He leaned against the wall in the waiting room and closed his eyes.

"You okay, my friend?" Dante eyed him. "You look exhausted."

"It's been a rough few days."

"What you said was beautiful," Becca whispered, reaching out to wrap her arms around him. "You're one of the strongest, most wonderful men I've ever known."

"Thank you." He kissed the top of her head. "I don't feel very strong right now."

"That's okay," Zakk said gently. "We'll hold you up until you're ready to take on the world again."

"Thanks." He sighed. "I should get back to Jamie..."

"Everything okay?" Dante asked as they walked towards the elevator banks.

"He's struggling," Viggo admitted. "As hard as this has been on me, it's been a hundred times harder on him. Chances are, his hockey career is over. His kidneys are failing and the thought of dialysis for the rest of his life is daunting. The idea that I might have to support him financially is more than he can stand. And our relationship is one thing I can't help him with—he has to come to terms with what it means for us to be together on his own."

"You want me to talk to him?" Zakk asked.

"No." Viggo smiled faintly. "When I said Jamie isn't gay—that wasn't some bullshit I made up for the media. It's the truth. He's just a guy who fell in love with another guy and is completely unprepared to deal with it. Imagine if you woke up one day and realized you were in love with a guy but had never acknowledged that kind of attraction before. How would you handle it?"

"Jamie's bisexual. He may never have admitted it, but I always kind of had a feeling—I'm not sure why."

"Maybe *you* did, but Jamie never recognized it—never gave it a name—and now it's overwhelming."

Zakk nodded. "And that's why he needs his friends just as much as he needs you. The rest of us are going to be there for both of you and eventually he's going to realize it's okay. It's okay to be different. It's not easy, but it's okay."

# CHAPTER 28

Viggo wasn't sure what to expect when he got back to Jamie's room, but the tall, broad-shouldered man holding his hand wasn't it. He paused for a moment, caught off guard, but as the man turned, he had to smile. Jamie looked so much like his father, there was no doubt they were related. He held out his hand as he approached.

"You must be Jamie's father."

"And you're Viggo." James shook his hand. "It's nice to meet you. Jamie's told me a bit about you since I got here."

"I've heard a lot about you as well," Viggo nodded. He looked down at Jamie who met his gaze and mouthed, "I'm sorry." Viggo just winked and turned back to his father.

"How much longer will you be able to stay?"

Viggo sighed. "I should fly home soon. I need to talk to Coach about my hand. The doctors here think I should take two weeks off."

"You need to go so you can skate with the team and be ready," Jamie said quietly.

"Please don't start this," Viggo muttered under his breath.

"I'm going to leave you two for a minute," James said, recognizing the uneasy tone between them and making a hasty exit.

"No, listen." Jamie held out his hand. "I'm sorry I've been a dick—it's not about us specifically. I would feel this way no matter who I was in a relationship with. I don't want to rely on someone else for something this serious. I hate the idea of my lover—man or woman—taking care of me to this extent. This isn't like when I was puking and you helped me to the bathroom. I can't even wipe my ass, man, and I don't want my mom to do it either. I want to go to a rehab center—" Viggo started to protest but Jamie held up his hand. "Please, just listen."

Viggo grunted but nodded.

"I don't want to be a burden on *anyone* I love. I'm 27, not 97. If I can work it out with the insurance and the team, and all the medical logistics, I'll find a place in Vegas. I'm willing to compromise, but not on this: Until I'm able to take care of my basic bodily functions, I want doctors and nurses taking care of me. Once I'm past that, I'll come home, either to you or my mother, depending on the insurance and how I'm doing. Can you live with this?"

Viggo slowly nodded. "I'm willing to do anything you need, but if this is what you really want, then yeah, I can."

"Come on—my mom shouldn't wipe my ass. It's gross." He made a face. "You want your mom wiping yours?"

Viggo wrinkled his nose. "Nah, you're right. We can afford help, so there's no need for that."

"If I can't work it out with the insurance so I can be in Vegas, I'll only stay in a facility like that short-term, I promise. Maybe a month. If I'm not well enough to take care of basic stuff after a month, we'll come back to this conversation."

"I love you, Jamie." Viggo sat on the chair next to the bed and rested his head on Jamie's hip since his ribs hurt too much to put any weight on his chest. "I can't stand the thought of us being apart while you're going through this—I need to be here for you."

"We'll be okay," Jamie whispered, stroking his hair. "I'm scared to death that I'm not going to get better, but as far as you and I go, I know you're there for me."

"I guess I should tell you I gave an impromptu press conference."

Jamie made a face. "What did you say?"

"I hope it winds up on the news somewhere so you can listen. I don't think I can repeat it accurately." He paused. "And Dante spoke as well. He's a good friend, Jamie."

"I know." Jamie listened with a faint smile as Viggo recounted his encounter with the press.

DANTE KNOCKED on the door later that day and Jamie waved him in with a smile.

"Hey!"

"How are you feeling?"

"Like someone beat the crap out of me," he chuckled.

"Jamie, how much do you remember of the night you were attacked?"

He frowned. "Not much. Why?"

"There's a woman downstairs. She's been trying to see you for two days. We've sent her away but today she looks as though she's been beaten, and Becca feels she's legit. I offered to allow her to write you a note." He handed him a piece of paper.

Jamie opened it curiously.

*Jamie, I need to see you. My court date is tomorrow and I can't even afford a motel room to take a shower. Please help me. -Misty*

He sighed. "Yeah, send her up."

"You're sure?"

"Can you stay? Just in case? I mean, I think she was a victim that night too, but I'm not up to taking any chances."

"Of course." Dante left and came back 10 minutes later with Misty shuffling in behind him.

Jamie had to close his mouth to hide his shock. He'd never seen her look so terrible. Her long, thick hair was matted and greasy and she had two black eyes. Her clothes were torn and dirty, fingernails broken, and even her sneakers had holes in them.

"Oh, Jamie, I'm so sorry!" Tears splashed down her cheeks as she approached him.

"Did you set me up, Misty?" he asked quietly. "Tell me the truth."

"No!" she whispered, shaking her head vehemently. "I would never—you're my friend! I didn't want to involve you, I tried not to, but...they took my son. They took Chance. My ex, he used to be one of them, part of their stupid group of Aryan assholes, but when I got pregnant he stopped drinking and everything was really good for a while. About 18 months ago, Trent was in a car accident and couldn't work. I had to start stripping to pay the bills and he was so jealous and depressed he started drinking again. That's when he started hitting me. I left him but with the help of his stupid friends, he made the courts believe I'm an unfit mother. He got custody of Chance and I've been fighting to get him back for a year, but with Jill's father being the judge, they've managed to stop me. Since those guys got arrested for what they did to you, Collin's father has been in constant contact with Jill's father and last night a couple of guys showed up at the club and beat me up. *Again*. It was my first day back to work—they won't let you work if you have black eyes—"

"Look at me." Dante's deep voice interrupted her rambling and she turned, blue eyes filled with tears. "Do you know who I am?"

She frowned slightly but nodded. "The baseball player," she whispered. "I don't know a lot about baseball...Dante something?"

"Yes. I'm Dante. Right now, the only thing Jamie is allowed to think about is getting better. If there's a problem, I'll be handling it." He fixed a look on Jamie. "Do you want me to take care of this?"

Jamie nodded wearily. "Yeah, whatever she needs."

"Jamie, I'll pay you back—"

"This isn't about money, little girl." Dante's eyes glittered as he assessed her. "This is about loyalty and friendship. Either you're with us or you're not. If you're not, and you're somehow trying to hurt Jamie, I will deliver you right back to your Aryan friends without a backwards glance. You understand me?"

"I just want to run," she whispered. "But I can't leave my son."

"You understand I have the resources to find out if you're lying? To check out every single thing you've said?"

She nodded, a tear trickling out of the corner of her eye. "If you bring me my son, I'll disappear and you'll never see me again."

"That's not how we do things in our family," Dante said with a faint smile. "Come. You are in desperate need of a shower, medical attention and food. Then I'll get someone to look into this." He cut his eyes meaningfully towards Jamie, who gave a slight nod.

"Jamie?" She turned to him uneasily, a touch of apprehension on her face, unsure what to make of the strikingly good-looking but scary as hell baseball player.

"It's okay." He reached out his hand. "Dante's family."

She put her hand in his and their eyes met. "I'm really sorry," she whispered. "I tried not to involve you...but they took Chance from Trent and I'm afraid they'll hurt him."

"Go with Dante," he said gently. "As long as you're telling the truth, you have nothing to worry about."

"Okay." She nodded.

"What was all that?" Viggo asked, coming back into the room as Dante and Misty left.

"Long story."

"I was listening outside...who is she to you?" Viggo's voice was calm but the twitch in his cheek belied his annoyance.

Jamie felt a smile tugging the corner of his mouth as he looked up. "Is that a twinge of jealousy, Mr. Sjoberg?"

"No!" he growled in response, though his eyes darkened. "But I'm guessing you slept with her."

"You and I agreed I would date while we were apart," Jamie said gently. "She came on to me at a party and when I tried to say no, she whispered in my ear that if I didn't do her, one of those other guys would force her to."

"They were forcing her to have sex? In exchange for what?"

"To get an hour of time with her son."

"She had to sleep with all of them?"

"The leader of the group, Collin, seemed to be in charge of who and when."

"The blond with the swastika tattoo?" Viggo asked suddenly.

Jamie narrowed his eyes. "How do you know about the tattoo?"

Viggo felt a flush creep up his neck. "Let's just say Chains had a hand in making sure they were caught."

"Is there something you need to tell me?"

"How squeamish are you?"

Jamie chuckled. "If he chopped them up into little pieces, I might be a little squeamish..." Suddenly he frowned. "He didn't, did he?!"

Now Viggo chuckled. "No. They're in jail. But I have something to show you. I don't know how you feel about...revenge. Vigilante justice. That sort of thing. Knowing you to be the gentle soul that you are, Chains and I thought perhaps we should keep this from you, but I've reconsidered. You're a grown man, and you've made it clear I shouldn't try to protect you from things. So, I can show you what was done, I can tell you, or we can leave it like this—you know revenge was served but you don't know the details."

Jamie knitted his brows thoughtfully. He didn't like the idea of revenge or vigilante justice, but what those men had done to him went beyond a simple beating. It had been a cruel, brutal attack meant to kill him, or at the very least end his career and publicly shame him. It didn't sit well with him, and though he hated violence, as he looked down at the cast on his wrist and imagined what his back looked like, he felt anger surge through him.

"I need you to do something for me first," he said quietly.

"Of course. Anything."

"Take a picture of my back."

"What? No!" Viggo shook his head.

"You just said you'd do anything for me!" Jamie protested in exasperation.

"It serves no purpose! You can have the scars lasered off or covered with tattoos, or—"

"And I plan to," Jamie interrupted patiently. "But I need to see everything they did to me before I see what was done to them."

Viggo sighed. "I'm not comfortable lifting you into a sitting position and then leaving you to sit up long enough for me to take a picture."

"I could help," Zakk said, standing in the doorway. His eyes were dark and filled with a strange combination of anger and emotion. "I apologize for eavesdropping, but I want to see too; I want that image, whatever it is, burned into my brain so when we sit in a courtroom with those motherfuckers, I can imagine every way I want to hurt them."

Viggo smiled faintly. "When you see what I've got, you won't feel that need anymore." He put his phone in his pocket and lowered the rail on one side of the bed. Zakk moved to the other side and together they helped Jamie into a sitting position. He was able to move his legs so they hung over the side of the bed and Zakk sat beside him.

"Can you sit up?"

Jamie started to nod but began lilting to one side. Zakk easily slid an arm around his waist, holding him up. Jamie felt an unfamiliar rush of shame at his friend's touch and lowered his eyes.

"I'm okay with touching you," Zakk said in a light, teasing tone. "We've been friends for three years and you've never put the moves on me. You think I'm worried about it now that I can outrun you?"

Jamie had never been more grateful for Zakk's friendship, but instead of letting it show, he narrowed his eyes playfully. "Just admit how broken-hearted you are that I have a boyfriend now."

Zakk's eyes filled with humor and the look of pleasure on Viggo's face made the discomfort disappear as they all chuckled.

"Relax." Viggo's touch on Jamie's shoulders was soothing. "I'm going to have to untie the gown and remove a few of the bandages."

"Not without me, you're not!" Brenda, the nurse who'd been with Jamie every day since he'd arrived, gave them a dirty look. "Move your hands, you big oaf! I don't know what the three of you have gotten into, but I'll take care of this. You take your pictures." She worked gently but efficiently, removing the bandages that were still covering the deeper wounds. "Ahhh, these are healing well," she said after a moment. "From the perspective of the skin, Jamie, these are going to heal nicely. I'm sure a year from now, after you've done whatever you're going to do to cover them, you won't even know they're there."

"I'll know," Jamie whispered softly.

Viggo snapped a few pictures, his stomach churning as he looked.

"I need to look too," Zakk said after a moment. "I want to see the real thing. I want to remember what hate looks like so it never, ever touches anyone near me again, as long as I'm around to stop it."

Jamie felt emotion building in his chest, and willed himself not to cry, not in front of Zakk. With Viggo or his parents it was different, but he hated showing weakness to his friends.

"Everyone should see this," Brenda snarled, her face contorting angrily. "I hate those men right now. I don't hate anyone, but I hate those men."

"I'd like a 'fuck-you' picture," Jamie whispered.

"A what?" Viggo asked, but Zakk was smiling.

"Yeah? You want me to rally the troops? We have to hurry 'cause we're leaving for the airport in about 15 minutes."

Jamie couldn't help but nod. "Yes. Please."

"Lie back," Brenda said. "It'll take a few minutes to get everyone in here."

"I'll handle it. Be right back." Zakk left the room and Jamie relaxed against the pillows, realizing how exhausting it had been to sit up.

"I know you're tired." Brenda touched his arm. "But the fact you sat up that long is really good news. Dr. Levesque probably won't be pleased we did this without his permission, so let's not tell him, okay?"

Jamie nodded. "Okay."

"You want to see it now?" Viggo asked, holding out the phone.

"Nope. I want to wait until my friends are here. Is my mom nearby?"

"Yes, and Maddie too."

"Will you text them?"

"Of course."

## CHAPTER 29

Five minutes later, Brenda was scurrying around nervously, peeking out the door and ushering in Jamie's friends.

"This is morbid, no?" Vladimir asked Toli in Russian, frowning.

"This is him taking back his pride, with the help of his friends," Toli responded.

Vlad nodded. "I would like just five minutes alone with those bastards."

Toli squeezed his shoulder. "So would we all."

Zakk and Brenda got Jamie into a sitting position again, and his friends gathered around him. It was a large, eclectic group, but the smiles on their faces spoke volumes. Coach Barnett and Chains had already returned to Las Vegas, but they seemed to be present in spirit.

As Brenda raised the first of several phones with which she would be taking a picture, the entire group raised their middle fingers. She smiled as she snapped each shot. Even though Jamie couldn't twist his body enough to have his face in the picture, he leaned his head on Viggo's arm, his heart so full of love at that moment he barely remembered what they were doing or why.

"Okay, playtime is over." Dr. Levesque came into the room with a stern look on his face, but there was a faint smile threatening to emerge. He narrowed his eyes. "I can have you all thrown out, you know."

"Doc, please—" Jamie began worriedly.

He held up a hand. "Relax, son. I'm joking. This is totally against hospital protocol, so you all need to make a quick exit, but I see what you've done and I understand. Now all of you—out!"

Everyone said hasty goodbyes, reaching out to pat Jamie's head or manage a quick fist bump. Then it was just Jamie, Viggo, Dr. Levesque and Brenda.

"I'm sorry, Doctor," she said softly.

"Sometimes what a patient needs goes beyond protocol," he said gruffly. "Now, it's time for Jamie to rest and Viggo to have his hand checked."

"But I haven't—" Jamie began.

"I don't want to—" Viggo said at the same time.

"Just stop, the two of you! You're worse than my kids. Viggo, go with Brenda and have your hand looked at by the orthopedist. Jamie, lie back and shut up."

"Yes, sir." Jamie widened his eyes but was laughing as he glanced at Viggo, who was holding his hands up in mock surrender.

"So." Dr. Levesque pulled out a clipboard and studied some papers carefully. "I've been in touch with a colleague from Harvard, who happens to live in Vegas now. There's a rehab facility he's affiliated with and he said they can get you in. I don't think you're strong enough to travel yet, so it will be at least two weeks before I can release you. However, I have some good news."

"Yeah?" Jamie looked up.

"It's slight, but there is improvement in kidney function. You're up to 25% in one and 40% in the other."

"Is this good?"

"I'm pleased. Although there's a chance this is merely a positive reaction to the dialysis, I think there's a very good chance that function is returning."

"Thank God," Jamie whispered.

"I didn't want to say that in front of everyone, because you may not want to get their hopes up, but I wanted to let you know. I know what it's like to have people making decisions for you, and it seems that kind of thing bothers you."

Jamie nodded. "Yeah. I mean, I want Viggo involved, but I need to be able to take care of myself."

"Well, assuming you continue to heal at this rate, we can get you transferred to the facility in Las Vegas around mid-February."

"How long do you think I'll be there?" he asked.

"Let's see how things go, eh? Don't try to rush this, Jamie. Five days ago I thought I was going to lose you."

Jamie nodded. "Yeah, I know. Thanks, Doc."

JAMIE WAS DOZING when Dante slipped into the room and motioned to Viggo, who went to the doorway to talk to him.

"Do you know a friend of Jamie's named Josh?"

Viggo frowned. "No. Who is it?"

"He's stopped by every day and asked about him. He said he'd like to see him but understands if he's not up to it."

"Do you have a last name? Any details?"

Dante shook his head. "No, but I took a picture of him and told him I'd show Jamie."

"Show me what?" Jamie rasped from the bed, yawning as he came awake.

"It's not important," Dante said quietly. "We can—"

"Come on, you guys, stop treating me like a delicate flower," Jamie rubbed a fist across his eyes. "What were you going to show me?"

"Do you have a friend named Josh?" Viggo asked, bringing Dante's phone to him and holding it out.

Jamie grinned. "Yeah—is he here?"

"He is," Dante nodded. "Said he would wait. He didn't want you to think he hadn't checked on you."

"Send him up, please," Jamie said.

"I'll get him." Dante disappeared out the door and Viggo frowned. "Who is he?" he asked. "A teammate?"

"No." Jamie smiled and held out his hand.

Viggo narrowed his eyes as he took it. "Why do I get the feeling I'm not going to like this?"

"Josh is gay," he said softly. "We went out a few times and—"

"This is a *boyfriend*?!" Viggo almost swallowed his tongue trying to keep his voice level.

Jamie laughed. "You're gonna be the jealous type, eh? Relax, big guy—nothing ever happened. *Nothing*. Can you please stop looking like that and act like you trust me? You didn't freak when I told you I had sex with Misty!"

Viggo breathed in deeply but nodded. "You're right. I'm sorry." He paused, a nerve in his jaw twitching slightly. "I've never been jealous before, so I'm not sure what to do about it."

Jamie was still chuckling. "It's okay. I tend to be a little jealous too, but Josh and I are just friends. He helped me deal with a lot of my shit...helped me figure out that my feelings for you don't change who I am. I can call myself bisexual, but I don't have to just because of this. He taught me that *bisexual* is just a word, but loving you is part of my soul. He's the reason I reached out the night of the attack."

Viggo met his gaze and gave him a wry smile. "I don't have to act like I trust you—I do."

A soft knock on the door made him turn and he smiled at the tall, handsome man who stuck his head in.

"Hey, Josh!" Jamie called out. "Come on in."

"How's it going?" Josh approached him and a faint scowl covered his features as he took in Jamie's pale, bruised body. "Damn, I'd like to take a stick to those motherfuckers!"

Viggo couldn't help but warm to him immediately and he held out his hand. "Viggo Sjoberg. I'd like some private time with them as well."

Josh shook his hand. "Josh LeBlanc. I've heard a lot about you—I'm glad you're here with him."

"Me, too." Viggo turned and winked at Jamie. "Look, I'll leave you two to visit and—"

"Stay," Josh said, a knowing look in his hazel eyes. "You don't know me and I'm sure you're feeling fairly overprotective right now."

Viggo swallowed. "Yeah, a bit."

"We have nothing to hide." Josh sank into the chair next to the bed and reached out to squeeze Jamie's arm. "So, how are you? Give me the real answer, not the bullshit I'm-a-tough-guy version."

Jamie laughed. "I'm definitely not a tough guy."

"Sure you are," Josh said with a grin. "Aren't all hockey players tough guys?"

Jamie playfully rolled his eyes. "Dude, we've had this conversation. We're not all goons and some of us still have teeth."

"I don't buy it," Josh deadpanned, folding his arms across his chest. "I have no proof that you have all your teeth."

Jamie gave a put-upon sigh. "Well, you're gonna have to take my word for it, eh?"

"Whatever." They chuckled quietly before Josh leaned forward, squinting slightly. "Tell me what the police said?"

Jamie sighed for real this time, shrugging slightly. "They've been charged with attempted murder with a hate crime added on. The preliminary hearing is coming up and my attorney—whom I've never met—says that it will definitely go to trial."

"How do you feel about that?"

Jamie raised his eyebrows. "They almost destroyed my life—they can rot in hell for all I care."

"That's not what I asked," Josh said gently. "How do you feel about being part of a very public trial, where your sexuality is going to be discussed, along with your past transgressions, steroid use and anything else they can find to make you look bad."

Jamie took a breath and steeled his resolve. "They can bring it. There is nothing I've ever done that makes this okay." He held out his casted arm. "I may never play hockey again. They fucking carved something evil into my skin—I'm pretty sure making a sex tape with a beautiful woman I was in love with doesn't warrant this kind of retribution. Plus, nothing I did was illegal. Not even the steroids I took; they just aren't allowed in the league. So they can bring it. They don't scare me."

"I'm proud of you," Josh said, nodding.

"As am I," Viggo said, speaking for the first time. "I've been hesitant to ask you about all that and now I feel like a fool for not trusting you to do what's right."

"Did you think I would drop the charges or something to hide my sexuality?" Jamie stared at him.

"I was thinking you've been traumatized and hurt—both emotionally and physically—and I wasn't willing to say or do anything that would upset you." Viggo looked slightly sheepish.

"Babe..." Jamie frowned.

"That's his job," Josh said gently. "As your partner and lover, his job is to support any way you might be feeling or anything he might think you need to do to get through this. As your friend, I can approach it differently."

"I guess that's true," Jamie nodded, glancing at Viggo.

"So, what can I do?" Josh asked. "Do you need anything?"

"I have what I need," Jamie's eyes never left Viggo's. "But you coming to visit means a lot. I hope you visit often."

"As often as you like."

"When Viggo has to go—"

"I'm not leaving you!" Viggo grunted.

"You have to play!" Jamie said.

"My hand is broken!" Viggo held it up, pointing to the bandage.

Jamie made a face. "The doctor said it's a hairline fracture and it'll be fine in a couple of weeks."

"In a couple of weeks, I'll go back."

"Viggo..."

"Jamie..."

They glared at each other until Josh snickered. "Sorry," he covered his mouth. "Had a tickle in my throat."

Jamie laughed. "Yeah, right." He glanced at Viggo. "Don't you think Joe and Josh would make a good couple?"

Viggo chuckled. "That could be arranged."

Josh groaned.

# CHAPTER 30

It was several hours before Viggo and Jamie had a chance to be alone again. The Sidewinders had a game tomorrow and the guys who'd come to Ottawa had left. Viggo was reluctant to go, but he was only staying another day. The team doctors were anxious to look at his hand and determine how long until he could play.

"I hate leaving you," he admitted, wrapping his uninjured hand around Jamie's.

"It's just two weeks," Jamie said. "And there's a road trip, isn't there?"

Viggo nodded. "East Coast."

"If everything goes well, I can try to arrange it so that I arrive right after you get home. You'll barely miss me."

"Like hell!" Viggo grunted. He leaned over and his mouth hovered over Jamie's. "I need to touch you," was all he said.

"Me, too." Jamie closed his eyes as Viggo's lips claimed his. It was sweet, tender, holding the gentle promise of so much to come. He opened his mouth slightly, letting the tip of his tongue touch Viggo's. Though they didn't intend for it to become heated, their mouths locked together instantly.

When Viggo brought his hand up to cup Jamie's cheek, an inadvertent moan left him, his tongue snaking in to grip Viggo's possessively. They lost track of time, kissing as if the world around them didn't exist, but it was Viggo who finally pulled away, one hand traveling to Jamie's groin, where his erection was tenting the bedsheets.

"I guess there's one part of me that's not broken," Jamie smirked, glancing down.

"Not at all." Viggo leaned over and kissed the tip, right through the sheets, mischief in his eyes. "Soon, lover—I'll have that perfect cock in my mouth again soon."

"Not soon enough," was all Jamie said. They pressed their foreheads together, looking into each other's eyes. "You never showed me the pictures of my back, babe."

Viggo moved away reluctantly but nodded. "Yeah, okay." He pulled out his phone, found the picture of the whole group and handed it to him.

Jamie smiled at the picture, all of their middle fingers in the air, lessening the blow of the reality of his back. He took a breath and scrolled back a few pictures, knowing the close-up was there. He swallowed, taking in the scabbed over skin, the ugly discoloration and dried blood. Though he'd had sponge baths, he hadn't had a real shower yet so there were still remnants of the horrible ordeal.

*FAGGOT*. The word burned into his eyes and he fought the emotion welling up inside of him yet again.

"You're not, you know," Viggo whispered, obviously as emotional as Jamie.

"I don't give a fuck," Jamie whispered back harshly, tears stinging his eyes. "If it means I get to have you, they can call me anything they want."

"No, they can't—I won't allow it. You're not. You're you. I'm me. We love each other. Who the fuck are they to label us? I won't have it!" His voice broke and Jamie reached out with his good arm to loop it around Viggo's neck and pull him closer.

"I love you," he whispered in his ear. "I don't care who knows it. I don't care what they call us."

"I do," Viggo whispered back. "I've been bisexual all my life and I'm tired—tired of being different, tired of having a name other than Viggo, tired of explaining that I love both men and women, so fucking tired. There's a thing now —a terminology referred to as 'gay for you'. It's ludicrous. It means that you're only gay for one specific person, as if that somehow makes a man loving a man easier to swallow. You know, like saying, well, I wouldn't be gay if it wasn't for you...fuck that. *Fuck them.* I'm not gay for you and you're not fucking gay for me. We're just Viggo and Jamie, yeah? We're just us. In a few years, when my hockey career is winding down, that's going to be my life's work. I want to change the perception, change the way people think. I want a better world for my daughter...for all of us. Before I die, I want it to be okay to be gay or bi or transgender. I don't know how I'll do it, but that's my goal. Are you in?"

"God, yes." Jamie didn't hold back his tears anymore, nuzzling his bare head against Viggo's neck.

"I love you."

"I fucking love you too."

ONCE VIGGO LEFT, Jamie, Dante and Brenda got into a little routine. Dante would work out in the morning while Brenda tended to Jamie's needs, including sponge baths, changing bandages and making him walk a few steps at a time. Then the three of them would hang out in between her rounds with other patients. Jamie and Dante played cards most days, mostly to kill the monotony, but also to force him to think and concentrate. Though it was mild, the doctors were keeping an eye on his concussion because he'd had another one just a few months before. He hadn't had headaches or nausea this time but the doctors were watching closely.

A week after Viggo had left, Dante came in looking more serious than usual and Jamie glanced up with concern.

"What's going on?"

"I'm worried about the situation with Misty. I need you to tell me how far I should go to help her."

"Is her story legit?"

"Oh, yes. A much more serious situation than I'd anticipated. Her ex-husband is a punk and another one of those Aryan skinhead types. He's tightly immersed in that little brotherhood of assholes, and I'll have to call in some favors to get the boy."

Jamie frowned. "She's my friend. When I had no one else to talk to, she was there, telling me it was okay. She's the reason I met Josh...and it's obvious they've been hurting her too. How much would it cost to get her and her son out of Canada?"

Dante grimaced. "It's not the money, but the legalities. She can come to the U.S. for a visit, but the child doesn't have a passport. We would have to sneak him into the country and if the father found out, he could cause a lot of trouble. For all of us."

"I can't just leave her here."

"I don't believe they'll hurt the boy. I think we have to take her to Vegas and get her settled—a job, a stable life, maybe even get her in school. Then we can hire lawyers to help her get custody, or at least visitations."

Jamie sighed. "I don't know if she'll leave him."

"She has no choice. Those men are going to kill her to try to get to you."

Jamie waved a hand. "Then do what needs to be done. Tell her I'll take care of her."

"Is there something romantic between you?" Dante asked carefully.

Jamie shook his head. "No. I've slept with her, but that was me trying to prove I was still a regular guy and her doing what she hoped would make those assholes happy. I can pay you back—"

Dante held up a hand. "Not a dime. We handle our business as a family. If she's your friend, then she's family as well."

Jamie squinted slightly. "You feel guilty, don't you? You think this is your fault, that if you hadn't asked me to get traded instead of Becca resigning, this wouldn't have happened."

"This wouldn't have happened in Vegas because you wouldn't have been alone. You and Viggo wouldn't have been making out in a hallway—you would have been in the privacy of your home—and you would have had the protection of the team and your friends."

"I'm not with the team or my friends 24/7," Jamie reminded him gently. "I was alone a lot in Vegas too."

"It was different," Dante ground out, setting his jaw. "You were never truly alone in Vegas, but here they knew they could get to you."

Jamie shook his head. "It's done, Dante. Agonizing doesn't help anyone, least of all me."

Dante met his gaze. "Becca hasn't slept well since it happened. She may never forgive herself, and this is something I can't fix. I agonize because what they did to you was reprehensible—and how it's affected my wife is not acceptable. We're trying to get pregnant and I don't want this for her. I definitely didn't want it for you."

"I'm okay," Jamie said softly. "I'm getting better and, even though I'm still getting a grip on my sexuality, I'm in love. Really, truly in love. I'd let them do this to me a hundred times over if it meant having Viggo's love."

"That should never be the trade-off for love, my friend."

THE MOVE to the rehab facility was done discreetly, with Lonnie Finch once again sending a chartered plane. Dante, Jamie, and Misty flew to Las Vegas from Ottawa, completely under the radar. No one knew Jamie had left Canada and he was whisked straight from the airport to the care center, where Viggo was already waiting. It had been a month since Jamie had been attacked and he was finally able to walk without assistance for short distances. He got up from the wheelchair they'd used to take him to his room and walked slowly but steadily straight into Viggo's arms. They kissed gently, aware that some of the staff as well as Dante, Becca, Emilie and Misty were watching.

"I missed you," Viggo said quietly.

"Back atcha." Jamie smiled and allowed the nurses to help him into bed.

"We have something for you," Dante said once Jamie was settled.

"I know you're going to be unhappy about this," Becca said, sitting on the edge of the bed. "But this is more for me than you, so I hope you'll accept it graciously."

"I don't need money, guys," Jamie said gently. "I have plenty and Viggo—"

"This isn't actual money," Becca said. "In fact, I want money from you."

Now Jamie was confused and with a frown he took the envelope she proffered. He opened it and had to read the papers twice. He blinked and finally looked up. "I don't understand," he said. "You're selling me 25% of Club Inferno? For a ridiculous amount of money?"

Becca ignored him. "Here's the thing... Dante won the club and gave it to me so that I would never have to worry about money, or feel dependent on him. He wanted me to have the same power he has, independent of him, so that we would always be equals. This is me giving you a portion of my independence because you took the fall for me. I should have left the Sidewinders, not you. I married a millionaire—I didn't need that job, but you did."

"Becca, I can't—"

"I would have just *given* you the shares," she interrupted. "But legally that could have gotten complicated, so we decided to do it this way. You should have your lawyer look at it but you'll see that you get a quarter of everything the club makes. It's already extremely profitable—the ledgers since it opened are included and they show that you'll make a nice profit each month for doing nothing."

He shook his head. "I can't just take part ownership and do nothing!"

"You're welcome to spend time at the club in whatever capacity you like. I still have the final say on major decisions, but you can be as involved as you want."

"That's not what I meant," he protested. "These shares are worth way more than 10 grand; this is just you feeling guilty! But it's not necessary. I'm okay. I still have money and will get my salary for four more years. Viggo is making money and if we invest wisely, we won't have to worry."

"And this is just a little insurance policy," Becca said, taking both of his hands in hers. "Please, Jamie, let me do this for you the way you did what you did for me."

Their eyes met and Jamie reached out to hug her. "Okay," he whispered against her hair. "But you have to name your first kid after me."

She giggled. "You'll have to ask Dante about that."

Dante's eyes narrowed. "You are *not* having another threesome with my wife!" he grunted, pretending to be annoyed.

Jamie chuckled, cutting his eyes to Viggo. "I think I have my hands full, thanks."

"It's my way of thanking you for what you did," Becca said. "If you say no, I might cry, and women supposedly already cry a lot in the first trimester."

Jamie blinked, cocking his head slightly. "Wait, are you—"

"What did you just say?" Dante growled, his face growing slightly pale as he stared at his wife.

She turned, her steel-blue eyes twinkling. "I said, women in the first trimester of pregnancy are prone to crying a lot. Why?"

He advanced on her in an instant and pulled her up against him. "Is there something you want to tell me?"

Her eyes widened innocently. "I don't know what you're talking about. All I said was—"

"Becca!" His eyes narrowed. "Are you pregnant?"

"Maybe." She giggled. "I bought a box of tests to take later."

"*Querida.* Sweetheart." His voice softened as he pressed a kiss to her forehead. "How long have you suspected?"

"A week or so, but we've had a lot going on." She squeezed his hand. "We'll find out together, okay?"

He nodded, somewhat overcome with emotion he was reluctant to show in front of their friends.

"So Viggo and I will talk about this and let you know, okay?" Jamie said after a moment.

"Of course." Becca leaned over to kiss his cheek. "You just rest and keep getting better."

"I will."

"I'm going to be Simone's nanny," Misty told Jamie. "I want to earn my keep but no one can legally hire me because I don't have a green card. We're already working on getting me one, though."

"She's going to live with us for now," Becca said. "Until you guys get a bigger place."

"We haven't gotten that far," Jamie admitted. "I don't know where we'll be living."

"We have a little time to figure it out," Viggo said gently.

"I know." Jamie reached out his hand and Viggo took it.

"I think we should let you rest," Dante said with a smile, wrapping an arm around his wife's waist. "We're going to get Misty settled at the house."

"Thanks. All of you."

When they were alone, Viggo crawled onto the bed beside him and wrapped his arms around him. It was the first time he'd been able to hold him in what seemed like forever and though there were staff members just outside the door and they were both fully dressed, there was an intimacy between them that had never been there before.

"I'd probably be really horny if I wasn't so tired," Jamie murmured, his eyes closing.

"That's okay. We have the rest of our lives to be horny."

"Have you been faithful all this time?" Jamie asked sleepily.

"You have to ask?!" Viggo demanded, lifting his head and glaring down at him.

"What about Emilie?"

"No. We agreed we would only do that with you. None of us has had any and it's starting to get old—get some sleep so you can get better and all of us can get laid again!"

"It's okay if you want to sleep with Emilie."

"No." Viggo kissed him. "Not going to happen without you. Either we do her together or not at all."

"Tired," he sighed, yawning through a smile.

"Sleep. I'll be right here."

## CHAPTER 31

Jamie got stronger every day and worked hard to do everything the doctors instructed him to do. His kidneys were functioning normally now, so he no longer needed dialysis and three weeks after he got back to Las Vegas, he was allowed to go home. Home was Viggo and Emilie's place, even though he'd protested and offered to rent an apartment. Emilie had insisted and moved Simone back into her and Viggo's room. They would give Jamie his own room, a private place to rest and unwind, even though there was no doubt Viggo would be sharing it with him.

He was excited to be going home and couldn't wait to be able to sleep without interruption. Sleeping next to Viggo would be nice too, although Viggo had spent many nights with him at the rehab center. They hadn't had sex, though, and Jamie made sure to ask the doctor about it when he spoke to him before his discharge. Getting the go-ahead had been both exhilarating and terrifying because things would change now. Mentally, he was ready to give himself to Viggo completely, but the physical part was still a little scary. He hadn't admitted that to him, though, so as they got ready to walk out to Viggo's waiting truck, he was lost in thought.

"The press has gotten wind that you're leaving," one of the center's attendants said as they got out of the elevator. "We've managed to keep them outside but there's no way for you to get to your vehicle without them seeing you."

Jamie groaned.

"It's okay." Viggo touched his shoulder. "We got this."

"I need my hat," Jamie fumbled in the bag at his feet, pulling out the baseball cap he'd been wearing for the last few weeks. He had hair again, but it was still barely a buzz cut on his head and he hated it.

"If you don't want to talk to them," Viggo said gently, "you don't have to. We can say no comment."

"Security can walk out with you," the attendant said.

"No. Let's do this. I'm not going to hide. I was the victim, so I don't have anything to be ashamed of."

"This means you're officially out," Viggo reminded him. "People already know but it will be you admitting to being in a relationship with a man, in front of the whole world."

Jamie took a breath and smiled up at him. "I *am* in a relationship with a man—let's go."

Viggo nodded.

Jamie swallowed hard but gave the attendant a thumb's up. He had to sit in the wheelchair until they got outside and he hated the idea that the press would see him that way. He would get up, though, as soon as they got past the doors. Although he didn't want to appear weak, he also didn't want them to get the idea that what those men had done to him was no big deal.

"Ready?" Viggo asked as the automatic doors opened and a group of reporters started moving towards them.

Jamie held up a hand and they all stopped moving. "I'll walk," he said quietly. "They may have knocked me down, but everyone's going to see that I've gotten back up."

Viggo stepped aside, understanding that Jamie needed the dignity of standing up without help.

Jamie faced the reporters calmly, though he was a little queasy and his palms were starting to sweat. Journalists immediately began firing questions at him and he approached them without hesitation. Though he was still a little wobbly on his feet, he refused to let them see it and allowed them to surround him, cameras and microphones everywhere.

"How are you feeling, Jamie?"

"Will you be able to play hockey again?"

"Has there been a hearing yet for the men who attacked you?"

"How long are you staying in Las Vegas?"

"What's the status of your relationship with Viggo?"

Jamie held up his hands, grateful they weren't shaking. "I can't talk over you!" he called out. "If you want me to answer, you need to ask one question at a time."

There were some more questions fired at him, but someone started shushing people and eventually they were quiet.

"First, my health. I'm a lot better, but still need a lot of rehab, especially for my wrist. As you can see—" he held up his casted arm. "It's going to be a while before we know anything, but it's healing. That's all I can tell you about that or about my ability to play hockey going forward. I'll have more news when I get the cast off in four weeks."

"When are you going back to Ottawa, Jamie?" someone called out.

"Right now, I have permission to stay here, so until we get more definitive answers about my wrist, I'll be here."

"Are you and Viggo moving in together?"

Jamie nodded. "Yes."

"What about his wife?"

"As Viggo has said repeatedly, questions about Emilie are off-limits."

"Is Viggo threatening to take custody away if she doesn't say that she's supporting your relationship?!"

"Is there a custody case going on and is Viggo going to use Emilie's porn career to take their daughter away from her?"

The questions came out of nowhere and Jamie looked back at Viggo in a panic. Viggo was already pushing through the crowd to get to his side. He had a dark look on his face and Jamie momentarily worried he was going to hit someone.

"When he said there would be no questions about Emilie, he meant it," Viggo growled, keeping his voice as steady as possible. "But for the record—of course I'm not threatening to take custody away from her! She was never a porn star—those videos were made without her permission and this topic has become tiresome. As for custody of Simone—that's ludicrous. I'm on the road constantly and in no way able to care for an infant by myself."

"What about Jamie?" someone shot back.

"Jamie plans to be back at hockey as soon as possible—although we can't predict what will happen with his wrist, the plan is for him to play. And anyway, he's not my babysitter."

"But he is your lover?"

Jamie rolled his eyes. "Okay, seriously, if you guys want to talk to me, you need to knock this off. You already know we're a couple, so why would you ask if we're lovers? Rhetorical questions aren't necessary. Yes, we're lovers, in love, a couple, whatever you want to call it. I'm not going to play games. The truth, in a nutshell, is that I fell in love with my friend. Yeah, it's hard to come out like this, in front of the whole world, but we haven't done anything wrong. We fell in love. That's it. I'm not sure why I need to say anything else. If one of us was a woman, this wouldn't even be happening. If you want to talk about my attack, my health, hockey, any of that—go ahead. If you're going to ask me about being in love, I'm going home."

"What do your teammates in Ottawa think, Jamie? Have they been supportive?"

"Everyone has been supportive. What happened to me was hateful—and what you're doing here today is part of why it happened. Granted, the press isn't responsible for what ugly, mean-spirited people do, but by perpetuating the idea that two men being in love is newsworthy, it makes it that much more taboo. Let's be more accepting of our differences and think more about right and wrong. Love is right; trying to kill someone is wrong. It shouldn't be more complicated than that."

"What will you do if you can't play hockey?"

Jamie shook his head. "Honestly, I can't go there. Hockey is all I've ever done, and all I've ever wanted to do. My only goal is to be able to play again. Until at least five doctors tell me I can't, that's what I plan to do."

"Is it true you're trying to get traded back to the Sidewinders?"

Jamie started. "I haven't had a conversation like that with anyone. Obviously, with Viggo and me being together, it would be better if we could be in the same city, but that's not mandatory. We understand what it means to be professional athletes and we may have to live apart during the season. That's part of the life. Ottawa has been really great throughout all of this, so I would never discuss leaving without talking to them first."

"I think we're done here," Viggo interjected mildly. "He's been on his feet for a long time and needs to rest. If you want to talk to him, contact his agent or the PR department in Ottawa." Viggo gently but firmly led Jamie away and they got into his truck.

Jamie was exhausted, immediately leaning back and closing his eyes.

"I wish you hadn't stood so long," was all Viggo said.

"I'm okay." Jamie reached over and rested his hand on Viggo's thigh. "Having you beside me is all the strength I need."

"Damn, whenever you say something like that, I get hard."

"It might be because you've been without sex for...how long?"

"Seventy-two days."

Jamie chuckled. "Maybe not tonight, but soon. Promise."

"I'll wait as long as you need."

THEY GOT HOME and found Emilie waiting in the parking lot for them. She leaned against the truck when Viggo rolled the window down.

"Can we go for a ride? It'll be quick, but it's important."

"I'm okay," Jamie said when Viggo hesitated. "As long as I don't have to face the press again."

Emilie shook her head. "Absolutely not."

"Let's go."

Emilie climbed into the backseat and directed them to the highway.

"Where are we going?" Viggo asked.

"Humor me for a bit?"

Viggo shrugged. "Okay."

They pulled up to a big sprawling house in a quiet, gated community. Emilie got out of the truck and motioned for them to follow.

"What's going on?" Viggo asked, turning off the engine.

"Are you all right to walk a little?" she asked Jamie. "It's not much and you can sit when we get inside."

Jamie nodded. "I'm fine." He got out steadily but was grateful when Emilie took his arm. They walked up to the front door and Emilie pulled a key from her pocket.

"Em, what—" Viggo began.

"Two minutes and I'll explain," she said softly.

He nodded even though he was frowning.

"I had a thought," she said when they got inside. "Let me finish before either of you say anything." She motioned to the living room. "Go ahead and sit, Jamie, so you don't get tired."

"Okay." He sat on the chair to their right and looked at her curiously.

"I had this idea," she said quietly. "But I figured it would be easier to show you than tell you. All of our lives have been turned upside down, but given the bond we share, I think it would be beneficial for us to move in together. Here. This house —" She held up a hand when Viggo started to speak. "Can I just say what I need to say? Then we can discuss or get up and go."

"Yes, of course." Viggo was still frowning, but he was willing to listen.

"This house was built for a family that had to back out. We can get it for a steal, immediately. It's something you two can afford—nowhere near as expensive as some of the houses our friends live in, but still a beautiful home. It has a huge master bedroom with a big en suite bathroom, dual walk-in closets and lots of windows. There's also a room that's deemed some sort of private living room but has an attached bathroom, walk-in closet and separate mini-suite, which would be perfect for me and Simone. There are two extra bedrooms for guests or anything else we need. It has a three-car garage, gourmet kitchen and a fabulous patio in the back where we can add a pool if we want. There's also a pool in the neighborhood."

"You've sold me on the house," Jamie smiled. "But what are you getting at?"

"I can't be on my own yet," she whispered. "And with all of us working, traveling, Jamie's medical issues, the press—everything going on—it would be better for Simone to be with all of us. She would be in a slightly unconventional but loving family with her mum and two dads. We would shut up all the people saying that you've deserted me or are trying to take Simone away. We would be there for each other emotionally—and as messed up as I am, Jamie is still struggling too."

"It's actually quite brilliant," Viggo admitted. "But, love, are you sure? You and I have loved each other since we were kids...how will you feel watching me in a serious relationship with someone else?"

She smiled, though tears puddled in her eyes. "I've loved you since I was 15. I thought if you just weren't bi, you would love me back. Turned out you loved me all along, but that what we felt was the sweet, innocent love of two children. Now that we're grown, and actually married, I see that our feelings have been one big, messed-up conglomeration of friendship, comfort and practicality. Watching you fall in love with Jamie has shown me what we don't have—I don't feel for you what you two obviously feel for each other—so I'm not going to be hurt. I'm actually very, very happy that I didn't have to hurt you by admitting I don't love you that way. But right now, until I find a way out of the darkness inside me, I can't be alone. I can't." A tear slid down her cheek and she hung her head. "Please don't leave me yet."

"No!" Viggo whispered raggedly, dropping to his knees to wrap his arms around her slight form. "I told you, as long as Jamie can be with us, I won't go anywhere."

"I can't share emotionally," Jamie admitted softly. "But I don't have a problem with the three of us having a home together, taking care of Simone, and each other."

"I'm not even capable of romantic love right now," she admitted sadly. "The only one I feel anything that intense for is Simone. The rest of me is pretty much dead."

"We're going to get you past that," Viggo said firmly.

"And in return..." She lifted her head, wrapped the fingers of her left hand around one of Viggo's and held out her right to Jamie. She waited until he took it, and scooted over to sit closer to her, before continuing. "In return, I can give you the one thing I know has weighed heaviest on your mind."

He frowned. "What?"

"A child." She put a finger on his lips and shook her head at Viggo when they both tried to speak. "Simone is Viggo's child. If I was to have *your* child, then you would both have your own children but they would still be related, half-siblings. When the time comes that we don't live together anymore, the children would either be with their biological fathers, or their biological mother. There wouldn't be confusing situations, holidays or any of that. The three of us would share two children, raise them as one big family. Even if I remarry or have more children, they would *all* be related, half-siblings. We wouldn't have to deal with awkward legalities, surrogates or any of that."

Viggo didn't say anything, glancing at Jamie to gauge his reaction. Jamie looked startled but also thoughtful.

"I adore Simone," he admitted. "And one biological child would make me really, really happy. Are you sure you want to have a child with a man you're not involved with?"

She reached out to cup his cheek with her palm. "But we are involved, aren't we? We have a friendship, you're in love with my daughter's father, and to be fair, we've had a healthy sexual relationship. Whether or not that changes now is irrelevant—it currently exists so it's not like we don't care for each other."

"I love the idea," Jamie said after a moment. "But I need a little time. I need to know if I'm going to have a hockey career and what I'm going to do if I can't."

"I understand," she said. "I'm busy at the club and Simone is a handful, so we have a little time, but we can't wait too long because eventually I'm going to move on. I've started seeing a therapist and am trying to work through my issues. Maybe in the next year?"

He nodded. "I'm okay with this if Viggo is."

Viggo nodded. "I think we should talk with your therapist about it, make sure that having a child for us won't set you back."

"I already talked with her about the house and she thinks it's a good idea." She reached into her purse and handed Viggo a card. "I've also contacted our accountant to let him know that this realtor may be calling him, but you should talk with him too. We'll get a lawyer to draw up papers saying that I have no right to the house when we split. I've already spoken to an attorney and she thinks it would be best if we divorced. It could be a little complicated, but it would protect both of us and allow you to be in a public relationship with Jamie without looking like you're cheating."

"No matter how we handle this legally," Viggo said gently, "we're going to draw attention. Two gay lovers living with the one man's wife...we're going to be in the gossip columns for sure."

"I don't care," she shrugged.

"We don't have to make it public," Jamie said. "We can keep our lives private. I plan to stay as private as possible. Not because I'm afraid of what names they might call us, but because I can't focus on getting better if I'm constantly under scrutiny. I want to be with the man I love and our friends. I'm happy to live together and help with Simone and the club, but I don't want to be in the spotlight. I just want to be a regular guy, without a new label every time I turn around."

For a while they were quiet, thinking about the changes and how far they'd come in such a short time. After a bit, Emilie stood up and held out her hands. "Do you want to explore the house? It's really, really nice."

"I want a California king bed," Viggo muttered. "That's nonnegotiable. Other than that, the two of you can pick everything."

Jamie raised his eyebrows. "You seem to be under the misguided impression that I *know* something about decorating a house. All I want is a really big grill for the back."

"And a top-notch security system," Viggo nodded.

"My TV's in Ottawa," Jamie groaned. "And it was really fucking awesome."

"We'll ship it back," Viggo said, following when Jamie wandered towards the kitchen, completely forgetting about Emilie.

"I like stainless steel appliances," Jamie was saying.

"Me too. And look—this is the perfect place to set up the Xbox..."

Emilie watched them with a faint smile as they disappeared around the corner. It was going to be all right, she thought. Somehow, the three of them were going to be all right.

## CHAPTER 32

Jamie slept for most of the first two days he was home. Without nurses and doctors checking him all the time, he was able to actually rest. Viggo was busy with hockey and Emilie was at the club most of the time, so he took advantage of the chance to sleep. After the third day, however, he was restless.

He managed to take a shower without any help or getting his cast wet. He looked in the mirror as he shaved and made a face; he really hated having what amounted to a crew cut. Though it was growing out, it was slow and he'd never had hair this short as an adult. He wore a knit cap or a baseball cap any time he left the house and today he pulled on the one he'd gotten when the Sidewinders won the championship last year.

Had it only been less than a year, he thought to himself as he got in Viggo's truck to go pick him up. Emilie had dropped Viggo off at practice before she took Simone to Misty. Jamie had agreed to pick Viggo up when practice was over but he was going early. He yearned for the smell of an arena, the sound of skates scraping across the ice, and more than anything, to see his friends. He'd begun to feel isolated now that he was getting back on his feet, but he still tired out easily and today was the first time he'd felt well enough to drive.

Pulling into the gate at the arena where the players parked, he felt a twinge of melancholy for the first time. Would he ever play again? Would he ever drive into the players' entrance at an arena to get ready for a game? Not knowing gnawed away at him, but until they took off the cast and began rehabilitating the wrist, there was no way to answer that question.

Focusing on seeing his friends, he walked in, waved at the security guard and headed towards the ice. He wouldn't let anyone see him yet; he just wanted a peek at the game he loved, and missed, so much. He wasn't sure what he would do if he wasn't able to play anymore. It really wasn't even the money; he didn't know anything else. He'd gotten the equivalent of a high school diploma while playing in the juniors.

He'd always assumed he would coach or work in the back office after his playing days ended, but at 27, he wasn't sure that would happen. There was simply nothing else he wanted to do, and even though he now owned 25% of Club Inferno, owning a club wouldn't fulfill him the way hockey did.

Forcing the negative thoughts out of his mind, he sank into a seat behind the bench, far enough away that the guys wouldn't notice him right away but still close enough to see what they were doing. As always, he spied Viggo first, shooting the puck at the net. His hulking frame was hard to miss and the wisps of red hair sticking out from under his helmet made Jamie smile. Zakk was easy to spot too, all six feet seven inches of him, flying across the ice at breakneck speeds.

He watched for a while, losing himself in the only thing he loved as much as Viggo. It was nice to be in this arena, listening to the coaches yelling out plays and drills, but it made him realize how close he was to losing it. Finally, knowing practice was coming to an end, he headed to the locker rooms.

Zakk saw him first and raised a hand in greeting. "Hey! What are you doing here?"

"Came to say hi."

"Good to see you." Zakk nodded. "How's the wrist?"

Jamie shrugged. "We'll see in a couple weeks."

"Hey, Jamie!" Cody waved as he set down his gloves.

"Jamie!" Toli waved and gave him a grin. "You look good!"

"Thanks!" Jamie waved.

"When are we going to trivia?" Zakk was asking him.

"Up to you," Jamie grinned. "You're the one with a new baby at home!"

Zakk laughed. "Why do you think I want to go to trivia?"

They laughed together.

"Jamie, my boy!" Lonnie Finch appeared in the doorway with a big smile. "Just the man I was looking for. Will you take a walk with me?"

A strange silence fell over the room. Lonnie almost never came down to the locker room, and certainly not after a practice.

"Uh, sure." Jamie exchanged a glance with Viggo but followed the older man into the hallway and towards the elevators.

"How are you feeling, my boy?" Lonnie asked after a moment, looking up at him.

Jamie nodded. "One day at a time. It's been a rough few months but I'm getting through it."

"Let me ask you a hypothetical question," Lonnie said as they walked into his office and shut the door.

"Okay." Jamie sank into one of the plush leather chairs.

"Would you like to come back to Las Vegas for good?"

Jamie frowned. "Well, yeah, but—"

"I simply want to know if you'd like to."

"Why?"

"I'm always looking for ways to make my team the very best it can be," he said lightly, thumbing through some papers on his desk.

"Sir, I don't even know if I'll ever play again..." His voice trailed off as he struggled to even say those words.

"Do you *want* to play again?"

Jamie looked away. "Come on...really? Having to retire after getting attacked by a bunch of thugs? Instead of on the ice, the way a man should be able to leave a game like this? To be able to say goodbye to his teammates, his fans, his coaches... of course I want to play again! Even one more game. One more chance to have some closure." He cleared his throat. "Anyway, it's going to be months before I know anything. Right now, I can't even hold a stick."

Lonnie's head came up. "Sometimes a team needs more than stickhandling and goaltending."

"You have great coaches, a fantastic staff and some of the best players in the league," Jamie said. "There's nothing missing on this team."

"Maybe," he said vaguely. "Maybe not."

"What was that about?" Viggo asked him when they were finally in the truck heading home.

"No idea," Jamie admitted. "He was being pretty cagey."

"The team hasn't been the same this season," Viggo said lightly. "It's obvious something is missing. With both you and Marco gone, plus all the new guys, it's not the same."

"I don't think anyone misses Marco," Jamie said dryly, referring to their late goalie, who'd been an epic asshole.

"No, but they miss you."

"I think you're a bit biased."

"There are many things I'm biased about when it comes to you," he responded quietly. "But when it comes to hockey, my personal life is always separate. I wouldn't say it if it wasn't true. They talk about you—if Jamie was here, he would've seen that coming...when Jamie was on the line, we were faster...every single practice, almost every game. They haven't yet figured out how to compensate for what you brought to the team."

Jamie looked out the window. "Well, I guess they're going to have to."

"Stop." Viggo reached out and took his hand. "I know it's hard, but you have to be positive. You can't give up before the cast is even off!"

"My size has always been a problem. Then two back-to-back concussions and my wrist broken in eight places. I haven't used steroids in a year and I'm thinner than ever now that I'm not working out. Even if the wrist heals, I don't know how I'll ever get back to what I need to be."

"You've got me, Zakk and all your friends to help you get there."

"I have you, but they're busy...with hockey and their own lives. No one has time to baby me."

"I do. Dante does. Chains is an animal in the gym—I'm willing to bet he'd help you too."

"I guess." Jamie leaned his head back and closed his eyes. He wasn't really tired, but now he was even more depressed than he'd been before his visit to the arena.

"What are you thinking?" Viggo asked, glancing at him.

"Nothing. I'm gonna take a nap."

"Bullshit." Viggo tugged his hand. "Don't shut me out, Jamie. That doesn't cut it in a relationship like ours."

"I'm not. There's nothing to say. We can talk all day about how much I miss hockey, but there's nothing we can do until I start rehabbing my wrist. And we have to meet with the lawyer in the next couple of days if we're going to go forward with the house."

"You want to buy it, don't you?"

"Sure." Jamie shrugged.

"Jamie!" Viggo looked at him in exasperation.

"What do you want from me?!" Jamie snarled, whipping his head around to glare at him. "I want you, I want the damn house, I want to be here! I don't know what more you need from me! Shit, it's always something!"

The silence in the car was charged with frustration the rest of the way home and Jamie stormed into the apartment, slamming his bedroom door behind him. Hands on either side of his head, he sat on his bed, resting his elbows on his thighs. What the hell was wrong with him?

None of this was Viggo's fault, but he seemed to take it out on him regularly. Damn, he hated being an asshole, and the last person in the world who deserved it was Viggo. He wondered for what seemed like the hundredth time if he was making a mistake. Being in love with a man made no more sense to him now than it had two months ago, but there was no way to deny his feelings or even consider walking away again.

His doubts were fleeting but the accompanying fear and anxiety were not. Although he hadn't had any headaches this time, he was beginning to see a pattern in his behavior; depression, anger and frustration crept in regularly. There was obviously more going on than he wanted to admit and he glanced at the phone warily. He needed to call his doctor to talk about medication.

They'd brought it up multiple times after the first concussion, but he'd shrugged it off, insisting he was fine. However, there was a lot more at stake now, and he refused to let it continue. He wasn't stupid. He was well-aware of the kinds of mental and emotional damage concussions could cause and he was starting to worry it would derail his life the way it had the lives of many other athletes.

Without any more hesitation, he picked up the phone and dialed.

## CHAPTER 33

When he came out of his room half an hour later the apartment was quiet. He wondered if Viggo had left or if he was napping, something he often did after a particularly strenuous practice. Jamie was still trying to figure out how he was going to apologize as he opened the door to what was technically Emilie's bedroom now. Viggo was on the bed, hands behind his head, staring at the ceiling. When Viggo heard the door open, he glanced in his direction and Jamie approached slowly.

"I'm sorry," Jamie whispered. "I don't know what's wrong with me. I made an appointment with the doctor for tomorrow. I'm having a hard time with my temper and you're the only person I have to take it out on. I don't mean to."

Viggo simply held out a hand and Jamie reached for it as he slid onto the bed.

"The depression is getting bad, yeah?" Viggo had done a lot of reading about the after effects of both concussions and a traumatic experience like the attack, and Jamie was beginning to show some of the classic symptoms of PTSD.

"Yeah." Jamie closed his eyes. "I'm sorry, babe."

"It's all right, we'll figure it out." Viggo pulled him close.

"Every time I look in the mirror I see what they did to me," he said. "I can feel them digging the knife into my back even though I was out cold when they did it. I'm embarrassed by my stupid hair. I tried to jerk off last night and couldn't get it up."

"It's all right. I'm here and we're going to do whatever you need to get better."

"How?" Jamie buried his face in the pillow. "I was an emotional mess *before* this happened. I'm destroyed now."

"No. You're feeling vulnerable, afraid—you were brutalized, traumatized and humiliated. I won't pretend to know what you're going through, but whatever it takes, no matter how long it takes, I'm not going anywhere. We *will* figure it out."

"I don't want to be the weak one in this relationship," Jamie groaned with frustration. "We have to be equals or it will never work."

"We are equals." Viggo moved closer to him, flipping onto his stomach so he could press the side of his face against Jamie's. "You're healing right now—it's going to take a bit for you to be physically strong again. But you will be. They broke your wrist—not your spirit."

"Today was the first time I was scared." He was whispering again. "Today was the first time I couldn't shake the feeling that nothing would ever be right again."

"Tomorrow we'll talk to the doctor; today you hold on to me. Physically, emotionally, whatever you need."

"I need to feel alive again. I feel like I'm drowning in a pool of self-pity, doubt and fear. It's really fucked up, Viggo."

"What can I do?" Viggo looked down at him, wishing there was a way to trade places with him; he loved him that much.

"Kiss me?" Jamie raised his head to meet his loving gaze. "That's what started all of this. I knew right then I would never be the same, but even though I was confused, it was a good feeling—a once-in-a-lifetime feeling. I'm so scared right now I don't remember what that felt like."

"Like this?" Viggo moved in, his lips grazing Jamie's tenderly. He rubbed his hand over the short but soft hair on his head, pausing to run his thumb along his temple. He watched as Jamie's gorgeous eyes got hooded, darkened, and began to glint with need. When Viggo bent his head again he brushed kisses from his jawline to his throat and up the other side, watching as Jamie's head fell back.

GENTLY GRIPPING him by the shoulders, Viggo pulled him close, finding his mouth and sucking his tongue in deep. When they kissed, there was much more than their mouths involved; it was a full-contact sport and he wasn't sure if he was winning or losing because they became something else when they touched; all that existed was the reality of knowing they could find this much happiness together. These were the moments Jamie was talking about, when nothing else mattered but the two of them. Sex had never been anything more than a pleasurable joining of bodies before Jamie; now it was a mating of souls that was somehow as literal as it was figurative.

Lifting to his knees, Viggo pulled off his shirt and reached down to run his fingers lightly along the rim of Jamie's sweats. Jamie lifted his hips and Viggo pulled them free of his body before undoing the top button of his own jeans. Jamie reached up to slide down the zipper with his good hand, grimacing at the awkward movements since it wasn't his dominant hand.

"Let me," was all Viggo said, wanting to spare him anything else that would distract him from what they were doing. If he could help him get lost in how it felt when they were together, he would do almost anything. Watching him suffer today had been as hard on Viggo as it had been for Jamie.

Undressing himself and then Jamie was a glorious diversion, and looking down at his lean body, Viggo's eyes rested on his cock, already full and thick.

"Looks like jerking off is the problem, not your dick," he said, one side of his mouth tilting up.

Jamie glanced down. "Thank God. If that was broken too, I'd be in deep shit."

"Nah. We'd bring it back to life." He bent his head and sucked it into his mouth in one swift motion that had Jamie drawing in a deep breath.

"Fuck..." he breathed, arching against him.

Viggo took his time, running his lips down the lengthy shaft and using gentle fingers to massage his balls. Jamie shuddered against him, so he backed off, anxious to make this last longer than usual. Instead of continuing to suck him deep, he teased him with his tongue, licking just the tip and gripping the base with his hand. Jamie moaned, arching up expectantly, but Viggo held back.

"God damn, that's good," Jamie groaned.

"Just enjoy," Viggo whispered. He reached for the bottle of lube and poured some on his fingers before reaching back to part Jamie's tight, sexy cheeks. He slid into him easily but felt Jamie tense so he used his other hand to lightly jack his cock, distracting him from what was probably a faint burn. Jamie was tighter than any guy he'd ever been with and it had been nearly two months since they'd been together, so he had to move slowly.

JAMIE TENSED AGAIN when he felt a second finger slide in next to the first, and he gripped the sheets with his good hand. He'd gotten past the fear of ass play, but after being without for a while, it was almost new again.

"Easy," Viggo murmured. "Breathe out slowly."

Jamie squeezed his eyes shut as conflicting sensations ran through him: the pleasure of Viggo's warm body close to his, the occasional zing of rapture when supple lips grazed his cock, and then the faint burn as he stretched to take another finger. Viggo curved them up and found the spot that made Jamie's hips shoot up off the bed and a growl leave his throat.

"Oh, fuck yeah...more of that! Shit!"

Viggo worked on him patiently, pulling back until Jamie was all but humping his hand with his ass. Two fingers, one finger and finally nothing as he ran his knuckles over his rock-hard dick.

"More..." Jamie rasped. "I need more."

"What do you need, lover?" Viggo kept his grip on Jamie's cock gentle, blowing lightly on the tip.

"I need you to take me—no more holding back."

"You're sure?"

"Fuck yeah."

"I don't want to hurt you—my own first time wasn't great."

"I trust you."

VIGGO FUMBLED for a condom and slid it down his aching shaft, his heart shifting into overdrive as he realized what this meant: Jamie was finally giving him 100%. Whatever his reservations were about them, they obviously weren't as important as his need to be with him, and that was all Viggo had been waiting for. He really didn't want to hurt him, though, and something told him his wide girth was going to make this a little harder than it had been when he'd done it with men who were experienced; it suddenly occurred to him he'd never been with an anal virgin before.

"Bend your knees," he said softly, pressing a kiss right at the base of Jamie's shaft and running his lips across the sensitive sacs beneath.

With Jamie's knees bent, Viggo used his hands to push them back a little, bringing his ass up to the right level. He poured a stream of lube right over the crack, rubbing it in and then put more on his dick. He moved over him, pressing his cock against the entrance but not going any further. He leaned down on his elbows, letting his body cover Jamie's, and found his mouth. Their tongues did a familiar dance and Jamie looped his arm around Viggo's neck. That was his favorite thing to do when they kissed, and Viggo let him guide their pace.

"Now," Jamie breathed when the intensity and longing became too much. "I want you."

Viggo looked into his lover's eyes and pushed. To his surprise, instead of clenching tighter, Jamie let out a long breath and relaxed, never moving his gaze. As the head slid in, he hissed slightly, but when Viggo tried to stop, Jamie gripped Viggo's ass with his left hand to hold him in place.

"Keep going," was all he said.

Viggo sank into him inch by inch, and Jamie stretched to take him. He squeezed his eyes shut, unable to believe how good it was, or that he was even doing it. All his reservations faded to nothing as he lost himself in this beautiful man he loved and the feelings they aroused when they were together. Nothing had ever been this intimate, this sexy, or, so help him, so damn good. What he'd thought would be painful and awkward was instead taking him to the brink of something almost impossible to describe.

"You're not breathing..."

"Not sure I can..."

"I've got you, lover, just let go." Viggo leaned down to run his lips across Jamie's jaw and the side of his face.

The stubble from his unshaven cheek chafed against Jamie's skin, but he didn't care. Being back in the arms of the one person who made him feel whole was such an immeasurable pleasure, he barely noticed. How he'd ever thought he could live without this was beyond him, even as the physical discomfort grew. The burn had begun to intensify as Viggo filled him and Jamie fought to take a deep breath. A moan escaped his throat when he winced and Viggo stopped, running his hands up the side of Jamie's torso.

"Too much?"

"No, it's good. I want it. I want you." Jamie grit his teeth against the foreign sensation, the discomfort, the burn—everything except Viggo—and forced himself to relax again. This was his man, the guy who loved him against all the odds, and this was a moment he would never forget. The love in Viggo's eyes, coupled with his concern and restraint made him want it that much more and he grabbed Viggo's hips. "All of it," he rasped. "Every damn inch of your fucking cock inside me. Now."

"Easy, lover...it'll be better if we take it slow." Viggo leaned down to kiss him, unhurried and sensual, the familiar tangle of lips and tongues bringing Jamie back to the pleasure spot he'd been in before it got overwhelming. "Now breathe out like you did before."

Jamie did exactly that and Viggo thrust in deep, bottoming out with such force they both grunted.

"That's it, baby. You've got all of me." He reached down to stroke Jamie's throbbing erection, using the pad of his thumb to rub the pre-cum leaking from the tip.

"*Fuck.*" Jamie arched against him. "It burns but I want to feel you moving."

"Yeah?" Viggo's lips curved into a smile. He brought Jamie's legs up and rested one on each shoulder, giving him the perfect angle to slide in and out.

"Oh shit!" Jamie's eyes rolled back when Viggo began gliding in and out with deep, firm strokes. "Oh fuck, yes!" He started to move with him, bringing his hips up each time Viggo thrust in. He'd never experienced anything like this, his entire body on fire, nerve endings so sensitive he felt tiny pinpricks of heat across his skin. This wasn't like anything else he'd ever done—exquisite torture, the likes of which he'd never believed possible. His cock ached painfully for release and he reached down to grip it with his fingers.

"No." Viggo pushed his hand away. "You lie there and take it until I'm ready for you to come. You made me wait a long time for this—you don't come until I do. You hear me?"

"Fuck..." Jamie panted hard, overwhelmed with emotion and lust, unable to articulate another word. "Please..."

"Please what? Tell me what you need, handsome."

"You...oh shit, let me come, dammit!"

"Soon, lover..."

Jamie writhed against him, his breath coming in gasps as Viggo dug deeper and used his big hands to hold him in place, making sure Jamie felt every inch when he pushed in and withdrew. He did it over and over, letting tension and excitement build before he finally paused, balls deep, and rotated his hips so his cock swirled inside of him.

Jamie groaned. "Viggo..."

"Say it," Viggo growled. "You want to come? Tell me what you feel."

Jamie's eyes fluttered open and though they were hooded and heavy with desire, he smiled at him with everything he felt in his heart. "No sex in the world changes that, big guy. I fucking love you."

"God damn." Viggo gripped Jamie's cock and began stroking it in time to his thrusts, watching Jamie's gorgeous face as he let go and came with a guttural howl. His cum spurted over both of them, running over Viggo's hand and onto both their chests. Viggo shot off at the same time, shuddering through an orgasm that didn't seem to stop, semen shooting out so hard he nearly lost his balance.

Viggo gently lowered Jamie's legs and collapsed on top of him, finding his mouth for a soul-shattering kiss that nearly undid both of them. "Mine," he whispered between kisses. "I took that virgin ass and I'd better be the only one who ever does."

"Other than my doctor," Jamie teased with a contented smile.

"Maybe," Viggo grunted, nipping at the soft skin on his neck until Jamie jumped. "Mine," he repeated.

"Yeah, yeah." Jamie dug his fingers into Viggo's hair. "All yours, babe. So fucking yours it's embarrassing."

"Was this embarrassing for you?" Viggo's face immediately filled with concern.

"What?" Jamie's eyes rounded as he shook his head. "No. That's not what I meant! I meant it's embarrassing how much I love you because I want to say and do all kinds of sappy shit, and it grates on my already chafing manhood."

"Like what?" Viggo relaxed now, continuing to nip and suckle Jamie's neck and throat.

"Can we get married?"

"Of course. I have to take care of Em first, but yeah, getting married is on the list of shit I want with you."

Jamie snorted at the casual reference to such a major decision. "And we have to sort out finances. I can't be a kept man."

"Slow down, babe." Viggo stroked his cheek as he leaned up to gaze into those passionate, loving brown eyes. "We're in this forever. We'll get married, have kids and that totally traditional life we've always wanted. One thing at a time, though. You're still healing—you don't know that your wrist won't be 100% again. Let's give that a little time first."

Jamie shook his head. "I'm gonna have to come to terms with never playing again."

"No." Viggo put a finger on his lips. "You don't know that. The body can do miraculous things. Be patient."

"I'm trying to be realistic. Retiring at 28 is going to be the hardest thing I've ever had to do but I need to get used to the idea."

"Your contract will pay you a good chunk of money for four more years," Viggo reminded him. "You can use that to go back to school or start a business—we'll be smart with our money and you won't ever feel like I'm supporting you."

"Yeah."

"Come on, I just got off with my favorite guy in the world," Viggo whispered against his ear. "Let's not talk about serious stuff."

"You just want to do it again," Jamie snickered.

"Oh yeah."

"I'm probably gonna be sore, huh?"

"Maybe, but I'll kiss it and make it better, if you are," Viggo teased.

They laughed, moving together as they kissed.

# CHAPTER 34

Jamie was surprised to hear from Lonnie Finch's secretary a few weeks later, asking if he was available to meet the following morning at 9:00. Viggo was leaving on a road trip, so he didn't say anything about it, wondering what Lonnie could possibly want. He and the Sidewinders' owner hadn't been particularly close when he'd played here; Lonnie wasn't fond of Jamie's sex tapes and steroid use, but he wasn't hostile about it either. He'd been almost fatherly when he'd warned Jamie that the sex tapes didn't just tarnish the reputation of the team, but it detracted from Jamie's career as well. He'd been more matter-of-fact when their late goalie, Marco Rousch, had blackmailed him with copies of a failed drug test.

Then Jamie got caught with Dante and Becca and there was yet another sex scandal. When Dante asked him to get traded so that Becca could continue to show her face professionally, he'd done it. He'd gotten more money too, which was odd considering the circumstances, but he'd done it as a favor to Dante and Becca so he didn't question it.

It probably would have been okay, too, if he hadn't gotten the concussion. And hadn't fallen in love with Viggo. And hadn't been attacked for being...different. He still didn't like to call himself bisexual. It didn't seem right because he didn't feel any different than before—he was just in love with a guy. A great guy who loved him back.

Pulling on his favorite baseball cap, he grabbed his keys and headed out. He'd been pleasantly surprised this morning when the doorbell rang and a delivery man had handed him the keys to his truck. Dante had had it shipped from Ottawa so now he didn't have to borrow Viggo's or Emilie's and he felt a lot more independent.

When he arrived at the arena and got to the floor where Lonnie's office was, his secretary waved him in.

"He's expecting you," she said with a friendly smile.

Jamie nodded and went in, holding out his left hand.

Lonnie shook it and smiled. "Can I get you anything to drink?"

"No, I'm good." Jamie sank down in the same chair he'd been in last week.

"I'll get right to the point then." Lonnie put his glasses on and pulled some papers out of his desk. "I'm willing to buy back your contract from Ottawa, if that's something you'd be interested in."

Jamie's mouth fell open and for a moment he simply sat there. "I don't understand," he said at last. "Why would you do that? I may not play again. Ottawa has to honor the contract, but you don't!"

"Your presence here has been missed," he said simply. "It doesn't look like we're making the playoffs this year and I believe part of that is because of you. When you're on the ice, you make things happen. Without you, the boys have been off. I don't know exactly why that is, but we all feel it."

Jamie flushed, both happy he was missed and frustrated he might never play again. "Mr. Finch, I don't know what to say."

"First, call me Lonnie." He took his glasses off and put them on the desk in front of him. "Let me be blunt here, my boy. I like you. You're like the golden child who can't help but get into trouble...always into mischief but so good-hearted and talented everyone loves you anyway. When that nonsense got out with you and Becca, I was frustrated, but I figured Becca would be the one to leave since she was getting married. Then suddenly you'd gotten a deal in Ottawa and were leaving us. I thought at first you just wanted to start fresh, after all your different ordeals, but I started to hear rumblings that you were unhappy, didn't want to leave the team. It was too late, of course."

"It was complicated."

"It was Dante," he corrected mildly. "He coerced you, I assume—" He held up a hand when Jamie started to talk. "At this point it doesn't matter. Becca is pregnant and probably leaving the team, but even if she stays, it doesn't matter to me. What matters is that you come back. Even if you can't actually play again, you will play at least one more game. You'll have the choice of whether or not you feel up to the task—the coaches won't have to tell you if you're not getting the job done. You'll know and you'll do what's right. But those Aryan assholes don't get to dictate the timing of your last game. That will be *your* choice."

Jamie hated the emotion building up inside him, wishing he was strong enough to hide how overwhelmed he was. "I don't even know what to say," he rasped, trying to control his shaking voice.

"Say it's okay for me to send this along to your agent. I've already spoken to Ottawa, explained that this is about showing support, showing you and the rest of the world that we don't *hate* in Las Vegas—it's not about business or even hockey, really. You were an integral part of this team and we've missed you both on the ice and in the locker room. We also don't give a flying fuck who you're in love with. It's ridiculous to even bring that up with respect to the game."

"And Ottawa is okay with trading me back?"

"We missed the deadline for now, so this is all unofficial, but come this summer, you'll be a Sidewinder again. We're going to send them Barrows."

Jamie blinked. Barrows was a rookie, an up-and-coming player they'd picked up to help the team grow as he matured. "Really?"

"He's nowhere near the player you are, Jamie, and this is something I feel I need to do, for you and for myself. I play tough in business, but life is short—and what those thugs did to you will not get swept under the rug on my watch."

Jamie swallowed. "There aren't any words..."

"Have the contract looked at by your people. Talk to Viggo. Once we can make trades again, we'll make it official. In the meantime, I want you to rest and heal. Enjoy the fact that you're still alive. Forget about what happened in Ottawa. Forget the media and all that other bullshit. Just take care of yourself, Jamie."

"I still don't understand why you're doing this," Jamie said in a voice thick with emotion. "I get that there's a lot of sympathy and empathy about what happened, but this is your business—a professional sports team worth millions. Why would you put yourself out there like this for me? I'm a good player, but there are a lot who are better."

Lonnie smiled. "Jamie, I've been in business for almost 40 years. I started with nothing and built everything I have. I'm 62 years old and technically I should be getting ready to retire. Instead I brought hockey to Las Vegas. Because I love the sport and this city. I thought it would be fun, and if it turned out to be a dud, I'd get a big tax break. Then it became a family and we won a championship. I've got the money to do anything the hell I want, and I've spent years kissing asses for exactly this reason. Now that I have the money and power, I'm going to use it for things that are important to me, business be damned."

Jamie could only nod since he was so choked up.

"So, I hear you're buying a house?" Lonnie easily transitioned into another topic.

"Uh, yeah." Jamie told him about it and they talked casually about random subjects for a while. Finally, Lonnie glanced at the clock.

"I have another meeting, son, so I'll need to get going."

"All right." Jamie rose and shook his left hand again. "Thank you. For everything."

"It's always better to do what's right than what's easy," he said quietly. "And for the record, I don't think there should be labels either. I've been a closet bisexual all my life and now that I'm powerful enough to make a stand, it feels like it's too late."

"Aren't you married?"

He smiled. "To the same woman for over 30 years. You truly can't help who you fall in love with, son. That doesn't mean I don't appreciate the fact that you have a nice ass and Viggo has a big dick."

Jamie's mouth fell open and he blinked before he realized that Lonnie's eyes were twinkling with mirth. "Are you really bisexual?"

"What do you think?" He winked and gestured towards the door.

---

JAMIE DIDN'T TELL Viggo anything about the trade back to Las Vegas while he was out of town. Instead, he waited until he got back, early in the evening that Sunday. Emilie was at the club and Simone was sleeping, so he wrapped the new contract in a pair of his boxers and tied it with a piece of ribbon he found in Simone's room. He hoped it wasn't anything important, but it was kind of funny to see his black boxers wrapped with a piece of pink ribbon. He'd ordered a nice meal for them and it was warming in the oven, along with a bottle of champagne that was chilling in the refrigerator.

He'd planned a quiet, romantic evening and wondered if that kind of thing worked with a guy. He'd enjoyed romantic evenings when he'd dated women, but now that he was learning new things about himself, he speculated on just how different he really was. Was being bisexual something that made him less masculine? He found that hard to believe because Viggo was all man, from his size to his personality to his mannerisms. There wasn't a feminine thing about him, not even when he called him "babe" or "lover."

When he heard a key in the lock, he leaned against the wall in the foyer, folding his arms across his bare chest, a smile playing on his lips.

Viggo stopped when he opened the door, taking in Jamie's hip-hugging jeans and shirtless torso. "Hey." He shut the door behind him and dropped his bag. He walked over to him and pressed his lips hard against Jamie's. "Been waiting for me?"

"Well, duh."

Viggo slid his tongue along Jamie's lower lip, pausing to nip at it. "I'll make you very glad you did." He started to unbutton his shirt. "*After* we eat. Please tell me there's food."

Jamie smiled. "Of course. Go change and I'll get everything ready."

Viggo was back two minutes later, grinning at the feast Jamie had set out in the dining room. "What the hell is that?" he laughed, spying the strange package on his plate.

Jamie chuckled. "You should open it."

Viggo reached down and untied the ribbon, squinting. "You realize this is the ribbon my mum gave Simone when we baptized her, yeah?"

Jamie grimaced. "I didn't jerk off on it or anything—it was the only thing I could find to tie it up with!"

Viggo shook his head as he studied what was in his hands. "Are these your *boxers?!*"

Jamie snorted. "Maybe."

"What the hell..." Viggo frowned as he unrolled the contract, trying to focus on the English legal terms. "Jamie, what is this? Is it your Ottawa contract?"

"Nope." Jamie couldn't help the grin that spread across his face.

"Give me a break, yeah? Reading in English is still hard and this legal shit is beyond me."

"The Sidewinders," he said gently, taking it from him and pointing to a specific line. "They're buying my contract from Ottawa."

Viggo stared at the papers and then at him. "Do you mean...?"

"I'm staying here. They want me back, even if I can't play again."

"That's wonderful!" He put down the papers and reached over to grab Jamie by the shoulders. "Aren't you happy?"

"So fucking happy I want to cry—but then I'd feel like a pussy so I'm not going to."

Viggo chuckled. "I told you! Things are going to be okay. You're getting better and the meds have stabilized your moods. We close on the house soon. You're staying here permanently...this is all wonderful, yes?"

"Yeah, it is." Jamie nodded.

"But?" Viggo narrowed his eyes.

"Nothing. I'm just a little overwhelmed by...everything. The support from our friends. The way Emilie treats me like a second husband—and not in a creepy way. Dante pulling strings for me, for Misty. What Chains did to those skinheads. Now this contract from the Sidewinders even though I might never be the player I was before...I never thought I'd find this kind of thing outside of my family."

"It's a good thing, isn't it?"

"Oh, yeah." Jamie met his eyes and smiled. "But you're the best thing. Thanks for putting up with me. I know I'm a pain in the ass."

"Maybe." He smiled back. "But you're my pain in the ass."

## CHAPTER 35

July – Ottawa

JAMIE'S HANDS trembled as he tried to make his tie straight. After the fourth attempt, he tugged it in frustration and yanked it from around his neck, throwing it across the room. He tried to breathe steadily though his heart was beating double time as he stared at his shaking hands. He couldn't remember ever feeling this nervous and he clenched his fists in frustration. His attorney had called to say the jury had just come back with their verdict and that the judge expected them at the courthouse after lunch for the announcement.

"Hey." Viggo's deep gentle voice washed over him and he felt tender hands on his arms. "You're shaking."

"I think I'm gonna puke," Jamie whispered, hanging his head.

"It's okay. I'm here." Viggo wrapped his arms around him from behind and squeezed him tight. "They can't hurt you. No matter what happens today, they can't touch you."

"I don't know if I can sit there if they're acquitted."

"You don't have to go—you're not the one on trial—but I think you need to be there, babe."

"If they get off..." Jamie turned, his brown eyes filled with pain. "I don't know what I'll do if they're not convicted."

"It doesn't matter," Viggo whispered, gripping him by the shoulders and making him look at him. "We have each other, our friends, our families—and next month you'll be able to play hockey again."

"I'll be allowed to hold a stick," Jamie corrected mildly. "There won't be any hockey involved."

"Shut up, will you?" Viggo leaned down and looked into the soft brown eyes he'd grown to love more in the last few months than he'd ever imagined possible. "We've got this and no matter what happens, I've got your back."

"I know." Jamie leaned up and kissed him, welcoming the relief that always came with Viggo's touch. No matter where they were or what was going on, the moment Viggo touched him everything was less complicated.

A sharp rap on the door interrupted their intimate moment and Viggo nearly growled with frustration as Jamie instantly tensed. "Relax," he whispered. "I'll get rid of whoever it is and be right back."

"Okay." Jamie bent to pick up his tie.

VIGGO STRODE to the door and opened it with a scowl. Everyone knew how stressed Jamie had been over the course of the trial and today was going to be either the hardest day or the best, depending on the verdict. It was hard to believe someone was bothering them right before they had to leave and—he froze as he stared at the people standing in the hallway. Because of the publicity of the trial, they'd rented the entire floor of the hotel, with security guarding the elevators and stairs so that no one had access to them. No one except their mothers, apparently. Evelyn had a big smile on her face as she stood beside Viggo's mother, Claudia.

For a moment Viggo couldn't comprehend the two women standing in front of him until he heard Karl's rumbled laughter. "I'm thinking you're about to get a smack," he called out. "You should say hello to your mother."

"Shit," Viggo muttered under his breath, reaching out to hug his mother. "Mama, what are you doing here?"

"Did you think we would miss this? We were to be here yesterday but the flight was delayed and we missed our connection!" She hugged him tightly before looking up into his tired face. "You look exhausted...this has been hard on you."

"Not nearly as hard as it's been on Jamie," he sighed. "He's not doing well..."

"Is he okay?" Evelyn was immediately concerned and glanced around worriedly.

"Physically he's fine, but emotionally..." His voice trailed off. "I'm going to need a minute, yeah?"

"Viggo, who's—" Jamie came out of the bathroom with his tie hanging loosely around his neck. He stopped abruptly, smiling at the two women in the room. "Oh, hi, Mom."

"Jamie." Viggo reached for his hand and pulled him forward. "This is my mother, Claudia."

"Mrs. Sjoberg..." Jamie stared at Viggo's mother and noted the resemblance; the same red hair and blue eyes, the same smile and stocky build.

"Please, call me Claudia." She smiled, reaching for his hands and immediately noticing they were ice-cold. She took them in hers and squeezed tightly, moving closer to him and looking into his eyes. "My English is not so good," she said gently. "But I see you are nervous?"

"Yes, very."

"Do not worry," Claudia said, searching his face intently.

"I'm trying," Jamie admitted. "But it's not easy."

"Come." Claudia slid her arm through Jamie's and guided him towards the couch. "You will tell me why you are feeling..." Her voice grew faint as they moved into the main room.

Watching his mother so lovingly tend to Jamie made Viggo happier than he'd been in months. He and Jamie hadn't been able to make a trip to Sweden to meet Viggo's family because of Jamie's physical therapy and rehab, but now his mother was here, as if she'd known how much he needed her. He hadn't asked her to come, but he realized she must have sensed that her presence would soothe him at a time like this. The trial had been brutal, and though he'd remained steadfast for Jamie's sake, it hurt to hear the things people said about them. Deep down, it stung to hear the details of what some people thought of two men in love. He never let Jamie see how it affected him, because Jamie's pain cut much deeper, but Viggo had been struggling too; he hadn't had anyone to lean on throughout this ordeal.

His mother's presence calmed him. As a child, he'd done everything in his power to protect her from his abusive father. In turn, she'd taken many a beating to protect him. They'd remained close over the years, even after she remarried and had another son. His stepfather was a good man, who'd never treated Viggo any differently than his own son, but after Viggo's sexuality had come out, he'd grown apart from his stepfather and half-brother. He missed them, but now that he was involved with a man that he was most likely going to be with for the rest of his life, he refused to beg them to accept him. Either they did or they didn't; he didn't have anything left after taking care of Jamie the last few months. It had been the hardest thing he'd ever had to do, and he'd basically been on his own because Emilie had spiraled out of control after they moved in together and got legally divorced. He'd been playing hockey, taking care of Jamie, sharing duties in Simone's care and having to keep an eye on Emilie as well. By the time Jamie had gotten back on his feet to some degree, Viggo hadn't been sure how much longer he would have been able to keep up the breakneck pace.

Emilie's recent disappearing act had almost been the last straw. She'd taken off after they'd come to Ottawa for the trial. Luckily, Emilie's mother, Anya, had come from Sweden to help Karl and Kate with their three-month-old twins for the summer so she'd also been able to lend a hand with Simone and give Misty a break. All of it put together, however, left Viggo feeling like he was being pulled in a lot of different directions and it had already been a long, difficult summer. Jamie was doing better, but even after a second surgery his wrist was nowhere near ready for hockey and that was all Jamie thought about most days. Emotionally, it had begun to take a toll.

"Are you okay, Viggo?" Evelyn spoke quietly, putting a gentle hand on his forearm.

Viggo turned, his most pleasant smile in place. "Yes, of course."

"Don't lie," she said softly. "I know how difficult this has been on you. Jamie tells me how much he relies on you and how much you've had to take on during his rehab. He feels terribly guilty and knows how lucky he is."

"We're lucky to have each other," Viggo said. "It's been a trying time, but as hard as it's been for me, it's been 10 times harder for him...the therapy, rehab, the counselor for his depression and PTSD. He's been through so much and he's still fighting to come through the other side."

"And with Emilie gone, how are you dealing with being a single father?"

Viggo smiled. "I'm not—Jamie has stepped up. Simone has two daddies now and I don't think she'll ever know the difference."

"Is Emilie not coming back?" Evelyn frowned.

"I don't know," he admitted. "She left without any warning, although Chains says he thinks he knows where she is. He couldn't go get her until the trial was over because it wasn't fair to leave Franny and Becca alone at the club. Especially with Joe, Dante and most of the Sidewinders here with us, but he's leaving for London today, I believe."

"It would be great if everything didn't hit the fan all at once, you know?" She made such an irritated face Viggo couldn't help but laugh.

"Tell me about it." He leaned over to kiss her cheek. "Thank you for being here for us."

"If Emilie isn't back when hockey season starts, I'll come to Las Vegas to help with Simone. Your mother and I already decided we would take turns. I know it's a bit of an invasion of your privacy, but you and Jamie both have a lot to do when the season starts and a toddler isn't easy to care for. Once Jamie is 100% again, we won't be such nuisances."

"You're not a nuisance, but if Emilie isn't back by October," Viggo muttered, "I'm going to give new meaning to spanking her!" He stalked off into the living area to see Jamie and his mother laughing on the couch. She had a small photo album out and Viggo had a feeling their laughter was at his expense, but that was okay; seeing Jamie laughing and at ease on a day like today was worth any small embarrassment on his part.

"I need to fix my tie and we'll be ready to go," Jamie said, standing up.

"I'll be right back, Mama," Viggo said to her, following Jamie into the bedroom and shutting the door. "Hey."

"Hey." Jamie turned, glancing over at him as he worked to make some semblance of decency out of his tie.

Viggo noticed Jamie's hands weren't shaking anymore and he sent a mental thank you to his mother for making that happen.

"I didn't know she was coming," he said quietly.

"I know." Jamie continued to work on his tie, not looking at him. "I arranged it as a surprise."

"You what?" Viggo frowned at him. "Why?"

Jamie cocked his head and glanced up. "Because you've been so busy taking care of me and Simone, there's been no one to take care of *you*, and I figured it was time."

"Jamie..." Viggo felt emotion welling up in his chest.

"Since we've been together, I've done nothing but take," Jamie said, securing the knot at his throat and then turning to look at Viggo intently. "First I was terrified of admitting I was bisexual and what that would mean to my manhood. You waited for me to figure it out while I played games with your heart. Then I jerked you around some more while I came to terms with the idea of being in love with a guy. When I was attacked, you not only had to deal with my very fragile ego, you also had to worry about my physical injuries and the emotional bullshit that went with it. You've had to work your very demanding job as a professional athlete, love me enough for 20 men, take care of your infant daughter, buy a new house and deal with all the fallout from basically coming out in the league. And you've never faltered. Not once." Jamie leaned up and kissed him, his lips gripping Viggo's firmly. He nudged them apart with his tongue and slid it inside his mouth. For a moment, everything else disappeared as their tongues mated with gentle and loving familiarity.

"Jamie..." Viggo's breath hitched slightly.

"Shh." Jamie pulled away but looked into his eyes. "Do you realize you've never raised your voice to me? Never lost your temper? Never told me no—and I need you to know I'm aware and I'm grateful and as soon as this is all over, I'm going to make it up to you."

"How could I lose my temper while you were fighting for your life?" Viggo asked in confusion. "Why would I raise my voice when it took every ounce of strength you had to get out of bed some days? And say no to what? You're not a child—you're perfectly capable of doing what you like."

"You know that's not what I meant," Jamie smiled faintly. "But you need to know that all the shit I've put you through hasn't escaped me. I *know* how hard it's been and I promise it won't be like this anymore."

"Loving each other means we do what's necessary. You don't have to make anything up to me. All I want is you."

"You have me," Jamie said earnestly. "You know that, don't you? You know I'm all in."

"Of course I know." Viggo ran his knuckles across Jamie's cheek. "Have you been worried about us? Have you thought that because of everything that's happened I would lose interest or something?"

"How could you not think twice about this disaster?" Jamie asked, looking away. "Everything about us has been a fucking mess, man. I don't want you staying with me because you feel sorry for me!"

"Stop it!" Viggo hissed through his teeth, grabbing him by the shoulders and claiming his mouth more fiercely than he intended. His lips were almost brutal as they captured Jamie's, forcing them apart again and practically demanding his tongue. His kisses were hard, punishing, and he didn't let up until Jamie breathlessly pulled away.

"Okay, big guy," he gasped, panting. "You made your point. You own me. I get it." His quirky smile was enough to make Viggo shake his head in frustration despite the beginning of his own smile.

"You think I'm still here because I feel sorry for you?!" he asked, not quite ready to let it go. "You can't be serious?"

"People fall in and out of love," Jamie said slowly. "It happens. We were so new when all this happened—what if you were having second thoughts? How could you leave me in the middle of the nightmare that was my life?" He held up a hand when Viggo started to talk. "Seriously—think about what you would have done if you'd realized you didn't love me that way, that it had only been a fling? You're a good guy and you never would have walked away from me when I was so down and out."

Viggo rolled his eyes but nodded. "Yeah, you're right, it could have happened, and I wouldn't have walked away during your recovery. But it *didn't* happen—I love you more every day. The thing is, we were friends first and I would have found a way to let you know that while things weren't working romantically, I never would have abandoned you. If anything, I would've started looking for a beautiful woman to distract you."

Jamie made a face. "You think my love for you would be tested by something as simple as a beautiful woman?"

"Someday we're going to have to talk about that," Viggo chuckled. "But not today."

"About beautiful women?"

"About the fact that both of us enjoy pussy as much as we do cock."

Jamie shrugged. "Being in love means I don't care about whether you have a vagina or a penis—I only care about this." He put his hand over Viggo's heart.

"I know. Like I said, that's a conversation for another day." He covered Jamie's hand with his own. "Thank you for bringing my mother. It means a lot."

"I'm glad. I wanted to do something special for you."

"Let's get through today, yeah?"

"Yeah." Jamie took a deep breath and reached for his jacket, sliding it on and adjusting it.

"You're sexy as fuck in a suit," Viggo murmured under his breath.

"Just in a suit?" Jamie teased.

"The muscle you've put on during rehab is pretty hot too," he chuckled, running a hand across Jamie's broader chest. "And I admit to being fond of these..." He ran a hand along the area where one side of the "V" that ran down Jamie's impressive abdominal muscles was.

"Tonight we'll celebrate," Jamie whispered. "Win or lose, it'll be over, and that's reason enough."

"You realize our mothers will be here?" Viggo arched a brow. "I'm pretty open about all things sexual, but I draw the line at having sex while my mother is in the same hotel room."

Jamie burst out laughing. "Oh ye of little faith! Your mom is in a suite on the *other side* of the hotel, babe! Do you believe I can even think about sex with my mom in the room?!"

"What are we going to do when they come visit?" Viggo asked, a pained look on his face.

Jamie chuckled. "That's different. That's our home, where we live. We share a life, a house, a child and, yes, a bed. They know this. We'll just have to be quieter, and obviously, there'll be no bending anyone over the living room couch, but there will absolutely be sex."

Viggo leaned down and slowly, deliciously, licked Jamie's lips. He ran his tongue along the full lower lip and then the underside of the upper lip when Jamie's mouth opened. "I love you," he whispered. "Win or lose, I love you."

"Then it's a win," Jamie whispered back, meeting his lustful gaze. "Now knock it off—my mom's like 20 feet away!"

"Is everyone ready to go?" Viggo asked as he and Jamie joined what had become a small crowd in the living area.

Their mothers had been joined by Jamie's father, sister and brother, along with Karl, Dante, Josh and Joe. Joe had come to organize security for them for however long they were in Ottawa for the trial, and he and Josh had been spending time together. Jamie had been too distracted to ask him if they were dating, but he was planning to today. Based on their body language, he was almost positive something was going on, but obviously, this wasn't the right time.

"So, before we go," Jamie stepped forward and looked around the room, "I have one more surprise for Viggo—who's been more than just my rock the last six months." He turned and smiled at his confused lover before looking at Karl and nodding. Karl moved to the door and opened it.

Viggo's mouth fell open when his father and brother walked in. He glanced at Jamie and knew he might cry if he said anything, so instead he gave him a grateful nod before taking three big steps towards his father, who gripped him in a tight hug. Jamie couldn't understand what they said in Swedish, but Mattias spoke English when he stepped up.

"I've been a boor and I apologize," he rumbled in a deep voice, holding out his arms. Viggo grabbed him and pulled him into the hug with their father and the three men said nothing for a few minutes. Finally, Claudia joined them and the four of them shared an intimate family moment, speaking quietly in their own language before Viggo lifted his head and reached out his hand to Jamie. Jamie hesitated for a moment, not wanting to intrude, but when Viggo's father also reached for him, he had no choice but to move forward.

"My family," Viggo said in a voice thick with emotion. "My father, Stefan, and my brother, Mattias. Papa, Mattias, this is Jamie."

"My English is not good," Stefan said, hugging Jamie tightly. "But I will learn, yes?"

"And I'm trying to learn some Swedish," Jamie smiled.

"My English is fine," Mattias grinned, shaking Jamie's hand. "While Viggo's been playing hockey, I've been attending university in England."

"That hockey has been paying for," Viggo grunted, punching him in the shoulder. Mattias swung back, catching him in the gut. Both of them raised their fists and immediately began a faux fight, swinging and laughing as they tried to best the other.

"Since they were kids," Karl muttered, rolling his eyes. "Viggo is eight years older and I swear, at four years old, Mattias would sucker punch him in the nuts and then run to their mother and pretend Viggo started it."

Mattias snorted with laughter as Joe cleared his throat. "Unless you gentlemen want to be late, I suggest we head out. There are three limousines waiting outside the maintenance entrance so we need to go."

"Three?" Jamie frowned.

Joe smiled. "You have a lot of friends."

"Come on." Viggo straightened his jacket and tie. They filed into the hall and down the elevator, getting off on the second floor instead of the first and transferring to a cargo elevator. They got to the ground floor and Joe's security team led them through private hotel hallways until they got to the exit. Joe opened the door and let Jamie and Viggo go out first. When Jamie saw what awaited him he stopped abruptly, causing Viggo to stumble into his back.

"All right, babe?" Viggo murmured, squeezing his shoulder.

"No." Jamie had to take a moment to compose himself. Standing in a huge semicircle that enclosed the area just inside the three parked limousines all the way to the building where they were exiting, were Jamie's family, friends and teammates. Members from the team in Ottawa and some of his friends when he'd played in Minnesota were there, interspersed with almost the entire Sidewinders organization. Coach Barnett and Lonnie Finch stood in the middle, with Assistant Coach Gagne, General Manager Pierre Bouchard, Doc Levine, equipment managers, some of the sales and marketing team and all but a few of the players. Zakk and Tiff stood off to one side, smiling broadly, and the first person to move was Rachel Kennedy. She pulled away from Vlad and walked up to Jamie, placing a kiss squarely on his lips as she cupped his face with her hands.

"Straight, gay, bi—I don't give a shit," she whispered. "You were my lover and my friend, and I don't give a flying fuck who knows it. I'll always treasure the time we spent together and I hope we'll always be friends."

Jamie nodded and bent to kiss her forehead. "Always. Thanks, babe."

She winked and walked back to Vlad, who slid a possessive arm around her waist despite the smile on his face.

The next person to move was Zakk and he approached Jamie with a grin. "I'm not going to kiss you—sorry, my fiancée gets jealous—" Tiff burst out laughing as he continued. "But whatever happens today, you win. There is too much fucking hate in this world and together, we will knock down that hate one person at a time. Together we're stronger. Together we can and will make a difference. And here's my donation to No Labels for Hate." He handed Jamie a check before walking away.

"Wait—what is this?" Jamie frowned, staring at a check for $20,000.

"You're not the only one with surprises," Viggo said quietly. "Our first step towards bringing acceptance to the LGBTQ community and beyond is our new charity organization—No Labels for Hate."

"We all have checks," Lonnie Finch called out. "But we'll get them to you after the verdict."

"For now," Viggo said, "we wanted you to walk into that courtroom knowing that it doesn't matter if you win or lose. We still win. Because of what they did to you, it's now something tangible for us to fight against and No Labels for Hate is just the beginning. We'll make it big, make it well-known and make it a haven for those who have nowhere else to turn. The money we raise will not just bring awareness, it will help eliminate labels like gay, bisexual, transgender and more. Our goal is to make the idea of love simply that—love. No labels, no differences, and absolutely no hate. No more."

"God, I love you," Jamie whispered, looking into Viggo's eyes.

"And I you." Viggo wanted to kiss him, but refrained. Not for any other reason than he had a feeling it might make Jamie cry, and as far as they'd come, the one thing Jamie held on to was his masculinity. Crying in front of this crowd would embarrass him, and that was the one thing Viggo didn't want.

"You can kiss me," Jamie whispered, as if reading his mind.

Viggo smiled. "I don't have to show the world I love you—they already know."

Jamie nodded. "They do, but showing them is okay too."

"When they announce the guilty verdict, I will shove your sexy ass against the wall and suck your tongue so deep into my mouth you won't be able to breathe."

"I'm going to enjoy that," Jamie chuckled.

. . .

When the guilty verdict was announced, Jamie felt the stress, anger and humiliation of the last seven months drain out of him in one fell swoop. The anger radiating from Collin and the others on that side of the room was hard to miss, but it didn't matter. As his friends and family let out whoops of joy and laughter, he felt something inside of him let go. He wanted to cry but couldn't do it here; later, when he was alone, he would let it out, but right now he wanted to be strong, and show the world he was okay with who he was and that what they'd done hadn't broken him.

He glanced over at Viggo and was startled to see tears in his eyes. His large body was barely holding back the need to break down after so many months of keeping everything bottled up.

"Not here," Jamie whispered to him, squeezing his hand. "I need you to be strong just a few more minutes, babe. We don't show weakness in front of these assholes."

"Fuck them," Viggo whispered back, but he was nodding. "But yeah, I'm okay."

They filed out of the courtroom and into the crowded hallway en masse. There were reporters everywhere and Joe and his team efficiently escorted Jamie and Viggo to a back elevator. Once inside, Viggo pushed Jamie against the wall and kissed him, hard, just as he'd promised he would do and Joe cleared his throat as they got to the bottom floor.

"Enough, you two—get a room!" he teased.

Jamie chuckled, putting a hand on Viggo's shoulder. "Later, big guy. Lots of that later."

They stepped out and headed for the exit where more reporters waited like a hungry mob. Joe glanced at them. "Do you want to do this?"

"No." Jamie shook his head. "I'll do interviews one-on-one when I get home, but not like this. Let's get out of here."

Joe nodded and pulled out his radio, letting his team know the plan.

Viggo reached out and took Jamie's hand, glancing down at him as if asking permission. Jamie smiled and gave him a brief nod, squeezing his hand to let him know it was okay. This was who they were and the world already knew it. Hiding it was ridiculous and they weren't willing to live that way. Besides, after today, it didn't make sense to hide anything; this was their life.

Sliding into the limo with Joe and their parents, they pulled down the street and for a moment everyone was quiet.

"This is a great day," Joe said after a while. "Good to know that the legal system has our backs, even if a lot of people don't."

"Definitely." Jamie nodded.

"So," Evelyn said after a moment. "How shall we celebrate?"

"Dinner!" Mattias said with a grimace. "I've had, like, a sandwich since I got here!"

"Alcohol!" Jamie's brother, Dwight, said. "After the last two weeks, we need to get shit-faced."

"Amen to that!" Viggo laughed.

# EPILOGUE

"So, what kind of conversation do we need to have about beautiful women?" Jamie asked late the next morning as they awoke after a long night of celebrating.

Viggo grunted. "I've got the hangover from hell and a raging hard-on, and you want to talk about beautiful women?"

"You said we had to talk about it, so I figured this was as good a time as any." Jamie turned onto his side and looked at Viggo's large, muscular body with appreciation. "Because right now all I see is a gorgeous, sexy guy with a big dick. I'm not sure I remember what a pussy feels like."

"Liar." Viggo opened his eyes and smiled.

"Okay—what's the deal? You think I'm going to start missing sex with women?"

"Well, just because I knew I was bi doesn't change the fact that I've never been in a relationship with a man," Viggo said. "I've never gone without sex with a woman for any length of time. *Ever*. And since I'm the only guy you've ever been with, neither have you. Don't you think we're going to think about it now and again?"

Jamie frowned. "I suppose. We're probably not thinking about it yet because we've been sleeping with Emilie, but eventually that's going to stop."

Viggo nodded. "When we settle into regular life, without all the added drama, do you think we'll miss it?"

"I don't know." Jamie looked at him. "Are you starting to miss it already?"

"I'm not missing it, but I think about it," he admitted.

"Me too," Jamie sighed.

"We have to be honest about this stuff," Viggo said gently. He turned onto his side so they were facing each other. "Look, here's the deal. I've always been pretty experimental in the bedroom. I enjoy a lot of sex, with both men and women. At the same time, I have no desire to sleep around and I want very much to have what we have—love, commitment and a family."

"I feel the same," Jamie said. "I'd never had sex with men, but I was always curious. Now that I have you, to be honest, I'm not curious anymore. I definitely don't want to sleep with other men."

"I don't either," Viggo admitted. "And the thought of you being with another man makes me insane."

"But?"

"You're into spanking and that's not my thing—you know that."

"I don't have to—"

"Wait, let me finish." Viggo touched his face. "If you wanted to go to the club and find a woman that likes to be spanked, I think I would be okay with it, assuming I was with you."

"And maybe you got to be with her as well?"

"I don't know. We have to see what happens."

"Your thing was multiples, right? Threesomes? More sometimes?"

Viggo nodded slowly.

"So, if we found a woman who wanted me to spank her, and then you got to fuck her, it could satisfy both of us, right?"

"I don't know." Viggo was hesitant. "We have to be sure we can add something like that to our relationship without it coming between us."

"Nothing will *ever* come between us," Jamie said. "What we have goes so far beyond sex. The last six months proves that, doesn't it?"

"I just think we have to be careful. We're in new territory with this and we have to put our relationship before anything else."

"You come before *everything* else," Jamie whispered, leaning over and brushing his lips across Viggo's. "I will never love anyone but you—I know that as sure as I'm breathing."

"Fuck, I fall more in love with you every goddamn day," Viggo rasped. "Marry me, Jamie? Like, soon?"

"When?" Jamie dug his fingers into the other man's hair. "Today? Tomorrow?"

"We can get married today if you want to. No waiting period in Ottawa."

"You looked?" Jamie arched a brow.

"Yeah."

"Most of our friends and family are here with us."

"Except Becca and Chains."

"You just got divorced," Jamie frowned. "Are you sure you want to jump right in?"

"I jumped in the first time I kissed you," Viggo admitted. "I knew you were straight but I wanted you and wanted you to want me."

"I already wanted you," Jamie whispered. "I just didn't understand it. That little bit of temptation was all it took—and now I'm going to fucking marry you. Today."

"Today? Really?" Viggo squinted slightly and leaned up on his elbow.

"Yup." Jamie pressed another quick kiss to his lips and sat up. "Wait—we don't have rings."

"Yeah, we do." Viggo felt his cheeks redden.

"You bought wedding rings?" Jamie stared at him.

Viggo got up and padded over to his suitcase, digging around until he found a small box. He brought it over to the bed and handed it to Jamie.

Jamie opened the box and smiled. "Brushed titanium," he said quietly. "How did you know?"

"I asked Rachel."

Jamie blinked at him. "You asked my ex?"

"You two were going to get married, so I figured you must have talked about rings."

Jamie could only nod.

"I asked her and she said you were fond of titanium and the darker colors, not traditional gold or silver."

"What about you?"

"I want whatever you want," Viggo shrugged. "And I thought these rings were masculine, like us, but also beautiful and exotic, like our love."

"Yes. To everything." Jamie closed the box and got to his feet. "Yes, to these rings. Yes, to forever. Yes, I'll marry you. Today. Right fucking now."

"After a shower," Viggo grinned.

"Becca and Misty are gonna be pissed," Jamie chuckled, heading for the bathroom.

"We'll have a party when we get home," Viggo said, following him.

"Are you sure?" Jamie stopped abruptly and turned, causing Viggo to run into him. Standing chest to chest, they stared into each other's eyes.

"Yes." Viggo placed both hands on Jamie's shoulders. "To everything."

"There's no one in the NHL that's *out*, much less two players that are married to each other."

"Then it's time."

"We're going to get a lot of shit."

"Bring it."

"For every wonderful day we have together, there are probably going to be two bad ones."

"Name one married couple that doesn't have bad days." Viggo reached up to rub his hand over the short strands of hair that were just beginning to curl. "We've got this."

"I don't want to change my name."

"I don't want you to."

Jamie turned his head to kiss the inside of Viggo's wrist.

"Anything else?" Viggo asked softly.

"Our lawyers are going to freak if we get married without prenups."

"If you leave me, you might as well take everything because none of it will matter without you."

"You realize I could really screw you over financially?" Jamie tried to sound stern, but his voice cracked, belying the overwhelming feelings surging through him.

Viggo shrugged. "If that's what it takes to make you happy."

"*You* make me happy. None of that other bullshit matters."

"Then let's go get married."

For a long moment, they continued to stand close together, their eyes locked for an interlude so intimate there was no reason to speak.

"Say it," Jamie whispered. "And then do it."

Viggo smiled, knowing exactly what his lover wanted.

"I. Fucking. Love. You." He spoke slowly, enunciating carefully. Then he kissed him.

****THE END****

If you'd like to keep up with me and my characters, books and appearances, subscribe to my newsletter at www.katmizera.com. Subscribers see covers and excerpts first, get bonus content and can enter in monthly contests!

YOU CAN ALSO FOLLOW me on social media and Book Bub:
www.facebook.com/authorkatmizera
www.twitter.com/AuthorKatMiz
www.bookbub.com/authors/kat-mizera

# EXCERPT FROM REDEMPTION'S INFERNO

The nightmares came almost every night. Full of blood and gore and the pungent smell of death. The wind howled like in the storms of 1950s horror movies, ripping through trees and rooftops until only tiny parcels of destruction were left. People screamed and cried, begging for mercy, as havoc rained down on everyone and everything. The sound of a baby crying played like a soundtrack set on repeat; the same piteous wail reverberating through the walls of her mind, keeping rhythm with her body as she thrashed on the bed.

Even in her dreams, Emilie Sjoberg could sense the Grim Reaper looming, so close she felt his breath on her neck as she ran. She was always running, darting around corners and hiding in the shadows, but he managed to find her. Just before she found the baby, or shelter from the wind, or a safe haven to protect her, he was there, pulling her into the abyss. No matter how much she begged and pleaded, he merely held out his skeletal fingers, beckoning to her. The more she resisted, the closer the fingers got to her face, their icy moisture skimming the tip of her nose. She screamed over and over, until she woke with a panic-laden shriek, heart pounding like a jackhammer, hands protectively covering her face.

Breathing deeply, Emilie lay back and tried to calm her frantically pounding heart, hands clenched into fists as she struggled to relax. Another nightmare. The fourth in the last six days. They were becoming more frequent, more repugnant, and much more terrifying. She'd never been afraid of, or even put much thought into death, but now it lurked inside of her as if it were tangible. She couldn't fight anymore; if her life was a swimming pool, she was becoming too tired to continue to tread water. She had to do something, and soon, or she was going to drown.

"I can't do this anymore," she whispered into the darkness. There was no relief and no light at the end of the tunnel. No matter how hard she tried, and in spite of all the wonderful things happening in her life, she was losing the battle waging within her.

Glancing towards the open door that led to the adjacent room where her 15-

month-old daughter was sleeping, she knew that would be the hardest part of what she had to do. She had to go away in order to find the answers to what haunted her, and that meant leaving Simone behind. There was no way to know how long she would be gone, and the end result would almost definitely be prison. Which meant Simone could be without her mother for a very long time.

That had to be what the Grim Reaper represented in her dreams: prison. She was terrified of even the thought of being incarcerated, but that would be the only way to pay for what she'd done. Otherwise, she would never be free and never be able to enjoy life again. The problem, of course, was that she didn't know exactly what she'd done. Her first mission would be to find out what had happened, and once she knew the details, then she would accept whatever punishment was necessary.

Decision made, she closed her eyes and thought about what she needed to do to make this happen. Her ex-husband, Viggo, and his boyfriend, Jamie, were both professional hockey players so they were off until mid-September. It was mid-July now, and they'd just gone to Canada for the trial of the three men who'd beaten Jamie and nearly killed him. It was impossible to guess how long the trial would last, but the attorneys estimated no more than two weeks. Although this wasn't an ideal time for her to get away, if she waited much longer it might leave them in the lurch with childcare when they started hockey practices in September. Her mother was here in Las Vegas for the summer, helping Emilie's brother Karl and his wife with their newborn twins. She would probably be able to help Simone's nanny as well until Viggo and Jamie returned. Hopefully, by the time hockey season started, Emilie would know what was going to happen to her, giving them time to make preparations for Simone's care if Emilie couldn't come back. In the meantime, she had one other thing to do, but that could be done on the way to London. She just had to make sure no one knew her plans until she was gone.

*JULY*

WALKING up to the large brick building, Emilie pulled her lower lip between her teeth and took a deep breath. She stared at the bleak, windowless walls and wondered what it was like inside. She would only see the visitors' area, but that would be more than enough. She'd never been inside a prison before and just the thought made her a little queasy.

Forcing herself to put one foot in front of the other, she paused and turned to her friend Becca Lamonte. Six months pregnant and literally glowing, she stood next to Emilie patiently, her silver-blue eyes following her friend's as she looked towards the building.

"It's all right," Becca said gently. "She can't hurt you."

"Sometimes words are more painful than weapons," Emilie said quietly.

"You don't have to see her," Becca reminded her. "We can turn around and drive right back to New York."

"No, I have to," Emilie said, clearing her throat. "I need to ask her some questions, maybe get some closure."

"I still think you're crazy," Becca murmured, thinning her lips into a flat line of disapproval. "We found out just how crazy she was during the trial—why do you need to revisit this?"

"I don't know." Emilie stared off into the distance with almost sightless eyes. "I just do."

"All right." Becca squeezed her arm. "I'll be waiting for you in the car. Do what you need to do."

"Thanks." Emilie gave her a faint smile. "And thanks for coming with me—I don't think I could have done it alone."

"That's what friends are for."

Emilie hadn't seen Therese in two years. Two years ago, almost to the day, Therese Anderberg had tried to kill Emilie and her older brother, Karl, in Las Vegas. She'd stabbed him with a needle containing a lethal dose of a sedative and it was only because the paramedics had arrived quickly that Karl had lived. Emilie could still see his large body falling to the ice that day, struggling to stay conscious while Therese laughed and laughed, as if him dying was the funniest thing she'd ever seen.

Today Emilie wished she had it in her to laugh at Therese, but she didn't. All she felt was pity as her old friend came into the room. Therese had always been tall and thin, but she was practically emaciated now. Her orange jumpsuit hung limply on her body and her face was pale and drawn. Her blue eyes sparked with energy when she spotted Emilie, though, a smile lighting what had once been a beautiful face. She seemed harder now, as though prison had truly changed her, and Emilie could only stare with a little bit of shock, a little bit of fear and a lot of pity. This woman had almost destroyed her life but looking at her now she couldn't seem to hate her.

"You came!" Therese said happily, as though seeing Emilie made everything okay.

"You said it was important." Emilie sat in the chair across from her, folding her hands in her lap.

"I thought we were besties! Why haven't you come before now?" Therese demanded, cocking her head.

Emilie frowned. "You know, that whole thing where you tried to kill my brother? And me, for that matter."

Therese waved an impatient hand. "I wasn't medicated then—but now I am, so we can be friends again!"

Emilie raised her eyebrows. "I don't think so, Therese. Too much has happened. You killed people, threatened me, tried to ruin my life. That's hard to forget."

"I didn't know what I was doing," Therese protested, her lips forming a small pout. "Please, Em, can't we be friends again? I don't have anyone else here in the U.S."

"Have your parents been to see you?" Emilie delicately changed the subject.

"Not since the trial." Therese sighed. "They say it's too far to come to visit once a week for 30 minutes."

"You must write?"

Therese shrugged. "I haven't the patience. Mama deposits a little money in my account each month so I can get a few things, but it's not enough. It's rough in here—I could use a little help, Em. You're the reason I'm here, after all."

Emilie rolled her eyes. "I didn't kill anyone, Therese."

"You're the reason I came to the U.S.!" Therese grunted. "You told me I had a chance with Karl!"

"That was the first time you came," Emilie said patiently. "The second time he was already married to Kate and you knew better."

"They say I'm a paranoid schizophrenic," Therese said after a moment. "I used to suffer from delusional thinking and hallucinations, and that's why I believed Karl abandoned me while I was pregnant and all those other things. Now that I'm medicated I don't get those symptoms. You don't have to be afraid—I'm okay and don't want to hurt anyone else."

"That's good to hear," Emilie nodded.

"I heard you and Viggo got married." Therese suddenly looked like a teenager again, her smile sweet and her face almost angelic. "Are you totally in love?"

Emilie sighed, trying not to show much emotion. "We divorced last month. We only got married because of the baby—our daughter."

"You had a baby!" Therese's eyes widened. "Can I see a picture?"

"I wasn't allowed to bring anything in with me," Emilie held up her empty hands. "But I'll send you one in the mail." She would do no such thing, but Therese seemed to accept that at face value.

"I'd love that!" Therese suddenly frowned. "Why did you get divorced? You've always loved him. Wasn't he faithful?"

"It was a mistake," Emilie said softly, trying to keep Therese engaged without giving her too many details. "What I felt as a teenager wasn't the same now that we're adults."

"He couldn't stay away from men, hm?" Therese asked knowingly.

"No." Emilie figured there was a good chance Therese would read about the trial online and hear about Jamie and Viggo anyway.

"Well, you're better off," Therese shrugged. "You were too good for him."

"Then why did you get me involved with him? It was your idea that I hook up with him at the club that night..."

"That was when I was having the hallucinations and such," Therese hedged. "I thought I needed those compromising photos and by involving Viggo it was easy to get you to play along since you'd always wanted him."

"I still don't understand why you did that. Even if you occasionally had those delusions, you had to know that I couldn't make Karl love you... Back then we were close—why would you do that to me?"

"I thought I was in love and holding on to you was the only way I felt I could hold on to him."

"But you involved Viggo and Otto."

"Viggo meant nothing to me and Otto is a pig." She shrugged.

"So you ruined my life, and almost Viggo's as well, for no reason?" Emilie felt herself getting angry all over again. "Why? There had to have been a reason!"

"I don't know!" Therese shot back. "Jesus, haven't you been listening? I'm schizophrenic! I barely know what that means—but they give me these damn meds that make me twitch sometimes and feel dizzy all the time... I just do the laundry a few hours a day, go outside an hour a day, and I get an hour a day in the library. That's it—I have nothing thanks to this stupid disease, so asking me the same questions over and over is a waste of time!"

"Then why am I here?"

Therese paused. "I could use a little money."

"Money?" Emilie blinked.

"Not a lot, maybe a hundred dollars a month. For tampons and toothpaste that doesn't taste like ass... Come on, Em, it's not a lot."

Emilie pretended to think about it as she realized Therese had just played right into her hands. "Tell you what," she said. "If you can tell me some things I need to know, I'll get you some money."

"Like what?"

"Do you remember when we ran into each other in London? About eight years ago? You were on holiday with a couple of your girlfriends and we went dancing at that club with the dance floor on the roof?"

Therese nodded. "Oh! Yes, of course. You were frightened—something about a bondage session gone wrong."

"What do you remember about that?"

Therese frowned. "You asked me to go to that hotel and see what was going on... The police were bringing out a body but no one had any information. A young man had died under suspicious circumstances."

"I left the next day," Emilie said. "And you promised you'd try to find out more. You told me at one point that they were looking for someone—there had been fingerprints in the room that they couldn't identify—but you said they stopped looking relatively quickly."

"It was a while ago, but from what I recall, the search died off almost immediately. You thought you were somehow involved, yes?"

Emilie nodded.

"Why are you thinking about this after all this time?"

"I need to know, one way or another."

"Let it go," Therese hissed, glancing around. "You don't want to wind up like this."

"Do you remember anything else? His last name? Any details?"

Therese rolled her eyes. "Seriously, you're such a bleeding heart... Who cares? It was years ago and no one knows anything about it."

"What do you remember?!" Emilie pressed in frustration.

"There was nothing to remember! It was a non-story within a day."

"You brought it up once, when you were getting me to sleep with all those men." Emilie tried not to squirm at the memory.

"I was trying to make you do what I wanted—there was no new information."

Emilie sighed. "All right. I'll find out how to send you money when I leave."

"You'd better." Therese's eyes suddenly glinted like they used to in the old days; cold and maniacal, as if she was planning something sinister. Again.

"Threats mean nothing anymore," Emilie said.

"I still know things. And people."

Emilie scowled. "You haven't changed at all, have you? Always ready to hurt someone."

"It's your fault I'm in here and, damn you, I deserve better!"

"Better? What about Trey Montoya? Did he deserve better? What about Larissa and her baby? Did they?"

"They deserved what they got and so will you!" Therese growled. "Just wait. I'm not done with you! And I can still reach the authorities in London, even from here!"

"Then give it your best shot," Emilie replied.

With nothing else to say, Emilie got her things as quickly as she could, made arrangements to get Therese a little money, and was grateful to step out into the bright sunlight. She took a few deep breaths, and momentarily closed her eyes, letting the warmth of the sun take away the chill that had settled deep inside of her. She knew what she had to do and she would do it. Even if she had to go to prison, one mistake, made when she was just 19, wasn't going to control her life anymore. She was done. She was going to London and she would face whatever was waiting for her. One way or another, she was going to be free of this and then she would take Therese's advice to make the most of whatever time she had when she was done.

SITTING at the desk in her Manhattan hotel room early the next morning, Emilie drummed her fingers restlessly on the keyboard of her laptop as she tried to figure out what to write. Yesterday and today were her days off from the club she managed, and she and Becca had arrived in New York yesterday morning on the red-eye. Becca wasn't just her boss and the owner of Club Inferno, she was also one of Emilie's few confidantes. Though she couldn't tell her everything, she trusted her with a lot and was grateful for her companionship during the prison visit. Afterwards, when Becca had gone to the Westchester home she shared with her husband when they weren't in Las Vegas, Emilie had gotten online and found a flight that was leaving for London this afternoon. She had no idea when she would be able to come back; if the authorities were looking for her, she might even be apprehended at the airport. She wasn't sure what to expect, but she needed to leave some kind of message for both Becca and Viggo.

Sighing, she opened the email program and started the note to Becca first.

*Hey. Thanks for coming with me yesterday—you have no idea how much I appreciate it. My conversation with Therese reminded me that I have some unfinished business in Europe, and I'm leaving today. I apologize for not giving you any warning, but this is important. I'm not sure how long I'll be away, so I'm okay with you not paying me while I'm gone and I hope you can forgive me for being vague. You're my best friend and I hate not confiding in you, but you know I've had a lot on my mind lately. Please don't worry, I just have to sort through some things. I'll call soon, I promise. Give me a little time to figure out what I'm doing—I need to be away from everyone and everything in order to do that. Thanks for being my friend. Love, Em.*

She read it several times before hitting send. Then she opened another message and sighed. What to say to Viggo was harder because although they were no longer married, they were extremely close and were raising their daughter, Simone, together. He would know something was going on because there was no reason for her to disappear like this. He would undoubtedly be worried, but she couldn't help that. She'd already sent her brother Karl a note, saying she was going to Europe for a few weeks for vacation. Since their mother was in Las Vegas right now helping with Karl's newborn twins, instead of home in Sweden, Emilie didn't have to worry about her expecting a visit. Her other brother, her fraternal twin Sebastian, would most likely make a fuss if he realized she'd disappeared but she was counting on no one telling him just yet. It was just Viggo that would be a problem.

*Hello, love. I wanted to let you know I'm taking some time for myself. I'll be traveling around Europe, hoping to clear my head. It's not about us, the divorce, or you and Jamie. You know I adore both of you! It's just time for me to come to terms with the past. Therapy hasn't been a big help but it made me realize how far I've begun to spiral. I need a different kind of help, and part of that is finding closure on a few things. I can't explain it properly, so I'm asking you to give me a month or so to try to find answers. I won't leave you hanging with Simone, but I'm not sure when I'll be home. Please don't tell Karl or Mama the truth—they think I'm on vacation and it's easier this way. I'll stay in touch. You can send a text if you need something or if anything comes up with the baby. I won't have cell service all the time, but I'll make sure to check my phone once a day. Give my love to Jamie and good luck with the rest of the trial. Em.*

She hit send and slowly closed the laptop. Tomorrow would be the beginning of the end of her past; she would make sure of it. Somehow, she would find peace for what she'd done and if that meant going to prison, she was okay with it. She regretted possibly being away from her daughter for a long time, but Viggo and Jamie were good, loving men who would take care of her. When it was all said and done, she couldn't live like this anymore. Somehow, she had to be free of the guilt, the memories and the fear of discovery. It had been haunting her for eight years and she realized now that almost all the bad decisions she'd made back then had been because of what she'd done, or what she feared she'd done, in London. It was time to put that behind her, even if it meant giving up her freedom.

A FEW DAYS LATER, Emilie sat in the London townhouse of a man she'd known for nearly a decade. Sitting across from him, she thought her old friend looked tired. Warren Bern was a good man, and she trusted him implicitly, even though she hadn't seen him in several years. In his mid-70s now, he was still handsome but something had changed since she'd seen him last. Running a sex club obviously kept him young, but the lines around his eyes had deepened, he'd lost far too much weight, and there was something almost gaunt about him. She felt a flicker of concern as he paused to cough several times during their conversation.

"Are you all right?" she asked gently, frowning.

He scowled. "It's a tickle, love. Nothing to worry about—no need to mother me."

She rolled her eyes. "You've parented me enough times; it seems to be my turn."

Now he rolled his eyes. "Not even a chance, little one."

She grinned. Though he was a well-known, experienced dom in the BDSM world, they didn't have that kind of relationship. He'd met her at one of her brother's hockey games when she was just 17 and had given her a pass to his club for her 18th birthday. He'd even paid for her ticket to London from Stockholm, although there had been no sex involved. He'd said he simply wanted to expose her to something she might enjoy because there had been no doubt that she was already sexually active. Emilie had fallen into the role of a dominatrix naturally, and he'd made sure to let her explore every aspect of the lifestyle under his supervision. He'd never participated in her sexual exploits, but he'd overseen everyone she was with in the beginning, making sure her exposure to BDSM was a healthy and positive one. Fortunately, he had no idea how far off course she'd veered over the years.

"The wheels in your mind are spinning so fast I can practically see them turning," he said softly, gazing into her bright blue eyes with his tired brown ones.

"I need a favor," she said after a moment. "But I'm struggling with how to ask."

He frowned. "You're afraid to ask me for something?"

"Not afraid," she shook her head. "Embarrassed."

He cocked his head. "Considering the lifestyle I live, what I do for a living and how long we've known each other, I'm almost afraid to ask what could possibly embarrass you or me."

She looked down. "Will you allow me to be your slave for a short time?"

His mouth fell open and he blinked rapidly. Then a loud, bellowing laugh escaped his belly as he threw his head back. "Okay, you got me! It was a good one, too."

She shook her head rapidly. "No, Warren, you don't understand."

"I'm 74 years old and you're like the child I never had, despite the fact that I've watched you have sex dozens of times. But I did that so that I could assure myself you were being trained properly! It isn't the same as actually having relations with you myself—that's a line I would never cross! What on earth are you going on about?" His clipped British accent got more distinct as he became obviously agitated.

"I know, but there's no one else I trust."

"Emilie, even if I was willing, and I assure you I'm not, we're both dominant. Though you've been a switch in recent years, at your core you're as much a dom as I am." A switch referred to the BDSM term for someone who could be either a dominant or a submissive.

She averted her gaze. "I need to do this. I can't keep going the way I've been." She got up and began to unbutton her blouse.

"Emilie." His voice was a quiet but firm protest.

"This isn't what you think," she said with a shake of her head. "I only want to show you what happened."

He frowned but nodded as she dropped her blouse. She heard his soft gasp as he practically leapt from his chair, coming around the desk to stand behind her. "Emilie, what have you done?" He ran gentle fingers over the ugly purple bruises that had begun to form on her skin.

"I got carried away."

"You got carried away?! Who did this to you? Someone in the scene here in London? I want a name."

"Not his fault," she whispered. "He's a novice and I offered to work with him for the evening—his master had the flu—and I ordered him to do it."

"You ordered him to beat you until he broke the skin and left marks like this?!"

She nodded, rapidly blinking away tears as she pulled her shirt back on. "You don't understand; this is the only way I get relief. Not even release anymore—just relief."

"Relief from what, dearest one?" He put his big hand on her cheek and cupped it almost lovingly. "What could be so bad that you seek this kind of pain?"

She swallowed. "It doesn't matter. I just need to find another solution before it consumes me."

"It does matter and I won't allow it. I'll lock you in my personal dungeon here at the house before I allow this to continue!" His eyes darkened angrily. "You may be a dominant, but you're not stronger than I am. I can and will force you to stop."

"I want to stop," she whispered. "I just don't know how. The emotional turmoil bottles up until I can't stand it and then I look for relief any way I can find it."

"Emilie, that's not what this lifestyle is about. You know that."

"Yes, but it's short-term, until I can sort out this...issue."

"What issue? Whatever it is that has you twisted inside will still be here at the end of every day."

"I got married and had a child and that didn't help. I've been in therapy for months and it's not helping. I have a fantastic job making a great deal of money and that makes no difference either. I can't find any relief from the guilt, and I'm afraid I'm going to let someone hurt me badly. Maybe even permanently."

"What could you possibly have done that was so terrible?" he asked.

She shook her head, tears spilling down her cheeks. "I can't, Warren. I can't tell anyone until I sort it out inside me first."

"Did you tell your therapist?"

She shook her head no.

"Then perhaps this is why she couldn't help you."

She looked down, so despondent it nearly broke his heart. "Sweetheart, you know I'd do almost anything for you, but what you're asking... I can't. Even if I wanted to. There's cancer. I can't perform, and to humiliate you just for the sake of watching—not with you, little one."

Her eyes widened and she was momentarily distracted from her troubles. "Cancer?! Warren! Why didn't you tell me? How bad? Oh my God!"

"I had surgery and I'm doing everything the doctors tell me. They think they got it all, but I haven't had an erection in over a year."

"I don't care about that!" she hissed. "I only care about you!"

He smiled. "You may not care, but it's been a bloody nightmare for me!"

She smiled unwittingly. "I can imagine, but still—can't they do anything?"

"At my age?" He shrugged. "I haven't the faintest idea and, frankly, that's way down on my list—I don't want to die. Unlike you."

She flushed. "That's not my intention. I simply have a lot to answer for and the guilt is getting the best of me."

"You want me to allow you to be humiliated and used as a slave because this will assuage your guilt?"

"It will distract me. Once I give over control to a master I won't be able to think about my own issues. It will be all about what he wants, which gives me a temporary reprieve."

"Why not just do whatever it is you're going to do—why add this step?"

"Because I deserve it," she whispered.

He sighed heavily, at war with himself. A sex slave and humiliation rituals were nothing new. Some women actually enjoyed them, but as a strong, dominant woman, Emilie most likely would not. She was punishing herself for something and using her involvement in the BDSM world for something it wasn't meant for. Yet her desperation tugged at him, and he understood the need for relief.

"Please, Warren. There is no one else I trust like this and until I find the answers I need, I feel so much shame! You must know someone who would be willing to humiliate me—even if it was just once."

"Of course I know people, but I wouldn't dream of leaving you there alone, and to watch that..." He scowled. "You're not just some random member of my club—you're my friend."

"And I'm asking you, as my friend, to help me. Afterwards, I'll be searching for the answers I need to make this go away."

"I could help you with that more easily."

"No. I have to do this on my own." She looked away. "Maybe I should just go to the police and turn myself in."

"You've been sending me pictures of your little girl for how long now, Em? A year?"

She nodded, pulling out her phone and opening a picture. "She's 15 months."

"And she's with her father?"

"Yes. It's summer so Viggo isn't playing hockey. He's with a partner now, and they're both wonderful with her."

He stared at the picture for a long moment. "If you go to the police and they arrest you, what will happen to Simone?"

"Her two fathers will take good care of her," she whispered.

"Won't you tell me what you've done so I can perhaps find a way around—"

"No! I've found a way around it for eight years! No more. I have to face it."

"And what of your daughter? Even with the world's best father, she'll miss her mother. A little girl needs a mum and a dad."

"I know, but she needs a healthy mum, and that's not me. I'm far from healthy emotionally."

"Emilie, I will agree to this for a very short period of time, but you will—you must—try to sort out your situation. If you don't find a solution, or tell me exactly what it is you've done, I will end it. Do you understand?"

She swallowed. "Yes."

"Tell me something, little one." He sat back in his oversized leather chair and narrowed his eyes. "Look at me."

She met his gaze. "What do you want to know?"

"Do you believe a few days or weeks of pain, submission, humiliation—all of that—will change anything? If you've committed a crime, you'll still go to jail. If you haven't, it will be a big waste. And if it's something in the middle, what do you hope to gain?"

"Punishment just feels fitting," she whispered.

"Then I'll ask again—why not go straight to the police and turn yourself in?"

She swallowed. "Because I'm more afraid of that than this."

Warren hesitated. He had the means to find out what she was hiding and he would use every tool available to him to do so. In the meantime, he was loath to allow her to do this, but he could tell she was determined. If he didn't deliver what she wanted in a safe setting, she would undoubtedly find strangers to do it, and that would be more dangerous than anything he could provide for her. "You get a few days, Emilie. Then this insanity ends—do you understand?"

She nodded.

"All right. I have to make some calls, but in the meantime, how about spending the day with a perverted old man who wants a sexy 25-year-old on his arm to show off to his mates?"

She actually smiled, her face lighting up for the first time. "I'm turning 27 soon, but I would love that. I'd like to freshen up a bit first. May I use your powder room?"

"Of course." He nodded and watched her disappear into the bathroom. Quickly, before she came out, he sent an email to a mutual friend. Perhaps it was time for more than one of his young friends to exorcise their demons.

Click now to find out what happens with Chains and Emilie! Find the links on my website!
https://www.katmizera.com/inferno

Made in the USA
Columbia, SC
19 February 2024